MORNING SPY, EVENING SPY

Also by Colin MacKinnon

Finding Hoseyn

MORNING SPY, EVENING SPY

Colin MacKinnon

ST. MARTIN'S PRESS
New York

www.stmartins.com

Library of Congress Cataloging-in-Publication Data

MacKinnon, Colin
    Morning spy, evening spy / by Colin MacKinnon. — 1st ed.
        p. cm.
    ISBN-13: 978-0-312-35576-0
    ISBN-10: 0-312-35576-9
    1. Qaida (Organization)—Fiction. 2. Terrorists—Middle East—Fiction. 3. Mid-
dle East—Fiction. I. Title.

    PS3563.A3176M67 2006
    813'.54—dc22

                                                                    2006040590

First Edition: October 2006

10 9 8 7 6 5 4 3 2 1

CONTENTS

AUTHOR'S NOTE

Sincerest thanks to my agent, Phil Spitzer, for his belief in this work and for his wise advice; and to my editor at St. Martin's Press, Diane Reverand, for her enthusiasm, insight, and meticulous editorial care.

I'm grateful also to Gene Poteat and John Waller of the Association of Former Intelligence Officers for our conversations about how spies live their lives.

My warmest gratitude, however, is due my wife, Diane, whose love, understanding, and unfailing support made all the difference.

In writing the al-Qaeda sections of this work I've drawn on *The 9/11 Commission Report* (the *Kean Commission Report*), W. W. Norton, 2004; the *Report of the Joint Inquiry into the Terrorist Attacks of September 11, 2001, by the House Permanent Select Committee on Intelligence and the Senate Select Committee on Intelligence*, S. Rept. No. 107-351, 107th Congress, 2d Session, H. Rept. No. 107-792; congressional testimony by FBI director Robert S. Mueller III (Statement for the Record, Joint Intelligence Committee Inquiry, declassified September 26, 2002); and the memorandum dated May 21, 2002 to Robert S. Mueller from FBI special agent Coleen M. Rowley, Minneapolis Chief Division Counsel, until her retirement in December 2004.

In ancient times, men observed a body in the sky they called the Morning Star, which appeared around dawn, and another they called the Evening Star, which appeared at sunset. It took a keen observer, probably some intelligent Babylonian, to realize that they are actually one and the same planet. Yet each name means something different, even to us. Now, how can that be?

—Karl Schleicher

The mind-set is, when one of your guys is popped and you know who did it, you go after them. Nobody [in Washington] ever has to hear about it. No memos, no signatures. Nothing ever goes into the files. . . . You just do it or you find somebody else to do it.

—American counterintelligence source

MORNING SPY, EVENING SPY

PROLOGUE

DECEMBER 24

A Man Called RUTHERFORD

The Mall

Peshawar

North-West Frontier Province, Pakistan

They shot the American, Powers, at 9:23 a.m. on a broad, tree-lined avenue called the Mall. Powers had just come out of a Grindlays Bank and was standing at the corner by the bank's large front gate, fiddling absently with a bright orange airline schedule and squinting up and down the Mall as if thinking which way to turn.

Then it came. At the margin of his vision, Powers glimpsed flashes of white-pink and blue, circles so rapidly expanding, so rapidly gone, leaving nothing but a void. And before he could understand what the flashes meant, he heard the angry, hammering burst of fire and felt searing pain as six 7.62mm rounds tore into his right arm, chest, and stomach. One lone, final round, catching Powers in the face as he fell, shattered his jaw and exited his right temple in an explosion of crimson mist.

Powers, a tall, lanky man, collapsed indecorously onto the pavement while passersby panicked, terror-stricken, screaming at the sound of gunfire and the sight of masked men brazenly shooting assault rifles.

Beyond Powers's hearing, a car door slammed, heavily.

And Edward Nelson Powers, born poor in Gary, Indiana, in 1948, by turns a lieutenant in the U.S. army, officer in the Central Intelligence Agency, and businessman, died, not knowing why, in this sullen, hostile city.

Provincial police did not name suspects in the crime and found no evidence beyond the fourteen spent shells they collected from the street, a slug they removed from Powers's spinal column, and the five slugs they retrieved from the façade and compound wall of the Grindlays Bank.

Witnesses told police that two men had leaped from a beige automobile—some said it was a Toyota—gunned Powers down on the crowded Mall, then fled in the same vehicle.

Shortly after the incident, police arrested and briefly held a beggar who had been soliciting in front of the Grindlays and who, witnesses said, had accosted Powers aggressively just before the shooting. The beggar, who was an Afghan and a veteran of the war against the Soviets in the 1980s, was blind in one eye and legless. He did his soliciting from a battered, four-wheeled cart that rode low off the ground. He was released the same day.

Police said they could determine no motive for the killing, which remains unsolved.

The American embassy in Islamabad issued a statement deploring the crime and pledging all assistance in finding the perpetrators, but otherwise had no comment.

Four days after Powers was killed in Peshawar, a team of special agents from the FBI's Washington Field Office broke into his town house, a large brownstone on P Street just off Wisconsin Avenue in Georgetown in the District of Columbia.

The agents searched the house for most of a day, seizing a large number of documents—business records, personal tax returns, bank and credit-card statements, phone bills, newspaper clippings—and three personal computers. In an otherwise empty desk drawer—office, second floor—they found Powers's Pentagon entry card and, with it, his color-coded and still-valid VNE (Visit, No Escort) badge, which, when Powers was alive, had given him access to numerous cipher-locked and windowless rooms of the inner rings of the Pentagon.

In a bedroom closet on the third floor the team found a shoe box containing two U.S. passports, one in Powers's name that he had reported lost and another issued in the name Guy Rutherford. It had Powers's photo in it but was no longer valid.

Stuffed into this second passport and bound with thick rubber bands were a Virginia driver's license with Powers's picture, various credit cards, a checkbook, and business cards—all in the name Guy Rutherford.

The passport also contained a snapshot of Powers standing with four other men. Africans. They are dressed in camouflage gear decorated with military insignia. They are standing in a bleached-out, desiccated landscape. One of the men, the one standing closest to Powers, is wearing a British-style officer's cap.

In the night table in the same sparsely furnished bedroom, the team found two other photographs. One, large and in color, was framed. It had been taken in front of what the FBI later determined was Powers's London town house, an expensive late Victorian off Drayton Gardens in South Kensington.

It is a sunny day, the town house a brilliant white. Powers is standing in the courtyard in front of the house. He is bent toward the camera, awkwardly, as if not knowing what to do with his arms, but grinning.

He has an almost handsome face. He is a tall, slim, gangly-looking man, big-framed, but trim at the waist. He has thick red-blond hair that's receding a little. A mustache. He is wearing wire-frame glasses that give him a studious, half-intellectual air, the air, some might guess, of a smart lawyer. He looks to be in his fifties.

Behind him, parked on the beige gravel of the courtyard, is a classic, silver-gray Bentley, and leaning her hips on its passenger-side hood, her arms crossed, is a beautiful woman wearing a black-and-white, tweed business suit, a white blouse, a small red bow tie. She is perhaps in her late thirties. She has long black hair and fine features. She is staring at the camera, unsmiling.

The other photograph, not framed, showed a young woman, naked, lying prone, sunning herself on what looks to be the deck of a sailboat. The young woman's face is turned from the camera. Her oiled back glistens in the bright sunlight. She has short, reddish hair and trim, young legs and buttocks.

The day the FBI searched Powers's Washington town house, Muhammad Atta, a thirty-three-year-old Egyptian national, and a colleague named Marwan al-Shehhi, ten years younger and a citizen of the United Arab Emirates, began training on a Boeing 727 flight simulator at SimCenter, Inc., an aviation school located at Opa-Locka Airport, outside Miami, Florida. Atta had entered the country on June 3, 2000; al-Shehhi on May 29, 2000.

At SimCenter, Atta and al-Shehhi each trained for ninety minutes.

In its advertising, the school promises to produce "airline-qualified pilots in the shortest time possible."

Between training sessions at SimCenter, Atta and al-Shehhi drove north to Fort Lauderdale and bought four portable GPS-3 global positioning devices from Tropic Aero, an aviation supply shop. Such devices, they thought, might allow them to guide aircraft from point to point without having to rely on radio beacons or advice from control towers.

PART I: MORNING

(FEBRUARY 12-APRIL 27)

1

"Will we ever . . . I mean *ever* . . . figure that asshole?"

Bill Cleppinger, sour this chilly morning, shoots me a look when he asks this, then goes back to staring out the window of our government-service Chevrolet at the rain—a sullen, sloppy February drizzle—descending on the George Washington Parkway.

I shrug: beats me.

We're talking about Ed Powers. And with Ed—well, the more you know, it always seems, the less you know. Even now.

Clep and I are being driven from CIA headquarters in Virginia into the District of Columbia. We are both officers with the Agency—Clep heads the Antiterrorism Action Committee, ATAC in the jargon, and I am special assistant for counterterrorism to the director of the Agency.

We have a midmorning appointment on Capitol Hill with a Senate aide named Jim McClennan. McClennan is chief of staff, Senate Select Committee on Intelligence, whose members are supposed to watch over our doings. McClennan has told us he wants to "talk over" what he calls the "Powers thing."

Bill and I have gamed this morning's session, and we know pretty much what we want to tell McClennan about Big Ed. He will hear that and no more.

We are both, nevertheless, deeply uneasy. Powers, a private businessman, had been working for us on contract when he was murdered. He had been in the thick of an operation code-named

NOREFUGE, a program we are running out of Peshawar. We think his connection to NOREFUGE may have gotten him killed.

NOREFUGE is beyond sensitive. Its object is to capture an Arab named Osama bin Laden. We have four presidential directives, formal executive orders, tasking us to do the job, and we want to, badly.

NOREFUGE, as befits its purpose, is an elaborate and tricky project, relying on telephone and other electronic intercepts and a small network of human informants we've been able to develop with much delicate work. Through NOREFUGE we have gotten to know who some of bin Laden's top people are and their addresses. We have even learned some of bin Laden's operational style, the way he travels, what his personal security procedures are.

Powers, who knew many strange people in this world, got some Afghan tribals to attack a convoy carrying bin Laden outside Kandahar, his city of choice in southern Afghanistan. Rather than go for a capture, the tribals simply slammed a rocket-propelled grenade into one of bin Laden's Toyota Land Cruisers, incinerating the thing. Wrong Land Cruiser, though—the great man escaped.

But then, a few months later, Powers died. Clep and I, some other people at ATAC, don't like the timing. We think bin Laden's group, al-Qaeda, may have killed Powers in retaliation for the attack on their leader. If so, it means al-Qaeda and bin Laden are onto NOREFUGE and know at least some of what we've been up to. Powers's death may therefore signal the unraveling of the operation.

Terrible, if true. We are getting increasing chatter—ambiguous phone intercepts, vague reports from dubious sources—suggesting that al-Qaeda is planning something very large, perhaps in the United States. We can't tell what. We are beside ourselves.

It is a delicate time, and we do not need a Senate committee barging in on this.

———

I look over at Cleppinger. "We never found out. About McClennan."

"Huh?"

"McClennan. Why he never got told Powers was Agency."

Under current protocol, enshrined in two official memorandums of understanding between us and each oversight committee, House and Senate, we should have informed them when Powers was murdered that he had been an Agency contractor. We did not.

Cleppinger snorts. "McClennan didn't get told fast as he wanted. So what? McClennan's a big boy, he'll get over it. And we're telling him now." Clep makes a dismissive *pffft* sound. "This is all such bullshit."

About a month ago McClennan got wind somehow that Powers—crooked, slippery Ed Powers—had been on the Agency payroll. When he called over to find out if the stories were true, he got what he thought was a runaround from some of our people at Operations. I do not know—still—exactly what Operations told him, but whatever it was, it did not make Jim McClennan happy.

McClennan, who is ex-CIA himself, is normally a friendly guy, not given to outrage at his former employer, but when he got what he thought was the okeydoke from us, he, or somebody, persuaded committee chairman, Senator Dennis Coale, to send the director of central intelligence a stiff letter (hand-carried, secret courier—the works) demanding an accounting. Hence our trip into town this dank morning.

Clep hates dealing with the Hill and should not be sent on these missions, but McClennan asked for him specifically. Len Davidson, who runs Operations and is Clep's boss, ordered him to show up. Davidson asked me to tag along. I am being sent to keep the proceedings with McClennan civil, which may not be easy.

Clep, who was born pugnacious, is red-eyed and snarly this morning and looks ready for a set-to. Clep is sixty maybe, paunchy, squat, and heavy. He has buzz-cut, graying hair and a gray, suety, all-business face, which he keeps in neutral much of the time, though he is a bundle of middle-aged hypertension.

A mordant smile suddenly flits over that chubby face. "Well," he says, "not to worry. We have a secret weapon: this, our Briefing Book"—he taps a thin, blue loose-leaf binder he is holding in his lap. "We will hand them this. This book and what it contains"—tap tap tap—"will make all these troublesome people happy, and they will all go away and leave us alone."

Clep knows the Briefing Book is a crock. It is mostly background material on Big Ed, highly edited, along with some routine cables on Pakistani politics. Len Davidson had the thing put together, hoping it would be some kind of proof of our bona fides. There is nothing of any note in it. If committee is really interested in Powers's death, this stuff will not satisfy them.

Cleppinger's smile has disappeared.

My name is Paul Patterson. I am Ohio born and bred.

I'm heading for fifty—the big five-O—and look it. I'm getting heavy at the edges and thick at the jawline. My hair, blond once, has browned and is beginning to whiten. These days, too, I catch a hint of my mother's squarer, German face (she was an Aultz) moving into, re-placing the more angular Patterson shape. It's not a shock anymore.

I like to say I'm the son of a truck driver, though my father, when he died of lung cancer in 1970, had worked for years as the very sedentary manager of a local freight-hauling firm in Columbus. In the late 1940s, though, when he was a young man, not yet married and probably a little wild, my father had driven trucks for a living, and he claimed he knew all the roads and towns between Pittsburgh and Chicago.

When he married my mother, he took an inside job—she insisted on that—and settled down to domestic life. Now and then, though, he would reminisce fondly about his driving days. I recall winter evenings in our small, old-fashioned kitchen, warm from the gas stove, and I hear my father in his gravelly voice telling me of the towns he used to pass through—Wheeling, Zanesville, Dayton, Toledo, Terre Haute—and of the behemoths he would pilot, telling me about what he hauled, about the companies he worked for.

I think my father had a wanderlust, a need to roam that for a time sent him driving from town to town in the Midwest, which I inherited. And for me, a little boy with no sense of the world's immensity, the names of those modest places had the ring of the far, far away, of romance.

About a mile from where we lived, just south of the Columbus city limits, was a small U.S. army base, long since closed, with a contingent of troops. On summer nights with the windows open in the Midwest heat, I would hear the sound of taps coming over the slow water of the Scioto River. The soft, far-off sound of that lone bugle expressed everything I thought was brave, manly, and patriotic, and I would fall asleep, lulled by its somber tones.

I went to college at OSU, and it was there that I managed to live the dream of every Ohio boy in those days. I played football for Woody Hayes, the greatest coach that ever was, that ever would be. Senior year, I was first-string tackle, offense and defense, on a crushing, almost always victorious team. By this time my father had died, but my mother in her earnest, dutiful way, collected all the clippings of Buckeye games from *The Columbus Dispatch* and kept them in a large, fat scrapbook, which I still have.

At OSU I did Marine Platoon Leaders' Class and between junior and senior years put in part of a summer at Quantico. As soon as I graduated, I joined the Corps over the objections of my mother. I served at Camp Pendleton in California, then Okinawa. I did overseas training in Iceland and France. In all, I gave the Corps three years of happy fealty. And the Corps—its unconditional love of country, its fatalism, its willingness to kill—entered my being and has never left.

"Pray for war," we used to yell as we jogged down the trails at Quantico. We meant it.

I have worked for CIA for almost twenty-five years, mostly overseas in various dusty Eastern capitals. Once in the early nineties, a *Wall Street Journal* reporter who was covering one of the spectacular trials we used to generate asked me why I'd joined. I told him because work at CIA promised me endless war on Communism. At CIA, I said, we were privileged to fight that war day in, day out. And we fought it everywhere—not just in Moscow or Beijing. We fought it in Cairo, Jakarta, Bogotá, Tehran. We used everything, every weapon, every rock and brick we could pick up off the ground to fight the bastards with.

My speech impressed the guy no end. He seemed to believe me—he got the quotes right and ran them pretty much as he'd heard them. And what I told him was true enough as far as it went.

But I didn't tell him about my wandering father or those Midwest towns, far-off and exotic in a boy's imagination, or the sound of taps in the summer night.

"Word in from an embassy. There's been a killing, you'd better get back in. We can't talk over the phone."

Stu Kremer, Cleppinger's deputy at ATAC, called me at home the day Powers died. Christmas Eve—leave it to Big Ed.

Most of the ATAC office staff, like almost everyone else in the federal government, had gone home that day in the early afternoon, buzzed, some more than others, after an office Holiday Happiness party.

When I got back to ATAC's Fusion Center that dreary evening, four or five other officers had returned to headquarters and were at work in the warren of gray cubicles that surround Cleppinger's suite. They were on their phones or popping away at their keyboards, trying to pull in what we knew about Ed and what he had been up to for us over the years.

Stu, out among them, also at a keyboard, just waved me a distracted hello.

"Peshawar," he said. "Ed Powers. They killed him."

Stu shoved an embassy cable at me describing the murder. I do not surprise easily, and I doubt that I showed much reaction, though even then I sensed the depths of trouble this might cause us.

Cleppinger, tie loose, shirt popped out over his gut, was sitting alone in his office, the only light in the room coming in through his half-open office door. On his desk stood a big, half-empty plastic bottle of Gilbeys he had rescued earlier from the party. He had stayed behind that afternoon to read cables—his way of spending a holiday.

I didn't bother to say hello. "This was not random terrorism," I said. "This was something else."

Not responding to that, Clep said, "He'd been to Peshawar a lot, five, six times in the last year, and it wasn't NOREFUGE work—we got that figured out at least. Jesus Christ, what the hell was he doing there?"

"Making enemies."

"Well, I guess."

"And got himself murdered in Pakistan—no surprise, the place is such a shooting gallery."

Cleppinger nodded. Other Americans had been killed in that country: four oil company employees in the early nineties, two consular officers in Karachi in 1995, and then in 1997 a CIA officer, a young woman named Terri Talbot, who had been working under embassy cover, also in Karachi. She was shot while being driven to work one morning. Some minor accomplices in her murder have been captured.

"Bill, it was al-Qaeda and it was some kind of payback. Maybe NOREFUGE. Maybe somebody got him for that—what do you think?"

Cleppinger made a muffled noise that sounded like agreement and looked away from me out his window, which runs the length of his office. Black sky by 5:30 p.m., worst goddamn time of the year. Outside in the cold evening, mercury arc lamps had come on to illuminate our grounds. The lamps' chilly blue light melded oddly with the reflection of Cleppinger's round face swimming in the shiny dark of his window, and it looked to me as if a bodiless Cleppinger, nonplussed by an agent's death, was hovering out there above our snowy campus.

Beyond the lamps and the zone of visibility they created, hidden in pine trees and darkness perhaps a quarter of a mile away, ran the ten-foot chain-link fence that defines our perimeter, and beyond the fence, more pine trees and the first hints of the Langley suburbs, out there where it was Christmas Eve.

Next morning, I got an early call at home from Robert Fowler, terrorism honcho on the National Security Council. When Fowler calls, it means the White House is calling.

"What have we got here?" he asked. "Another shooting in Pakistan? What the hell's going on over there?"

"I don't know, Bob. We'll get the station reporting shortly. I've talked with them over the phone, but the Paks have the info. We don't know a lot yet."

Fowler said nothing for a time, just made an impatient humming sound, not much liking my answer. Let him hum, I thought. We know what we know, Bob.

Before coming to NSC, Fowler was at State doing something with arms transfers, for or against I do not know. The rumor is, State wanted to get rid of him and suggested to him, strongly, that he take up the antiterrorism slot at NSC.

Fowler has pale blue eyes, pale white skin, close-cut, wavy red hair that's gone almost white, and a prim little rosebud mouth. He looks like death. He is also a tense, nervous piece of work.

"Who was this Powers?" Fowler asked finally.

"An American businessman."

"Who did it? What do we know? We know anything at all?"

"Right now not much."

"Don't we have assets? What are they telling us?"

"We'll get it together as soon as possible, Bob, and get it to you, promise you that."

Fowler made another impatient little hum, then said, "Right, okay. Talk to you, Paul," and hung up abruptly.

We have a lead on Powers's murder. One. It isn't much, and we are not sure what it means.

On December 19, five days before Powers was gunned down, a wanted international killer entered Pakistan. He goes by the name Liamine Dreissi. Dreissi is not his real name, but it's the one we've got, and until we know better, it's the one we'll have to use.

Dreissi, we believe, is a high-ranking operative of al-Qaeda. We have caught rumors that he engineered the deaths of those four American oil company employees gunned down some years back in Karachi. He is a man we badly want.

A day after Dreissi entered Pakistan, we got a Priority One alert from Islamabad Station reporting that he'd been sighted at the airport.

Hyperlinked with the alert was a black-and-white police photo of Dreissi we have in our archives. The photo shows Dreissi flat on, but he is holding his face tilted back from the camera, his mouth half-open. His black hair is unkempt. His eyes, empty, say nothing, seem to focus on nothing. He has a long, untrimmed beard; his cheekbones are very high. He is wearing a white shirt with a narrow, stiff little collar that he has left unbuttoned. He looks tired.

The photo is captioned, "Supplied by Algerian Sûreté," the main Algerian security service—they have a dozen or so. We got the photo through regular liaison in Algiers.

The photo shows no background, just a flat, dark gray matte. It is time-stamped bottom right—PM 6:44:59 and is dated March 1994. Two years after the photo was taken, Dreissi somehow escaped from his Algerian jail. Bribery or a breakout, we don't know which, but he's been on the loose, dodging the world's police and intelligence services, for five years or so.

Islamabad Station cabled us a confirm on the shot: two months back a Pakistani source in Peshawar had picked it out of a pile of various photos, various faces:

IDEN A, AN ORDINARILY RELIABLE SOURCE ON MATTERS ISLAMIC, RECOG-NIZED THE INDIVIDUAL IN THE PHOTOGRAPH AND TOLD STATION THAT HE IS KNOWN AS LIAMINE DREISSI (SPELLING?). IDEN A COMMENTED THAT HE DID NOT KNOW THE INDIVIDUAL'S AFFILIATIONS BUT THAT HE THINKS HE IS A MEMBER OF AL-QAEDA LEADERSHIP AND THAT HE IS "STRONGLY ANTI-AMERICAN."

Dreissi has an uncertain bio. CIA records attached to the file say he was born in Algiers. Speaks Arabic, French, some English. Associated with the Armed Islamic Group, an underground movement in Algeria. Residence in Sudan, residence in Afghanistan, residence in Yemen. Fought the Russians in Afghanistan. He seems to be an al-Qaeda operations chief, an organizer, maybe a recruiter. He has traveled in the Philippines, Thailand, Pakistan, Malaysia. Possibly Bosnia, Chechnya. Age: unknown, midforties maybe.

Dreissi had been sighted first in Bangkok, Thailand, ticketed to Karachi, Pakistan. According to Karachi Customs and Immigration, he entered Pakistan through Karachi International Airport, flying PIA. He was carrying a Moroccan passport. They did not pick him up at the airport—Thai security people notified the Paks too late, say the Paks—and he disappeared into the slums of north Karachi. The Paks told Islamabad Station that they had no further information on his ticketing, and they didn't know where he had gotten to, that he had simply slipped out of their surveillance.

Then Powers died. We want this Dreissi.

Clep tosses the Briefing Book scornfully onto the seat between us. "Here's a Powers story," he says, his face brightening. "One time we're at a dinner, Bea and me." Bea is Cleppinger's wife, a heavyset, blue-haired baritone, taller than Clep by six inches or so, and one formidable lady.

"Cairo. Ambassador's residence. Big feed. Powers somehow gets himself invited, and they put him next to Bea. So Bea and Powers are talking about this and that. Now, Bea'd never met Powers before, and I don't know how they got onto it, but Bea tells Powers she was having to put her aunt in a nursing home, right?—told him how she loved her aunt and how it was killing her to do it and all that—this business with her aunt, by the way, really did hurt, major trauma for Bea.

"Anyhow, goddamn Powers tells Bea about putting his *father* in a home, how it really tore him up, how just before he drove him out to the home, the old guy walked out into his backyard to take one last look at the sunset through the sycamore trees that he'd planted there long, long back. I learn later—no shit—Powers's father'd been dead thirty years, and Powers hated his goddamn guts. Sunset through the sycamore trees! Je-sus *Christ,* what a bullshitter! And he had no reason to unload all that crap on her, he just did."

A French intelligence officer, a suave and canny fellow, who knew Powers well once said to me, "Your Mr. Powers is very intense, very charismatic, a very charming person. He has energy, dynamism. And dreams, visions, plans. He is a man people believe, because *he* believes. You think that what he is saying must be true. He has the eyes, you know—the eyes of a man telling the truth."

He did. Powers had the gift—I suppose that's what it is—of talking himself into believing his own lies. People who can do that are the best liars in the world.

Cleppinger shakes his head, chuckling. "You got to admire it, Patterson, you really do. Ed Powers was the mother of all fuckers. And Bea thought he was the greatest. 'Poor guy,' she says, 'mourning his father.' Bea, hell, she's a sensible lady, takes no bullshit in this life, but there you go—Powers all the way!"

Bea Cleppinger has loyally followed her short, fat husband from CIA station to CIA station around the world, often teaching—her subject is math—in the overseas American schools. Cleppinger and Bea must have had their ups and downs, but their long marriage is happy as far as I know.

Not so mine.

My wife, Nan, partner and bedmate of twenty-four years, has decamped—fled—to a fancy and expensive apartment down in Crystal City close to Reagan National, leaving me alone in our house in north Arlington.

She blames me for the death of our one child, David, who died eighteen months ago in an automobile crash. The classic accident: 3 a.m. on a summer night, a car full of drunken kids. It was that waiting time between high school and college, when a world of possibilities lies before you and you think you will live forever.

The driver—it wasn't David—lost control of their vehicle on a long stretch of road in north Arlington. The police figured their car was doing 115. Of the five kids in the car, David was the only one who died. All the others were badly injured, one paralyzed from the waist down.

Nan, as I say, blames me. I was, she believes, the absent, work-obsessed daddy, a common enough phenomenon in Washington, the kind of daddy that produces disturbed kids.

I think about it. It's not implausible.

David, once a graceful, good-humored boy with a sweet smile, had begun to show some disquieting signs, though nothing really alarming, mostly, I thought, the marks of the adolescent male. He kept his distance, seemed a little secretive, listened to music beyond our ken. He had friends, some of them in the car with him that night, who were not all that great.

When David died, I was out of the country, in Athens, at a regional meeting of Middle East counterterrorism officers. Nan went to the hospital alone.

Through the trees to our left, I catch glimpses of the ragged cliffs across the river in Maryland. A house appears now and then, and one white church steeple pops up out of the trees. Far below us and out of sight is the river itself, running through the chasm it has cut in these granite rocks, down to tidewater and the Chesapeake Bay. The rain has stopped now, and a fine, silky mist hangs in the air.

I came to work today from my home in Arlington and from the arms of my love, Karen. She and I have a my-place, your-place relationship these days, serious to the point of each having a key to the other's house.

I have told Len Davidson at the DDO of the romance—we're supposed to let the Agency know these things—and told Karen that I have told him. Karen, whom I met by the chanciest of chances five months back at a shindig on the Hill, is a reporter with *The Washington Post*. She does national politics for the *Post* and is well regarded in the profession.

When I let Davidson know I was dating a reporter, he seemed unsurprised, but I know the structure at Langley would just as soon I weren't. One of the polygraph questions we put to our new recruits these days is "Do you have friends in the media?" Our preferred answer is no.

I think of Karen this chill, dripping day—her hair ash blond in the early light, tousled there on the pillow. I picture her face when, in the early morning's sleepy time, she opened her eyes halfway, smiled, and, closing them again, nestled into my side.

We are in Arlington County now. Across the river on our left Maryland has become the District of Columbia, and we get our first glimpses of the radio towers and the taller buildings over there.

A small, familiar sign—it's there, then it isn't—announces that we are passing over Glebe Road, a street name I do not hear or think of easily. David died on Glebe Road.

For a time after the accident I would drive that long, straight stretch of road in suburban north Arlington where the police said they must have picked up speed. I would drive past the guardrail a hundred yards farther north that they careered off. And I would pull off the road and stop across from the big oak tree they smashed into, its bark noticeably lacerated from the accident. And there, sitting in my car, I would weep, my heart like lead, and I would repeat his child's name, "Davey, Davey, Davey," a name we hadn't used with him for years, embarrassing and also surprising myself at how easily the tears came. As we pass the sign today, it makes me think, as it always does, Davey.

When we crest a rise, the silvery towers of Rosslyn come into view and beyond them, across the river in the District, the Washington Monument and the baroque crenellations of the Watergate building.

"Look at *that* fucker," Cleppinger says, gesturing with his head at a black shape outside our Chevrolet's window. "Goddamn aircraft carrier, isn't it?"

The shape is a stretch limo that glides soundlessly past us in the

gray light and mist, its long bank of dark windows hiding everything
and everyone within. Some Virginia real estate brigand, I think. From
the limo's trunk rises the V of a radio antenna that sweeps back like
the tail of some great sea monster, disdaining lesser creatures in its
wake, including, most emphatically, government-issue Chevy Subur-
bans.

A smaller car, a black Oldsmobile, rides just in front of the limo,
and the two, in the sparse midmorning traffic on the GW, seem to
move in tandem, swerving quickly into the right lane in front of us.
Both are going very fast. Then a second smaller car, also black, fol-
lows and pulls in quickly behind the limo, and the three—lead car,
limo, and chase—go sailing off in the icy mist.

This flotilla is too fancy for a real estate brigand, even the Virginia
species. It dawns on me now that the limo, the other vehicles, had
government plates, probably G-12, our usual number, and that all of
them are Agency. The director of central intelligence has just sped
past us down the GW.

"Lindsay," I say.

"White House?"

I grunt, then say, "A little late today. He's usually there by eight."

"Going there in style, isn't he? New buggy? I like it. It's regal.
No, no, make that imperial. Yes, indeedy, that's it: imperial. Fits him.
Well, good luck to the president."

Paul Lindsay was confirmed DCI six months back, after a short,
happy day's worth of testimony before Senate Select. He had been an
assistant secretary of defense, one among many, and has no known
enemies on the Hill.

Lindsay started coming to town long back, when he was a bright,
young engineering professor at Cornell, shuttling in regularly to be
on this or that science commission at the Pentagon. In the eighties he
worked upper-level jobs at Defense and made friends there with
some rising stars, then headed back to Cornell, though always keeping
in touch. Four years ago, after cashing in chips at every table in town,

he got himself appointed an assistant secretary and impressed enough people of both parties to rise to his current eminence.

Lindsay's an intense, driven man, balding, short, and built like a lightweight wrestler. His love in life is clandestine surveillance: photorecon, imaging, electronic eavesdropping. At the Pentagon he was in charge of some of DOD's blackest boxes, oversaw the spending of billions of dollars, and was a powerful member of the inner circle that runs that place.

At the Agency, though, he is very much an outsider, and many of the troops, especially the older ones in Operations like Cleppinger, were ready to hate him even before he came in. Lindsay, abrasive at the best of times, has already clashed with some of the upper-grade officers.

This touches on me, because in a big way I am a Lindsay man. A year back I lateraled out from CIA to Defense Intelligence and worked down at the Pentagon in their counterterrorism office, where Lindsay and I got to know each other. He liked my work and liked me personally and persuaded me to come back to headquarters, back to the Agency, as his special counterterrorism adviser, partly because I know the territory at Langley, partly because I have some old friends here—I think.

My job is to review ongoing operations, particularly at Near East Division, which everyone considers a vermin pit, and give Lindsay a heads-up on problems just appearing on the horizon. I am also operations special coordinator (OPSPECCO in the cable addresses), a post not on the older organization charts that Lindsay created for me when he brought me back from DOD. As OPSPECCO I am to run projects not quite in the chain of command, pretty much what I did at the Pentagon.

None of this, despite my long years with the Agency, endears me to the structure at Langley, from which I've gotten some chill breezes now that I'm back. I sense that even Cleppinger, a buddy of twenty years, resents my presence and considers it just one more proof that Lindsay's an asshole.

When we get to Rosslyn, we swing left off the GW and onto Roosevelt Bridge, which takes us across the river, broad here and slate-colored in the midmorning winter light. To our right, rising up over the river, is the Lincoln Memorial, to our left, the Kennedy Center and the Watergate. Suddenly we dip down onto Constitution Avenue in the District, just across the bridge at Twenty-third Street, where we stop for the light.

Even in this sorry weather three or four panhandlers, one wearing a black garbage bag to keep off the wet, are out waving plastic cash buckets, hustling the traffic as it comes in over the bridge. All are African-American. One of them, who is tall and skinny, wearing a purple exercise suit and a big, blue, peaked woolen cap, carries a cardboard sign that reads SUPPORT A HOMELESS VIET NAM VET.

I watch him as he walks up and down between the two leftmost lanes of cars, shaking his bucket at the drivers, stoically, almost cheerfully moving on as no one rolls down a window. He has a short, gray, nappy beard and a pushed-in nose, and he looks benignly purposeful. I make eye contact with the guy just to see what he will do, but he glances on quickly, knowing I'm no customer.

He could have been in Vietnam. He looks about the right age.

As the light changes, traffic eases onto the straightaway of Constitution Avenue, and we leave the panhandlers behind in the sodden morning. I wonder about them. Funny how they show so little menace.

We are now in the District of Columbia, in the Washington that the country sees at the movies, and we proceed along Constitution. To the right of us is the Mall, two miles of open green space edged by museums and punctuated with memorials and gardens, a kind of officially approved national memory stream and one of my favorite places in this city. Just out of sight, down below a grove of oak trees, is the black slash of the Vietnam Memorial, its unseen presence announced by a modest brown Park Service sign.

Cleppinger's gone silent. He's been that way, it now strikes me, since we first sighted Rosslyn. Brooding maybe, thinking of McClennan.

Far over the Ellipse on our left I see the White House, where Lindsay and his flotilla have presumably arrived. We proceed now in the slow morning traffic, past all those federal departments and agencies that lie on the north side of this broad avenue: Commerce, Internal Revenue, Justice, the Federal Trade Commission—what you think of when you think of tedium.

Ahead of us, the Hill comes into view, rising gently over all the rest of this city, with the Capitol sitting high up there like a shining temple, as the Founders had wanted it to do, and on the very top of its great white dome the statue of Lady Liberty.

"Spin City," Cleppinger says finally, as much to himself as to me. Then: "Truth scares these people."

---

2 **JUNE 8, 1978**
The Attempt to Kill Me Was Kept Quiet

"You're gonna be all right, sir, you're gonna be all right, we'll just walk in here."

A marine guard—he's red-haired, pink-faced, maybe twenty years old—calmly pulls me toward a chair and sits me down in it. I'm unsteady on my feet, my face is streaming blood. Iranian urban guerrillas have just tried to kill me.

It's 1978, and this is my first brush with terrorism, though not my last.

I'm a young officer laboring for the Agency at the American embassy in Tehran. I arrived in this country three months ago.

Each morning when I report for work, I see on the yellow and blue tile walls of our embassy lobby a large photo of Jimmy Carter, solemn-faced for this his presidential portrait, not grinning that Bugs Bunny grin of his.

The tiles on the lobby wall are Persian-made, the pattern on them a filigree of looping arabesques that repeats endlessly like the ornate and persistent political ways of that strange country, that strange region.

The terrorists who have just tried to kill me will soon tie Carter and his presidency in knots, but no one knows this yet.

My cover is political officer, U.S. Department of State, POLOFF on the cable routing list. I work on the second floor, three doors down the hall from the ambassador, who at this time is Bill Sullivan.

My job is to track Soviet-bloc personnel operating in Iran, a crew of hapless and ineffectual Russians, Poles, and Czechs, who are vastly outnumbered and outspied by the Americans and Iranians. We have been told by the Shah to keep our noses out of Islamist politics, and we do. We know little of the gathering storm that over a few short months will sweep the Shah and the Persian monarchy away forever.

Summer, late afternoon. The city is all shimmering dry heat and dust. I am in an air-conditioned embassy Oldsmobile headed for an appointment in the far north of the city with an Iranian banker who is a well-plugged-in informant.

My Iranian driver, a large man, almost as tall as I am, has just pulled our vehicle out the rear gate of the embassy compound, past the PX, where I've done some shopping. After the appointment, I figure on heading home to the large villa, also in the far north of town, that I share with Nan, my bride of one year. We pass through the wide, regular streets north of our vast embassy compound.

I still remember the sharp, sweet smell of cigarette in the car from an Iranian brand the driver smoked.

On our right we pass the Chetnik Restaurant, on our left, a confectioner's shop and a florist.

Then this: A motorcycle pulls even with us on the driver's side, but does not pass. It hangs there, coasting with the rear window of our Olds, coasting with me. Two Iranians are riding it. The one in the rear turns his face to me and—this I will always, always remember—catches my eye and, connection made, displays an ecstatic smile.

Then this: the machine pistol—it had not been there, now it is, stubby and ugly—and the smiling man on the rear of the cycle has it pointed in my face.

Things go fast as the man focuses his black eyes on me and, still smiling that ecstatic smile, fires a short burst from the weapon, five rounds, we decided later, shattering the rear passenger window, but missing me—I've ducked to the rear floor—and the driver.

My face was badly scratched by fragments of flying glass, but I had no other wounds. Miracle.

When the window shattered, my Iranian driver, well trained by Agency security people and a cool head, brought his foot down hard on the accelerator and the Olds shot forward. Then, to shake any following vehicle, the driver jerked the steering wheel left, braked hard, and spun the Olds around in a 180-degree turn, its tires screaming, burning the asphalt, and took the vehicle fast back toward the embassy.

But there was no following vehicle. As if it had never been there, as if no crazy had smilingly put a machine pistol in my face and pulled the trigger, the motorbike had vanished.

The usual thing to worry about, embassy security had told us, was a van or a car running in front of you, stopping you, and a second vehicle running in behind you, keeping you from pulling back, and then somebody emerging fast from one of the vehicles and closing in for the kill. That did not happen this time. This attempt seemed amateurish.

The Iranians' clothes, the shapes of their faces, the color of their motorbike—these I cannot remember, could not for the debriefing just after the attack. But to this day, I remember the black eyes of the man with the machine pistol.

And that smile.

The attempt to kill me was kept quiet, though scuttlebutt about "an incident" got around the embassy and eventually out into the larger American community.

From time to time I've wondered what happened to my would-be murderers. The Iranian security services seem never to have caught the pair. Who were they? What brought them there? Why did they think I deserved to die?

More than anything, I wondered about that smile, its enigmatic confidence. What did that smile mean?

In the embassy after the attack, after the marine security guard had walked me into the infirmary and parked me in a lounge chair, then, only then, did I begin to quake with terror, as with palsy, my hands shaking, my voice not my own, not under my control.

3

FEBRUARY 12

"Waters Close over This Thing"

"Hiya, Marie."

"Ooh, hello, Mr. Patterson, Mr. Cleppinger. You are awaited. I will let him know." Marie, the sloe-eyed receptionist at Senate Select, buzzes McClennan to tell him in her golden-honey Southern voice that we are here. Marie is a buxom brunette somewhere in her fifties and maternal-looking. Marie's a fixture at Senate Select, where she's been doing one thing or another at least since I started showing up ten years back. She's been married twice, I think, though at this point in her life she apparently has no husband.

"Nasty morning, isn't it, Mr. Patterson?"

"Was, Marie. It's kinda stopped."

"Oh, when I came in it was raining animals out there. Ba-a-a-d weather coming."

"Way it goes." A sudden cold snap will fall on our town tonight, bringing snow with it. After all the wet weather, the city will be solid ice tomorrow, slick and polished like a mirror and hell for the commuters. It happens every few years—our lovely, temperate city gets slapped around this way by the elements.

Just as Cleppinger and I park ourselves on Senate Select's long, black, fake-leather sofa, McClennan springs out the one door leading from committee offices and greets us with brisk, firm handshakes—a "H'lo, Bill, how you doing?" for Cleppinger, and for me, punching at my upper arm with his left hand, a "Hey, Paul, how's it going, guy? Good to see you—been a while."

McClennan's about my height but with no bulk to him. He's fortysomething and balding and, with his thin face and piercing, intelligent eyes, looks like a college professor of the meaner sort, the sort you wouldn't want. He wears silver-rimmed glasses and crisp buttoned-down shirts that give him a trim, precise look and add to the effect.

"Hey, come on back"—he gestures with his head—"we got the room set up."

"Back" is not Senate Select's regular offices. "Back" is the SCIF (Secure Compartmentalized Information Facility), just around the corner.

The SCIF in Hart is Captain Midnight's Secret Chamber, two thousand square feet of floor space inside a seamless steel box that you enter and leave through a steel-flanged door that could work as an air lock on a submarine. Raised on brick stanchions and double-walled, the SCIF is bugproof and impenetrable, as secure a space as you get in Washington, maybe anywhere in the world.

Here personnel from CIA, NSA, and other, even shier intelligence services come in to display in secret the family jewels to the representatives of the people.

We troop with McClennan into our usual venue, a side chamber off the main hearing room, and sit down at the long, glass-topped conference table, as familiar to Cleppinger and me as a piece of old family furniture, in chairs that are more comfortable than they look. McClennan sits down at the head of the table, as if about to preside over a board meeting of some small company; Cleppinger and I settle in on each side. A Senate Select aide, a pretty young woman wearing a white blouse and silky gray slacks—I note her high-cut panty lines, Clep ignores her—smiles her way out past us.

She's deposited three legal-sized yellow notepads, each with a blue Bic, on the table plus a thermos of coffee, a cylinder of styrofoam cups, paper napkins, and a box of jelly-filled doughnuts.

Clep, who down deep is a lump of cold fury, is slouching comfortably back in his chair away from the table. He has put a friendly, affable look on his face as he regards McClennan. He could be eyeing a favorite nephew.

Just the three of us, I notice. Usually when we make our jaunts up here, other people from committee, one of the lawyers maybe, or a political analyst or two, sit in on the sessions.

Not today. Today it's just McClennan and us. I wonder about that.

"Here—for your bedtime reading," Cleppinger says, pushing our sad binder of clippings over in front of McClennan. "The Briefing Book summarizes what we know about Edward Powers. It is classified and partly redacted. It's got to be held at committee level." "Committee level" means the material is to be kept in the committee's safe and is to be looked at only by committee members and cleared staff.

Cleppinger's language is pro forma, a short set of phrases Mc-
Clennan has heard intoned many times before. Then, less pro forma,
Cleppinger passes McClennan a receipt for the binder, which Mc-
Clennan signs perfunctorily with one of the Bics and hands back.

McClennan ignores the binder, though, letting it lie on the table.
He's got a pretty good idea what it's worth.

McClennan was a CIA officer for eight years. He's served in
Bangkok and elsewhere in East Asia and has received a couple of ci-
tations for distinguished service. Ten years back he quit CIA to work
on the Hill for Senator Dennis Coale and, thanks to Coale, has become committee staff director. Cleppinger and I awe him not at all.
McClennan knows the deal at Langley.

"Sure took a while, Bill," McClennan says. "How come?" It's
been a month since Coale's letter arrived on Lindsay's desk.

"Hey, not that long," Cleppinger says, his face all geniality.
"Gimme a break. Paper isn't all that easy to track down, as we know,
and the Briefing Book had to get vetted. We had to call a goddamn
lawyer in over the weekend to get the stuff looked at. And my private chaplain here, Paul Patterson"—Cleppinger gestures stagily at
me with both his pudgy hands—"had to pray over it, make sure it
was okay."

McClennan smiles. So do I, uneasily. Cleppinger—I know him
well—gets jokey when he's tense. I wonder if McClennan senses
that.

"Praying over it couldn't have taken that long," McClennan says,
"not forty days and forty nights, anyhow." He splashes coffee in a cup
and looks at Bill, then over at me. "Guys want some?"

Cleppinger takes the cup; I wave off.

"Glad you were hard at work," McClennan says, "but you might
have let us know—we got nothing but silence there for a while.
Black hole over there in Virginia? Phones down?"

Cleppinger's response is to say, "Ho ho," slurp his coffee, and
stare back. I don't react.

" 'Ho ho' indeed," McClennan says, smiling but with not much mirth. Then he says, "Okay, subject of the day: Edward Powers. Was he Agency?" McClennan looks over at Cleppinger.

Cleppinger, who is stuffing a doughnut into his face, eyes McClennan and says, sloppily, mouth full, "In a manner of speaking."

" 'In a manner of speaking.' What the hell does that mean?"

Time to break in. "Jim," I say, "let's start with this: we are into a sensitive area here. With Powers, I mean. We are trying to be forthcoming, we really are, but there are ramifications with this."

McClennan does me the courtesy of seeming to ponder what I've said, looking at me silently for a moment, then says, "Okay, point noted. But, again, was he Agency?"

I say, "He was on contract, yes. He was not an officer."

McClennan nods. "Okay, he was a contractor. Fine. Good to know. Now, second question: Does the death of this guy mean any damage to ongoing operations? We got a problem with this thing? What's the assessment?"

I think NOREFUGE, I think Dreissi. "We're looking at that," I say. "Frankly, could be, but we don't know yet. Sometimes you find out years later, as you know, Jim. Sometimes stuff comes back at funny angles."

"So it does." McClennan glances back and forth at Cleppinger and me. "Well, are there any 'funny angles' here? Anything ricocheting back—like operationally?"

"We're looking," I say. "We haven't found anything, but we're looking. Again, Jim, this is sensitive stuff."

McClennan seems to buy that. "Okay, third question: Could this have been random terrorism?"

I shake my head. "We don't think so. If you want to make a terrorist statement, you don't shoot Ed Powers. You blow up an embassy or grab a bunch of tourists—something like that."

Cleppinger breaks in, "McClennan, the man had enemies. You start thinking about the possibilities, you don't stop thinking—could have been a lot of people. Ask me, it could have been a commercial killing—business dispute, that kind of thing."

"They must take business really seriously in Pakistan."

Cleppinger suddenly leans forward, eyes on McClennan. "Jim, one-line wisecracks get us nowhere. Face it, Powers was a secretive fucker and business-wise he was all over the goddamn lot. No telling how many enemies he may have had. We may find out who the perps were, we may not. I think it's pretty obscure and may well stay that way. Ask me, likely thing is, the waters are just going to slowly, slowly close over this thing."

" 'Waters close over this thing,' " McClennan repeats, rubbing his thumb on his chin just below his lip.

"Possibly," he says distantly. "And nobody's claiming responsibility."

"No," I say.

McClennan drums his fingers on the Briefing Book, eyes adrift around the room, then says, "So how'd he get killed?"

"Paks report the slugs were 7.62 caliber," Cleppinger says. "FBI people who were there confirm this. Unfortunately, 7.62s are consistent with a whole lot of weapons—pistols, assault rifles, whatever. And there are guns all over that goddamn place—you know what it's like. No weapon recovered. Guess is, two different AK-47s were used. Right after Powers got killed, they arrested some people, then released them. Tallyho."

As we have gamed it, Clep also tells McClennan that Powers had flown into Karachi on a British Airways flight out of London, then immediately caught a local PIA flight to Peshawar, and that Powers had a return flight to the U.K., also on British Airways, booked for a week later.

Also as we have gamed it, Clep does not tell McClennan that Powers had phoned from London four days before and set up a meeting with CIA Peshawar Base chief Pancho Reiner and told Reiner that he was onto something, a "major deal," that it was about Osama bin Laden, that he couldn't talk about it on the phone.

McClennan doesn't have to know any of this, or that early in the morning on his first day in town, the day he was to meet with Reiner, Powers walked out of his hotel, Dean's, into the dust and hubbub of Peshawar and died ten minutes later.

McClennan puts his hands behind his head and leans back in his chair, face turned up toward the ceiling. "Well," he says ruminatively, "we've got a problem with this company, this airline he had—what's it called, Triple A Air? Been around awhile, hasn't it?"

Ed's airline. A sore point.

Cleppinger says a simple, guarded "Yes."

"How'd it get started?"

My turn again. "It was a proprietarial to begin with. It was a small, Agency-owned company. We set it up in the late seventies. Back then it was called Global Air Freight. We used it in the Middle East and Africa. Ed was an officer with the Agency back then—not contract labor, a real officer."

I notice as I speak that McClennan is nodding pseudo-helpfully, like an adult urging a child who's done something bad to come clean. It's McClennan's way, and I've seen it before, but I don't care for it. I wonder if he's doing it to bug me, then decide he probably isn't, but who knows?

"He joined CIA in '75," I say, as McClennan nods that nod, "and left in '91—twenty years and out. You'll see all this in the Briefing Book. Ed took Triple A over in '87, '88—something like that, ran the business while he was still an officer with us. When he quit CIA, we sold it to him."

McClennan stops nodding and cuts a look at me. "Sold it to him?"

"Yes."

"Uh-huh. And when 'we' sold it to him, what did 'we' charge him for it?"

"He paid one dollar."

"Oh, my. Oh, my, my."

"Just the name," I say. "No equipment. When we sold it to him—for a dollar—it had no airplanes, it was just a rented office in Florida. Ed took over the lease, which was easy since we'd been paying it in his name anyhow. Just some office space and some letterhead, that's it. All this is in the Book."

Ed held the company together somehow, then built it up in the middle and late eighties, buying or leasing DC-6s and other old clunkers, and running them out of a grubby office at the Dania, Florida, airport, the service port for Fort Lauderdale.

To get its name up front in the yellow pages Ed renamed the company AAA Air Freight Services. Since Powers's pilots flew a lot for us—cashing in on his buddy network and flying for us is probably what Ed had in mind in the first place—people started calling the company Aid and Abet Airlines. Somebody in the know back then made up a jingle that went the rounds: "It matters not what or where, Aid and Abet will get it there."

"Well, it's nice he didn't have to take out a loan, isn't it?"

I nod, smiling.

"Look," Cleppinger says, "he worked around Africa, the Middle East, lotta places, with all those baloney companies he had, including this one, this airline, which he ran out of his ass. Triple A was one of the ways he got to know people."

And the people he knew—Taliban "officials," old mujahideen fighters, wealthy Gulf Arabs with an itch to contribute to Islamist causes—gave him entrée to some pretty strange circles and helped us put NOREFUGE together.

McClennan says, "He also serviced the U.S. government with this company?"

"He did."

"CIA?"

"Yes, indeedy. He got Agency contracts."

"Recently?"

Cleppinger looks over at me.

"Last one was two years ago," I say. "It ran out after a year."

"Nothing since then?" McClennan asks.

"Negative."

In fact, we let him go, cut off the relationship with Triple A by letting a contract lapse and never picking it up again. DDO Len Davidson had started worrying about Powers, about some of the deals he'd heard Powers was doing, and got worried about blowback. There is no formal burn order in Powers's file and nothing on paper about needing to end the Triple A contract. Davidson simply let it go, hoping the contract and Powers and Triple A would all slip off into the fog of bureaucratic amnesia.

But they are back.

"McClennan, we are being very cryptic this morning," Cleppinger says. "What are we barking about? Tell your old buddy Bill."

McClennan pauses, maybe for effect, then says, "We think Ed Powers, former CIA officer, CIA contractor at the time of his death, owner of former CIA proprietarial airline—we think Ed Powers might have been a player in the South Asian heroin market. You hear anything about that?"

Here we go. Purpose of the morning. This is really why we are here, not some question of protocol. McClennan has of course sandbagged us nicely.

Cleppinger is incredulous. "Aah, come on!"

"Serious accusation, Bill."

"Just how the hell do you figure that?"

"We heard."

"I don't believe it—who's *we*?"

"Committee staff fieldwork. Just rumors so far, no hard evidence.

But the people who are spreading those rumors are talking like they know."

"Who, may I inquire, says that asshole was running dope?"

"Right now that's closely held. But CIA may be in deep trouble here. Powers was one of yours."

Cleppinger stiffens at this, his hands gripping his chair arms, and, his face gone red, he glowers speechlessly at McClennan, then chokes out, "That . . . That is so . . ." Then still infuriated, but gaining some control over his voice, he says, almost hissing the words, "McClennan, this is bullshit, goddamn it! Remember 'dope from the contras'? Remember CIA dealing in South American cocaine, birthing crack babies in L.A.? Remember how talk radio got it? All that gossip in the black barbershops? So? Story never worked out, pile of shit. Some asshole reporter out in California blew it up, up, up with his own helium, and then the balloon exploded, leaving him aloft without a chute. Same with this. McClennan, this is disgusting."

Eyes shooting back and forth between the two of us, McClennan asks levelly, "What's going on? You got anything on this? Cables, scuttlebutt—anything at all? Gotta know, Bill, Senator Coale wants it. Some of the senator's constituents—African-Americans—do indeed think CIA's selling dope in our fair cities. Think about it—what do you really know about this guy? If there's anything to it—I mean anything at all—it could be a major hullabaloo."

"I don't believe you."

"I know, but it's a problem."

"Well, it's bullshit."

"Are you sure? Are you very, very sure?"

And of course, we're not.

Leaving Senate Select, Cleppinger and I silently exchange glances. Cleppinger puts on a tight, little I-told-you-so smirk, then blanks it out.

Silence in the elevator, silence in Hart's cavernous open atrium as we walk over the polished rose-pink marble floors through the tourists, staffers, and Capitol Hill police. And silence as we pass through the big doors that lead out to C Street and the misty, gray morning.

Our driver, who's been alerted by Marie, has already pulled our Suburban out of Senate Hart's underground garage, and it is here on C Street waiting for us, engine purring.

"McClennan knew a lot before we told him," I say in the car. "I don't care for that. Committee's been doing some work. Something's going on, Bill. I don't know what, but something."

"It's bullshit."

"Media's on this." We've had calls from the press, *The Post, The Times,* ABC News, about Powers. Nothing serious—the usual people doing the usual checking—but they're out there, looking.

"That doesn't make it any less bullshit."

"They may find something. 'Waters close over this thing'—are you out of your goddamn mind?"

Cleppinger says nothing.

4

FEBRUARY 12

"I Think We Need to Get This Over With"

"Hi, it's me."

Hi, it's me. My wife, Nan, announcing herself to me on the phone the way she always has. After nine months of separation, the habit seems strange, and the phrase has come to sound far away in time, like dialogue from an old movie. Nan catches me late in the day, sitting at my desk, thinking of Powers and Triple A Air. And of Dreissi and the death of NOREFUGE.

"Hi, Nan. How're you doing?"

"Oh, fine—how about you, Paul? Are you all right?"

"Just fine." These days I tend to do monosyllables with Nan.

"Paul, have you talked to Mailer? Lloyd sent that settlement agreement over to you three weeks ago. What on earth is going on?"

Three weeks ago, Nan's slick lawyer, Lloyd Gerstenbach—Fairfax, Virginia, old friend of the Radfords', Nan's blue-blooded New England family—sent a revised proposal for our divorce settlement for me to look at and forward to my lawyer, Eliot Mailer—Arlington, guy on the Agency approved list of attorneys—who has yet to issue an opinion on it. Nan wants me to goose Mailer.

Mailer, though, was heading off for a vacation somewhere when I let him know I was sending Gerstenbach's latest handiwork over to him. I told Mailer, no skin off my nose, it would be fine if he vetted Gerstenbach's proposal a few weeks down the line.

"I've done it, Nan, sent it over. Mailer's skiing somewhere this week, Colorado, if I'm not mistaken." I have no idea where Mailer is, and I doubt that he skis.

"Well, I think we need to get this over with."

"So do I, Nan, but, look, hey, we got three months before we can even show the thing to a judge. There's no great hurry here."

"Oh, Paul, for heaven's sake! I *know* you, you're just doing this."

Our trope: phone calls that start politely enough like this one, somehow regularly and swiftly descend into snottiness.

"I've looked at it, Nan. I will check with Mailer when he gets back and see what he says. I will. I'm sure things will be fine."

"Paul, you don't stop, do you?"

"Meaning?" I ask, though I'm fairly sure I know the answer.

"Oh, Paul—your games. You're always gaming the other party, always trying to seize the high ground, trying to be in control—that's what this is all about. This settlement agreement—you're playing it like it's some Agency need-to-know thing. Everything's on a need-to-know basis with you, Paul, and you're the guy who decides what other people need to know. It gives you control over them and it lets you keep your distance, which is what you want—distance. It goes way, way beyond the Agency stuff, Paul—it's how you've lived your life, including life with me."

I let that pass. It's been Nan's refrain, and I have no answers I haven't already given.

Nan is in her midforties and is still a most beautiful woman. She is trim, slender, and athletic and still has good, sexy-looking tennis player's quads. In her black hair just above her left temple there's an oddly asymmetrical starburst of white. She parts her hair there in the white, and the effect is elegant.

Nan's father, Jack Radford, is long gone. He died in California in a freak horseback accident when Nan was sixteen. The horse took a tumble jumping and gored Radford on the saddle horn. They didn't knew how serious it was and got him to the hospital too late.

Nan's mother, Evelyn—Evie—a woman of no generosity, is sitting in their big place in Greenwich, ailing and senile, hitting the sherry and accusing the help of stealing it. The family can afford home care for Evie, so that's what they do, though Nan and her brother, Teddy, and sister, May, would probably just as soon put Evie away somewhere.

May, married to a cardiologist and living in Darien, is overseeing the home care and probably resents having to do it, though it can't take much of her time. Nan, who doesn't like May or Evie, stays out of it.

"Well, it's over," Nan says out of nowhere—she does that—"and I'm glad. I piled up a lot of losses in that life, I really did, Paul, and shouldn't have." Then: "In my time I've made choices, and some of them have been very wrong ones." Heavy pause here. One of those very wrong choices, I am given to understand, was yours truly.

"You're lucky she's got money," Mailer told me.

Nan, a rich man's daughter, needs no support from me. Her

wealth is how she managed to move to her fancy, furnished apartment down there by the airport. In the settlement, your basic no-fault from Gerstenbach, she's going easy on me, though not out of mercy. She just wants out, and quickly.

Under Virginia law, one year of separation does it. Prove to a judge you've been apart for a year, apart from "bed and board" as the statute says, and the judge, he or she, stamps the decree, and you're sundered, no other questions asked. Minimal fuss, minimal money.

I'm going to have a financial problem, though. I want to stay in the house. To do that I will have to buy her out, and the equity in the place has ballooned like crazy since we bought it. The plan is, I will give her some money up front, then refinance and give her some more money. Maybe do a second mortgage on the house with her holding the deed, an arrangement I think she'll spring for, though Mailer's not so sure. Even so, the deal will probably come close to cleaning me out of savings, but then my lifestyle these days is government-issue Spartan, and I don't give a damn.

"So how's Charley?" I ask.

Nan has let me know she is "seeing" someone—Charley Bennett, real estate tycoon, private-airplane pilot, sack of shit. She's on the verge of "getting serious" with Bennett, she tells me, which is Nan talk for marriage. Bennett is an acquaintance of ours from church, no friend of mine, whose wife died suddenly about a year back. He is ten years Nan's senior, portly and fat-faced.

At church, the only time I see him, he dresses well in a kind of casual, blue-blazered, moneyed way. He is flush from local investments and is forever mentioning his Arlington and Fairfax properties— letting you know.

"Charles is fine." I hear umbrage in Nan's reply. She has been defensive about the guy from the get-go.

"You two 'working on your relationship'?"

Silence here.

"Jesus Christ, you say you want honesty in a guy, and you take up with a real estate huckster."

Bennett, a good old boy from central Virginia, somewhere around Farmville, is more than that. He is actually a major player in local real estate circles. You see Bennett's name on new condo and town-house projects around northern Virginia, even way out in Loudoun County. I wonder about his talents in the sack, though. Pills, I suppose. I can't really believe Nan will marry this guy, but who knows?

"Well, say hello to Chuck for me."

"Oh, go to hell."

Nan and I are both technically adulterers, though of course neither of us looks on it that way. The concept would hardly bother Nan, who comes from a family milieu, horsey Connecticut gentry, where there was a lot of that as well as plenty of alcoholism and a suicide or two.

In my stolid, Midwestern family, adultery, "playing around" they would have called it if they had talked about it, which they did not, was unknown. So was divorce. My father, to the day he died, was a teetotaling, four-square Baptist. After he met my mother, life on the road and its temptations, whatever they had been, seemed not to attract him, and he got out of the truck-driving business early in life. He may have had a wilder youth than he let on, but if he did, I'll never know. During their marriage, he was as faithful to my mother, I am sure, as she was to him.

As I was the first in my family to graduate from college, I am, too, the first to divorce. My mother, my father, that whole older generation, gone now, what would they have thought of this?

5
FEBRUARY 23
The Commercial Representative

On February 23, 2001, Zacarias Moussaoui entered the United States at Chicago's O'Hare Airport, traveling on a French passport that allowed him to enter the country without a visa and stay legally for ninety days, until May 22.

Moussaoui was carrying a letter of introduction from a Malaysian businessman, Yazid Sufaat, naming Moussaoui as his commercial representative in the United States.

Sufaat was a high-level operative of al-Qaeda. In January 2000, he had allowed a number of known al-Qaeda members—Moussaoui was not one of them—to use his apartment in Kuala Lumpur, the capital of Malaysia, for a strategy meeting, a gathering that had been surveilled by the Malaysian security services and the American CIA, which was aware of Sufaat's affiliation with al-Qaeda.

Immediately after arriving in Chicago, Moussaoui traveled to Norman, Oklahoma, and on February 26 began flying lessons at Airman Flight School in that city.

6
FEBRUARY 26
Home with Karen

Evening, Karen's row house on the Hill. Snow is falling gently in windless air as I arrive for a night with my love. I park at the rear just off the alley, in a graveled space marked by a small sign, 428—Karen's street number—which hangs askew from the weathered redwood fence surrounding her back plot.

Out of the car, I pause and look around carefully, checking my surroundings, a game I sometimes play. Back here, two brick-paved alleys merge. One enters from the north and bisects the east-west passage I have just come in on. I see nothing moving at first, just the falling snow, glimmering in the light of a streetlamp at the intersection.

Then, there: from the north, a small, lone car turns into the alley and creeps quietly down toward where I am standing, the sound of its motor muffled in the soft silence of the snow. When it reaches the intersection and streetlamp, it halts. It's a foxy, little Honda CRX, black, D.C. plates, the driver a black chick wearing a black leather, Afro-style pillbox cap. I check her license number ("District of Columbia, AD 2989, Taxation Without Representation") and memorize it. Our eyes meet: hers are hard, practiced, urban, barely noticing. She turns left, heads toward Twelfth Street, disappears.

Game over, though I will know that plate number tomorrow.

Entering Karen's back plot, I skirt the crazy, snowed-on shapes of her old, wooden lawn furniture and pause just before going up the stoop. I see Karen in the warm light of the kitchen. She's working at the sink. Her face is pleasant and concentrated. She doesn't see me, a dark shape out here in the falling snow. She is in her thick, blue terry-cloth bathrobe, a garment I'm well familiar with by now. It is loose and open at the front this evening. Her blond hair is wet and dark from a shower. She is transfixing.

Up on the stoop, I bang on the back door—I always give a warning, three rapid knocks, she knows who it is—unlock the door, and enter the back hallway.

"Hey, ho."

"Hey, Big Boy," she yells from the kitchen. I go in to the light and the warmth, and we kiss. She has been chopping cucumbers, peppers, and tomatoes on a white plastic chopping block, feeding herself from the veggies, and her mouth tastes fresh and good. Her hair smells of shampoo. She is bright-eyed, sharp, and happy looking. It is Monday, a day off for her, private time, when she does her bills, cooks, gets domestic.

"Good day?" I ask.

"Ooooh, perfect."

I know why perfect: "Hey, I liked the Dieterich piece."

Karen has just done a long profile of Representative Bob Dieterich, a congressman from Illinois, who these days is acting suspiciously like a presidential candidate.

The Post ran the piece this morning, front page, left column, with a big color shot of the tall, skinny Dieterich standing in a cornfield somewhere downstate. The piece looks good in print. Karen, despite being a veteran—she's worked for *The Post* for five years and has done these things before—is happy as a clam. Appearance on the front page gets her every time.

"Ooooh, thank you, yeah, yeah."

Karen smiles and pulls her head back, looking up at me at an angle as we still hold each other, groin to groin. She brushes snow from my hair with the back of her right hand.

"And your day, Big Boy, how was yours?" she asks, still holding on to me and smiling.

"Meetings all day. That's about it. I'm telling you, I spend sixty percent of my goddamn time sitting around tables listening to other people's bullshit. And my own."

The rule is, beyond generalities I do not talk about my day or the run of events in my world. As with Nan, I tell Karen nothing of my working life that you cannot read in the papers. Like a good Agency wife, she seems to accept it.

Truth: I'm edgy as hell, but very high. We've just gotten a capture report. An al-Qaeda operative has been seized by the Jordanian Mukhabarat, the country's internal security service, in Amman. The first news is incomplete and we're waiting for the full story, but provisionally the take from him looks good.

This we know: A week back, Jordanian police captured this man, an al-Qaeda member whose name is on our Terrorist Register and whom we wanted. He and three others, whose identities we have not yet confirmed, had been hiding in a safe house in a poor neighborhood in east Amman, out past the airport. There had been a gun battle. Three of the men died, but one, this man, was taken alive. We got news of his capture the day it happened.

The captured terrorist, a Palestinian named Waleed Abu Nejmeh, is lucid and began talking two days ago. A cable on his debriefing came in this morning. He has confessed to training at an al-Qaeda camp in Afghanistan, a place called Khaldan. Abu Nejmeh has had operational contacts with other persons we believe belong to al-Qaeda. The names, including Liamine Dreissi, the man we think killed Ed Powers, check out on our rosters. We're waiting for interrogation transcripts.

Under the Amman safe house, in a basement they'd had enlarged, they had stashed large plastic barrels containing sulfuric and nitric acids in massive quantities, more than two tons of the stuff in all. You could have filled a couple of trucks with it.

When sulfuric and nitric acids are mixed, the result is an explosive more powerful than TNT. Though the terrorists had kept the two acids in separate containers, over time a number of the containers had leaked, and the two fluids had mixed on the basement floor. If someone had thrown a cigarette down there, the whole house would have blown and taken half the neighborhood with it.

Abu Nejmeh, the others, had bought the sulfuric acid gradually, in small quantities, on the open market. The nitric acid, which in Jordan only gold dealers can buy, they purchased using a forged gold dealer's license.

At first we didn't believe the story of the leaky barrels and mixed acids, but we now have a confirm from Amman Station.

Jordanian police also found five Toshiba two-way radios, bought in London, they learned, and modified for use as remote-control detonators. The four-man cell, Abu Nejmeh said, was planning to destroy a Safeway store in Shmeisani, an upscale neighborhood in the west of town. They wanted to blow the place up because it is American owned and because Western booze is on sale there. The liquor department is off in one corner of the store, sequestered behind thick curtains.

" 'Carrolls Sund.—beef strog, salad,' " I read aloud from a note on the fridge.

The Carrolls. I'd forgotten.

"Sunday dinner," Karen says. "And you're bringing the vino, okay?"

"Yep, right, gotcha."

The Carrolls, Joyce and Tim, are friends of Karen's from the near Maryland burbs. He is a lawyer, solid and unobjectionable, she an old high school mate of Karen's and also a lawyer.

How they pair in Washington, lawyers. Somebody ought to study the phenomenon; it can't be healthy. Like the press, so many of them don't talk to anybody else, don't even deign to fuck anybody else.

But then, when you think about it, we—we of the Agency—are like that, too. We intermarry. Our sons, and these days our daughters, follow us to join the Firm, often before we ourselves retire. And here in Washington at least, we socialize almost exclusively with our own, making the rounds of CIA houses scattered through the Washington suburbs—safe houses in a way—that form a kind of black archipelago from which we rarely venture.

The Carrolls know vaguely who I am, *vaguely* being the operative word. When asked what I do, I tell most people "I work for the government" or "I am with the intelligence community," statements that say, go no further with your questions. And most people, including the Carrolls, don't.

"I've taken Saturday off," Karen says. "I've got lots of time due me—several years of it. Jesus Christ, could I use a break!"

Her hair is clean-scented from the shampoo. I run my fingers through it, and we kiss again. Bed later.

I grab a Bud from the fridge and head for the living room. There, Karen's aging dog, Pooch, a large, black animal, mostly Lab, awakes from a snooze by the fireplace, sees me from afar, and thumps the floor with her tail in a sleepy attempt to greet a friend, albeit recently acquired. Then she closes her eyes and drifts back into the slumber of the elderly.

For a moment, standing by Pooch, I look out the big bay window down onto Karen's quiet street. Game time again: I take note of an unmarked van parked in front of the house. I've seen it before. I presume it belongs in the neighborhood. I have not had the plates checked.

Across the way, down at the corner on Pennsylvania Avenue, is a brightly lit Texaco station. Beyond it, the thick traffic on Pennsylvania is creeping east, out away from town.

I yell, "Bitch on the roads out there tonight. You're lucky you weren't out in it."

Karen, who's heading up the stairs, yells back, "I was. Safeway was packed. They're saying six inches by morning now. Scares the hell out of people, they all head for the grocery store to stock up for the big blizzard. Washington dorks."

The Safeway—Karen's store on Maryland Avenue, not far from here. I think of the other Safeway, the one in Amman that almost got blown up, thankful we don't have such mayhem here. Then I sink, tired, into Karen's puffy, old couch under the bay window. My day is catching up with me. The Bud tastes good.

For a time I noodle with my cell phone to check my home voice mail—could be news there, maybe something about Amman. It turns out I do have a couple of calls, but nothing earthshaking, both from evening-duty people at Langley who have routine questions about my scheduling. These I'll deal with later.

From Karen's cluttered coffee table—days-old newspapers, books, an empty Sprite can—I grab the Metro Section of today's *Post*, my end-of-the-day kind of reading: COUNSELOR FACING SEX CHARGE: PR. WILLIAM GIRL, 13, TELLS OF RELATIONS . . . CAR IN FATAL

CARJACKING RANDOMLY PICKED ON BELTWAY . . . BITE FROM PET COBRA ALMOST KILLS VA MAN.

Your better stuff.

Then I click Karen's TV on to *NEWS4 at 6,* the Washington NBC affiliate's local news program, which they run before they put Brokaw on. *NEWS4* is the TV equivalent of the Metro Section, but even better: you don't have to read anything.

As the sound comes up, Jim Vance's leathery, older Afro face appears, the face of a man who's seen a few things in this life. Vance is leaning into the camera, announcing a suicide story out of Pittsburgh. He warns us solemnly, a lugubrious look on his face, of "graphic footage in the following segment." Vance's look is probably faked, though how can you tell with TV people?—they fake it so much fake becomes real for them.

Then we see a taped shot of a man sitting on the white tile roof ledge of an office building, his legs dangling down. The footage has been taken from higher up on a neighboring building. Vance in voice-over tells us the man had been shooting randomly with a pistol at passersby in the streets below, though he hadn't hit anybody and the cops think he didn't really want to. The cops have cleared the streets. The man is, Vance intones, about to kill himself.

The man—a black man, it looks like, though the camera is far away and a wide-brimmed, red hat covers much of his face—sits on the ledge for a while, doing nothing, then calmly puts the gun to his heart. We see him twitch and relax and fall forward off the ledge, his body bending in flight, jackknifing, as if he's trying to touch his toes. Fluttering in the air behind him his red hat falls more slowly, down, down, down.

And that's the story. On comes a commercial for some fancy new SUV GM is pushing. You wonder who he was, the falling man, what demons drove him to do what he did. We never learn, we never will learn. The footage was basically pointless, just *NEWS4* exploiting a bit of urban tragedy their Pittsburgh affiliate caught on tape.

The Falling-Man Story is like many of our Agency narratives: it has no beginning and no real end, no explanation. You can't tell what it means.

"Hey, Dieterich going to make it?"

Karen's in the dining room now, setting the table. She's changed into a man's buttoned-down white-and-pink-striped shirt and a dressy pair of stonewashed jeans, tight over her ass. Her belt is a white leather thing, my gift to her for Christmas two months back.

"Maybe. He's sure got a structure out there, you can see it easily, they're not hiding it. He's got plenty of friends, probably get the money. Illinois's hard to launch from, though. Hasn't happened in a generation. More. Stevenson in the fifties. Nobody since then, and Stevenson lost."

Dieterich's a youngish Democrat. Karen tells me he's liked in the party, works hard, that he's smarter than the average. Friends of Bob, an ever-expanding group, are said to be traveling the country, making more friends, feeling the national pulse for a presidential run. The guy thinks ahead.

And is lucky. He's on the *Lehrer NewsHour* this evening, which is no coincidence: PBS newspeople seem to get most of their news and all of their ideas from the day's papers. Dieterich's appearance tonight was Karen's doing.

"You got him, babe," I say, "national coverage in the paper this morning and now he's on the tube tonight." I whistle a little tootle of admiration. "Double whammy, Kare—guy owes you."

Karen's standing now in the big doorway between the dining room and the living room and is watching, with an ironic, corner-of-the-mouth smile, as Ray Suarez lobs softballs—it's a News-maker Interview—at Dieterich, who plucks Suarez's questions gracefully out of the air, like a star ballplayer, and sends them softly back.

"Dieterich's a quick man to say yes to a TV producer," Karen says. "His people probably arranged it this morning. And look at him—great candidate, comes across beautifully." Karen doesn't hide her hopes: if you're a reporter and you get in early on a serious candidate, as Karen has with Dieterich, he takes you up with him.

As she stands there watching Dieterich perform, her lovely face becomes less ironic, more calculating, the face of someone who's placed a bet on a good horse and is waiting for the gate.

Karen's face.

On the wall of my den I have hung an eight-by-ten, glossy photo someone from the *Washingtonian* took of Karen about a year ago when Jake Podesta, their features guy at the time, was doing a piece about *The Post*.

They shot the photo on a third-floor balcony of the Senate Russell Building. Karen, facing the camera, is standing in front of a white marble balustrade. Looming over her right shoulder is the Capitol, then as now Karen's professional hunting ground. Far in the distance, out of focus and grainy, rises a church steeple, the tall octagonal spire of St. Dominic's down in the depths of the L'Enfant Plaza area.

Karen is wearing a demure white cotton blouse—high collar, puffy sleeves, frills down the front—and a conservative dark skirt. Her House and Senate press pass, embalmed in yellow-tinted plastic, is hanging around her neck on a chain entangled with a string of fake pearls. Her hair is combed back, slightly mussed, blown by the wind.

She's put on minimal makeup and is wearing no earrings. The early-morning light is striking her wide, intelligent forehead and has caught her high cheekbones.

She is looking directly into the camera, her eyes confident, forthright, honest. A face a spy could love.

———

After dinner, we kick back on the living room couch, both of us a little muzzy from the chardonnay.

"Thing in the office?" she asks softly.

"Hey?"

"'Hey'? Hey, Paul, you're off somewhere." She pauses. "Even when you're here, you're off somewhere. Lot of the time."

"I hear Nan talking."

"Well, maybe Nan had something."

I say, meaning it, as I used to say to Nan, "You know the drill: just ask. It's okay, it's not a problem. I don't think you're the agent of a foreign power. I'll tell you what I can tell you. What I can't, I won't."

"Mmhmm. So—was there a 'thing' at the office today."

"Yes."

"Mmhmm. What was it?"

"Foreign news."

"Good foreign news?"

"Maybe."

"Good." Then softly: "You know, a lot of you is top secret. More than the spook stuff." She closes her eyes, is quiet.

Nan talking again. "Your secret life is an excuse for you to be elsewhere," Nan would say. "You like being far away, like the song— remember the song?—'Faraway places with strange-sounding names . . . calling, calling me'? Remember? Bing Crosby? You're a faraway place yourself. You always have been."

You like being far away. I would object to this, and when I did, Nan would smile. We never settled it.

I caress Karen's forehead, lightly trace her eyebrows with the tips of my fingers. She opens her eyes halfway, closes them again.

Our fling was never supposed to turn into anything much, but it has. Karen tells people, "Don't ask. We slopped into it and stayed there, what can I say?"

I had caught her between lovers. With the last one she'd had a bad good-bye and was in no easy mood.

We met last September at a reception on the Hill, a fête of sorts for Representative Tommy Finn, an earnest, rust-belt Democrat from Ohio, expert on the U.S. census, of all things, and dull as dishwater. Finn was being honored by an Afghan relief organization for support he'd given for them in and out of Congress.

By chance, I had come into D.C. that afternoon to confer with House Appropriations people—budget targets, eye-glazing. Since Finn is on Appropriations, I thought I'd stick around and see if I could work him a little.

Finn showed, and we exchanged pleasantries, but before I got a chance to massage him, he moved on smoothly to work the room. It was then that I noticed her: tall, slender, blond. Good face. Ass and legs to die for.

She seemed to know Finn. She walked up and started talking with him, listening carefully to what he had to say, writing it down in one of those long, narrow spiral notebooks press people whip out when they're at work.

A reporter.

In my trade, when we are trying to turn some foreign target, we sometimes call it "making a pass" or "romancing." I know no word or phrase for an intelligence officer using his background to make a real pass and stir up a real romance, but that's what I did.

I waited, not too obviously, for Karen and Finn to split, then approached her and said hello. I told her a little, not much, about myself. I suggested I might be a source on the Afghan troubles, about which she knew nothing. I got her work number, she got mine.

Since we were both leaving, I walked her out to Independence Avenue—the reception had been in House Rayburn—said good-bye, and watched her walk up the Hill in the rain, avoiding the puddles. She had a firm, direct step, and her calves were good under her tan raincoat. They'd be good, I thought, around me.

A week later I took her to dinner at The Dubliner, on Mass Ave near Capitol Hill. We had onion soup and fish and chips in the big, dark, wood-paneled dining room away from the noise and the crush of college kids at the bar.

It was too early for the live entertainment—a local group, Irish Cream, would be on at nine thirty—so the management had the jukebox going, playing at one point "Black Velvet Band," a kind of Dubliner anthem. I knew the words of the chorus, and as the jukebox played, I repeated them to her:

> *Oh, her eyes they shone like the diamonds,*
> *You'd think she was queen of the land,*
> *And her hair hung over her shoulder,*
> *Tied up in a black velvet band.*

The song, I told her, is about a naughty lady in Belfast who would steal watches from gentlemen in pubs and plant them for safekeeping in the pockets of unsuspecting and innocent young lads. Now and then an innocent lad would be taken to be an accomplice of the naughty lady and as a result find himself in Australia, working in a penal colony.

"You've got to watch naughty ladies in bars," I said.

"Only if you're an innocent lad," she said, cocking her head.

Smiles. We talked of this and that, where we were from—Ohio, Kentucky—where we'd been in our lives, that I had a wife, Nan— "We're separated for good, it's over, divorce under way," I said—and that "long back" Karen had had a husband. My "intelligence community background"—the phrase I used—attracted her. She liked it, liked the mystery, maybe even danger, it hinted at. The mystery and danger of my trade allure some women. It gives you a handle.

That first date, straight-out and up front, Karen told me she would never give up her career for a marriage. Never. Principle One of her life. "Been there, didn't work."

At thirty-five Karen is fourteen years younger than I am and introduces me to her friends as "my old man—my new old man." A joke of sorts, but down deep we both know my days are past the best and that those fourteen years are a problem.

Will she take a walk? When?

They—Dreissi and some others—are trying to break into our bedroom. I am up, struggling to keep the intruders out. I have my left shoulder against the door, my legs braced, right leg back, left hip on the door.

They, on the other side, outnumber me and are managing to force the door ever more open.

A knife's edge of light, expanding, cleaves the cold pitch-black of our room. They are al-Qaeda, and they are winning. I want to pull a gun and don't have one.

The change comes when I realize that in this room or out of this room, they will die. That's the deal: because I am who I am, I will make them die. The thought comforts me.

I drift then down a silver river, a soft stream of spilling, shimmering bubbles, into a zone that is not quite wakefulness.

Karen's there. She breathes deeply. I feel her rhythms.

It's cold in our bedroom, but the snow has stopped, and the night is very quiet.

---

7 **FEBRUARY 27**
Lurch

"Got a sec?"

It's Lurch poking his huge head into my office.

I always have time for a monster, I am thinking.

Lurch's real name is Rudolph Thurneysen, but his buddies call him Lurch because he's six and a half feet tall and has massive, boulderlike shoulders and hands like Texas steaks. He combs his pitch-black hair straight up and back, a style that makes him look—I'm pretty sure this is intentional—like an ape. Lurch also has a deep, booming voice that carries through walls and down corridors.

Lurch seems to fit.

Lurch commands the FBI Liaison Group assigned here to ATAC, where he occupies, almost fills with his person, a small, windowless room in the middle of the Fusion Center. His office is surrounded by cubicles full of Agency and Bureau people, notably a pair of aides re-assigned from the Hoover Building downtown, two dour, black-suited Mormons named Gary Petty and Clyde Arbuckle, who follow him around like twin angels of doom. He is alone now, without his Mormons.

"Just came in, take a look," he says. He puts a document on my desk and eases himself into the scruffy, beige wing chair, a hand-me-down from General Services Administration, that sits opposite my desk. The document is entitled "Interim Report on Investigation into Causes of Death of American National Edward N. Powers." It's from the Pak police, presented to our embassy by InterServices Intelligence.

As I leaf through it, I give Lurch a questioning look.

"Powers," Lurch says, "Paks say the Indians did it."

"Huh?"

"Indians—Hindus—killed Powers."

"You're shitting me."

"Nope. They're blamin' *'agents provocateurs'*—pardon my French—*'agents provocateurs* of a foreign power.' That means India, if you wondered. They say the *'agents'* have disappeared from Pakistan. They're quoting 'sources' and 'informants' we ain't allowed to talk to. They say the case is still open, but the perps have gone." Lurch makes a fart-ing noise with his mouth. "Buncha shit. Way I figure it, the 'Interim Report' ain't no interim report. I figure it's over on the Pak side. They are done working on this, though they don't say so in so many words."

I feel a hot, molten anger rising in me as I flip through the pages—there are four, the Paks are being succinct—and see that Lurch is right. They've blown off the investigation. "Why the fuck are they doing this?"

"Ah, the mysterious East," Lurch says. "Curtiss called over to give me an alert on it." Tom Curtiss is legal attaché, Islamabad, also an FBI officer. "Curtiss's pissed, everybody's pissed."

Lurch has had time to calm down, but I'm seething. You cannot trust the Pak services. For some reason they're pulling back, screwing us.

"Ain't no help, are they?"

I don't answer.

In early January, maybe ten days after Powers died, Lurch showed up in my office with the same "Got a sec?"

"Got the Powers stuff, sneak preview," Lurch said then, parking his fat briefcase on my floor and seating himself in my wing chair.

The "stuff" was some of the FBI's take from Powers's town house in the District, mostly copies of photos and other documents. "Sneak preview" because Lurch would go on to present this material later that day to a session of the Working Group, an ATAC committee that reviews operations, a meeting I would have to miss because of an appointment I had with the Saudi ambassador, a guy who seems to avoid Washington—I grab him when I can. Lurch, it pleases me to note, knows the pecking order here at ATAC and is always treating me well.

After the Bureau seized this material, CIA requested it from the FBI formally through channels. Happily, it took the Bureau no more than a week to get it to us, a fast response for them, apparently one of the fruits of our new, respectful relationship.

Smiling evilly that snowy January morning, Lurch pulled two photos out of his briefcase.

"For your album," he said, tossing them onto my desk.

One, a blurry Polaroid, was of a young woman. She is naked. She is lying facedown on what looks like the deck of a boat. Her skin is dark and shiny. Lovely ass, sleek, perfect legs. Beyond her, sunlight on the water breaks into slivers of silver. Hot day.

"Taken on Powers's sailboat," Lurch said. "He used it for parties, the boat. Powers's old lady hasn't been on it in years."

Lurch puts on a face. "They're estranged."

"I bet they are. And the cookie? She Ed's niece?"

"I figure not."

"Know her name?"

"Not yet. She may be hard to track down. I think he had a lot of these bunnies. Though"—evil grin again—"maybe this one was something special and dear to his heart."

I grunted. "Lifestyles of the rich and famous."

The other photo, a color five-by-seven, showed Ed with a stylish, shrewd-looking lady. She's dressed for success: black-and-white, tweed suit, white blouse, little red bow necktie. She's leaning her hips on the front hood of a silvery, expensive-looking automobile. She has her arms crossed. Ed's next to her, grinning that used-car-salesman's grin he had, as if he's just sold her the car. The lady, icily self-confident, is staring at the camera, unsmiling, though she doesn't seem unhappy.

"The picture," Lurch said, "was taken in London, front apron of Ed Powers's town house."

You can see some of the building in the background, a classic, beautifully kept late Victorian. High-quality real estate. The house is gleaming white. It has black shutters at the windows, black wrought ironwork on the porch. Red geraniums are blooming in big, white wooden flower boxes set on the traffic apron.

I know the place well.

"Andrea Rodriguez," I said, thinking immediately I might regret saying it. I went on quickly, "She ran his office in London. American. I've met her. Anybody talk to her?"

"Brits did in London, so'd we. And we'll see her again here— she's coming back to the States. Arrival of the lady is imminent. Here's a transcript"—Lurch dropped a manila folder on my desk— "of what she had to say to the Brits and to us, which turned out to be not much."

I leafed through it quickly. My copy, I gathered. I would read it later.

Ten years back, London was a town I saw much of. I was often there on assignment from my job at Langley, where I worked in what was then known as the Counterterrorism Center.

One of my tasks in London was to meet people like Ed and collect what they had to say of their ramblings through countries of interest to us. I'd see Ed over drinks in a pub in Chelsea we both liked, the Cross Keys. Andrea, ice-cool, alluring Andrea, would sometimes tag along, maybe have a pub lunch with us. Typically after a beer or two Ed and I would take a stroll in a park near the Thames and get down to cases. Andrea would leave us and head for the shops up on King's Road or wherever.

The merest, briefest of glances can signal desire.

At one of those lunches, as Andrea sat next to Ed and across from me in the pub's back room, I thought I saw something in her look, caught some split-second lingering of her glance that suggested . . . what?

What indeed? I thought.

When I knew Ed was out of the country, off drumming up business in one of his hellholes, I phoned Andrea.

"How about lunch?" I said. "I'd like somebody to talk to. You free?"

She said, as I thought she would say, "Sure, sounds good. Where?"

In that "sure" was just a millisecond's catch of excitement.

"I know a place just off Brompton Road, not too far from you."

She hesitated: Then: "How about here?" she said, as I hoped she would. "I could fix us lunch. Be fun. Why not just come over here?"

In the sunny bedroom on the second floor of that South Kensington town house, as I was about to leave, she caressed my cheek and lips with the backs of her fingers. When I told her she was lovely, she reacted, honestly, I think, as if surprised, as if unused to compliments. We kissed softly at the front door and then I walked out into Drayton Gardens.

Nan never knew. Neither did Big Ed. No sweat, I thought. I have always had the feeling—against all logic, I know—that if I didn't tell someone that something had happened, it was as if it had never happened.

"We also got a bunch of phony documents," Lurch said, "passports and shit—here's a list and some Xerox copies—in the name of one Guy Rutherford, which I understand was his alias."

"One among many," I said. "It was the latest. And last."

"Now have a look at this." Lurch pulled out yet a third photo.

"Show and Tell Day, Lurch?"

"What do you think? What do you make of it?"

In the photo were five men, Powers and four Africans, standing in the sun. Behind them were scraggly bushes and low, thorny trees. I recognized one of the Africans. The photo had to have been taken in Sierra Leone, a sad country on the hot, mosquito-ridden coast of West Africa. The man, my African friend, was named Samuel Kontay Edgerton. Lurch was happily surprised that I knew him.

Sam Edgerton had been one of ours. We thought Sam and his New Africa Rally would go places. They didn't. Sam, I told Lurch, was probably still alive, but I was not sure.

"Like to check him out," Lurch said.

"Hard to do. I'll see what we got."

Theoretically Lurch has access to our records, but we both know it doesn't work quite that way. My own clearances allow me to rummage in our files, both paper and electronic, far more easily than an outsider, even one with Lurch's status. I told him I would do a look-see and give him what I could find. Powers had worked Sam, I knew. So had I.

"Know the others?"

"Nah," I said. "But I'll dig around. We may have something on them."

We probably do. They were our men. Once.

"His wife's a piece of work," Lurch said. "Know her?"

I nodded.

I bump into Vye Powers now and then. She is getting up in years, a little older than Big Ed was. She lives in Kenwood, a tony suburb just over the District line in Maryland. She owns a boutique in Georgetown—PJ's—and is wealthy.

The marriage had become a shambles. Vye knew of Andrea and probably knew of some of Powers's other mistresses and girlfriends. Vye had come to hate Powers and had a cool contempt for Andrea. "That little Chiquita banana," she once called her—Andrea was born in L.A. and her father was Mexican.

"Wants to sue us for bustin' in," Lurch said. "Said she'd have given us the keys, right? Well, hell, who knew? Didn't even think of her. We had to go in fast, had a warrant, which we got in the middle of the night, lotta goddamn trouble. In we go, we find out later the bitch is pissed. What can you do?"

Lurch then fished a sample of corporate stationery out of his briefcase—for a firm called InterTech, the company Ed housed on P Street. The fifteen or so names listed as "associates" in fine print in a column on the left read like a Pentagon roster ("Admiral Edward S. Bricker, USN Retired," "Lt. Col. Richard Mullins, USA Retired," others like that).

Ed, who knew the economic value of reputation and rank, had recruited these men after they'd left the services and had gotten them to pitch their old offices and cronies for sales. Some were probably working for him illegally, since retired military are supposed to have no business contacts with any of the services for five years after they go civilian. Some of them either ignore the rule, which is hard to enforce, or find ways around it. Big Ed would have helped them.

I said, "InterTech was such a fucked-up company. Why would anybody work for an asshole like Powers?"

"Hey, think about it. Military retirement ain't all that great. These guys are used to pushing hundreds of people around, daily basis, right?—and getting saluted and yes-sirred all over the fucking place. Then all of a sudden, poof, gone is the glory. Golf course bores the shit out of them and all they got to do otherwise is sit around the house and listen to the old lady, which is worse. Maybe also they're on their second or third wives, and they've got alimony or something to worry about, so they say, 'Hey, here's this company, needs experts, what the hell, give it a try.' We've talked with some of them. We'll track down every last one of them, the ones that are alive anyhow. Couple are dead."

Lurch grinned when he said that. "In my fair city Chicago the graveyards vote, right? At InterTech they work for Ed Powers. Also, Powers was sole proprietor. When Powers died, so'd the company. One of his U.S. lawyers is handling it, paying off the employees. They're all pissed. Amazed at the murder and pissed. What can you do?"

I drop the "Interim Report" on my desk. "Lurch, I don't believe it, I just don't believe it."

"They're such assholes," Lurch says. He means the Paks. "Dead case as far as they're concerned. Like, the folder's open, but there ain't gonna be no movement. End of the show."

Lurch shifts his voice into a soft basso profundo and whispers in his conspirator mode, "Kinda makes you wonder, don't it?"

I nod. The Pak secret services' ties with their country's Islamists are close. Whoever killed Ed Powers may well have a protecting angel.

I tell Lurch we have a report from a source, an officer in the Border Police, who has been reliable up to now. The guy claims that shortly after Powers was murdered, Liamine Dreissi passed through a town in western Pakistan called Bannu, headed for Afghanistan. Not much, but there it is. I tell Lurch he'll get an analysis of the report from someone in the DI. Lurch has no comment.

We mull all this over, remarking on the general crummy quality of our Pakistani connection, then go silent and sit for a time.

"Hey," Lurch suddenly says, "Reggie Wims retiring—goddamn milestone, man, what are your guys gonna do?"

"Oh, yeah, Jesus, sure is. 'Skins'll really go into the hole, won't they?"

Reginald DeVonne "Miracle Man" Wims is the Washington Redskins' star cornerback. He is pure grace on the field, faster than the wind. He is all-time leader for the 'Skins in both interceptions and interceptions returned for touchdown. But Reggie, at forty-one, is just too old for the job. He has just announced that he is stepping down, one more tragedy for the home team, whose record of late has been lousy.

When we're not talking business, Lurch and I like to dissect the pro teams. He knows I played for Woody Hayes way back when and is mightily impressed by the fact. Lurch is a Bears man, a team that did considerably better than the 'Skins this season, but, living in Washington, Lurch pays attention to our home team—you have to, you can't escape them.

"Greatest goddamn interceptor in the history of the 'Skins," Lurch says.

"Probably. No Miracle Man—what the hell are we gonna do? Be murder out there. We'll end up bottom of the league."

I look aside. As I think of Wims and of downfield passing, I feel the motion of my arm, feel the release of the ball, and see it spiraling tightly, lifting, then dipping, to my son, who has placed himself just right, about twenty yards down from me on the Yorktown High athletic field, and who pulls the ball cleanly, no bobbling, to his stomach, his face earnest, businesslike. When he looks to me for approval, he gets it. The kid's a natural.

The vision of David's young face lasts for an instant, then vanishes utterly, leaving only inexpressible pain.

I see Lurch has gone. I must have said good-bye.

---

8 **FEBRUARY 28**
Meatball on the Line

Cleppinger storms into my office with the news: "Meatball just called. O-o-o-oh, yes."

Meatball is our name for the *New York Times* reporter Marshall Robertson. I have no idea why; it goes back.

"Out of the blue," Cleppinger says. "Five minutes ago. Guy calls me up and tells me Ed Powers is CIA, that there's a 'thing' coming—a 'thing.' That's not what he says the call's about, but that's what the call's about. He starts out, 'How's it going, Bill?'—you know that goddamn unctuous way he has. 'Just touching base,' he says, 'just want to talk,' and we talk about not much till finally there's this big pause and then he says, 'Say, by the way, Bill, anything new on Edward Powers, guy killed in Pakistan? He was Agency, wasn't he?'

"And I say, 'Who the hell told you that?' and he says, 'O-o-oh, there's talk around, it's pretty definite, you got a comment?' "

Cleppinger does an eye roll at the ceiling. " 'Talk around'! 'Comment'! Jesus Christ! I fish him a little to see who's doing the goddamn 'talking,' but he doesn't bite, so then I tell him I don't get into that kind of crap with anybody, not even deep philosophers like him. End of conversation."

You've got to watch Meatball. We have friends in the media, and up to a point, Meatball is one of them. As he should be. He lives off us and the stories we feed him.

He is also a pooh-bah in the fat and sassy Washington news establishment. His editors regularly give him front-page status, and once in a while you see his pudding face and heavy, torpid eyes on *Washington Week,* as he discourses knowingly on America's secret agencies and their role in the great events of the day.

This glory is as much our doing as his, and for that reason he is ordinarily highly polite to us. But like all reporters, Meatball is ever ready to dance off the reservation if a juicy enough story beckons. In Powers he may have one.

I'm pretty sure I know where Meatball heard his "talk."

"Bill, two weeks after we head over to committee on the Powers business, we get this call from Meatball. About Powers. Ain't no coincidence, they're feeding him over there—you just know it."

Cleppinger is nodding. "You want to kill them," he says.

"And you know who, too—fuckhead Grayson."

Merritt—"call me Bob"—Grayson is Jim McClennan's opposite number on the minority side. Merritt's a wiry little shrimp, maybe five foot five on a good day, with a way-too-superior air. And Merritt—I don't call him Bob—never misses an opportunity to give us trouble. Merritt's guardian senator on committee, Edward L. Donovan, for reasons best known to himself, is an implacable foe of ours. Donovan is forever claiming, in committee, on the Senate floor, sometimes in print in the op-ed pages, that CIA, like the Berlin Wall, is a relic of the Cold War and, like that wall, ought to be torn down.

For the last decade or so Donovan has talked about zeroing the Agency out of the budget, breaking us up, and shifting our functions to State, Defense, and elsewhere in the government. If Donovan got his way, the Agency would cease to exist. It's a loony scheme that will go nowhere, but then that's Donovan for you. A lot of our troubles with committee, including, we are pretty sure, negative leaks of classified information, come straight from Donovan or his boy Merritt.

Cleppinger's face has gone stony. "Merritt Grayson. That rat-faced little turd. I will piss on his goddamn grave."

Bill just might. Once in Rome, years back, after a heavy night in the bars somewhere in Trastevere and a wild ride through town with drunken cronies, Bill famously had the car they were riding in stopped in the Via Gaeta in front of the old Soviet embassy and, no doubt caught in the act by the KGB's closed-circuit TV cameras, urinated on that building's ornate wrought-iron entrance gate.

Those who saw the performance say Bill took his time, executing the act with a smile, and, after zipping up, bowed politely to the camera. Next morning Bill professed to be deeply embarrassed—"Jeez, is my face red!"—but there were no complications. The Soviets lodged no complaints, though they knew it happened and knew who did it—they knew our whole Rome Station, of course—nor did Bill's career suffer for the deed, which, in time, became part of Agency lore.

"Grayson's doing something with Powers," I say. "Think about Powers's backgrounder, it reads like a police report—best you can say is, he never got indicted. Thing's made for Merritt."

"'Made for Merritt.' So it is. Our little Merritt." Cleppinger shakes his head, then looks over at me, incomprehension on his face. "Honest to God, I don't see it, I just don't. I mean, yeah, this could be a PR problem because of the guy's, call it the guy's business practices, but we use fellows like Powers all the time, always have. They know that on the Hill, those assholes, why don't they grow up?"

Committee chairman Dennis Coale (Republican, Alabama) is not a problem for us. Coale is a true believer in the Agency, a man we spend much time stroking, though it is hardly necessary. Coale, like most other members of the committee, is circumspect and does not ordinarily poke into who our spies are and how they operate. Leaks horrify him.

"Patterson, these people on the Hill," Cleppinger says bitterly, "staff, our noble and courageous representatives up there—these people are not interested in the truth or in reason. They are Wild Willies. And"—right index finger in the air now—"they let stuff out—little stories, little tips to buy face time with the press. They think it's harmless when they do that. Then when these 'little stories' they put out screw operations, endanger lives, then—then—they act surprised." Clep shakes his head. "None of those clowns are ever polygraphed and for goddamn good reason—half of them couldn't pass. The Hill cannot be trusted."

Cleppinger is old guard and his bitterness toward Congress—you find the same feeling all through the older cadres in Operations—goes way back. Clep will never forgive Congress, the Senate in particular, for the hearings of the seventies and eighties and the court trials that followed, some of which engulfed his friends.

These days our relations with the Hill are smooth. We are treated with respect by committee members, save throwbacks like Donovan, and we get all the money we want, sometimes even more than we want.

But Cleppinger hasn't forgotten. For Cleppinger, the relationship between CIA and Hill is Ancient Hatreds, like the Serbs and the Croats.

I say, "When one reporter calls, there's usually scuttlebutt going around."

"Yep. Could work into a feeding frenzy at some point—know that?" Clep looks away, gazes out my window. "Oh, those assholes."

9

FEBRUARY 28
Enter Sonny

"Powers had all kinds of deals going in that part of the world—Taliban, Paks, everybody. Lots we didn't know about. So maybe he simply screwed somebody in Peshawar—in some 'business' deal—and got whacked for it. Hell, you knew Powers—perfectly plausible, right?"

Sonny Desmond, plans officer, ATAC, is talking in his furry Boston accent. We're in a booth away from the bar in J. Gilbert's, an Agency watering hole in McLean. Sonny's invite.

It's late afternoon. Sonny and I are playing hooky because Sonny wanted to get out of the building "for air" and, I think, to push his theories of Ed's death. Sonny's on his second double vodka on the rocks, a drink he favors, which he calls a rammer.

Sonny's one of our older officers. He has thick, arctic white hair, which he keeps long and lets spill over his ears. He wears trifocal glasses that cut across his sad, pouchy eyes like broken windows. His cheeks are hollow-looking and are crisscrossed with a tracery of wine-colored, broken capillaries—alcohol, I swear, is the true hazard of our trade.

Sonny's theory, that Powers died in some business dispute, is more or less what Clep suggested to McClennan. Sonny, though, seems to find it believable.

He leans forward now and says softly, "Anyhow, we're spending way too much time on this al-Qaeda-killed-Ed-Powers business."

"You don't buy it."

"Shit, no. Al-Qaeda's Bill Cleppinger's Great Cosmic Sugartitty. For Bill the armies of bin Laden explain all the world's evil—suicide bombers, dandruff, low-cal food, you name it. I mean, yeah, sure, you and Clep are right to worry about NOREFUGE, I grant you that, and maybe al-Qaeda did go after Powers. And maybe they did it 'cause some tribals blew away one of Osama's Land Cruisers and maybe somehow they connected Powers to that op. Maybe, maybe, maybe—it's possible, I'm not saying it's not.

"But think about it. We have just one indicator that al-Qaeda might be involved—friend Dreissi. And how come Dreissi? Well, Dreissi entered the country—Pakistan—about the time Powers was killed. Entered the country! Shit, Osama's people enter and leave that place every damn day of the week. We don't hear about it most of the time but we sure as hell know it. Dreissi might have been up to something else, had nothing to do with Powers. And we're not thinking about what else. Major mistake. You guys' hang-up on Dreissi and Powers, this single-minded focus on NOREFUGE—it's tunnel vision, Paul, and it's skewing everything."

"Majority view."

"Conventional wisdom. Where's the evidence?"

I shrug.

Sonny bows his head to me in mock graciousness: there you are.

"Well, I'm out of the loop on this, so you and Bill and Kremer can go play the cops and robbers." Clep has purposely excluded Sonny from "the Powers thing." "Sonny's plans officer," Clep said, "it's what he's good at, not counterintel. Working Group'll do the head-scratching on this."

Sonny catches the eye of our waiter, who is pudgy but cool-moving and who jumps our way through what is now a growing, yammering crowd of young people. Sonny orders a third rammer. When the waiter gestures toward my beer mug, I shake my head no.

"I keep telling Bill we could be barking up the wrong tree," Sonny says, "I keep pushing it with the Wizards"—Sonny's term for the Working Group—"which our boy Bill chairs, but he never listens. Never."

Our boy Bill.

Sonny and Bill can't stand each other. That's part of what this is about. How or when the feud got started or over what I don't know, but its underlying themes are style and class. Sonny was born to wealth. He went to Yale and dresses like a lord. He was handsome once and even today, with those flowing locks, looks like an aging Greek god. Bill was born prole in Somerville, Massachusetts, in the forties and went to Northeastern. He wears off-the-rack suits that never quite fit him and has a face like a potato.

You can't shake your origins, not even here at the Agency, where we dispense phony names and cook up bogus personal histories with ease. Even here no one reinvents himself.

Sonny shuts up—message delivered, I suppose—and starts munching on a hard pretzel, one of the foot-long jobs they serve here in big black ceramic cups.

I wonder about Sonny, about this invitation off campus "for air." I think maybe Sonny has a dog in the Powers fight, but I can't think what.

I first met Sonny in Athens, late seventies. He was second-in-command, Beirut Station, and I was a young and lowly foot soldier in Iran. Athens was where Agency officers working in the Middle East would meet and exchange notes and info. I wondered at the time why in hell a forty-five-year-old man was still called Sonny, but his given names are Declan and St. John, and I suppose that's the reason.

Sonny's well-off family is headquartered in one of those comfortable towns on the coast south of Boston—Scituate sticks in my mind. Everybody in his large Celtic tribe down to his nephews and nieces seems to be in stocks and bonds, investment banking, and the higher forms of real estate.

Sonny told me once that some such line of work had been in his future when he was a kid. His father was a no-nonsense, imperious guy who owned a small but highly prosperous securities firm. "It was run by Micks, not WASPs," Sonny told me, "and the old man was damn proud of that." His father had more or less commanded that Sonny follow him into the business, and the young Sonny, more obedient then than now maybe, promised he would. But, suddenly, shockingly, Sonny's father died at his desk in his midforties of a massive heart attack.

Sonny was just out of Yale and was touring Europe when it happened. He took the opportunity not to follow dad into the stock and bond business, a line of endeavor, as Sonny saw it, that promised a life of endless boredom.

Like me, Sonny joined the Marine Corps, probably to prove

something obscure to himself or to his family. Though eminently draftable, he could have found a safe place in the National Guard if he'd wanted. He did two tours in Vietnam in the late sixties and won a Distinguished Service Medal and a Purple Heart. When he was discharged from the Corps, he came straight into the Agency.

For more than thirty years Sonny has moved from station to station, out in the wild places of the world, Beirut being the most dangerous. Along the way he earned top ratings. He was brave and effective. And he was clever: he masterminded some of our riskiest operations in the Middle East, exploits no outsider can ever get a hint of. When we sent his résumé over to Senate Select recently, four pages of it were blacked out.

Three years ago in a quiet ceremony on the seventh floor, the DCI made Sonny a Distinguished Officer, our highest honor.

In his long career, though, Sonny got known for what we call "creativity." That is, he acquired a rep for ignoring rules and breaking laws. A veteran of the DO once told me, "Oh, Sonny's one of our best. If you've got a dangerous or tricky job you want done, Sonny's your man. Just keep a lawyer around."

When Lindsay came in as DCI, he started sharpening his knives for guys like Sonny, older combatants, who Lindsay thought were a little too flip and a little too smart, and who had reputations for arrogance and mendacity, virtues of a sort in the old days, less so now. When Lindsay moved to can Sonny, though, he met resistance from the upper layer in Operations—"You can't fire a Distinguished Officer, you just can't"—and he backed off. And Sonny, kissed by fortune as usual, escaped the executioner.

Like me, Sonny's a product of the Cold War and has the ice of those times in his veins still. Now with his Russians gone, he's turned to terrorists and is waging the same deep, intense war on them that he waged against the Soviets.

He puts in twelve-hour days at Langley. On weekends, he'll be in the Fusion Center reading cables, sending out queries to the field—

"Are we tracking so-and-so? What are they saying about threats to installation X? How secure is embassy Y?"—and dreaming up new ops.

Sonny's wife, Clarisse, a short, chubby woman with a button nose and meaty, little legs, divorced him some years back. I figure she left him because he spent too much time on his ops, ran off too much in the night. Like me, again.

Sonny has fathered three kids, who have all grown and left. As far as I know, he has no woman friend or hobbies. Life for Sonny now is just Agency. He lives in a rented town house in McLean, near CIA.

"You know, Powers had this broad in London," Sonny says, "his 'office assistant.' Hot piece of ass apparently. Ever meet her?"

I check Sonny's face at this and see nothing. I say, "Oh, yeah, Andrea something. I knew her. I'd see Powers in London. Regular thing. I was one of the collection officers assigned to him, so I'd give him a buzz now and then and sometimes Andrea'd be around. Good-looking lady."

"Andrea," Sonny says, as if retrieving the name out of deep memory, "right, right, right."

I don't care for this. Sonny's memory, especially for names, is spectacular. I'm looking at a performance, a clumsy one, and inevitably the thought passes through that Sonny is yanking my chain here.

But over a ten-year-old fling? Why? Who'd care? Still, at Langley we're always assessing each other, we always want to know. And things add up, even love affairs of yore. I keep my eyes on Sonny, wondering.

People always know more than you think they know.

"She was with him in Dubai off and on," Sonny says. "She'd fly in from London to straighten out his Dubai operation. Hated the place. I don't blame her, nothing for a poor girl to do in that sandbox, right? But she'd come in every once in a while and straighten things out, or try to anyhow, as much as anybody could. Powers said she was a goddamn good manager and also one good bang for the buck." Sonny chuckles here, looking at me, eyes merry and bright.

Sonny's a man you always wonder about, and reading him is never easy. That smile of his, even when he asks an innocent question, is always canted and a little off true level. Kind of like Sonny himself.

"Synergy, right? Course, he treated her like shit. He had other ladies, even in Dubai. Thai, Filipina hookers. Andrea'd be in the office working hard for Ed, doing the books or trying to collect bills or stall creditors or something, and there Ed'd be, off in some borrowed villa banging a little nut-brown sweetheart. One time, I swear he had three different women in town—his wife, Andrea, and some hotel hooker he'd found in the Holiday Inn—all at the same goddamn time. I don't know how the hell he juggled all that."

Sonny drops the subject of Andrea, leaving me to wonder what this foray was all about. I'll probably never know.

We shoot the shit and watch J. Gilbert's fill up, both of us eyeing the pretty girls coming in out of the February winds. In our lazy chatting Beirut comes up, as it does with Sonny and me. We talk of Bill Buckley, our Beirut Station chief, and of the others murdered there. For both of us that city is one long, lingering ache.

As we ponder those tragedies, Sonny's furry voice grows ever more intense, and his eyes, sad, haunted, obsessed, film over like those of a man who has stared too long at the sun.

10
APRIL 19, 1983
In Beirut I Walked in Blood

Blood is a lubricant. It is thick and slippery. When you walk in it, your feet slide, your step is hard to control. The sensation, if you've ever felt it, is unforgettable.

In Beirut on a warm April afternoon in 1983, someone driving a Mercedes-Benz delivery truck loaded with explosives pulled into the driveway of our high-rise embassy. He drove the truck up the front stairs of the building, crashed it all the way into the entrance hall, and detonated the explosives, taking down the central part of the building in a rumble of falling concrete and crumpled steel girders.

Sixty-three persons, seventeen of them Americans, died. Among the dead were the entire CIA Beirut Station, the most people the Agency has ever lost at one time.

I had been visiting incognito from Istanbul, where I was posted, and—miracle again—I had not attended the Beirut Station meeting, but was lunching instead with a Lebanese informant, a journalist of sorts named Danny Rizk, at a nearby restaurant, Chez Michel, on the Corniche in Ain el-Mreisseh.

Chance governs all.

The sound of the explosion, starting as a low moan, ended as a colossal, metallic clang. The force of it shook Danny and me, shook our table and everything on it, and set the restaurant's hanging lamps in motion.

"Jesus Christ!" Danny yelled, fear in his sallow olive face. "Jesus Christ!"

Rizk and I dashed out of the restaurant into the bright early-afternoon sunlight—it was just after 1 p.m.—and ran up the Corniche, heading for where a cloud of dirty gray smoke was rising and quickly spreading into Beirut's blue sky. I knew before seeing it that the target had been our embassy.

Pounding along, not feeling my street shoes cut into my ankles, I encountered grim-faced Beirutis, some running toward where the smoke was rising, some away, some simply standing and staring down the Corniche.

A young mother, one of Beirut's well-dressed upper register, was walking toward us, pulling two kids along, a little boy and a little girl, one on each side. The little girl was wearing a gauzy, white party dress and silvery fairy antennae in her hair; the little boy was in a child's blue, pin-striped suit, looking like a tiny Lebanese banker. They were on their way to a birthday party, I suppose.

When Danny and I turned left at a corner, we saw the wreck of the building. The embassy's center section, all seven stories of concrete flooring, had collapsed onto itself, crushing to death almost everyone inside. In the wreckage a few floors up, a man was pinned alive between two huge slabs of concrete, his upper body hanging down and out over the central drive, motionless in the afternoon sunlight.

And in the street: severed limbs, blood, charred bodies, groans, cries, smoke, pain; passersby trying to care for the maimed and the dazed; in the distance, approaching us, the singsong wail of the French-style sirens the Lebanese use in their ambulances and police cars.

The blast shattered windows for miles. Far out in Beirut harbor, the battleship USS *Guadalcanal* rocked in the water from the shock.

I came up behind Dave Windham, a State Department political officer and now deputy chief of mission. Like me, Dave had been out of the building when the truck detonated.

The anguish in his face must have been reflected in mine. Neither of us could say anything when we saw each other, we just shook our heads silently. Danny, when he caught up, kept softly saying, "Goddamn, goddamn."

I smelled the chemical odor of the smoke all around and the concrete dust; then something else: the sickly sweet odor of blood and body parts. Underfoot I felt something slippery, which turned out to be a narrow rivulet of blood, pressed from the victims in the building. I can still feel the sensation. In some of my better nightmares I still experience it.

In that atrocity I lost a friend, a man I will call Doug. Doug, who had a fine, subtle mind, was our chief Middle East analyst. He was in his midforties when he died. He had been born in Beirut of missionary parents and had lived in the region for years. He knew as much about the Middle East and its ways as any Agency officer.

He was the kind of officer I wanted to be. He liked me and became something of a mentor to me. At Langley and elsewhere—Beirut, Tehran—Doug taught me a lot, particularly humility about the Agency, a sense of our limitations.

The Agency, Doug would insist, is too secret. We live isolated in our black world. We therefore have trouble sensing important public facts—like popular will and changing political moods. Journalists—like my love Karen—are better at gauging these things. They're forever out asking questions openly, talking with all kinds of people. They know important truths that we often miss.

And, Doug would say, stealing someone else's secrets is doubtless a fine and necessary art, but often when we've stolen them, we find they don't add much to our view. Going after secrets, we can miss the real world in front of our faces.

More than anything else, we miss out on the private intangibles—feelings, passions, fears, rage. These are not filed in our targets' archives or databases. No one leaks them to us.

To know our targets, really know them, we have to live in their world. We have to be fluent enough in their languages to read the local papers with our breakfast and pick up on the nuances in the press—often a press that speaks in code—then venture forth into this foreign world and try to make sense of it.

We have to hang out, we have to talk, not just with politicians or Foreign Ministry and military types, but with everyone—dissidents, Islamists, businessmen, shopkeepers, plumbers, human rights workers. Everyone.

To know the world, Doug would say, you have to go there.

And be careful of Washington. It's a world muffled in fog, driven by its own imperatives, with no high regard for truth. They'll want you to lie to them. Resist that.

We confirmed Doug's death from the wedding band on his severed left hand. When I learned he was gone, I wept.

That fall, a smiling crazy driving a pickup van destroyed our U.S. marine barracks on the beach not far from our bombed-out embassy. He killed 241 young Americans. Almost simultaneously, another smiling crazy in another van killed fifty-eight young French soldiers in their barracks. The following spring terrorists brought down our embassy annex in East Beirut, which we thought was protected and secure. Later they kidnapped and tortured to death William Buckley, our Beirut Station chief. All the while in this same city and in the mountains over toward the Syrian border, Americans were being held hostage under cruel circumstances.

When Doug was killed, I knew my work. The work became me, who I am. Like Sonny, I have encountered the terrorists, and I hate their guts.

11
MARCH 1
Downtime

Our dank February slops into March.

We are intercepting conversations from people we consider al-Qaeda operatives, but the talk is cryptic. ("The game is tied," "Bring Sally her dresses"—that kind of thing.) We have no one on the inside who can tell us what this stuff means, if it means anything.

And we get no further take on Dreissi. He has slipped away.

So I do my job.

I brief Lindsay on this program and that, I do working lunches with Lindsay and his staff. I see congressional people like McClennan, sometimes their bosses, like Coale. I talk to a civics class at Langley High, I dine alone with the Turkish ambassador at his embassy residence, a fantastic old house on Sheridan Circle. When Clep and his crew do preliminary budget submissions, I read and comment on the god-awful stuff. I meet with officers from other services—British, Russian, German. I greet my Israeli counterpart, Uri Gal, at Dulles International when he comes to town. Lindsay puts on a lunch for him here at Langley.

Mostly, though, I read cables from our far-flung outposts and write replies. Picture of a spy, I tell Karen: a man sitting at a desk, doing his dismal work like any other paper-shifting federal schmo.

And I wait.

---

12 MARCH 26
Phoenix

In late March of 2001, instructors at Pan Am International Flight Academy in Phoenix, Arizona, contacted the Federal Aviation Administration about a problem student, a thin, sad-faced young man named Hani Hanjour. Hanjour, a Saudi Arabian national who had been living in the United States, mostly in Southern California, since 1996, claimed to have a commercial pilot's rating. In 2000, he had traveled to al-Qaeda's Faruq Camp in Afghanistan, where he'd described himself to Osama bin Laden and others there as a trained pilot.

At Pan Am, though, the instructors found Hanjour's flying so inept and his English so poor they couldn't believe he had a pilot's rating. When they asked the FAA about Hanjour's rating, the agency assured them that his commercial certificate was legitimate, that he had received it from Arizona Aviation in Mesa, Arizona, in April of 1999.

Nevertheless, supervisors at Pan Am told Hanjour they would not qualify him for an advanced certificate, though the school would allow him to pay to train on a Boeing 737 flight simulator.

Among themselves the instructors said Hanjour would be dangerous if allowed to pilot an aircraft.

13
APRIL 23
Enter Kareem

They sit on my desk, seven smudgy photos, one of them only partly in focus. All feature Liamine Dreissi, our putative killer, with assorted acquaintances. One standing with Dreissi, his arm around Dreissi's shoulders, is wearing Arab dress, an Egyptian galabia. He has heavy-lidded eyes that give his face a lizardlike, reptilian look.

Our German counterpart service, the BND, supplied us these pictures after we queried them on Dreissi. All were taken in Hamburg. Three of the photos were shot near a mosque, the al-Kods-Moschee, Steindammstrasse, in a part of the city called Harburg. The others are street photos, some taken outdoors at a couple of Arab cafés.

The Germans have identified five of the people who were with Dreissi—ten different individuals are in these pictures, not counting him—and have sent us their names with backgrounders, asking for comment. The Germans believe most are al-Qaeda sympathizers, if not recruits.

Clep is with me. He's sitting by my desk, reviewing notes ATAC has produced in response to the German Request for Information.

"Look at that one," I say, pushing toward Clep the photo of the Egyptian in the galabia with the lizard face.

Clep smiles. "Yeah, some duds—true son of the desert here, right? Well, hell, why not? You can get away with anything in Hamburg. Always could." Clep curls his nose in disgust. "What a face."

ATAC people have tried to do computer traces on these worthies, but except for Dreissi only two of them check out on our various watch lists. The lizard-faced Egyptian is not one of them. Embarrassing, maybe, but there it is. So we will add them, names, photos, and little else, to our databases, along with the details the Germans have sent.

The photos Clep and I are looking at are two to five years old. Six months or so after the latest was shot, Dreissi would leave Germany and disappear for a year and a half, gone utterly. Then somehow he would reappear in Pakistan in time for Powers's death, then would vanish into the mountains of Afghanistan. The trail on this guy is frozen over.

I notice one shot of two men, Dreissi and another whose name the Germans report they don't know. The two are sitting at a table at an outdoor café drinking tea out of little glasses in silvery metal holders. Dreissi is smiling. The other man has thrown his head back in laughter, but has kept his eyes—clever, piercing eyes—on Dreissi and has both hands on the table as if to anchor himself as he shakes with the joke.

Concentrating now on the shot, on the laughing man, I get a feeling like a cat's claw scratching at the back of my neck. "Shit!" I say under my breath. "Shit, I know this guy! Jesus Christ, I know this guy!"

Cleppinger looks up over the little half-moon reading glasses on his round face, suspends scribbling with his ballpoint on the German RFI.

"It's Kareem! It's goddamn Kareem! I ran him! This guy worked for us!" A kick in the stomach, this photo. "We gotta get the docs on this guy!" I dash out past a gaping Cleppinger into Stu Kremer's office.

The last time I saw Kareem he was standing on the back of a flatbed Pakistani army truck in dwindling twilight. The truck was parked in a muddy field by the gate of a mud-brick compound. Along the compound's perimeter wall old tires had been piled up for some reason. For storage? For sale? For burning? Who knew?

Kareem was addressing a group of his men who had gathered at the rear of the truck to hear him. It was cold.

Sadozai Refugee Camp, twenty klics or so northwest of Peshawar. Winter 1989. The Russians had just left Afghanistan, though the Afghan Communists still controlled Kabul.

Snowflakes were falling, but not sticking, and there was a wind. I had overseen delivery of a shipment of commo gear to a mujahideen group Kareem had somehow come to lead. I watched at a distance as Kareem spoke.

All around, across the rocky, treeless land, stretched hundreds of green and gray canvas tents in straight lines. From somewhere came the smell of burning kerosene, and from a line of latrines about fifty yards upwind wafted the faint smell of human waste.

The mujahideen had brought out two large propane lamps, which they lit and put on each side of Kareem as he stood on the truck. The lamps cast a bright, white light that played over Kareem's sharp Afghan features. Fifty or sixty mujahideen, wearing round Chitrali hats and with the usual blankets slung over their shoulders for the cold, had collected behind the truck. Most of them were carrying AK-47s, though some had older carbines that could have been Russian or British. They listened, straining to hear Kareem, who was hoarse from a cold he'd caught.

Standing face to the wind, dressed like his men, Kareem spoke in Pashto, rapidly and ecstatically, sometimes pausing to clear his throat and spit out phlegm. It seemed to be a pep talk. The men would respond to the points he made by shouting "Ha," which meant "yes," and nodding their heads in agreement. When he joked, they laughed; when he was serious, they gazed. When Kareem said something they liked, which was often, they rattled their Kalashnikovs approvingly.

I watched the show dumbly, understanding nothing.

Later, inside the compound, Kareem, some of his men, and I drank gloriously hot tea that was steeping in a pot on a kerosene heater, which, because the wick needed trimming—or maybe it had simply burned down to the end and they hadn't replaced it—gave off an oily odor and barely warmed the room.

Kareem seemed tired and weak that evening, perhaps because of his cold, but his speech had excited him. His eyes, his body, and the way he spoke with us displayed a raw, nervous energy.

"Quite a performance," I said. "I wish I could talk like that."

"I know them," Kareem replied. "They know me. They trust me."

He smiled confidingly and said, "Things are bad. But I don't tell them that. Why? Because they know that anyway. I tell them we will win. And that is so. We will. It is true we are weak, but the weak have a good weapon: the mistakes of those who think they are strong. When the snow melts, so will the regime."

He meant the Najibullah government, which the Soviets had installed in Kabul and had been maintaining, even after they'd pulled their troops out of Afghanistan.

Kareem was wrong. When the snow melted that year, Najibullah's regime didn't melt with it. But in time, one by one, all the cities in Afghanistan fell to the mujahideen, including Kabul. There they found Najibullah hiding in the U.N. compound. They beat him, castrated him, dragged him through the streets of the city behind a Toyota pickup truck, and hanged him finally by the neck from a lamppost across from the Ministry of Justice.

In the compound that cold evening, Kareem and his men lit up cigarettes and didn't talk much.

Kareem was also getting money and equipment from the Paks, who seemed to have a high regard for Kareem's group. The Paks, who controlled most of the matériel going into Afghanistan, supplied Kareem's men with all the classic guerrilla weaponry—assault rifles, shoulder-fired rockets, mortars, antitank guns, land mines.

The funding for this was arranged by Arab fixers, mostly Saudi, including Osama bin Laden. It was Arabs, with much help from CIA, who got the arms together, and Arabs who got them shipped to Karachi and trucked up to the Afghans. The Paks would distribute them among the groups they and the Arabs liked—Islamist Afghans and foreign Arabs of the right degree of religious fervor. CIA chose not to interfere in the selection of favored groups. We left that to the Paks, who took a dim view of Afghan secular nationalists. Afghan nationalists had dangerous ideas, particularly as to where Pakistan ended and Afghanistan began. Religion, said the Paks, is our common heritage. Religion is the better motivator. Much better than nationalism.

The Paks thought they could control the Islamists. They thought they could control the Arabs.

No one recruited Kareem. Kareem found us. He showed up one cool spring evening in the mid-1980s in the back courtyard of Dean's Hotel, one of a jeepful of raggedy-ass mujahideen that I as CIA liaison was to meet and get to know. They had pulled their vehicle into the back courtyard and were sitting in it, grinning and hugging their AK-47s and looking tough—all of them, that is, except Kareem, who was short and slender and soft-skinned and who had just the beginnings of a beard. On his right cheek was a scar, a small crater in the flesh about the size of a quarter, known as an Aleppo boil. You see them a lot in South Asia. They're from parasites transmitted by sand flies, and a mark of the region's bad hygiene.

Kareem spotted me as Agency easily enough. He leaped out of the jeep alone and stepped brusquely up to me, pulling close with that in-your-face way they have, and, fixing his eyes, clever and piercing even then, on mine, started reciting his résumé in good English.

"I am Abdel Kareem Yusufzai," he said, nodding his head once vigorously to emphasize the point.

"My father and mother are in the U.K. I was student in the U.K., in London, I have no money, I am engineer, I have come to fight the Russians."

At this point Kareem was hooked up with one of the mujahideen commanders in Peshawar, a breed known mostly for posturing and high talk. Kareem wanted something more, money and action probably, and thought we might supply both.

He was eager, energetic, and English-speaking, so we took him on and put him to work, first as a gofer around Peshawar, translating for us and running our errands. We paid him a little, not much even by Afghan standards, but the low pay seemed not to bother him.

We learned soon enough that Kareem was no engineer. He had taken a couple of electronics courses in a place called the Hammer-smith Technical College in London, courses that gave him a passing acquaintance with wires and electricity, but that was it.

Still, Kareem was smart, eager to master our Western gadgetry. Because we liked his enthusiasm, we let him handle the commo gear we were supplying to the muj then, burst-emitting and frequency-hopping radios, telephone scramblers, handy-talkies, and other electronics. Kareem loved the stuff, couldn't keep away from it, and was forever pestering us for instruction. We were happy to supply it.

After a time he left us. He crossed into Afghanistan and joined a resistance group operating around Jalalabad, and we had almost no contact after that. His group had fifty fighters or so at most, part of some larger outfit called the Afghan Front for Islamic Unity.

This I dutifully reported to HQ in a cable, one of a long series of elaborate studies I wrote on mujahideen groups and their ideologies, cables I am now sure no one back at Langley ever read.

At the height of the war there were probably two thousand of these groups across Afghanistan. Most were tribal, built up on clan and extended-family lines, and composed of brothers, cousins, and further distant relatives by marriage. They grouped and regrouped, shifted allegiance from one leader to another, sometimes merging, sometimes splitting apart. It was hard as hell to track them.

A year or so after he left us, we heard Kareem had managed to become commander—at nineteen—of the Afghan Front for Islamic

Unity. How he accomplished this feat I don't know, through simple force of personality maybe, or maybe he played on his stature as a man of technical learning. Maybe—who knows?—he had a knack for strategy. In any case, as commander of the Afghan Front for Islamic Unity he was soon claiming victories here and there in the war—a power pylon blown down, a convoy on the road to Jalalabad turned back to Kabul—and made a kind of name for himself. Hearing this, we got back in touch with Kareem, who was still eager for our gadgets, and put him on our drop list for equipment.

When I saw him last, that frigid evening at Sadozai Camp, I noticed he'd gotten scarred in the face, a deep triangular cut across his left cheek.

I pointed at it. "From battle?" I asked.

"RPG," he said. "Our own. It exploded fifteen meters from me. The man who was firing it died."

More than a decade later as I read the take on Kareem, I can almost see him standing there on that truck bed, in the dark and cold, coughing up phlegm, haranguing and cajoling a group of his adoring mujahideen.

But Kareem now is just a memory: elusive, vanishing, vivid as a dream and as ungraspable.

Back then he was a mujahideen commander, one of our paid men. But what is he now? The photo from that Hamburg café showing Kareem with Dreissi tells me that my old gofer is way too closely associated with al-Qaeda.

ATAC troops in the Fusion Center, as on the night when word of Ed Powers's death came in, have their eyes fixed on their terminals and are popping away at their keyboards, trying to pull in everything they can find on Abdel Kareem Yusufzai, CIA unilateral. They find a backgrounder on his work, a short bio, some, not all, of my old cables, in which he appears crypted as DODGER. Not much else. Kareem exits our stage when Najibullah was overthrown in 1992.

I stay in the Fusion Center until the documents peter out, which is early evening, then go home and try to sleep, thinking, Kareem knew Dreissi, Kareem is al-Qaeda, Kareem knew Dreissi, Kareem is al-Qaeda.

---

14 APRIL 23
Arrival of the Muscle I

On April 23, 2001, two young, male Saudi nationals, Satam al-Suqami and Waleed al-Shehri, entered the United States at Orlando International Airport in Florida.

Al-Suqami, a native of Riyadh, the Saudi capital, had spent time in Afghanistan and had trained at Khaldan Camp, a large basic-training facility al-Qaeda maintained near Kabul.

Al-Shehri was born and grew up in Asir Province, a poor, rugged region down on the Yemen border in southwestern Saudi Arabia. Asir, which is not well policed, is sometimes called the wild frontier.

Like al-Suqami, al-Shehri had spent time in Afghanistan and had received training in an al-Qaeda camp, the al-Matar complex, near Kandahar. He then served for a time in the al-Qaeda security force at Kandahar airport.

On their arrival at Orlando Airport, al-Suqami and al-Shehri were met by Muhammad Atta.

---

15 APRIL 24
WILDCARD

I'm back in the office by 7 a.m., fidgety after a night of bad sleep. As I dose myself with coffee and start rereading one of my old cables, a shadow sidles into my peripheral vision: Kremer.

"This turned up last night," he says. "Better read it."

"This" is a cable that Kremer, a look on his face, is holding out to me. I can't read Kremer's look, but his is not a happy face.

The cable dates from last summer. It was sent out of Langley and is addressed to Dubai Station. It describes a meeting Ed Powers was to have in Peshawar with an individual crypted WILDCARD/1.

"WILDCARD is Kareem Yusufzai," Kremer says. "Guy Rutherford's Powers. Powers was obviously working Kareem. We didn't know."

As I read, I get that cat's claw at my neck again. I can't believe this cable, I just can't.

S E C R E T 242349Z JUL 00 STAFF

CITE ISLAMABAD 481971. SECTION 1 OF 2.

TO: PRIORITY DUBAI

WINTEL RYBAT AJAJA WILDCARD/1

REF: DIRECTOR 459158

1. FOLLOWING IS UPDATE ON PLANNING FOR WILDCARD/1 OPERATION AND TRAVEL OF GUY W. RUTHERFORD (IDEN A) TO PAKISTAN TO MAKE CONTACT WITH WILDCARD/1. WE TENTATIVELY PLAN TO SCHEDULE RUTHERFORD TRAVEL IN SECOND OR THIRD WEEK OF AUGUST. TO REFRESH STATION MEMORY OF THIS LONG-DELAYED OPERATION, WILDCARD/1 WAS FIRST APPROACHED IN FEBRUARY BY RUTHERFORD IN ATHENS. WILDCARD/1 WAS TOLD WITHOUT SPECIFICS OR ACTUAL NAMES BEING MENTIONED THAT RUTHERFORD WAS A WASHINGTON-BASED U.S. BUSINESSMAN REPRESENTING A NUMBER OF TELECOMMUNICATIONS FIRMS AND AN AIR SHIPPING SERVICE.

2. RUTHERFORD WILL CARRY A LETTER APPOINTING HIM AS A CONSULTANT TO HUSSAYN KAMRANI, A PROMINENT U.A.E. BUSINESSMAN WHO HAS ASSISTED STATION IN THIS CAPACITY FOR SEVERAL YEARS. THE LETTER WILL INCLUDE TRAVEL AUTHORIZATION AND DESCRIPTION OF NATURE AND DURATION OF WORK RUTHER-

FORD IS DOING IN PAKISTAN AND/OR INDIA. MECHANICS FOR THE CORPORATE
COVER ARRANGEMENT WERE WORKED OUT WITH KAMRANI IN EARLY JUNE.

PAGE 2 DIRECTOR 481971 S E C R E T

3. RUTHERFORD IS SCHEDULED TO PICK UP ALIAS AND REGULAR PASSPORT 9 AU-
GUST. WHILE AT HQS HE WILL ALSO BE FURNISHED WITH SUPPORTING DOCUMEN-
TATION IN FORM OF CREDIT CARD(S), POCKET LITTER, IMMUNIZATION CERTIFICATE,
ETC. PROPOSE ALSO THAT RUTHERFORD TRAVEL PAKISTAN/INDIA VIA ATHENS,
WHICH HE KNOWS WELL. WE PLAN FOR RUTHERFORD TO BE IN PESHAWAR FOR
TWO WEEKS AT THE MOST, THE CONTROLLING FACTOR BEING HOW TO BALANCE
GETTING AS MUCH TIME WITH WILDCARD/1 WHILE AVOIDING AROUSING HIS SUS-
PICION THAT RUTHERFORD IS "HANGING AROUND." IT IS ESTIMATED THAT 60 PER-
CENT OF HIS TIME IN PAKISTAN WILL BE OCCUPIED BY COVER JOB WHICH WE FEEL
LEAVES AMPLE TIME FOR THE MEETINGS WITH WILDCARD/1.

4. FOR INITIAL PESHAWAR MEETING, RUTHERFORD WILL WEAR CASUAL CLOTHING
CONSISTING OF LIGHT TAN TROUSERS, SHIRT WITHOUT TIE. RUTHERFORD IS CIRCA
6FT 2 INCH, WITH SLENDER APPEARANCE. HE IS 53, OF ERECT POSTURE, BLUE EYES,
BLOND HAIR AND MUSTACHE.

FILE: 201-959289. RVW 24 JULY 00 DRV.1. ALL SECRET.
SECRET
   BT
#9815

HQ was running some kind of operation on Kareem, call
it Operation WILDCARD. Ed was the courier between HQ and
Kareem. Ed and Kareem met in Peshawar just last year. Ed died a
few months later. Kareem was a friend of Liamine Dreissi, who we
think killed Ed.

My heart is pumping hard. I am furious. I want to break Kremer's arm.

"What happened, goddamn it? This cable is Powers. We should have had it in January. It's fucking April! Why the hell are we finding this now?" I feel the heat in my face as I look in Kremer's serious eyes, as I search that scholarly demeanor. The guy seems lost, clueless.

"I don't know how we missed it—it didn't show up in the initial search. Sloppy work—I mean, really sloppy, I know that." Kremer shakes his head no, meaning no explanation. "Swear to God, I can't figure it." Kremer's voice is agitated, his look far-off, as if he can't believe this either.

"When we reffed the cable last night, maybe midnight, we found phone records," he says. "Kareem and Powers, they've been in touch. A lot. Twenty or so conversations, fairly recent—they all took place in the last year. Here's a list."

Police records from the U.K. tally twenty-three phone conversations between Powers and Kareem. Powers is always in London; WILDCARD—Kareem—with two cell phones seems to get around in the world. He's in Peshawar, Islamabad, Istanbul, Athens, London.

We don't have transcripts of what they said, only the phone records. Powers seems to have reported none of this to us.

"Stu, Jesus Christ!"

He waves his hand. "No, no, I know."

Kremer is not incompetent. The people under him seem to know what they're doing. This may be the fault of our filing systems and their attendant security procedures, which can be so arcane they defeat their purpose: too often once something is filed, it's gone.

At the Agency we purposely do not allow the right hand to know what the left is doing. Our computer systems have firewalls on their firewalls. But in a world where everything is need-to-know, no one knows enough.

Here is Kareem again, in our phone records and in this cable. Just last year. Further: the cable had to be Sonny's. No one but the ATAC plans officer could have written it.

When I bring the news to Cleppinger, he screws up his face, squinting at the cable incredulously and twisting his fat body as if pained with bowel cramps. "Jesus Christ, Jesus Christ! What the fuck's going on?" He shakes his head. "All that talking on the phone they did—Jesus, more'n twenty goddamn phone records! But we got no operations reports, no contact reports—big nothing. Where was the control on this?"

Our eyes meet. In cold anger Clep picks up his phone and punches a dialer button as if punching the chest of the person on the other end. "Sonny? Bill. . . . We got a problem. Major. . . . Yep. . . . Yep, yep, yep. Okay." Then to me: "The Silver Fox will be delayed slightly, but he will soon grace our gathering with his presence. You, me, and Sonny. Hey, let's get Kremer in here, too." Clep looks away for an instant. "No. Wait a minute," he says grimly. "We'll just make it you, me, and Sonny. We'll keep it cozy."

A feeling comes over me. "You know this Kareem—the drug allegations. Could be this—know what I mean? Al-Qaeda's in the drug business, right? Think about it, Bill—Kareem and Powers running heroin on the side."

Cleppinger doesn't care for this and says nothing in response, but his face tells me he acknowledges the possibility.

I decide to send out the word. We will put Kareem on our watch list, we will query our people in Europe, and we will query friendly services.

But first we will query Sonny.

"It was informal," Sonny says. "Powers's idea. We thought—Powers thought—WILDCARD was open to something from us—money, whatever. We thought WILDCARD was a way into al-Qaeda. Might have been—shit, you take a look at that photo with what's his face, Dreissi, you know he was a way in. I mean, goddamn it, if he looked pretty good then, ask me, he looks even better now."

Sonny, Clep, and I are at the big table in Clep's conference room. Sonny, a go-to-hell smile on his face, has his left leg up over the arm of his chair. I've been around Sonny enough to know this is put on. As Clep gets jokey when he's nervous, Sonny adopts a highly relaxed air. We all have our ways. Don't let the fuckers know.

By virtue of my better relationship with Sonny, I'm to do the talking.

"Powers's cover was pretty elaborate, Sonny—I mean, all this shit, passport, pocket litter, backstopped number, like he was a major agent and this was a major op."

"It wasn't. We just gave him his old crypt. People out there knew him as Guy Rutherford, so that's what we used. Like the cable says, he showed up here in August and got his legend. Got it back, I should say, it was old stuff. There's records on this somewhere, they're routine. The relationship was highly informal. Powers, as we know, had contact with all kinds of people. Check the NOREFUGE paper, you'll see a buncha names. Most of the people he dealt with never panned out. This Kareem fellow might have been one of them, I don't know. We paid them a little out of discretionary funding. That was it. Worth a try and we didn't lose much money. You can check the paper."

I will, Sonny, I will. "So this other guy in the cable, this Kamrani—who's he?"

"Old friend of the Firm. Importer-exporter in Dubai. I knew him pretty well. He's got a bunch of auto franchises—tires, parts, whatnot. We've used him a fair amount for cover. His bio's around."

Through all this Clep has been sitting forward, tensed, staring hard at Sonny. Now, fed up, face red, he shouts, "Oh, for Christ's sake! Sonny, you drafted this cable—why, pray, did we have to stumble over it?"

"Hey, I write a gazillion cables. You remember all the cables you ever wrote? WILDCARD was Powers's deal. WILDCARD wasn't that bright on our radar screen, not till he popped up in that photo from Hamburg. The relationship with him was highly informal. That, of course, was the problem. We never knew the whole deal. Powers, guys like him, have their own agendas. They're always a little off the flight path, you never know how far."

Clep isn't having this, especially from Sonny, who during his long career with the Agency has often been far off the flight path himself. "Sonny," he says, "there's this mentality around here that no paper means it never happened. Why is there so little paper on WILD-CARD? Last night we got nothing fresh—just old stuff down from the attic. How come?"

Sonny shrugs. "Bill, go ask Powers, we got what we got."

Cleppinger bugs his eyes at that.

I say, "Sonny, it is a problem. I mean, this cable, the phone records we got here—just got in, by the way—are from a year ago, no later. Everything else we got is from the Soviet period, 1987 at the latest, and a little from me in the early nineties. Nothing in between. We lose touch?"

"Looks like it," Sonny says. "Except for Powers. Powers knew him."

Cleppinger says, "Well, we don't know where this Yusufzai bastard is these days or *who* he is."

"Correct," Sonny says. "Wish we knew more."

"Lookit, goddamn it"—Clep's voice is low, he's glaring at some point in space—"it boils down to this: Dreissi pops into Pakistan. Soon thereafter Powers dies. Dreissi knew Kareem, Kareem knew Powers. In our world this is way, way too close. Prima facie case Kareem was in on it, at least knew something about it. Am I right?"

"You're broad jumping, Bill. In our world everybody knows everybody else, everybody's always dealing, always bumping into the next person, everybody's got two degrees of separation max."

"Look, we gotta get this Dreissi, because he has murdered our people. Would you grant the theoretical point that it would be nice to know what this shithook Yusufzai knows? Make sense?"

Sonny smiles an acknowledgment.

"Sonny," I say, "we got a Hill problem, the drug allegations and all, they're worrisome. This Kareem—he might be in the business, that might be the connection with Powers, Powers's 'agenda' as you call it."

"The allegations about Powers are nonsense," Sonny says. "Rumors and that's it. Hill bullshit. Nothing'll come of it."

"Don't give me that, goddamn it," Cleppinger says rapidly. "We got enemies up there. They may be few in number, but, as we all can attest, they are loud of mouth. And they're talking to the press—they've already started spilling their royal guts, and believe you me, if they can, they're going to leak and piss all over us. Pieces of NOREFUGE will find their way out into the shining light of day. Osama and friends read the goddamn papers and watch TV—so we can scratch that op and Osama can go to bed at night secure in the knowledge that we have once again fucked up. And further, if there's any goddamn truth to this drug business, any at all, we may end up having no friends on the Hill. Coale ain't happy."

"Bill," Sonny says, "we got no indications of drugs. Nobody, none of our people, has ever heard anything like it. Hell, rumors fly around, always do. Hazard of the trade—it's noise, radar snow. You gotta be able to overlook things, gotta know what to ignore. Being able to do that, Willie"—Clep doesn't flinch at *Willie*—"is the beginning of wisdom. Until McClennan or somebody else on Committee comes up with something real, I just won't believe it."

Cleppinger sits quietly for a moment, calming himself.

I say, "Well, to hear you tell it, Sonny, you'd think WILDCARD was a minor deal. But Jesus Christ, sitting there in Hamburg with this Dreissi character. Kareem is thick with al-Qaeda, may be one of them."

Clep, furious again, pounds his fist on the table, three times fast, and says, "You want to shoot these people, you really do." I'm not sure who he's talking about, Dreissi, Kareem, or—it could be—Sonny.

Sonny makes a noise. "Well, just remember, he doesn't look like a 'militant Islamist,' whatever that may be. He doesn't fit the template."

"Hey," I say, "he's been out of sight a goddamn long time. Funny things happen, guys get religion out of the blue."

"Ask me," Sonny says, "he was pulling some scam. He was working Powers for something, and that does fit the template. Be fun to know what. They might have been working each other. We never got much from Kareem, by the way, the relationship just fizzled out."

"Think he killed Powers?" I ask.

Sonny raises his eyebrows, a gesture he has picked up in one of his Eastern locales. It means, Hell if I know.

"Maybe we can haul him in," Cleppinger says, "put a squeeze on and haul him in."

"Gotta find him first," I say. "Germans don't know who he is or where he is—got no address for him. Could be Germany, could be Timbuktu, they don't know."

"Yeah," Cleppinger says, "asshole Krauts, their own fucking fault. He's probably slipped out, gone somewhere else."

"Ye old EU *problema,*" Sonny says. "It's so goddamn easy to skip around over there these days."

"Well," Cleppinger says, "we'll send our German friends a report on what we got, meager though it is."

Sonny taps his pencil on his teeth. "Okay, be it resolved: we try to find this Kareem guy and check him out. I'll get Division to have a look. Make him a project."

Cleppinger, appearing dubious, blows through his teeth and makes a sign of the cross in the air.

"I don't like the loose lines on these things," Cleppinger tells me after Sonny leaves, "these loosey-goosey, 'informal' things, using tools like Powers. They've got a certain swing to them you can't predict. Of course, Sonny loves them, gives him more control here at HQ." Cleppinger drums his fingers on the table. "You can't trust Sonny, that's the long and the short of it. He'll let somebody like Powers screw around."

Sonny Desmond's one of our best. Just keep a lawyer around.

I say, "Kareem was involved in Powers's death, you just know it."

Clep nods. " 'Two degrees of separation max,' " he says, and throws up his hands.

We will keep this cable from Lurch and the Bureau. Family jewels. We do not even let our own analysts, let alone personnel from other services, see operational cables. Nor will we tell Lurch of its contents.

I go back to my office, around the corner from Cleppinger's suite, and stare out my window at National Cathedral rising on the horizon way far away.

I believe that Liamine Dreissi and Kareem Yusufzai, for some reason, killed Edward Nelson Powers. Probably payback for NOREFUGE.

And I don't believe a word of what Sonny said. Not one word.

17

"Let's See If We Can Get This Thing Wrapped Up"

When I get back to my office, I stovepipe the news about Kareem and Powers to Lindsay, who calls me into his office immediately.

"Okay, Powers," he says, "our bad boy. I've read all the briefing materials you've given me on the guy. Good stuff, very interesting. But this whole new mess, this Yusufzai, his relationship to us, I mean, goddamn, it smells bad. What gives?"

I show Lindsay the photos from Hamburg and dutifully run through what we know of Kareem's strange and sudden arrival on the scene as a friend of Ed's. I say that Dreissi is al-Qaeda, that Kareem is connected to Dreissi and may be an al-Qaeda operative himself. That this is just another piece of evidence that al-Qaeda killed Powers and that NOREFUGE is compromised.

I keep Sonny's name out of this. When I get Sonny figured out, it'll be time enough to tell Lindsay.

As I speak, Lindsay's face gives off all the signals that indicate he is understanding what I say. He nods at the right times, seems to follow the details, which are many and complicated, and keeps his eyes fixed on mine.

Yet something in that bright face tells me he's not quite making the connections. Despite his years in technological spycraft, he simply cannot understand our flesh-and-bone black world of human espionage.

Lindsay has never been an operational spy, and I don't think he really understands ops. The old guard are right about him: he puts too much faith in his satellites and his sensing devices. He doesn't know how things work on the ground.

I say, "Let's turn up the voltage on Powers. Kareem really may be the key to this, to the Dreissi and Powers business and to those guys in

Hamburg. And he may be a way in to bin Laden. Let me see what I can do."

"Inquiry Team?"

"Let's do it out of channels, keep it informal—the fewer people here at Langley who know about it, the better." People like Sonny. "Let me pull in who I need on it, but keep it restricted—drug allegations and all that."

As I talk, Lindsay fiddles with his Scotch tape dispenser, a nervous habit he has. He tears off an inch or so of tape, folds it over on itself, then folds it over again, saying, "Right, right, yeah, right." He drops the tape, now a little ball, onto his desk, and looks up at me. "Understood. Ah . . . you'll have to do a lot of the work yourself. I know you been working hard on this anyhow, so that makes you the logical guy. We'll make this whole thing an object lesson, figure out what kind of lesson later." He nods decisively.

In his way, Lindsay wants to know what there is to know about Powers and his death. Lindsay, who is a compulsive note-taker and worrier, is scared by the sloppy record-keeping on Powers and, like the rest of us, is afraid of what might turn up. And though Lindsay will never understand field operations or the tricky world of Out There, he does understand what may come of "the Powers thing" in Washington.

Lindsay says, "Let's at least get a notional schedule going here. First off, and this should be doable, let's say a written summation of what we got now, including what you just told me this morning. Have that tomorrow—get some munchkin to put it together, the whole business, briefly, one page if you can. You give it a final read and sign off and let me have a look. Then let's see if we can get this thing wrapped up"—Lindsay starts ticking his right thumb on his fingertips—"(a) what the hell Powers was doing, (b) who got him— even if we don't really know, make some educated guesses, this Dreissi guy or Kareem or whoever—(c) why we let our guard down on this. And then, maybe most important, (d) implications for the

NOREFUGE thing and maybe other ongoing programs and operations, recommendations for action, that kind of stuff. Maybe pay a visit to Islamabad, check out the station, see what's what. Okay? Great. Cool."

18
APRIL 26
Stopped

On April 26, 2001, a state police officer in Broward County, Florida, stopped Muhammad Atta for speeding. The officer found that Atta was driving without a license and issued him a ticket. On May 2, Atta applied for and received a Florida driver's permit.

Atta's identifying photo shows him staring unemotionally into the camera, his lips compressed. His thick black hair is combed directly up and back. His left eye seems heavy-lidded, reptilian.

19
APRIL 27
Chain Bridge

Dawn. I'm standing in the pedestrian walkway on Chain Bridge, a long, low arc that stretches over the river and the old C&O Canal and connects Arlington with the District. It's a mile or so from my house.

Sometimes when I wake in the middle of the night, doomed to sleeplessness, I will walk to this place. The trudge up Military Road, then the quick descent to the bridge down the steep back streets here, gets my heart pumping and clears my mind, though, as now, I may be dead tired and facing a day.

This morning a chilly breeze comes down the river. The air is fresh, and it feels good on my face. The river is up and running fast, leaping and plunging over the rocks north of where I'm standing. For a time I watch the show, watch the early gulls circling and listen to their faint cries.

Above the dark tree line in the eastern sky, the Morning Star, Venus, has appeared alone, soft and white in the deep blue.

Kareem is somewhere in the U.K. The British, responding to a query from Sonny, tell us that one Abdel Kareem Yusufzai, Afghan national, entered the country on January 7.

They don't know where he is. At Heathrow Airport Kareem gave them a nonexistent address in Hull as "residence while in the U.K." He seems not to have opened a bank account, tried to get a driver's license, or done anything else that would require an ID or an address. The British at our request are now looking for him.

Kareem and Powers, Kareem and Dreissi. Clep is right—in our world, this is way, way too close.

I believe Abdel Kareem Yusufzai, my old agent, is an al-Qaeda operative, working for Osama bin Laden. He's thick with that gang in Hamburg—Dreissi, the lizard-faced Egyptian, the others. I think Kareem betrayed Ed Powers and arranged for Powers's murder. I think he probably used Dreissi to kill Powers. I can't prove any of this.

Powers's death and what it may mean for NOREFUGE add to the foreboding that hangs over us. We know al-Qaeda is moving money, perhaps to the United States. We don't know to whom that money is flowing or for what purpose. From phone intercepts and airport watches, we know al-Qaeda operatives—a Moroccan, a Lebanese, three Yemenis—are traveling unusually around Europe and between Europe and Pakistan. We don't know why. It's maddening.

I walk across to the District. At this hour traffic over the bridge is still sparse. As the vehicles pass, one by one, their weight makes the structure flex and bounce under my feet, its movement giving me an eerie, unsteady sensation.

Along Canal Road the streetlamps are still on, pearly in the haze, and the headlights of the early commuters coming in from Maryland glide smoothly toward town. On the towpath, a lone runner, a girl, mirrored in the motionless water of the canal, lopes easily.

PART II: EVENING

(MAY 1–JULY 30)

1

Kareem Did Not Know How the Passports Had Been Acquired

Ealing, Greater London

Kareem rode the lift down to the ground floor of his apartment building and exited into the dark entrance hall. When he pressed the *minuterie,* a dim fluorescent light fluttered on to fill the dingy space: old lime-green paint, dust. Here, four doors led to four separate flats. On one, the first on the far left, hung two signs: BEWARE OF CAT and WATCH CAT ON GUARD! An obese, hostile young woman lived there.

The hall went dark again as Kareem walked out into the chilly evening. For a time he stood in the front drive, hidden by the privet hedge from Hanger Lane. He could hear, but not see, the traffic rumbling past. Under his arm he held a small package. It contained two stolen Moroccan passports.

Down the hill, circling the Hanger Lane roundabout, were small shops and businesses: estate agents, a newsstand, the Pakistanis' convenience shop, the Indians' liquor shop, the Chinese restaurant, a launderette. Beneath the roundabout was the Hanger Lane tube station.

A good neighborhood, Kareem had thought, in which to disappear.

He looked at his watch: 9:50. The sky was overcast, the moon hidden behind the clouds.

Kareem kicked at a stone in the drive, sending it skittering into the privet, and waited awhile for nothing, then looked again at his watch: 9:55.

Go. Now.

Kareem turned and set off down the sloping back driveway past a newer wing, the "annex," that thrust out from behind the main building—the whole complex was T-shaped—and led down to a line of garages.

It was back here by the annex, when there was sun, that the Pritchards and old Mrs. Kennedy would sit, the three of them, wrapped in mufflers and woolen scarves, at a white metal table. Mrs. Pritchard, who plaited her gray hair in tight, ugly pigtails, always wore a floppy blue-and-gray knitted hat. She smoked and coughed. Mr. Pritchard wore, always, a small, round, black cap with a stubby visor. Mr. Pritchard's jaw was drawn with age. He had cataracts. Old Mrs. Kennedy had pale white skin and blue veins at her wrists.

They, the Pritchards and old Mrs. Kennedy, called Kareem "Joe," because he had told them that that's what people called him when they wanted to be friendly, and it was easier than his real name in his own language. The Pritchards would wave at "Joe" as he went past, and he would smile and wave back, sometimes bowing decorously. Kareem, who had a gift for chat, would talk with Mr. Pritchard of cricket scores, the weather, television. Always smiling.

Head down, carrying his small package nonchalantly, Kareem passed the long annex, where Mary, who lived on the ground floor back here, had been working in the flower beds that afternoon. She had been wearing her green exercise outfit. Her small car was parked by the annex, driver's-side wheels up on the pavement. She would be at home. He wouldn't knock.

When they were becoming friends, Kareem would sing to Mary in his language, a language of mountain people, men in baggy trousers who, he told her, carried ancient rifles and moved through the passes of mountains whose secrets they alone knew. He'd sing her songs of guns and hunting, of tribal feuds, of kidnappings, of women and horses and sheep carried off, and of marriages and bridal processions over stony mountain paths on agile horses. And he would sing love songs: "Why don't you love me, you whose face is like an angel's face?"

When she finally did, it made no difference.

Kareem was on the edge. A touch, a whisper, would send him into the abyss. Kareem dreamed sometimes in his troubled sleep that he was climbing a wooden ladder—it was always wooden—in a closed, suffocating space, a space in the wall of a building, an interior shaft of brown mud bricks, in which he was climbing, climbing, until, barely reaching some upper level, close to the top, he would lose his footing and his grasp. He could never remember what happened after that. Perhaps nothing. That would be death.

Past the annex, Kareem descended a second slope to the line of garages that paralleled the main building. Down here, away from the Hanger Lane traffic, it was quiet. When he reached his garage, third in from the end, he looked around carefully, then stood waiting. His watch said 10:01 now.

After a few minutes a stab of light illuminated the drive and the end garages. A vehicle had turned in. It came down to the garages, turned right, and slowly approached Kareem.

A van.

The van.

Two men were in it, the Kuwaiti and another, a man Kareem did not know, who was driving.

The Kuwaiti, who was wearing a dark-colored parka, got out.

"Muhammad?" Kareem said. It was not really a question; he knew it was Muhammad.

"Ahlan. Keyf halak?" Muhammad said, speaking Arabic. "How are you?"

Muhammad put his right hand out for a shake. Muhammad was slender, narrow-faced, thick-lipped. He did not smile.

"Long trip?" Kareem asked in English.

"Give it here," Muhammad said, gesturing with his eyes at the package Kareem was holding. Muhammad: always abrupt, always uncomfortable. A difficult person. Muhammad didn't like women, didn't even like looking at them. Muhammad took the package from Kareem.

Saying nothing, Muhammad got back into the van, glanced at Kareem, then looked away.

The driver pulled the van around and left.

One week earlier, a short, slender Yemeni had given Kareem the passports in the same manner—a furtive transfer at night in the Hanger Lane tube station. Kareem did not know how the passports had been acquired. He did not know who would use them.

Kareem lived in fear.

Fear was a small, persistent waif that came to Kareem at odd intervals and plucked at his sleeve. And if Kareem looked down, he saw only a child there with an empty, featureless face.

The child would say nothing, was nothing.

2

MAY 2

Arrival of the Muscle II

On May 2, 2001, Majed Moqed and Ahmed al-Ghamdi arrived at Dulles International Airport, outside Washington, D.C. Both were Saudi nationals.

Moqed, a university dropout, was from a small town called Annakhil, west of Medina. In 1999, he was recruited into al-Qaeda and trained at al-Qaeda's Khaldan Camp, near Kabul.

Ahmed al-Ghamdi was born in the al-Bahah region, an isolated and underdeveloped area some one hundred miles south of Mecca. In late 2000, he quit school to fight the Russians in Chechnya. In December of that year he saw his family for the last time.

After arriving at Dulles, the two stayed briefly in Fairfield, Connecticut, then traveled to Paterson, New Jersey, and disappeared in the Arab community of that city.

---

3   **MAY 13**
Out There

To know the world you have to go there.

The driver of our SUV takes us fast from the airport into Islamabad. An Agency officer named Wilkes is sitting next to me in the middle seat and is holding a 9mm Beretta semiautomatic down between his knees below seat level. Wilkes is tense and we say little to each other. The embassy, Wilkes tells me, is on high alert.

A beefy State Department security officer named Michael Beaudry has come along and is sitting up front. It is 8:30 a.m. on a hot morning.

"Carl would have come himself," Wilkes tells me, "but some business came up related to the alert, said he'd tell you all about it."

"No problem," I say. Carl Lindquist is chief of station, Islamabad. I have a dinner appointment with him this evening.

I'm groggy from the long, lousy flight, a DOD milk run out of Andrews A.F.B., that left Washington yesterday evening and stopped three times—London, Paris, Frankfurt—before arriving in the middle of the night in Karachi, where we sat around till 7 a.m. for maintenance and fueling before flying on to Islamabad.

As we are being driven in, Wilkes and Beaudry scan the streets of this dismal city, gaze at its long, wide avenues of disconnected buildings and its treeless, grassless open spaces.

Our driver heads for the east side of town, bringing us quickly to a guest villa, a large, salmon-colored stucco house, off Airport Road, in the diplomatic enclave, not far from the embassy.

Wilkes unlocks the front door of the empty house and ushers me in. Beaudry stays in the SUV.

Wilkes has a crew cut. His baby face makes him look young and wet, but then everybody new is beginning to look too young to me.

"The street's under surveillance," Wilkes says.

"By us I hope."

"At least."

"Surveillance" probably means another house up the street, most likely one with a view of a cross street, a situation we prefer. As we were being driven into this neighborhood, I noticed a branch of Habib Bank on the ground floor of a modest three-story building on the corner. The building, dull yellow brick, showed no signs of life on the upper floors. It had the look. It's where they'd put the video-cam.

"There's food and beer in the fridge in the kitchen, booze over there," Wilkes says, pointing at a shiny black credenza with mirrored backing on the far wall of the large main room. "Carl, I guess you know, has you on for dinner this evening at seven thirty, then a meeting at ten a.m. tomorrow in the embassy. Appointment with the ambassador in the afternoon. Carl'll have you picked up for dinner this evening."

I thank Wilkes for his help.

"No problem."

He leaves quietly. I go upstairs to shower, find a bed, and try to get some sleep.

Lying in the cheap bed—the mattress sinks in the center—I doze a little, wake, doze some more, sometimes think of Karen. Two mornings ago at her place, I kissed her good-bye—both of our mouths toothpasty—and told her that I was leaving next day for "inspection of stations," that I couldn't tell her where, but that it was no big deal and that I'd be back in ten days or so.

She smiled knowingly. "Mystery man, off on his foreign assignations, huh?"

She's not tired of this yet, of not knowing where I'm heading off to, or why, or for how long. It's still new to her. Maybe it'll never bother her.

4

MAY 13
Carl and Nora

Just before 7:30 p.m. I am driven the three hundred meters from our safe house to the Lindquists' residence on embassy grounds. Near the embassy gate we pass a Pakistani police jeep with two troopers lounging in it. They give us bored glances. A canvas tarp covers a large shape on its rear deck, presumably a machine gun. American marines—they keep getting younger, too—check us into the embassy grounds.

Lindquist greets me at the residence. He has a square, open, Swedish face. He is blond, blue-eyed, self-assured, a man who is good at looking good. This is his second tour of duty in Pakistan. He was acting chief of station in the late nineties. Lindquist's wife, Nora, is a tall, thin woman, with broody, questioning eyes and a distant manner. Her dark brown hair, which she parts in the center, falls flat down the sides of her head and scrolls in at the ends. She has fluttery hands and a high voice.

Over drinks before dinner—both Lindquists down a couple of large Scotches—Carl asks about Cleppinger. "Always liked him. Nore, you remember Bill Cleppinger, don't you? Bill and Bea? Cairo Conference?"

Nora blinks.

"He's short and stocky, she's—"

"Oh, yes," Nora says. "Much fun. Much fun."

"Oh, they're fine," I say, sticking to the social truisms. "I've known Bill from way back, wa-ay back. Good to be working with him again. I don't see Bea all that much, but, yeah, Bill and I are in each other's hair a lot."

Lindquist nods. "Well, he's got a rough job."

I nod agreement.

Lindquist has the air of a can-do, kick-ass officer, and he has no great blots on his record. The structure at Langley likes him, probably as much for the latter as for the former, and he seems still to be going places in the Agency. If he makes no future false moves, he could be headed for DDO.

My visit worries Lindquist. As one of Lindsay's special assistants, I am the bureaucratic equivalent of an aircraft carrier. I am floating danger and there is no telling what havoc I'm capable of wreaking. Lindquist is hoping that in the few days I'm here I will be the objective good guy and will see that Islamabad Station, contrary to rumor, is not fucked-up, and that, despite a disgracefully low level of staffing, it is doing its best, its level best.

At dinner Nora keeps up with Carl at the bottle of Chivas Regal—$5 or so from the embassy PX—which Carl has planted on the dining room table.

"Oh, Washington, I love it *so* much," Nora says, "all that green space, all of our monuments, all of that history. So does Carl—love it, don't you, Carl? But here we are." She gives out a grim little smile meant to be sardonic and funny, but which comes across as merely grim. "His work here is important, I know that, and of course I support it entirely, but at some point"—she lowers her head, keeping her eyes fixed on me—"we are going back." In this, as in a couple of other comments she makes during the evening—"picking up and moving so often," "flying horrors in the air here"—there is more than an edge of weariness with the Agency life. That life has turned out to be something she wasn't counting on—a string of postings mostly in forlorn third-world cities like Islamabad, where she is forever teaching little brown people how to lay the silverware.

"The heat gets you," Nora says. "So oppressive, just waves of it from now on until the monsoon. I leave in two days and I'm quite happy to be doing so. You've been here before, Paul?"

"Oh, yes, in the eighties, a year or so. Peshawar. Not all that long, I guess, but I was getting used to the place, kind of liked it here actually."

Nora smiles at that one. The thought strikes her as goofy.

I ask Carl about the embassy alert.

"We stopped a small operation two days back," Lindquist says. "They were photo surveilling an embassy worker's house here in Islamabad—parked van, camcorder. It took unbelievable gall or great foolishness to try it because we are very alert. In any case, we neutralized their operation. Pak security people hauled them away. Caught another one last night, middle of the night. Hiding in some safe house they had. We don't know who they are yet. We know they're local, not Arabs. More detail later. Stay tuned."

Lindquist is proud of the coup. I'm not sure why. It amounts to not much more than looking out your window.

Throughout the meal Lindquist, a talented raconteur, is garrulous, insistently friendly, telling me war stories to show he's been around and is a tough guy. He talks of Cairo whorehouses and trick pads, which were used to seduce and entrap East Bloc and Arab diplomats; of a phone tap gone wrong in Delhi ("We thought they'd caught on to us when the listening devices died, but in fact rats ate the connections"); of whiskey sessions in a Red Sea beach shack with a one-eyed Somali warlord—telling all these stories with enough vagueness so that Nora can be allowed to hear. The pièce de résistance is a tale of breaking, entering, and bugging an Abu Nidal safe house in East Berlin and the strange little Swiss dwarf CIA paid to pull off the job. "Fellow named Dieter, older fellow, still athletic at the time, though, contract employee, acres of experience working for us." We avoid talk about work, real talk.

Lindquist has been around the world. In addition to posts in Egypt, India, and Germany, he's worked in Somalia and Thailand, two years here, two years there. The result is he actually knows little of these places.

We discourage country expertise in the DO. An op is an op, we tell our new troops at the Farm, a target is a target, and they are all the same. Lindquist is of this school of thought.

As Lindquist talks of all the places he's been, I think of David, a missionary kid who grew up in Beirut and who spoke Lebanese Arabic like a Lebanese, down to his accentless Beirutisms. David knew his murderers well.

Lindquist seems relieved to get through the dinner and thinks he's made a friend. He hasn't.

When I thank Nora for the evening, she's well tanked but manages a gracious smile. I am driven the three hundred meters back to the safe house, where I try to sleep.

---

5 MAY 14
NOREFUGE

I'm with Lindquist in his third-floor sanctuary in the embassy. Though the building's air-conditioning is working, Lindquist's room is stuffy, and we're both sweating. Lindquist is sporting his Beretta in a chest holster.

I push at Lindquist, giving the headquarters assessment of NO-REFUGE, which is bleak.

"Tell me if I'm wrong, but we think NOREFUGE is off the tracks. When they got Powers, it meant a threat to that whole op. Juice has gone out of it. What do you think?"

"NOREFUGE is in trouble, not because of Powers—it's just in trouble, nature of the beast. Snatching bin Laden ain't easy."

Carl and I run through the NOREFUGE paper, the contact reports, the photos, the transcripts of electronic surveillance, our in-house analysis (charts, diagrams, family trees). Almost all of this is available at Langley, and I've seen it already.

As part of NOREFUGE we have hired some Pak army officers, including a Signal Corps engineer, a couple of upper-level police officers, a lawyer in Peshawar, an aide to the governor of the North-West Frontier Province. We have a small army of Afghan unilaterals—Af nationals who take our money and promise us information.

But we have no Taliban, nobody in al-Qaeda. And since Powers's death, the lawyer, the police officers, and a couple of our army informants have gotten skittish about dealing with us. We're not going to get any terrorists with these people or "preempt," as we like to say, much of anything. We don't have a program.

"Carl, I've tried and tried to light a fire out here. I know NOREFUGE is tough to keep going, and our problems aren't just here in Islamabad. I regularly come out to the region, have one-on-ones with the chiefs, run conferences. You've been to these things, same goddamn deal: Everybody admits there's a HUMINT problem. And nobody does anything about it. When I talk with these people, I could be talking to Health and Human Services. It's like swimming in Jell-O.

"Way I see it, we got four hundred to five hundred so-called agents out here, but only some of them, maybe a handful, produce useful intelligence. Most of these guys have been collected by officers hot to make their rep in counterterrorism or whatever. Well, 'agents'—they're cheap out here and easy to recruit. Get a bunch, looks goddamn good on your résumé. If they turn out to be worthless, that fact does not catch up with you in your new post or in your personnel file. Right?"

Lindquist stays poker-faced through all this. Pounding on Carl is like pounding on a bale of straw. He's soft, but unyielding. You can't even hurt your hand.

"Paul, six, seven months back a bunch of Afs almost got him, almost killed bin Laden. You heard about it. Roadside ambush just outside Kandahar. RPGs. They tagged the first vehicle, but missed bin Laden's. It was so close, I mean so close."

"These were the guys Powers came up with," I say, "and maybe that's why Ed died, that attack."

Lindquist shrugs that off, then suddenly says, "Look, those bastards are under a dozen layers of secrecy. They move around only at night, they've cut back on radio use, almost no satellite phone traffic anymore. They use look-alike decoys for Osama, they got fake convoys going here and there. And they use couriers. Know what we hear? We hear they carry messages written on paper, thin paper, in indelible ink stuck to the roofs of their mouths. I'm not kidding about that, and I don't doubt it. Paul, getting a line on these people is *hard*."

We're at a dead end on NOREFUGE, I see. I bring up Kareem and Dreissi.

"Yeah, Sonny's query came through," Lindquist says. "Our people—we've looked. None of our sources has much to say. This Yusufzai was here, now he isn't. He was into 'importing'—smuggling—stuff from Afghanistan, probably luxury items, electronics, maybe dope, which brings up another problem, as if we didn't have enough: DEA's kicking up trouble. Been going on ever since Tony Escudero arrived on the scene."

Antonio Escudero is the resident Drug Enforcement Administration officer.

"He's out of their Los Angeles office. Claims we're fucking up his work, and he's pulled some major shit because of it. First of the year a congressional delegation came through, International Relations, trade subcommittee. Escudero bent their ears on the dope wars—plenty. Told them State and CIA are conniving with the Pak and Afghan drug mafia to protect CIA sources. The asshole bitched to the congressmen about Ed Powers, told them Powers was probably

CIA and also probably in the dope trade, and that we 'winked' at Powers's misdeeds."

The reports on the Hill about Big Ed dealing in narcotics, I know now, are out of DEA, out of Escudero's shop. I wonder what DEA knows. I don't tell Lindquist about the rumors circulating on the Hill.

Lindquist seems honestly outraged. "I mean, come on. It's a joke; whatever you say about Powers, he was clean on this. We've never heard anything like it. There is nothing to the goddamn dope charge. At this point Escudero refuses to talk to us—I mean he won't talk. Paranoid moron.

"So, Ben McCall"—Representative Benjamin McCall, Democrat, New York, subcommittee chairman, and honcho on the Black Caucus—"screams and yells at the ambassador, 'Misery in Harlem's coming out of here, families are breaking up, CIA turns a blind eye, even encourages it,' and all that shit, so the ambassador has us all in, whole Islamabad Station, wants to know what the hell's going on. Well, nothing's going on and we told him that. Not enough arrests? The Paks are just being Paks—who knows why they do anything?

"Paul, we got enough trouble chasing down the Pak nuclear program and local terrorists, who by the way—the terrorists—if those guys ever take over this fine country, the crazies will have an A-bomb. It is scary, it is goddamn scary. I'm telling you, I'm just one lonely guy out here at the end of the earth shoveling shit for democracy. Assholes like Escudero don't make it any easier."

Escudero is "not around" when I want to see him.

In the morning I head for Peshawar on an Agency jet, a Gulfstream we keep in Bahrain.

6

In May 2001, though warnings of terrorism against U.S. targets were at their height and though Saudi Arabia was considered a major source of al-Qaeda recruits, the U.S. State Department began what it called the Visa Express Program.

This program permitted residents of Saudi Arabia, including noncitizens, to obtain U.S. visas through Saudi travel agencies, rather than from American consulates. In issuing visas, the Saudi travel agencies were allowed to apply standards that were less strict than those applied by U.S. officials. Applicants for visas at the local agencies, for example, had only to provide a photograph and fill out a short form. They did not have to submit proof of identity, as they would if they had applied through a U.S. consulate.

It was in the travel agencies' financial interest, naturally, to process as many applications as possible.

7

"It's over," Reiner says simply. "SIGINT, yeah, such as it is. But the people—if we get something up and running again, it'll be a whole new op. I mean, we keep after Osama, obviously, but we've been pushing our NOREFUGE rock up the mountainside here a long, long time. Keeps falling back."

Peshawar Base is a high-walled villa on Khyber Road in the Cantonment, once the British quarter, west of the old city and not far from where Powers was killed. The villa's courtyard is full of pink-flowering oleander, the walls climbing with bougainvillea.

Base chief is William Sebold "Pancho" Reiner. Reiner is a big guy, tall and heavyset, maybe fifty. He has a slightly crazy, wild look in his eyes and has a way of seeming antiestablishment, though he is basically very much a team player. He has been married twice and divorced twice, both go-rounds with diminutive, demure Asian ladies he met on his earlier postings.

Like Lindquist, Pancho carries a 9mm Beretta semiautomatic at all times. He has only two officers under him in the city and looks distracted and tired.

Pancho has been point man on NOREFUGE, among our other projects in this city, and is more pessimistic than Lindquist.

"Beginning of '97 we put together an action group in Peshawar to grab bin Laden. We were going to spirit him out of Afghanistan. So we recruited Afghans and Pakistanis to help us, but bin Laden got wind of it and decided to move away from the Pak border to the most secure areas he could find around Kandahar, where we had few assets. The op was suspended. We tried a couple times since, but we got nowhere till that thing with the tribals, when they blew away one of Osama's Land Cruisers."

Reiner has nothing new to say about Dreissi or Kareem. When I ask about Powers, he says, "We don't know what Powers was doing here last time through. They killed him before he could talk. On the phone he said he had a 'big deal' on bin Laden, that it might mean something, but he wouldn't tell me what it was. Seemed happy as hell with it. The usual Ed Powers—all laughs and bullshit. Then he came here and died."

Reiner balls his hand into a fist, releases his fingers one by one onto the glass top of his desk, making a little drumming sound, then thumps the glass once with his middle finger—the whole gesture indicating utter finality: end of Big Ed, end of NOREFUGE.

I pay off the triwheeler minicab at the junction of Police and Saddar roads, where the bridge crosses over the Peshawar–Rawalpindi railroad line. The tracks here run east-west through this dry, buff-colored town in a low-cut rail bed and separate the old city from the new.

It's the old city I'm headed for. I am alone now, a tourist, and no longer in the Agency bubble. In my tourist's day pack, among my maps, guidebooks, wallet, traveler's checks, and passport, I am carrying a locked and loaded Beretta 9mm and two full magazines of ammo.

Over the bridge, I turn left into the Khyber Bazaar, a street of transport companies and cheap hotels, and pass through what's left of the ancient brick Kabul Gate.

Strange to return to this place, familiar and yet not. As before, carpet sellers wander the streets, carrying their wares slung over their shoulders, and approach me hopefully. As before, pushcart vendors sell an array of Eastern street food: star fruit laid out on newspaper, sugarcane sliced into sections, mutton kebabs deep-frying in what looks like crankcase oil. Here and there in the dust lie crimson expectorations—Pakistanis, like Indians, chew the betel nut as a relaxant and hawk out the resulting red juice wherever convenient. Flies buzz everywhere.

The buildings here are two and three stories high and have trellised balconies that hang over the narrow lanes. Porches under the balconies serve as shops.

I pass clothing stores, stationers, dentists' offices, and one lone spice merchant who has set out trays of yellow turmeric, pale green cardamom, and black peppercorns. He sits behind his wares reading, not bothering to eye the passersby.

A beggar riding in a low cart pushes his way laboriously through the crowd. He looks like an Afghan. He is blinded in one eye and legless. He probably got that way in the war against the Soviets. You see a lot of them here, men maimed in that war.

I pause to inspect a flat pushcart piled high with Chitrali caps. Stopping gives me a chance to check my back. Across the way at a juice seller's stand I catch two young men watching me. They avert their eyes and turn away. That's all.

As I continue to rummage through the caps, a young man springs out of a doorway and says, "Are you into shopping? I will help." Cities of the East are full of young men like this, unemployed and unemployable, who stand around to "help" the foreign tourist. "I will help, yes? You want to see moskey, yes? You want to see moskey. I can show." This one has a tense, hoarse, overarticulated way of speaking, from desperation, I think. I wave him off and walk on.

I wander up a familiar lane toward the Andarshahr Bazaar, a market off the main streets, away from the shriek of the triwheelers and motorcycles. I head through the jewelers' quarter, where, yes, as I remember, the lane narrows to five or six feet, then opens again to a small courtyard, where quiet money changers squat on carpets. Behind them are glass cases full of the world's currencies—Saudi riyals, Swiss francs, U.S. dollars, U.A.E. dirhams. I leave this courtyard taking a narrow lane that twists up toward the white marble Mahabat Khan mosque.

When I turn a corner at a dried-fruit stall, I see just ahead and to my right the big gray stone lintel and, by the door, the old sign reading AMIRI TOURISTIC CENTRE. ORIENTAL GOODS.

I stoop and go down two steps into the low-ceilinged room, its floor just below the sloping stone walk. Even in the bright morning, it's dark and cool in here. A worn carpet, the same one as before, I am sure, covers the floor. Two trunks the size of footlockers sit opposite the door and flank a strongbox.

At the far end of the room, I see him sitting alone on the floor, cross-legged, toting up figures on an electric calculator. He looks up affably at the new customer, then quickly his eyes sharpen. After ten years he still recognizes me. He looks back at his figures.

"Something today?" he says in English. "You like carpet, yes?"

"*Na imroz,*" I say in my rusty Dari, a language he knows well. *Not today.* "*Yak nigah-e mekonom, ba ijaza.*" *I'll just take a look, with your permission.*

"Ah, then," he says, and gestures around his shop. "Command. I am at your orders." On the walls hang five or six *kamanchas,* the squawky, potbellied Eastern version of the violin, and around them, behind them, racks of silk cloth and cotton prints. On low tables that line three walls of the room are wooden boxes full of glass beads, papier-mâché pen boxes, brass hands of Fatimah, heavy silver jewelry encrusted with carnelian and lapis lazuli. On the floor: brass and copper bowls, teapots, samovars. On an easel in the far corner sits a large portrait of John F. Kennedy, painted on purple velvet.

You can't make a living this way. He fronts for smugglers.

"You are well, God willing, Mr. Bob?" he says.

"God be praised. And you?"

"God be praised."

For much of my life, including when I was working here, my cover name was ROBERT LANGER. To my informants and contacts, such as this man, whom I knew well back then, I was just plain "Mr. Bob." Strange to be called that again, years after I've abandoned the name, though once in a great while even today someone, in an airport, say, or a restaurant or out on K Street will come up to me and say, "Hey, Bob, how's it going? Remember me, buddy? I'm so-and-so." What do you say?

"Your business is good, I hope."

"Ey, I still breathe." His eyes crinkle. "You've come a great distance and after a long time. Remarkable to see you here again."

There's an eager wariness in his face. He knows I want something, probably knows what. This man should have been one of the people we talked to after Powers died. I've seen the contact reports. He wasn't.

His name is Abdul Ghafur, Slave of the Forgiving. Back during the war with the Soviets, when I was stationed here and busily writing cables on Afghan affairs, he appeared in them as an informant code-named RIDER. RIDER is a Ghilzai Pathan whose clan roots are from somewhere on the border north of town. Back in those days RIDER helped us arrange trucking for the war. He organized a small army of Afghan and Pak drivers who brought the Chinese and Egyptian weapons in from the seaport, Karachi.

The last time I saw RIDER was a decade ago during the Gulf War, when he was still on our payroll. Sometime after that, I'm not certain when, Islamabad Station dropped him off our roster.

In his day RIDER had a string of informants whom he paid with our money—we think. At least we collected receipts from him with their thumbprints on them, and we met occasionally with his suppliers.

RIDER had a smuggler's store of information and was one of our best sources on the mujahideen. Not the prima donnas, the so-called "commanders" who loafed around this city and arranged safe tours for foreign newsmen a few kilometers into Afghanistan. RIDER knew the tribal people far over the border, men who didn't speak English and to whom we paid little attention. These were the men who would go on to take over Afghanistan and who, no friends of ours, would shelter the likes of bin Laden and al-Qaeda. But getting information on the factions, my subspecialty, was never a priority with my bosses at the Agency. Perhaps that's why we dropped RIDER.

In the Eastern way, RIDER and I talk at random of this and that—the shocking price of land in Peshawar these days (RIDER, for all his complaining, is doubtless happy with the run-up of local real estate prices), of the evils of old age, the benefits and drawbacks of travel (it broadens the mind but narrows the purse).

As we chat, a boy carrying a censer of burning rue hops nimbly down into the room and without a glance at me brings the censer over to RIDER, who waves his hands in the smoke, capturing some of it in his beard. RIDER nods, and the boy leaves as quickly as he came in. Neither has said a word to the other.

Out of politeness, RIDER tries to interest me in a carpet, one of a pile of rough Afghan tribals on the floor, and I let him work me a little. You can't rush these people, and we both know the negotiation is a charade.

After a time, I break it off.

"A carpet I can't afford, Abdul Ghafur, and I need no more than I have. But information, yes, that I have need of."

"Well, I have that, too."

"The American who was killed here—you know who I'm talking of?"

"Yes, of course, God have mercy upon him."

"God have mercy upon him. You knew him."

"Ha."

"His death was a great crime."

"Ha."

"Against the laws of this country, against the laws of God."

"Ha."

"This crime, Abdul Ghafur, what do they say? How did it happen? How did he come to die? I know he was shot dead in the street, on the Mall, not two kilometers from here, but who would do this? And why? What can you tell me of this crime?"

He looks away—thinking what? The price a good story should command, perhaps? Or how to make a middling story better?

After a time he asks, "As in the old days?"

He means money, but from the look on his face, an almost imploring look, I realize also that he misses the game, just the game as game, and wants back in, that like me he takes a delight in conspiracy and secrecy, in knowing what is known only to a few.

"As in the old days," I say.

He smiles, puts his hand to his lips, and says, "Go, Mr. Bob. Come back. Come . . ."—that calculating look again—"come back this evening. After the prayers."

"Why not now?"

"You will see. Maybe. God willing."

I head for the Saddar Bazaar and kill time browsing in the Saeed Book Bank, buy Karen an ivory bracelet-necklace set from the antique dealer next door, and go back to my hotel to read a little. Then I get an early chicken tikka dinner at a restaurant, Lala's Grill, in Green's Hotel.

When I return in the evening to the Amiri Touristic Centre, RIDER has another man with him. The other man is large and coarse-looking. He has a flat, broad face and a thick, untrimmed beard, rusty with henna over the gray. He is wearing a gray karakul hat, a gray-blue *shalwar kameez,* and a black vest embroidered in silvery plastic threads.

"My friend Shah Dost," RIDER says. "A driver. He comes, he goes."

We shake hands. Shah Dost's paw makes me think of Lurch.

RIDER pulls a metal grate halfway down over the entrance to the Amiri Touristic Centre—it is now closed for the evening—and the three of us sit cross-legged in the rear, facing each other in a triangle.

Shah Dost, RIDER tells me, owns his own truck and does contract hauling. He has come from the truck and bus yard up where the Hashtnagri Gate opens onto the Grand Trunk Road and has a story for me.

Looking at me coyly, Shah Dost pulls out a little tin box in which he keeps his *naswar,* a mix of tobacco, lime, and spices beaten into a greenish brown sludge, which Afghans use as a kind of snuff. The box has a mirror in the top, and viewing himself in it, he twists and smoothes his mustaches, then begins, "I knew the *Emrikai.*"

The *Emrikai,* Shah Dost says, was built like a bull and wore spectacles. His name was Mr. Guy. He wanted trucking. He knew the Landi Kotal routes well and wanted a truck to go to Torkham up on the border, where the Pass to Afghanistan begins. The driver would meet another one coming down the Pass. He would take that man's cargo in his own truck.

"How do you know this? This is a story. Can it be true?"

"It is true. I am that driver. I have seen the *Emrikai.* The *Emrikai* and I shook hands. On my own soul, we did. And I saw his partner. I also saw the other trucker. Trucker, partner, *Emrikai*—I knew them. I saw the boxes taken from the one truck, the Afghan truck, that came down the Pass from Jalalabad, to my truck. And I brought those boxes here, to Peshawar, to a place by the Hashtnagri Gate."

"On the edge of the city," says RIDER.

"On the edge of the city, by God. Where I left my truck for a time."

"Then?"

"Well, then, after, when I returned, I had an empty truck. But I was paid for my trouble."

"The boxes, you say—boxes of what?"

"Televisions, electronics luxe. What did I care?"

Ed was not in the TV business. I'm thinking in among the TV sets, the computers, the camcorders, there must have been something else. I'm thinking heroin.

"It was goods," Shah Dost says, "who knows?"

I think this man knows.

I say, "The partner, Shah Dost—who was the partner?"

"An Afghan, not from here."

RIDER breaks in, "Why, you know him, Mr. Bob. He is an old mujahid—Kareem, Abdel Kareem Yusufzai. He is now in business."

Yes. Had to be. It makes sense.

At this, Shah Dost smiles, grasps my hand in that paw of his, and laughing, rises abruptly from the carpet. Bending low to get under

RIDER's grate, Shah Dost heads out into the dusk to whatever lodging he has arranged for himself in whatever dive up by the Hashtnagri Gate.

I have no idea why RIDER brought Shah Dost into this. Perhaps RIDER owed him something. Perhaps RIDER wanted to increase his own credibility with us. Perhaps it was a hint to me that a network may be out there that RIDER could again put together and run.

And I am left, as we often are, with a man's story. We have no documents, no other evidence of any sort on Kareem and Powers.

"What was the cargo, Abdul Ghafur? What were they bringing?"

RIDER nods his head to the side and spreads his arms low, palms up, meaning he may try to answer my questions. Or meaning nothing.

I slip RIDER $200 in cash, way too much for his help. I'll let Pancho and Carl know what RIDER had to say about Ed and Kareem and get Pancho to put RIDER back on payroll.

When I leave the Amiri Touristic Centre, all the lamps have come on.

9

MAY 18

"City of the Silent"

"Edward Powers took his secrets with him to his grave, didn't he?"

"That he did, Amjad. That he did."

"And now he dwells in the City of the Silent, as the poets say."

I am in a Pakistani reporter's apartment in the Cantonment. It is my last night in Peshawar. Tomorrow I head back to Washington with a stopover in Amman. We are drinking whiskey, which this man likes, though he drinks it sparingly. He has graying hair and a graying spade beard. He wears wire-rimmed spectacles and cultivates a precise manner. He is very smart.

His name is Amjad Afridi. He is based in Lahore, though he has this small pad in Peshawar. He covers South Asia for a newsmagazine in Hong Kong and writes occasional pieces for a daily paper in London.

The Agency trades in information with journalists. With Afridi, it's a barter economy. He gives us information, we return the favor. We've tried to buy him with cash, but have never succeeded.

Afridi has reported on Osama bin Laden for the better part of a decade and has traveled into some of the stranger byways of northwest Pakistan and eastern Afghanistan to do it. He thinks he knows just how far to go with these people. I think they'll kill him.

When I mention this possibility, he shrugs. "They know exactly who I am and what I do," he says. "I don't lie to them and I don't lie about them. They seem to respect that."

"You talk to us."

"They know that. They may think me a useful conduit."

"Let's hope."

He smiles.

"Why do you do it?"

"The work? Because I like it. I do it well. Almost no one else in the world can. Naturally, I don't write everything I know. There are some whispered truths I hear which are plausible enough, but which aren't really truths in the journalistic sense. I keep them in the back of my mind, but I don't write them. They are too vague, and they're often lies, not true at all. I don't even pass them on to you." He smiles again. "So. When the U.S. government sends you here, it means it is unusually interested in the goings-on in this city."

"Acknowledged. An American got killed here, late last year. Ed Powers. Tell me about Powers. What happened? What do you hear?"

"Very little. He called himself Guy Rutherford, by the way, but a great many people here knew he was Edward Powers. Using a pseudonym seemed to increase his importance, his secret life as perhaps an American agent. I reported the story of his death, of course. My paper in London took a passing interest, but let it drop."

"Did you? Let it drop?"

"Oh, no, it still seems quite interesting to me. I know what the police tell me, which is presumably less than they tell you. When you called, in fact, I was hoping to get a little enlightenment from the Washington angle. It's instructive that you're here, which means there is a CIA connection to Powers's death, which was likely anyway, but it's nice to see confirmation of that. Must be as good a story as I thought, maybe even better."

"Amjad, I think you know more about this than I do."

"As I say, I don't know the Washington angle. What is your view? You've concluded it's terrorism, obviously."

"We're looking at that. What do the police tell you?"

"Well, there are the 'official police,' the colonels and the generals and so forth who speak for publication, and then there are the other police, who don't, and whose word I trust to a degree. The police speaking for publication say a team of men, possibly as many as four, shot Powers and slipped out of sight. The police claim to know no motive for the murder, but say it was possibly an action perpetrated by the Indian services to embarrass Pakistan and stir up trouble with the Americans. Risible. This presumably is the same story they tell you.

"The other police, my friends, say this Powers was close to too many people, including Osama bin Laden and al-Qaeda. Also he was one of yours. Am I right? Don't bother to answer, he was or he wasn't, and you won't tell me either way. But he has all the marks of the CIA agent—the alias, the secretive business doings, and of course the official American foofaraw when he died: the big team of U.S. 'officials' who came in immediately after the death of this man, this 'businessman.' Not to mention your arrival and your going about asking questions.

"I do believe Powers had relations of one sort or another with al-Qaeda. Of course, this is quite a dark area. No one knew of these goings-on but a handful of al-Qaeda people and Powers, who is dead. But let's conjecture: Al-Qaeda may have suspected Powers of being a double, a betrayer. They may have let Powers go for a time, watched him, perhaps fed him bad information—I'm guessing, I don't know any of this—and let him betray himself. Whatever, somehow they concluded Powers had to be killed."

Afridi pours us more Scotch.

"Anyway, such are the workings of my lurid imagination. Imagination, however, can take one only so far in one's work. To do one's work one must start from facts."

Amjad has made his proposal.

I say, "He had a partner in some of his dealings here, an Afghan. They were trucking goods between Peshawar and Afghanistan. We'd like to know more about the business, more about the partner. He was a Yusufzai. His name is Abdel Kareem. We're not sure, but we think their business is significant. The partner may have had a hand in the killing."

Afridi regards me coolly and sips his whiskey.

I leave Afridi's apartment at nine thirty or so.

Afridi lives at the dead end of an L-shaped alley. His neighborhood is residential in the wealthy-Pak way: big houses, mostly, set back behind large, paved courtyards and surrounded by ten-foot-high walls. The walls have wide metal gates that let you bring automobiles in and out. The few streetlamps here are weak, and you can't see much.

Game time. I study the alley.

The foot of the L, where I am walking, is fifty yards or so long. At the heel, where the alley turns left, there's a narrow pedestrian passage that leads straight on to a lighted area, a commercial street, that looks far-off, where a yellow-orange neon light blinks dimly.

Standing by the entrance to the passage is a young man in Western clothing. He's simply standing there, his hands at his sides. What can he be doing? There is nothing to do in this alley.

I don't think hard about this, I just notice. As I pass I nod to him.

He eyes me—a little too slowly, I think—but he nods back, unsmiling and mute.

When I turn left, I see far up the alley a parked car blocking the alley entrance. Standing motionless by the car are two other men, doing nothing.

Then the young man behind me says, "Mister? Do you have the time?"

I know the voice. *Are you into shopping?* It's that same tense, over-articulated way of speaking. The guy was in the old city yesterday. Now he's here. He has two friends and a car blocking the entrance to this alley.

This is no game.

Hot in the face, heart pounding, I turn calmly to the guy—he's ten feet away—smile, and say, "Time? Sure, yeah, yeah," and walk slowly toward him, staring at my watch, not at him, studying it, holding it up at a streetlamp as if trying to make out the time. The guy is armed, has to be. I can't see the piece, but he has to have one.

When I say, "It's nine thirty-two," I'm on him, snatching at the wrist of his gun hand with my left hand, grabbing at his throat with my right, choking him hard. He's short, thin-boned, and weak. And a dumb shit who doesn't know what I'm doing to him. With no thought, I get a foot behind him, push him over and down, and come down on top of him. I pound his head on the pavement, and his piece, a chunky, Russian-looking semiautomatic, falls away from his hand.

On my feet, I kick the guy in the stomach—hard—and fold him in on himself. When he curls up, moaning, I kick him in the kidneys, and he begins to vomit, hacking and coughing, drowning in his own puke. I grab the piece.

The car is coming down the alley toward me, picking up speed, its lights off. The two men up the alley are pressing themselves flat into a metal gate. They don't know what's happened down here, but they don't like it.

Shooting is mental. You control your body by controlling your mind and your breathing. If you can do that, you can place your rounds where you want them. Holding the Russian semiauto in both hands, I crouch, aim, and fire, putting I think one round into the car, which is backlit from the far-off glow of the street. When I fire a second round toward the car, it stops. I've connected.

I see two simultaneous flashes—circles of white-blue light, expanding so fast, then gone—and I hear the nasty pop of the fire and the bumblebee sound of the rounds as they pass over me and smash nastily into the brick wall behind.

I fire a round, two, three, five, at the two men who are squashed into a metal gate and miss. Again I see the circular flashes of light, hear the buzzing of the rounds. I flatten into a gate, fire again, dash to a gate farther up, and try to fire off a round, but the pistol goes dead, clicking when I pull the trigger. As I am reaching into my day pack for my own Beretta, the car suddenly goes into reverse, backs crazily into the street, and disappears, and the young men, out of easy range, dash from the alley.

Panting, dripping with sweat, I turn and see that my friend with the tensed voice is gone and that Amjad and some of his neighbors have come out into the alley, standing aghast, staring at the large foreigner and his gun. Amjad gets me to Peshawar Base in his VW.

When I take the whiskey from Reiner, my hands are still trembling. He says, "You're very, very lucky."

"Born that way."

"You got a will?"

"Made one when I took this job."

"Time to quit—you're still ahead, but you ain't gonna stay that way. Someday or other, dice'll roll wrong."

The police, far too late, find no one and have no witnesses. We don't know who my attackers were. We'll never know what they wanted.

In the morning, the security interviews do not go well. The Rangers and Municipals send small delegations, both of which take depositions and otherwise fiddle and faddle. Midmorning we get an ISI colonel. He has a trim, British-style mustache and a high-and-tight haircut. He tsk-tsks a lot. "This is very unfortunate," he keeps saying, his tongue curled back in the roof of his mouth in that Pak way. The piece I took from my tense-voiced attacker, he tells me, is a Makarov 9mm, probably Egyptian-made. "Quite common here."

I spend the day talking to police, to Reiner, and by secure phone to Lindquist in Islamabad with Clep ("Jesus Christ, watch your goddamn back!") on the line at Langley. In the afternoon I write a short for-the-file report on the incident, with copies to Reiner, Lindquist, Clep, and Lindsay. It's worthless.

MAY 24

10 Flight Across Country

Beginning in late May 2001, Muhammad Atta, Marwan al-Shehhi, and Ziad Samir al-Jarrah, a companion of Atta and al-Shehhi's from Hamburg, took a number of cross-country trips between the northeastern United States and California.

Al-Jarrah, a Lebanese national, had entered the United States from Germany on June 27, 2000, at Newark, New Jersey, on a B1/B2 multiple-entry visa, then flown to Venice, Florida, where on June 28 he began training to fly large jets at the Florida Flight Training Center.

Al-Shehhi took the first trip, flying from New York to San Francisco, then to Las Vegas, on May 24. On June 7 al-Jarrah flew from Baltimore to Los Angeles, then to Las Vegas. And on June 28, Atta flew from Boston to San Francisco, then to Las Vegas. Each flew first-class in the type of jetliner they had been training to fly. Each flew to his destination using a one-way ticket. This did not arouse the suspicions of airport security personnel.

11

Sunday morning, McLean Presbyterian, a large suburban church surrounded by much asphalt for parking and so well-attended it uses
rent-a-cops to handle the traffic. It's a warm, buoyant day, drenched
in sun, profligate with life: azaleas, dogwood, laurel.

McLean Pres is a CIA church. I know a couple of the ushers here
from work and one of the Sunday-school teachers. Like them, I've
been attending for years. This morning I am seated toward the rear
right side, the perch Nan and I had, though Nan no longer shows up.
Where she is of a Sunday morning these days I have no idea—
probably in the sack with Charley. I don't drag my heathenish love
Karen here. Karen is a prosaic secularist with no religious sensibility,
though she tolerates mine, probably by putting it out of mind. The
transcendent seems to bore her.

Next to me in the pew sits a slender young woman, alone. She's
of high school age, a plain dresser who wears no makeup. I've seen
her here before, though I don't know her. We smile at each other.

"God's law thrills my socks off!" the pastor, a man named Beckmann, is saying. "Listen to this: 'I run on the path of your commands,'" he reads from a Bible in his left hand, "'because your Law
set my heart free.'" Waving his right fist in the air over his head, he
says, "Hey, listen folks . . . hey, that's not so bad. It's saying that if you
think your life should be measured by the Ten Commandments, they
won't hamper you, they won't hold you back, no, sir, on the contrary,
they set you free!"

Beckmann is new, from downstate somewhere. He's been at
McLean Pres only six months. He's tall and slightly overweight. His
hair is a lustrous gray, almost pearly. In his severe dark blue suit and
maroon tie, a kind of Beckmann uniform, he looks like a K Street

businessman. He has a mannerism, I've noticed, of running his tongue behind his lower lip when pausing to make a point. I've seen TV comics do that after delivering a punch line, waiting out the laugh, milking the joke. I don't like it. I don't know why he does it.

I'm still jet-lagged from the flight back from Peshawar and stopover in Amman, where our chief of station, Erik Abel, and I sat in on an interrogation of the terrorist Waleed Abu Nejmeh, the man captured last February in a raid on an al-Qaeda safe house in east Amman.

Abu Nejmeh is being held in a hilltop military prison in Jebel al-Armouti in rolling country south of Amman on the highway to the Dead Sea. His interrogation will be pro forma: both the interrogator and the subject know the questions and the answers by heart.

Abel and I watch from behind a one-way mirror as a Jordanian policeman pulls Abu Nejmeh into the room and sits him on a yellow plastic stool facing a gray metal desk, then stands behind him, slightly to his right.

Abu Nejmeh is wearing a kind of light green smock that reaches down to his calves. He's wearing rubber sandals on his feet. They've cuffed his hands behind his back. He doesn't like the look of the room or the closed-circuit TV camera, doesn't like the plastic stool. He looks away from our window.

He is short and slender, his hands delicate. I remark to Abel that Abu Nejmeh is in better shape physically than we expected, though as he was pulled toward the stool he limped on his left foot. There are also red marks on his face, and his lower lip is swollen on the left side.

Abu Nejmeh's eyes are hollow. For a brief time they skitter restlessly around the room, focusing here, unfocusing, focusing there, unfocusing. When he calms down, he smiles. He says, "Hoo hoo," once and smiles again. He's gotten something beyond a beating, probably electroshock and sleep deprivation. He may be on drugs.

"They're tough on the foreign Arabs," Abel says, "especially Palestinians. They seem not to like them." We don't ask our Jordanian friends the particulars, the Interior Ministry doesn't volunteer them. It's our working arrangement.

The room has a high ceiling. Just below it, in one wall, is a row of deep windows, each about a foot square. The walls are painted a light gray-green. Two large ceiling fans rotate slowly, whispering *tock . . . tock . . . tock . . .*

Abu Nejmeh has calmed down and is sitting still. His face is eager now, the face of a schoolboy, sure of his lessons, waiting to be called on by his teacher.

The interrogator, a large, solemn-faced man, enters and sits at the desk. He's military, a Colonel Joweini, but today he's wearing a brown business suit. As he seats himself, he looks at Abu Nejmeh and nods curtly, a kind of hello. He makes a note or two on a long pad of paper, considers the notes briefly, then looks up at Abu Nejmeh and says softly, "Let's begin."

The long interview is conducted in matter-of-fact tones, as if it were simply two men, friends perhaps, talking over the events of the day. The interrogation is done in Arabic and is simultaneously translated into English for us.

"Your name is?"

"Waleed Abu Nejmeh."

"You were born where?"

"Dheisheh."

"Dheisheh?"

"Dheisheh Camp, near Bayt Lahm, near al-Quds."

The Dheisheh refugee camp, near Bethlehem, near Jerusalem.

"When?"

"Nineteen seventy-eight."

Joweini proceeds deliberately and logically from topic to topic, point to point. Abu Nejmeh talks of his early life, of his religious devotion, of his conversion to militant Islam. He describes his family in

Dheisheh and the small cinder-block apartment that an uncle had built for the family.

He describes meeting fellow militants at a mosque in east Amman near the First Traffic Circle. He's been in Afghanistan, he says. He has trained at an al-Qaeda camp, he's met Osama bin Laden. He tells of renting a safe house, of buying nitric and sulfuric acids.

Abu Nejmeh's group had diagrams of the Shmeisani neighborhood in Amman and diagrams and photos of the Safeway store on Imam Bukhari Street. Someone else, from a different cell, had conducted the surveillance of the store. We don't know who they were. Abu Nejmeh claimed he had never learned his contact's name.

A man whose name the Jordanians haven't learned had left instructions at night in a dead drop near the Roman amphitheater, alerting Abu Nejmeh's group by putting a chalk mark on the route marker of a bus stop in Malik Faisal Street.

Yet another team was to arrange for a van to be left with Abu Nejmeh himself. The instructions in the dead drop told how to load the van with the explosives mixture that Abu Nejmeh's group had concocted and had kept in the safe house basement and how to connect the detonating devices that they were to find in the van to the explosives. The instructions also told where to position the vehicle. No one had yet delivered the van.

The Jordanian Mukhabarat have these documents as well as false travel documents and ID cards that had been supplied to the group.

There had to have been a coordinator, someone higher up who handled the two teams. Abu Nejmeh says that he was named Muhammad Hejazi and that he stayed briefly at the Cliff Hotel. The Cliff is a four-story building in downtown Amman. It has balconies on its upper floors, where in the evenings young Arab men sit looking down into the street, watching the passing show, yearning for excitement.

The Cliff's records turned out to be no help, of course, and the coordinator is gone, if he ever existed.

Now it's our turn. The interrogator asks the questions we want answered. Among the men Abu Nejmeh betrays today is our Algerian killer.

"You knew a person named Liamine Dreissi."

"Yes."

"Where did you meet him?"

"In the Khaldan Camp."

Khaldan is a dusty, rocky al-Qaeda training camp in the uplands far off the Peshawar-Kabul highway, near Kabul. We have aerial and satellite shots of it. One, taken by a U-2, shows men playing soccer. The resolution is so good we can count the players and see where the goals are placed. We can even distinguish the soccer ball.

But we've never gotten a man in there. For us, Khaldan could be as far away as Neptune.

"Tell us what you know of the man Dreissi."

"He is Algerian, a combatant. He is in the Osama bin Laden group."

"Al-Qaeda?"

"Yes."

"You saw him where?"

"In Yemen."

"And when?"

"Five months ago. About."

"What were your circumstances in Yemen?"

"We were staying in a house. Four of us."

"Did the man Dreissi stay with you in that house?"

"Yes."

"For how long?"

"Not long. Perhaps three days. Not longer."

"What did he tell you? Did he tell you about an operation?"

"Yes. He said there had recently been an operation against an American target."

"Where?"

"In Peshawar."

"When?"

"Two weeks before."

"Two weeks before you met in Yemen, before Dreissi arrived in Yemen?"

"Yes. That is correct."

"Did he take part in the operation?"

"He said he did."

"Alone?"

"With two other men."

Abu Nejmeh says that's all he knows.

The interview ends. The Jordanians have beaten, electroshocked, and possibly drugged this man, and we have doubts about what he's said, how good his account is. Under torture, people will say anything. The Jordanians have told us he volunteered Dreissi's name without their prompting. We can't be sure of that. On the other hand, we do think his account adds up. We are a small step closer to Dreissi now, and to Kareem, maybe to that whole gang in Hamburg.

As for Abu Nejmeh, the Jordanians will, after suitable due process, hang him.

Time for Communion. As bright sunlight streams into our austere white sanctuary, the pastor sings solo, and without accompaniment:

Amazing Grace, how sweet the sound,
That saved a wretch like me.

Beckmann's voice has a mild Southern ring to it. He carries the tune well enough, better than I would. His voice, though, is too throaty for me and has an unctuous quality. As he sings, the ushers, like stewards on an airliner, wheel a silvery cart bearing grape juice and saltine fragments up the aisle to the rear of the sanctuary, the little glasses on the cart softly clinking.

Beckmann sings:

I once was lost, but now am found,
Was blind, but now I see.

The girl sitting next to me sways a little with the music, eyes shut.

The service program reads, "Those who have yet to acknowledge Christ as their personal Savior will kindly refrain from joining in Holy Communion."

I take the little glass and saltine fragment and with the others, with the high school girl next to me, drink the grape juice and eat the fragment.

They are all innocents—Beckmann, the pretty girl next to me, others in the congregation. They do not know. They can't. There are some things moral men can't know.

---

1 2 MAY 28
"Itching to Take Over"

"Fowler called over this morning—on Powers. Again," Cleppinger says, standing in my doorway. He means Robert Fowler, the National Security Council terrorism man. "Says NSC wants more say on the Powers thing. Says he wants to 'broaden the responsibility base,' wants NSC to have 'more input, more viewpoint exchange.'" Clep grimaces when he says this. "You can feel it building over there, goddamnit, they want to grab the Powers investigation, take it away from us. Keep your eyes open for the snatch."

Cleppinger deals with Fowler almost daily. We are deeply suspicious of Fowler, who, now that he is at NSC, has a record of breaking in on things that we do and wanting to take command.

Since Powers's death, Fowler has been peppering ATAC personnel with phone calls and e-mail on the incident, irritating Cleppinger no end. Once in a great while, Fowler calls me as well. There is nothing overtly hostile in the calls—we all have to get along—but there is a subtext: move on this.

Sitting down by my desk, Clep says, "Fowler thinks he's King Shit and the rest of us in the grand scheme of things are minor turds. Mark me, he wants to step in, go operational on Powers, you can tell he's itching to take over, the fucker. 'Priorities have changed,' he says. 'We are now slotting this higher in our task matrix.' Task matrix!

"Well, at least he cares. The Oval Office—note my careful language—the Oval Office doesn't give a flying fuck about terrorism. Early on, we presented NSC—Lindsay did this when he took over—presented NSC with a list of threats and asked them to prioritize them from their perspective: what did they think was the absolute worst, what was the second worst, and so on. We'd work from that, we said, figure out how much time, how much money, to put into a problem, how to assign personnel, right? Well, all they cared about over there was China, Iraq, Iran. That's it, that's the goddamn NSC mantra—China, Iraq, Iran. So that's where CIA puts its time and the taxpayers' money. Terrorists, these boingos you and I have the honor of chasing around, come way, way down the totem pole. Except for Fowler—he thinks they're top priority." Cleppinger blows through his lips. "Well, what the hell—I suppose I should feel good when that asshole calls."

Fowler runs his operation—and I mean *operation*—out of Ollie

North's old suite in the Executive Office Building, a vast gray-and-white pile of Virginia granite a hundred yards or so west of the White House. The EOB was built in the 1880s and was known back then as the War Department. Fowler's digs are on the third floor, just around the corner from Lindsay's more modest pied-à-terre.

When Fowler first came on board at NSC, he rightly demanded a bank of new computers and new commo gear for his office. (We Feds are always behind the technology curve, sometimes as much as twenty years.) Getting the equipment put in place tied up half his floor for two weeks. Because the EOB's ancient interior walls are three feet thick and made of solid brick, when you have new cable put in, the workmen have to use huge drills, like miners digging out a coal face. It's noisy as hell and takes much time. It was one of many ways Fowler established his presence and bureaucratic gravitas. Lindsay avoided the building while the work was going on.

A reporter for *The New York Times,* Tom Avakian, recently did a pro-piece on Fowler headlined AMERICA'S TOP GUN IN THE WAR ON TERRORISM. Avakian, like Meatball, is a trooper in the large army of Washington defense-intelligence reporters, and we know him well. He is more than a little strange, but as far as we're concerned, pliable and generally cooperative.

The article earned Avakian points with Fowler I'm sure, but when Clep saw it, he was fit for a straitjacket. "Top gun!" he yelled. "Honest to God, that clown wouldn't know how to walk down the street in some of our better countries. He does not know the territory out there. He's pushed government paper all his adult—and kissed ass—all his adult life. That's not counting the backstabbing that got him where his is. 'Top gun'!"

The Post, not to be bested in obsequiousness by *The Times,* did a longer piece on Fowler a few weeks later, this one with several photos, one showing Fowler addressing the president in the East Wing under a portrait of George Washington. Fowler is his usual intense self, staring hard at the president, evidently instructing the president in the byways of terrorism, hand up to make a point. The president is listening earnestly, as to a great teacher.

" 'Broadening the responsibility base' my fanny!" Clep says. "More Washington bullshit. They are preparing to horn in on this and tell us how to do our jobs. They will come in here and screw things up, you just know it. Patterson, you've been alerted," Clep says as he leaves, a weary, knowing look on his face, "stand by for an NSC raiding party."

13

MAY 28
Arrival of the Muscle III

On May 28, 2001, Mohand al-Shehri, Hamza al-Ghamdi, and Ahmed al-Nami, all of them Saudi nationals, arrived at Miami International Airport and were met there by Muhammad Atta.

Al-Shehri and al-Nami were from the isolated and poor Asir Province in the south. Hamza al-Ghamdi was from neighboring al-Bahah. He was of the same tribe as Ahmed al-Ghamdi, who had arrived on May 2.

In the previous March, Hamza al-Ghamdi and Ahmed al-Nami had been filmed in a farewell video that was aired on the Arab satellite network Aljazeera. In the video, a number of young men swear to become martyrs. Though neither al-Ghamdi nor al-Nami speak, they are seen studying maps and flight manuals.

14

MAY 28
Al-Qaeda Wants to Kill Me

Karen is asleep, and I am not. The big red digits of her alarm clock read 2:08 a.m.

When we went to bed, there had been a hint of rain in the air, the promise of a spring storm. Now a wind has risen, and as its soft but insistent gusts hit Karen's house, the old place whispers and murmurs, its metal-framed storm windows thrumming softly.

I slide quietly from bed and pad over to the window to look down into the brick-paved alley behind Karen's house. I see no black chick in a CRX with DC plate AD 2989, "Taxation Without Representation." The alley's empty.

In Karen's cramped back plot, raccoons—dexterous little bastards—have once again gotten into the trash and have trailed pieces of crumpled aluminum foil, empty envelopes, and half a grapefruit rind around the small space. The garbage will be down there in the morning for the crows to take a turn with. They love the aluminum foil especially, have a thing for it.

Security Division thinks it was al-Qaeda that tried to kill me in Peshawar.

The evidence is SIGINT, an intercept we got today of an e-mail out of Pakistan. We think the e-mail was sent by an al-Qaeda foot soldier residing in Peshawar, but we are not sure—the source was a laptop, and it seems to travel.

The message—it dates from three months back, but was only translated yesterday—contained a list of twenty-one U.S. citizens, all of them foreign-service and intelligence officers. Two of them are retired, and the document treats them as still active—fucked-up Arabs, but then we do the same thing. The names hit a hot button with the computers at Fort Meade.

The cable called the twenty-one U.S. officials "individuals of potential significance," a cryptic phrase al-Qaeda uses from time to time and which ATAC considers hostile, though there is no clear evidence for that.

The U.S. officials cited are officers in CIA, Drug Enforcement Administration, and State and Defense departments and seem not to

have much in common except that all have worked in counterterrorism. I know a few personally—Tommy Hodges, Arnold Reisman,
both at the Pentagon—and Ernie Olson at CIA.

I am on the list. They have linked me with my old cover name,
ROBERT LANGER. They know who LANGER was, and to an
extent, what LANGER did. They have given an accurate physical description of LANGER. They know LANGER's phony background—
international trade lawyer—and an old telephone number
LANGER used, supposedly my business number, but backstopped
once long ago to an office at Langley. They have done a short but
fairly accurate bio of me, the real me, and have included it in the
document along with my current residence down to my street address and home phone number in Arlington.

They know all that. And they probably knew I was in Peshawar.
Al-Qaeda wants to kill me.

What if they learn of Karen? They won't, I tell myself. But what
if they do? They kill women. Terri Talbot, after all.

The e-mail went to temporary addresses on the Web. We know
the addresses of the sender and the receivers—cybercafés in Pakistan
and Germany—and we know the servers it went through. We do not
know the identities of those who used those cybercafés to send and
receive the message. They're gone.

Who of these phantoms is entering the United States? Since we
don't give lists of al-Qaeda people to the Bureau or to State or to
Customs, we can't know unless we track them ourselves, and we
don't track them. Nobody's minding the store.

I've raised the issue with Lindsay and Len Davidson, but top people in the structure just don't want to share the names with outsiders.
The names will get out, they say, and our enemies will know we
know. Got to keep the names tightly held. Family jewels.

So far Lindsay has refused to fight them over this.

As I stare down into Karen's dimly lit back alley, I think of our friends at that café in Hamburg—Kareem, Dreissi, that lizard-faced Egyptian in his galabia—and I wonder again, Who of these phantoms is coming in? And what will they do when they're here?

Watch your goddamn back.

I settle back in bed, quietly. The last I notice it is 3:12 a.m.

15

MAY 29

"Hands at My Throat. I'll Never Forget That"

Clep's raspy voice is on my intercom. "A break on your friend Kareem. He showed up in the U.K. I'm in Sonny's office, come on over."

Three weeks back, in London, Kareem violently attacked his girlfriend, a woman named Mary Ogilvie, then disappeared.

His girlfriend complained to the police, who queried MI5 on Kareem's status—he hadn't been using an alias—and his name came up on their watch list of terrorism suspects, put there thanks to Sonny's query. Our counterpart service, MI6, notified that Kareem has turned up in the U.K., has gotten back to us with the news. MI6 has also transmitted to us a police video of a statement the girlfriend made shortly after reporting the incident.

Kareem still may be in the U.K. He had been living in a condo apartment in West London owned by a Pakistani man with British citizenship, who claimed to have met Kareem at a mosque. The Pakistani said he had been looking for tenants for his condo and Kareem needed a place to stay. Kareem paid his rent in cash, not unusual among Muslims, even in London. The Pakistani landlord has no known terrorist connections.

Clep, Sonny, and I sit around a TV and VCR in Sonny's office, the first Americans to see this tape.

Mary Ogilvie, the girlfriend, is sitting at a table, arms folded in front of her, looking directly at the camera. She is attractive, in her midthirties. Her hair is blond and short, combed up straight like a boy's. She has high-arching eyebrows over blue eyes and high cheekbones. A pair of large glasses is hanging around her neck on a cord. The police interviewer, a man speaking with a soft Scots brogue, is off camera.

"What's your name?"

"My name is Mary Ogilvie."

"Where do you work?"

"I work at the Waterstone's in Ealing Broadway Centre. Before that I worked for them in South Kensington. So I'm a book person. I write, too. I write short stories."

"How did you meet Kareem?"

"We met in the parking apron. Eyes caught and we clicked. Or I did, anyway. We said hello. That's all. Couple more times, and there we were. He was very shy, very hesitant. I liked that. He said his name was Kareem. Also Yusuf, but he is called Joe.

" 'Like a walk?' I said once, and he said, 'Yes.' That's how it started. I mean the real thing. We started taking walks. We'd go down through Hanger Hill Park. There's a golf course there, and we'd go through. It's cool and green in the summer in the twilight. There are lovely short oak trees and hawthorns there and black beeches and it's very, very nice. Then we'd go out of the park and into a lane, past the nice brick houses all in a row, and they all had well-tended gardens with roses, and grassy lawns.

"So that's how we met. I've a ground-floor flat. Not much light. Excellent view of the side car park [laughs], nice if you like to look at other people's cars [laughs again]. Cheap stereo. John my ex took the good one. I got the Bach and the Handel CDs, a kindness on John's part, who liked Bach and Handel. And everything aesthetic.

"So I was hooked. His name was Kareem so I called him Cary, like in Cary Grant. I thought he was foreign and lovely. There was a time when I couldn't do things like that, but now I find I can. I'm thirty-five. And so we became an item."

"He lived in your building?"

"Yes. His place, Cary's place, had two bedrooms. He had a few clothes. You could put them all in a suitcase. One sport coat and a green mackintosh. He slept on the floor on a kind of pad. He had a TV set, which was on the floor, and we'd sit on the floor there in front of it and watch it. He liked American football. I thought it was fun, his lifestyle, I mean. Minimalism, right? Simplify your life, right? Electric fire in the kitch came with the flat. So did a refrigerator. So he cooked a little for himself. He spent a lot of time in my place. Once we got to know each other. Right. And it was all right, it really was. I cooked for him. He liked that."

"How did he present himself?"

"Present himself?"

"What did he tell you about himself?"

"He said he was a student. He was enrolled in some technical college in Chiswick, but he was doing English, doing that before his real studies. I thought he was polite and gentle. You know, dark eyes, mysterious East, Sufis, all that.

"Cary had been around, I concluded. What'll the neighbors think? Didn't matter.

"My days off I might go to Knightsbridge, Harrods maybe, and take him with me sometimes. He liked a scarf I wore round my neck, a silk thing, quite dazzling, from a boutique in Oxford Street. He liked it, said it was beautiful.

"I said I would teach him films.

"I garden in the plot that runs down past the new annex.

"John my ex was a nutcase. Total. Sweet in his way, of course, but off into his own thing. And utterly self-obsessed. Read books at the breakfast table. Professor of literature. Richmond U. Liked American grade-B fiction. Taught it when he could.

"You know who's friends to who in a divorce, don't you? The friends split, too. The Rusbridges—she's a bitch—the Howards, the Santorellis, all went with John. There you are [laughs].

"So, well, there I was. And there he was. I was ready for someone. Very. Cary's smile was a good one, good teeth."

"Did you know his friends?"

"He had friends. He wouldn't let me meet them. There were three that would come round a lot. I'd see them get into the lift. When they were there, I was always excluded, run out, told to go off and play like a good girl."

"What happened the night he attacked you?"

[Hesitates.] "There's a long hall in his flat that leads past a spare bedroom and the kitchen, then finally into the sitting room. One night they left him, and I suppose left the door open somehow, I don't know, and he didn't realize they hadn't closed the door properly, but they hadn't, and so I just walked in.

"And there he was kneeling on the floor, newspapers spread out on the floor, but not for reading."

"What did you see there?"

"A gun, a pistol. Big, large boxy thing. When he looked up at me I froze, not from fear of the gun, I don't suppose, though that was scary enough, but, no, from his look. I can't say the look, what it was. No smile. Frightened look, then a look of . . . I don't know—hate, something. Why that? Don't know. Then he sprang up and pushed me into the wall, hands on my throat, choking me. Couldn't breathe. I mean, I thought he'd kill me. I didn't get it. We'd been an item, you see. We had. Then he ran to the door and banged it closed. He came back at me staring, breathing hard, absolutely mad look on his face, mad, his eyes on mine. I didn't know. I mean, I couldn't get past him, and after the anger a different look, as if he were thinking what to do with me. I mean, we'd been an item. It was so raw, so different. How can people be like that? Don't get it. Can't.

"He looked down at the floor, hands down at his side.

" 'Go,' " he said. Just that, 'Go.' "

"What did you do then?"

"Moved out. That night. Went to a girlfriend's flat. Scared to death. Told her it was a row with a boyfriend. I'd been there three years, in the Hanger Lane flat. I didn't sleep that night. I think he might have killed me. He left that night, I think. He had nothing in the flat to take. Just that suitcase.

"I called the police the next day, not that night; should have, didn't. Stupid. There you are. They came round, I suppose, the police. I left. Friends moved me. Never went back. He doesn't know where I am. His friends don't. He never got to know my friends. Didn't last long enough for that.

"Hands at my throat. I'll never forget that. I never will."

"Crook or terrorist?" Sonny asks nobody in particular. "Can't tell from this, can you?"

"We've been through this," I say.

Sonny shrugs.

16

MAY 29
Divorce Suit

I enter my silent house from the garage, switch on the kitchen light, and go to collect the mail. When I open the front door, I see a large envelope taped to the outside of my storm door about chest high. The envelope is from Circuit Court, County of Arlington, State of Virginia. I know what this is: divorce papers. Gerstenbach has done his work. *Nancy R. Patterson v. Paul E. Patterson*.

Joanne Konner, a coffee-klatsch friend of Nan's from down the street, under questioning by Lloyd Gerstenbach, Esq., and in the presence of Nancy R. Patterson, complainant, has testified under oath to a representative of the court that Nancy R. and Paul E. Patterson have lived "separate and apart without any cohabitation and continuously and without interruption" for more than one year. Nancy R. Patterson on these grounds seeks a divorce. The court wishes to know if Paul E. Patterson, defendant, contests complainant's suit.

He does not.

Contrary to what my lawyer Mailer thought, Nan has accepted a hefty second mortgage on the house as part of the deal, her acceptance conveyed by her lawyer, Gerstenbach, to Mailer to me. Now she's moving on the divorce.

I sit for a time in the dim light of my living room. Off on a corner table is a framed shot of Nan and me, taken five years back on a blistering day in August on a beach on the island of Crete. David, at age fourteen, was the photographer.

The day before that picture was taken, the three of us, a trio of game tourists, had trudged thirteen miles of stony paths through the Sammaria Gorge, a dry creekbed in southern Crete, down to the light blue Libyan Sea. Next day, tired and achy from the hike, we were spending our time doing nothing at the beach near Khania, the little port town on the north coast where we were staying. And there David took his shot.

When we returned to our hotel in Kanevaro Street for an afternoon nap, David went to his room, Nan and I to ours. I waited until Nan fell into slumber. Then I slipped out and walked down to the quay, where I boarded a motor launch that took me far out in Khania Harbor to a large yacht, the property of a Saudi national named Ismail Hamawi, whom I had long cultivated.

The yacht was named *Samira* after Hamawi's daughter by a Saudi wife of another world. His Western wife was a young woman named Angelica, who resided in Rome and who had cinematic ambitions she seems never to have realized. Hamawi's girlfriend of the time, a pretty American named Cale, was with us on the boat. Her name, she told me once, was short for Carole. It was what she called herself as a little girl, and her "folks" called her that, Cale, forever after.

When I board the *Samira,* I find Hamawi and Cale sitting on deck. Hamawi jumps up and greets me warmly. He's all smiles.

"*Es-salaamu 'aleikum, ya sheikh. Marhaba katir!*" (Peace to you, respected one. Much welcome.)

"*Wa 'aleikum es-salaam, ya sadiqi.*" (And peace to you, O friend.)

Hamawi and I always play at speaking Arabic—it's not a language I'm comfortable with—when we meet, then switch to English.

"So good to see you, Bob. My love," Hamawi says to Cale, "you remember my old friend Bob."

Cale smiles and nods. Yes, of course.

The sun is glinting on Hamawi's bald head. He's holding a pair of folded sunglasses in his hand. He's wearing a white jacket with epaulets, a white cotton shirt, no undershirt—a puff of whitish hair peeps through at the chest—white trousers, white shoes, no socks. Cale is in white, too, a demure cotton skirt and a gauzy blouse. Her long russet hair is combed back.

Above them, on the upper deck, is a helicopter, baby blue with white markings.

Hamawi's boat, all teak and mahogany and beautifully brushed aluminum, is said to have cost him $34 million. I suppose I believe it, though I have no talent at estimating these things.

"My love," Hamawi says to Cale, "Bob and I have some very boring business to get out of the way, and we'll not tire you with it. Bob, let's retire for a moment or two."

In Hamawi's suite, where we have our talk, the couches are upholstered in lustrous green silk embroidered in a paisley pattern. The walls are beige chamois, and on them someone has sketched in black monochrome a Picasso-like idyll of fawns and satyrs and centaurs playing pipes for buxom maids with long, curly hair.

An Iraqi competitor of Hamawi's is undertaking a shipment of gyroscopes—missile guidance devices—to the Iraqi regime. Hamawi knows the ship, the *Sophia,* and the port of embarkation, Varna, Bulgaria. He also knows how and where on the ship the gyroscopes are hidden. As promised to Athens Station, Hamawi imparts this information to me. That's it, mission accomplished. Cale is called in to join us, and we all three have a flute of champagne. I am motored back to the quay at Khania.

We shared the information from Hamawi with the British,

French, German, and Israeli services. Two weeks later, the ship was stopped by the Turkish navy before transiting the Bosphorus and its cargo, including the gyroscopes, confiscated. Three weeks after that, Hamawi's competitor was found dead in the entrance to his modest sixth-floor apartment in Brussels. He'd received three .22-caliber rounds in the back of his head, execution-style, and had pumped very little blood. We don't know who did the deed, but we can guess. (We don't think it was the British, French, or Germans.)

When I slipped back into our hotel room, Nan was awake, reading.

"Where'd you go?"

"Out," I said, and kissed her.

"What'd you do?"

"Nothing." I kissed her twice. Her smile crinkled the edges of her eyes.

"Like a little boy," she said.

I kissed her some more.

In that picture David took on the beach, Nan and I are both wearing straw hats. Hers is narrow-brimmed and has a big checkered ribbon for a hatband. She's wearing it pushed back on her head and is smiling a bumptious, funny, girl's smile, having the time of her life. I have my left arm around her shoulder.

My mouth is set in a thin, hard line, my eyes hidden in shadow under the wide brim of my hat. You can't tell who I am. Nan's complaint, I suppose.

I look again at the communication from the Circuit Court, County of Arlington. Strange feeling. You think you have a certain kind of life. Then you don't.

As when my father died, I feel a steady, subdued ache, as continuous and sad as a pedal tone, for everything that cannot be unsaid or undone.

I suppose I want this.

17

"I Wanted to Leave Him"

"Virgin Mary." Andrea Rodriguez, Powers's mistress and my one illicit love of long ago, glances up affably at our perky little waitress—her name is Jenna, she has announced—who jots down our drink orders (beer for me) and sashays off to the bar, fanny wagging. It's a late, lazy Friday afternoon. We're in a Bennigan's in Falls Church, at a window table, far from the bar and the other customers. We look out onto an asphalt parking lot. Across the way are the usual: a Gap, an Omaha Steaks, a Pearle Vision. Bennigan's is Andrea's idea of an out-of-the-way place. People don't go there, she said, meaning People Like Us.

Andrea called me at home last night. She was in town, she said, and wanted to talk.

"About Ed and all that. Can I see you?"

That's all she'd say on the phone. "Yes," I said, "yes."

She's probably worried about federal prosecutors coming at her for some of Ed's shadier dealings. The FBI has been paying close attention to her, Lurch tells me. They're looking at Ed's arms trafficking and they smell a case against Andrea.

At the entrance to Bennigan's Andrea and I embraced, distantly and quickly, but in the feel of her right arm up on my shoulder and around my neck there was something of those afternoons in Drayton Gardens. That faint electricity between two former lovers, it never goes away. We both felt it, then broke the clinch.

"So how are you?" I ask.

"Oh, tired. I've been back three weeks now, would you believe, and I'm still in a daze. I'm in a town house in Falls Church. Place I own. I bought it as an investment a while back—for a rainy day." She gives her head a rueful shake. "Well, I guess it's a rainy day, all right.

The renters were on month-to-month, so when Ed died, I wrote them to leave."

Time has flattened her out and made her rangier, more angular. Her eyes and mouth have hardened, her features set. This is the way she's going to be from here on in.

And yet, and yet, there's still a hint, ten years later, of that sassy, sexy glance I remember. Born with it.

She shakes her head. "I'm such a dunce sometimes. I thought I'd get a job here in Washington, but now I'm not so sure I want to stay in the area. Too many ghosts. I shouldn't have kicked out the renters. They were really okay—nice people, you know? And now if I leave, I'll have to find new ones and that'll take some time and who knows what I'll get. And I probably will leave. My dad and mom live in L.A., and I've got a sister in San Diego, so I may go out there."

"To do what?"

"Dunno. Right now I'm still trying to figure things out. Go back to school maybe. I'm out of the business—Ed's. That's all over. His lawyers are 'winding it down,' like they say. Shooting it in the head's more like it. And I'm unemployed."

Jenna brings our drinks, Andrea's in a big glass with a celery stalk for swizzling the tomato juice and Worcestershire sauce, my beer in an iced mug. As she cranks with her celery, Andrea smiles at me. "I don't do alcohol anymore. Guess I've gotten to be some kind of a health nut."

We make perfunctory conversation. When I ask about Cyndi, Andrea's daughter by a marriage that ended before Ed came along, her face doesn't brighten. Cyndi I remember as a shy, moody child, ten or eleven years old, who never looked you in the eye. Even at that age the kid thought the world was lined up against her. You could tell. Andrea had put her in some private school in London that she hated and where she was doing badly.

"Cyndi's out in Chicago," Andrea says flatly. "She's been working at nothing jobs, been in and out of school, not doing anything real with her life. She's working now in a Mail Boxes Etc., if you can believe that. She'll do something else dumb later. She's living with a guy—this Eric, Jesus—who teaches music in an 'alternative school,' whatever that is, because he doesn't have a teaching degree. They pay him minimum, naturally. I visited them out there once, a year back. He—Eric—spent the whole darn time filing a recorder mouthpiece—you know, one of those whistlely things? Musical instrument? I think he taught it at his 'alternative school.' So there he sits in this bare, nothing apartment they have, not saying anything to me, just a bump on a log, all this time just making this *scritch-scritch-scritch* sound while Cyndi and I tried to figure out something to say to each other. God, the kid's only twenty-four and already her life's been a series of bad accidents." Andrea gives me a sullen look. "Where'd she get the talent, right?"

Then: "You know, I met Ed in L.A. Fifteen years ago now. Unbelievable. I mean, all that time." She says this with what sounds like genuine wonder in her voice. I know what she means. Time passes. You look back, you can't believe the distance, all your life stretching away, irrecoverable and unchangeable. Gone forever.

"Friend of a friend. A guy I knew who knew Ed." She tightens the edge of her mouth. "The rest is history."

"Why not come over here?" she asked. "I could fix us lunch. Be fun."

That bright afternoon with its crystalline sun in Drayton Gardens becomes a succession of afternoons, then evenings. The affair lasts a month, from a start in early April to a finish in May.

I am on assignment from my job at Langley, where I am desk officer for Turkey in the DO, working in London on temporary duty. My hotel, in which our embassy maintains a permanent bloc of rooms, is just off Grosvenor Square, giving me an easy walk to work.

Though I report in at the embassy in the morning, my job is to go out and interview U.S. and other businesspeople who, like Ed, frequent the stranger countries of the world and pass through London from time to time. I go where I please, and I set my own hours. For an office, I share a cubbyhole on the embassy's third floor with a gloomy Soviet analyst from the DI, Dale Grotz, who says little beyond "Good morning."

It took no time that first afternoon. In bed upstairs she is breathy, hot, burning, boiling over; she explodes quickly, thrashing, into moans and sobs. It brings on a kind of deafness, lust, when everything but the lover and the lover's touch, smell, and taste fade from your senses and the world is faraway, soundless.

After our first frantic love that afternoon, as she walks barefoot over the deep carpeting, I lie in the soft bed, up on my elbow, following her with my gaze. She is long and lanky, a little ungainly as she walks.

When she goes into the bathroom and shuts the door, I get up from the fluffy, pillowy bed and play that other game: I look down from the window through the drawn blinds into Drayton Mews and carefully check the street. Nothing there, no cars, no vans. The old cobblestones gleam in the early-afternoon sunlight.

Honey trap is what we in our black world call the sexual assignations we devise to entrap our unwary targets. It occurred to me that first afternoon that something of the sort might be afoot, but I decided that if "they," whoever "they" might be, tried to blackmail me, I'd simply tough it out, admit my roving ways if I had to, and tell them to go fuck themselves. A small test of courage, I suppose. Nothing happened.

Back, standing before me as I sit on the edge of the bed, Andrea smiles down, her hands resting lightly on my shoulders, her breasts tilted up before my face. On her right nipple she has a discoloration, a faint marbling of pink through the darker burnt sienna, some kind of birthmark.

Entranced, I kiss that imperfect nipple, more exciting because imperfect, then her warm belly, still flat and taut though she's had a child. Her pubic hair is a thick, dark patch, her smell musky. Nuzzling lightly, I kiss along the border between belly and pubis. "Lovely Andi," I say.

"When I had Cyndi," she says in a small voice, "they shaved me. Never thought it would grow back."

I kiss, then put an exploratory finger on a long, horizontal scar, a thin, whitish pink band of toughened skin stretching along her panty line. I look up at her questioningly.

"Cesarean," she says.

When we end it, Andrea is very cool. She has no regrets. It was a temporary thing and, I'm pretty sure, some kind of payback to Ed. "Once in a while you have a spring fling," she says. "No harm done."

It's a sunny May morning, some weekday. We kiss chastely, standing in the slate-floored foyer of that house in Drayton Gardens, and say good-bye. Ed's in Hong Kong and I have stayed the night. I head for my hotel, then Heathrow.

My flight back to D.C. starts in midmorning and stays always in a kind of ever-bright, eleven-o'clock time zone. I have a couple of drinks. I think of Nan. I think, It happens. And: It's over. No harm done.

If I didn't tell someone that something had happened, it was as if it had never happened.

I will never see Drayton Gardens again. Nor Andrea, until this Friday afternoon.

Andrea's eyes drift around Bennigan's. "I liked the neighborhood there," she says. "South Kensington. Pretty part of town. Ed and I'd stroll around the neighborhood in the evenings in the summer and smell the ivy in the gardens. That's one thing I'm going to miss, those pretty gardens. There was this Polish restaurant in Thurloe Square. They served Ed's kind of food—you know, heavy stuff, potatoes, sausages, big chunks of pork, Polish vodka. We'd go there rather than all the great little places in South Kensington. Ed didn't give a damn about food, he just didn't, but I didn't care, it was okay with me."

She pauses for a moment. "He had girlfriends, you know."

I don't react. I think of that young cookie on Ed's yacht, her beautiful ass, and beyond her, the blinding sun silvery on the blue water in the heat of the day. Lurch's colleagues at the Bureau seem not to have tracked her down and probably never will. Powers had, as Lurch said, a lot of them.

"I wanted to leave him," Andrea says. "I was about to. Then he died." Her voice is leaden, she looks miserable.

Time.

"Andi," I say softly. "Why the call? What's going on? What's up?"

She looks at me levelly. "I don't know who else to talk to. You knew Ed, the people around him. You're the only Agency guy—person—I know who did. Why'd he die?"

"I don't know."

"What are they saying?"

"I gather the belief is it's terrorism. Pakistan's a rough place."

"Do you know anything about it, what they're doing?"

"They?"

"CIA, FBI."

She's pumping me. She's worried all right.

"Well, FBI's got jurisdiction over his murder. It looks like it's terrorism against an American citizen. Even overseas, when it's terrorism, it's their deal. Omnibus Crime Act."

She lets that sit a moment, then asks, "What about CIA? What's CIA doing?"

At the Agency we do not like the terms *lie* or *lying*. We use euphemisms like *withholding* or we talk of "slanting the truth to make it fit the circumstances." After a while, slanting the truth becomes second nature. After a while, you don't even have to think.

"Hey, he wasn't one of our officers, Andi. FBI's leading the charge on this. I'm sure we want to know, but we're not the cops, they are." Then quickly: "You tell me. I'm curious. Who's doing what on it? Who've you talked to?"

"Well, I talked to the British in London, to the FBI there, too. Bad scene. I mean, Ed had just died, and I was almost catatonic. I'm like, What I am going to do? Where am I going to go? Just dazed and in such a fog. And then these guys show up—eight members of Her Majesty's Constabulary—at six thirty in the morning, banged on the door. It was an invasion. They took all the documentation I had, they took piles of my own paperwork—I mean, my own personal stuff, for God's sake—and they also took my computer, which they broke, and Ed's computer. They were polite on the surface, I suppose, the British, but they were not good guys. I mean, when I went in later the same darn day, they really gave me a grilling.

"Then those Bureau people in London came along and gave me another working over, like they're tough guys and I'm some kind of a criminal. It was . . . so . . . gross. And here, too—the FBI's been around a couple of times here, long, long interviews. I mean, I barely got here when they came over, came out to the house. They're really interested."

I've seen the transcripts of Andrea's MI5 interviews in London. In them she comes across as cooperative, and the British report describes her as "friendly." She had little to say we didn't already know.

We have requested the transcripts of the FBI interviews but have yet to see them. Lurch tells me the delay is no big deal, that they're on their way. "Problem of getting things typed, read, cleared through channels," he told me.

I like Lurch, and I don't think he's gaming me—not exactly—but the British services are more cooperative with us than our own Bureau. Cleppinger and I, some others, don't care for this treatment.

Then again, what have we told the Bureau about Powers? Not the whole truth, not all we know. Because Ed was who he was, an Agency operative, we are keeping as much of his story as possible in the immediate family.

She's scared, you can tell it. Gives you a handle. "Andrea, you ever do anything you knew was illegal? I'm not asking, just talking—know what I mean? You may need a lawyer."

"Yeah, I saw one of Ed's here in town. I talked with his attorney in London, too. Pisses you off to have to do it, I mean, my God, the expense!"

"Maybe you need somebody not so close to Ed."

"Maybe." She runs her hand back over her hair, patting it as if to smooth it, a gesture I saw first in the Cross Keys, our pub in Chelsea. Then later in Drayton Gardens.

"Who is it here in Washington? Good firm?" I try to sound only mildly curious, but I catch a look, a flick in her eye, that I can't read.

"Stanley Bress," she says. "Know him?"

I do. Stan Bress, of Creighton, O'Connell, Lobel, is an out-house Agency lawyer. His firm is on our preferred list. It figures Powers would use him. Bress has been in town since the Eisenhower administration. He has to be expensive. Bress knows who I am and probably knows what I'm doing these days. That flick in the eye—Andrea didn't just call me out of the blue.

"Good firm, good man."

"I didn't know what Ed was doing, not everything."

She shakes her head slowly back and forth, almost a child's gesture of denial. "He did his own business deals."

This will be her line. It's what Bress will lay on a jury if need be.

"Ed could be pretty mysterious about things," she says. "I mean, like the Brits grabbed the office records, but I bet they don't find anything."

"They're smart."

"Smart?" She rolls her eyes at the wall to signal she's talking to a dumb ass. "Paul, whether they're smart or not, there's nothing to find. Nothing incriminating's on paper. Ed's idea was to keep people—he'd take on partners now and then—keep people, the partners, everybody, in the dark. Ed did not run a well-documented ship. 'Keep everything invisible,' Ed would say, and that was the deal. A lot of what Ed did died with Ed. I never knew the whole score on anything. I mean, I was just the bookkeeper"—her eyes are large now and swarmy, confused—"and then the office manager."

Looking at me, she collects herself, then breaks into something close to a smile. "You know he used code? For his overseas deals? In faxes and e-mails and even when he was talking on the phone, it could have been a foreign language. And my God"—she laughs a little bell-like peal, first of the afternoon—"he used this phony name, Guy Rutherford, even with people who knew his real one. Guy Rutherford—so la-di-da. You wonder where he got it.

"Our phones were bugged, too. We never told the police about it 'cause we thought the police probably put them in, in the first place. I mean, what would've been the point?" She gives me a quick, sharp look. "Maybe you know this stuff already?"

"Hey, we didn't do it."

She laughs again. "No, no, you're the good guys, I keep forgetting. The rooms were always clean, though. Ed had a security company sweep the place every so often. They'd come in with little aluminum boxes—wires and doodads and antennas and stuff—and would work through the place. Then they'd go out to their van, and Ed would go with them and have a talk. I don't know what they ever found or what they did, but things were always okay."

MI5 has told us nothing about trying to eavesdrop on Ed, probably because they couldn't get working bugs into Powers's place or, if they did, Powers's people found the devices and neutralized them.

I probe around, ask some questions about Ed's deals, the partners he might have had. I am searching for Kareem. Andrea names people, some I've heard of, some I haven't, and describes them.

But not Kareem. Nobody like him.

"Well, I'll tell you, Andi," I say finally, "stick with a good lawyer and hope he doesn't have to do too much work. Stan Bress knows his business. I'll keep my ears open on Ed. Promise you that."

She seems grateful. When we part in the parking lot and head for our separate cars, we smile and wave good-bye.

She knows more.

---

18   JUNE 3   Antiques

Karen gets up, tousle-haired after a sleep-in Sunday morning, and leaves our bedroom briefly. She is naked. It's the way we sleep, a practice of hers that became mine. I watch her depart, then return smiling with two glasses of orange juice, which we drink lying in bed together—our morning juice ritual. Karen began the custom in her musty, narrow bedroom on the Hill our first morning after the night before, stepping gingerly over the clothes we had hurriedly scattered on her worn carpet, and we continue the rite now wherever we are, my place as it happens this morning.

When she finishes her juice, she puts her glass on the night table, turns on her side, and snuggles into my neck, lying in the crook of my left arm, nonchalantly, familiarly, as if we are a pair of old marrieds.

But I am no blasé husband. I am still the ardent lover, in awe of what has come my way.

Sleepily, though awake, she blows a puff of breath, a tiny warm gustlet, and shifts away onto her back. And there: her pubic area, a rusty variation on her lovely blond hair, trails off and down like a long teardrop.

Transfixing.

Karen has been married. Her ex is a *Legal Times* reporter named Peter Brock. They'd lived in a nice house in Glover Park, a neighborhood in the District's mostly white northwest, full of well-off young couples.

I've met Brock. He is tall and weedy, a man constructed to slouch. He has fiery red hair and beard.

Brock is not a bad reporter. He'd worked Washington for *U.S. News* during and after the Clinton impeachment and got some pretty good stories. Now and then you'd see Brock on TV at the congressional sessions, standing out in the crowd with that red hair and red beard, scooping up handouts and transcripts from the previous day, talking with the congressmen and their aides and the committee people.

But all was not well in Glover Park.

"I woke up one day," Karen told me early on, "and realized that I'd seen something in him that wasn't there, that I was caught in something, trapped in something that was a major mistake. We went in different directions. Too focused on careers, maybe, too many hours a day in our own separate worlds and too much traveling. We were apart too much, and our life just went kablooey."

My fear: that our apartness, our different worlds, her travels, mine, will end this.

"Media marriages," she said, "are lousy anyway, and I realized he didn't care that much for me. So I couldn't figure out why he was in it either. It didn't make any sense to me. I asked him what he saw in it, he couldn't answer. He thought about it awhile and said he didn't see anything, so maybe we ought to call it quits. No big tragedy. We're still friends."

I asked, "If he'd cared about you, a lot, I mean, would it have mattered?"

"He didn't."

"But would it have mattered?"

She considered this. "I don't know," she said finally.

I think she does.

While still married to Brock, she had a string of affairs out in the hinterland (wheels up, rings off, right? What happens beyond the Beltway doesn't really happen, right?) and one brief tumble here in town with a local *Los Angeles Times* reporter named James Jeffries.

This Jeffries I've met at media parties Karen has taken me to. He is four years younger than Karen and is boyishly good-looking though he has a pushed-in jaw and the beginnings of a double chin. Jeffries has a Southern accent and a slow, Southern manner that make people, maybe even Karen, a Kentucky girl who should know better, think he's shrewder than he really is. Jeffries is assigned to Congress so they're forever bumping into each other.

When Jeffries is in a room with Karen, he notices her and keeps on noticing her, looks her way a lot and doesn't make much effort to cover it up. I don't care for this.

Karen has told me that the affair's over. "I love you," she says, "you. You're my man."

"Your main man?"

"My man."

But Jeffries? What does Jeffries think?

After a lazy morning—*Post, Times,* coffee, we avoid the talking heads on TV—I drive Karen to Howard Avenue in Kensington, a street built along the south edge of a high railroad embankment and now given over to antique stores (Aunt Betty's, Carolyn's, Second Hand Rose), all of them quaint as hell. Though she seldom buys anything, Karen likes to poke through the old bottles and lamps, the tarnished silverware, the forlorn used books these places deal in; I am bored silly by it all.

We wander past the windows of junk—Seconds City, Renées—

some of it no older than I am: a spun-aluminum bun warmer, *Life* magazines from the sixties, a NIXON'S THE ONE poster. I'm as antique as these unwanted, dusty old artifacts.

Fleetingly the question recurs: Will she leave me? That age difference.

In one store, Time Past, a beautifully restored gasoline pump from the 1930s catches my eye—price tag $2,500, not for me. Standing next to it is a dark wooden statue of a woman, fake Afro style. She is three feet high and buck naked, her split vulva projecting like a penis.

"Catch the naked woman?" Karen asks, as we exit back out onto Howard. "Makes me think of Harry Dornberg. Doesn't look like him, I don't mean that, but it makes me think of him. Harry was staff writer on *The Courier-Journal*"—*The Louisville Courier-Journal* was Karen's first paper—"hack to end all hacks, believe me. Management tolerated Harry, I don't know why. He produced a thing called 'Town Talk,' all the big doings in Louisville. Jesus, it must have been hard to write. Maybe that's why they kept him on.

"Anyhow, there was this bar Harry and everybody else used to patronize, just across the street from the paper, down a little. It was called the Cheetah Lounge. Décor was White Hunters on Safari. Everything was shields and spears and tall grass and such. You'd love Louisville, Big Boy. They had this wooden carving on the wall about a foot high—naked lady, African, just like the one back there, only this one had little red tits that lit up electrically. Great place, the Lounge. So anyway I thought of Harry when I saw the lady.

"Harry was a major boozer. Every day he'd come into the office about one in the afternoon. That's when he started work. He'd come in and fiddle at his desk for a while, maybe make a couple of calls, probably to his bookie, then head straight out of the newsroom down to the Lounge and get plowed before really starting work. We called the route to the Lounge the Dornberg Trail. 'Where's Harry?' somebody'd ask. 'Oh, he's hit the Dornberg Trail,' we'd say."

"Hard-drinking press, huh? Your poetic souls."

She tosses her head back in a laugh. "Yeah, right—Harry Dorn-berg, Poetic Soul. Well, you can do that out in the provinces, maybe—the boozing—but not here in Washington. Everything's too serious here, everybody's too driven, always hustling. Drink too much, you can't keep up here. I mean, a few of the older types, yeah, they put it away, but not the younger ones. Way too serious, my gen-eration."

My generation, the phrase makes me uncomfortable. But Karen's right. You watch them at receptions, the younger press, they're always working. Our man Meatball, who may be forty at most, will take a big glass of whiskey and hold it in his hand all evening, always listen-ing, always watching, bring it to his lips now and then to encourage you to drink, and keep on listening, never really touching the stuff himself.

"Wasn't exactly what I was bargaining for," she says, "but I don't care, I love the biz."

" 'The biz'—I've always wondered what people see in your 'biz,' Kare. Bad hours, crap-ass pay. Even here in Washington it's only the big outfits that pay well—so why go in? Why do it?"

"Lot of reasons. Curiosity, for one. I wanted to know what was happening out there in the big world, know before anybody else did. And my beautiful ego. I like byline, like putting my name on a good story. And the stories themselves—I just like them. They explain things, make sense of the world, of life. I don't mean the usual news story, those things don't. The usual thing's some kind of snapshot you take in the middle of what's going on, but you keep at it, sometimes you can see the beginning and maybe know the ending, too. A lot of little stories sometimes make up the Big Story."

I say, "Seldom works out for us. A lot of our stories turn out to be nothing, just blind alleys or a bunch of lies. People we want to know about just appear for a while on the stage, play some kind of role, which half the time we can't understand, then drop out of sight. Gone. Never see them again, or hear of them."

Like Kareem, our Afghan.

Where are you now, Kareem, you little shit?

"Well," Karen says, "get the truth out to the public. That's the real point of being in the biz. 'The truth shall make you free.'"

"You believe that?"

"I do. I really do."

"We got that same quote carved into the wall at Langley, in the big entrance hall. Putting it up there was Allen Dulles's idea. I'm not sure Dulles believed it, but whether he did or not, he had it carved in stone up there for everybody to see. Book of John. The full quote is, 'Ye shall know the truth and the truth shall make you free.' I've always had a problem with having it up there. On our wall it's some kind of political statement. But the freedom the Book of John is talking about isn't political at all, it's spiritual."

Karen shows no reaction. *Spiritual* is one of those words, like *sin, atonement, redemption,* all the rest, that leave her cold, that simply don't figure in her worldview. She's too practical for theology.

I plunge on: "It's a claim basically that if you understand the truth, that is, if you understand Jesus' message, you will lead a Christian life and ultimately you'll enter the kingdom of heaven. I doubt Allen Dulles had that in mind as our mission, but up that quote went."

I never knew Dulles. Those who did say you couldn't believe a thing the tricky old guy said, sitting there behind his desk, smiling and smiling, light gleaming off his wire-rimmed glasses.

(Nan's take: "You guys, even when you're quoting the Bible, you're mendacious.")

I say, "The press twists the same quote the same way, Kare, gives it the same Enlightenment political interpretation. You're just like us— you guys read what you want to into quotations you don't understand."

"But the political interpretation is also true, truer than the original meaning, if you ask me."

"Rip it out of context and go with it, huh?"

"Hey, Big Boy, it's up there on *your* wall, not mine."

Spying wasn't my aim in life. I got recruited, long ago and far away: 1977, Bloomington. I am out of the Corps and am now an earnest student of international relations, IR we call it, at Indiana U., beavering away at a master's thesis on political conflict in South Asia, which I intend to make the basis of a Ph.D. dissertation.

A professor in the department, Sidney Drescher, author of two fat, unreadable books on Soviet economic history, had put me onto a campus recruiter out from Langley. The recruiter had flown into Indianapolis from Washington and had driven a rented vehicle over iced roads to Bloomington on a dark and dreadful day in what I recall as a dark and dreadful winter.

A storm had blown in the night before and had brought with it a foot of snow, which the wind had lashed into high, sloping drifts. By dawn the storm had spent itself, but a leaden, sunless sky hung over our university. The recruiter and I met in a small, overheated seminar room, a room Drescher had arranged, on the third floor of Woodburn Hall, the poli-sci building.

It didn't occur to me until much later to wonder what Drescher got out of the arrangement.

The recruiter was friendly, even jovial, and joked about the weather. He was middle-aged and pear-shaped. He had crew-cut hair, pale skin, and delicate hands. He wore glasses that had thick, black plastic rims. He spoke with a flat Midwest accent, like me.

"Sidney thinks a lot of you, Paul, thinks you're first-rate material," he said.

"Sidney," the recruiter said, not "Professor Drescher." All right to use Paul with me, of course, but *Sidney*? At that point I was still in awe of professors, and if Professor Sidney Louis Drescher and the recruiter were on a first-name basis, well, that made the recruiter quite a recruiter.

Drescher had already given them some background on me, and the recruiter was complimentary.

"You have a sharp mind," he said, "very focused. You've been in the Marines, good record there. You're a thorough patriot, that's clear. But your patriotism is not unsophisticated. Sidney says you ask good questions, genuinely questioning questions. You're a person who wants to know the truth. So do we. That's our mission. We want to know the truth so that our country can act wisely, can defend itself. We range worldwide—we view every culture, deal with every country in the world. Any conceivable place you're interested in, we're there, watching, evaluating."

As the recruiter spoke, it occurred to me that though I was writing on South Asia, I had never been there, knew almost no one from the region, did not speak or read any of the languages. It occurred to me that CIA, in the person of this pear-shaped bureaucrat, was promising me knowledge. Not only that, the Agency was promising me knowledge of a kind denied to all but a few. That promise of the esoteric, and the lure of far-off places with their strange-sounding names won me for the Agency and set me on my life's course.

I took my master's that spring, but let the Ph.D. go. Not for me the library, I wanted the street.

"I'm like you," I say to Karen. "I joined CIA, partly anyway, because I wanted to know what was happening. I wanted to know the truth."

"Well, you guys sure work hard to keep it hidden from the rest of us."

"Hey, you guys are supposed to learn the truth and inform the public. I am supposed to learn the truth and inform our government. We put out a newspaper, by the way—the National Intelligence Daily. Heck of a lot better than *The Post*. It's got maybe a hundred customers, which is what we call them, 'customers,' top guys in the government. No ladies' underwear ads. We just try to tell our customers the truth." Then I say blandly, hopefully, not so sure I believe what I'm saying, "Spooks and journalists, we're not so far apart."

She nods her head in put-on agreement—sure, sure, she seems to be saying. "You can be pretty sneaky and underhanded, right?"

"We can. We lie, we steal, we blackmail."

"Well, the spook world, all that lying you do, the cover stories, the phony names, the phony jobs, all that stuff, it never appealed to me. That's not the way we do business. Mostly we're straight up, straight-forward. 'Hi, I'm Karen Halliday, *Washington Post*. What's happening?'—that's mostly the way we do it. My attitude is 'I just want to know what's going on and I need some help.' No sneaking, no lying. What you see is what you get. Oh!" Karen punches me in the ribs. In the window of Second Hand Rose she's spotted a sparkling, snug-fitting, sequined top, three shades of blue, wavy-patterned, that looks as if it ought to be worn by a circus performer. "Outrageous! My black pants—you haven't seen them—palazzo pants, accordion-pleated, dull black silk—hooah, great combo!"

Karen buys the top for $5. "A steal," I tell her.

---

1 9   JUNE 5
Vegas, Arrival of the Muscle IV

On Tuesday, June 5, 2001, for the first time, Muhammad Atta, Marwan al-Shehhi, Ziad al-Jarrah, and Hani Hanjour all met, face-to-face. Joining them was a young Saudi national, Nawaf al-Hazmi. The five young men had taken rooms in an EconoLodge in Las Vegas, Nevada, not far from the old and, these days, less popular Strip.

Al-Hazmi had entered the United States January 15, 2000, at Los Angeles International Airport from Kuala Lumpur, Malaysia, with a companion, Khalid al-Mihdhar, also a Saudi national.

Shortly before entering the United States, al Hazmi and al-Mihdhar had attended an al-Qaeda strategy meeting in Kuala Lumpur, a meeting known to, and surveilled by, the CIA. It was held in an apartment owned by Yazid Sufaat, an al-Qaeda operative, the same man who furnished Zacarias Moussaoui a letter naming him his commercial representative.

At the time of the meeting in Kuala Lumpur, CIA was aware that al-Mihdhar possessed a multiple-entry visa permitting him to travel to the United States. CIA also knew that the meeting had been attended by a man suspected of helping bomb the USS *Cole* in Aden harbor, which connected al-Mihdhar and al-Hazmi to the operational cells of al-Qaeda.

Nevertheless, CIA, never willing to furnish more than a small fraction of its information about suspected terrorists to other U.S. agencies, did not provide the names of al-Mihdhar or al-Hazmi to the State Department, the Immigration and Naturalization Service, or the FBI.

After a short stay in Los Angeles in January 2000, al-Mihdhar and al-Hazmi moved to San Diego and began flight training there at the National Air College. At the time of the June 2001 meeting in Las Vegas, al-Mihdhar had left the United States.

Three days after the five men met in Las Vegas, two young Saudi nationals, Ahmed al-Haznawi and Wail al-Shehri, arrived at Miami International Airport in Florida.

Al-Haznawi, like Ahmed al-Ghamdi and Hamza al-Ghamdi, was born in the al-Bahah region of the Kingdom. The three shared the same tribal affiliation. All had begun university studies, though none had completed a degree.

Wail al-Shehri was the brother of Waleed al-Shehri, who had entered the United States on April 23.

20

JUNE 11
Lindsay Testifies

Monday, a stunning June afternoon. Len Davidson and I have joined Lindsay for a trip up the Hill to testify before a full session of Senate Select on "interagency responses to the international terrorist threat." The session, which is being held in Dirksen 419, is closed to public and press.

We're uneasy about today's event, not sure how it will go. Our congressional liaison office has been picking up negative vibes from some committee staff and a few of the senators. The senators are complaining about our "overreliance on signals intelligence" (Senator Blake), our "bureaucratic stultification" (Senator Webster), and the inevitable contribution from Donovan, our "fetish for secrecy."

Lindsay has ready a presentation that, though it does address the issue of the day—terrorism—will touch on as many of these other points as possible and fend off all the complaints we can imagine. Lindsay will do all the Agency talking today. Davidson and I are there to lend weight, silent weight, to the occasion.

Coale enters the hearing room first. He's tanned and looks beautifully fit. He's dressed casually in a brown tweed jacket, beige trousers, quiet necktie. His press guy, Norb Warner, is following him. Norb's been a Hill operator since the last ice age. He started working for Coale four years back. As ever, he's got an old-fashioned barbershop haircut that he's let go a little, and his doughy, baggy face suggests late hours, alcohol, cigarettes, and no exercise. He's wearing a cheap olive-drab suit with creases in the wrong places. Next to Coale, he looks terrible, making Coale look even greater, which, I suspect, is the idea, if there's an idea.

When he sees Coale, Lindsay's face lights up, and he goes to the dais and starts chatting with him. Coale is happy and relaxed and looks glad to see Lindsay. Len and I remain seated on folding chairs behind the witness table.

As other senators wander in, Lindsay glad-hands them one by one—Kennedy, Webster, Blake, Chamorro, others, then finally Donovan, last to arrive, tall, ruddy-faced, and jowly, followed by his evil genius Merritt Grayson.

Donovan looks moody, not completely in control of himself. He is in light blue seersucker. He is wearing his trademark bow tie, a navy blue affair speckled with white polka dots. His shirt is an expensive-looking white-on-white, and he has bright red suspenders. Trying to look like Uncle Sam, I suppose.

Donovan and I don't get along. We've clashed openly at hearings and once or twice at social gatherings, mostly over Donovan's insane ideas about dismantling CIA and splitting our functions up among other government agencies.

After saying hello to Donovan, who snaps out of his funk and breaks suddenly into warmth and cordiality, Lindsay comes back and sits at the witness table in front of Davidson and me.

As I sit on my folding chair, I have my right leg up on my left knee. Donovan, who has a drinking problem, looks well-lubricated this afternoon, red-faced, a little unsteady as he walks. He glances in my direction, then glares and bawls into an open mike, "Uncross your legs!"

I stare at him. My leg stays up. Lindsay and Davidson show no reaction, just immobile faces and silence.

Donovan stands glowering at me for a time, unable to think of anything further to yell, then slumps into his chair and looks away. Merritt's face is rigid, expressionless.

Davidson leans over to me and whispers dolefully, "Word is, Donovan favors doses of Tío Pepe these days because martinis are too high octane for him in his old age—they disturb his sleep patterns. Know what Donovan's staff says when he's back in his office tying on a Tío Pepe bender? They tell people, 'The senator's seeing the Mexican ambassador.' It's an in-joke. Doesn't make you laugh, though."

I am pondering this when Coale starts the proceedings with an affable little speech welcoming "our hidden warriors."

Lindsay gives a friendly, impromptu response to Coale, then starts reading his prepared text: "The Intelligence Community works closely with other U.S. government agencies and allied governments in countering terrorist threats overseas. These efforts include the dissemination of threat warning reports to overseas facilities and U.S. government agencies to support decisions on protective measures and other efforts to disrupt or mitigate the threat of terrorist . . ."

No one is paying attention to this. As Lindsay drones, Coale, Donovan, other senators whisper to aides, who wander in and out and who whisper back. At Donovan's left ear Merritt Grayson hovers like a small, squirrelly Iago. I try to make eye contact with Merritt, but he isn't having it. Donovan does occasionally look my direction, out of carelessness probably, because when he focuses and realizes who he's looking at, he shifts his glance angrily.

When Lindsay starts discussing Osama bin Laden, our senators perk up and give him their full attention, a measure of Osama's international mojo.

"Osama bin Laden," Lindsay reads in his monotone, "and his global network of lieutenants and associates remain the most immediate and serious threat. Since 1998, bin Laden has declared all U.S. citizens legitimate targets of attack. As shown by the bombing of our embassies in Africa in 1998 and his plots at the end of the millennium, he is capable of planning multiple attacks with little or no warning.

"His organization, al-Qaeda, is continuing to place emphasis on developing surrogates to carry out attacks in an effort to avoid detection, blame, and retaliation. As a result it is often difficult to attribute terrorist incidents to his group, al-Qaeda.

"Bin Laden and al-Qaeda are becoming more operationally adept and more technically sophisticated in order to defeat counterterrorism measures. For example, as we have increased security around government and military facilities, terrorists are seeking out 'softer' targets that provide opportunities for mass casualties. Employing increasingly advanced devices and using strategies such as simultaneous attacks, the number of people killed or injured in international terrorist attacks rose dramatically in the 1990s, despite a general decline in the number of incidents. They—al-Qaeda—are becoming more lethal."

Lindsay thinks to raise his head now, the first time this afternoon, and look directly at the senators. "We are now entering a new phase in our effort against bin Laden. We are at war with him and with al-Qaeda. We are sparing no resources or people in this effort, either inside CIA or the wider Intelligence Community."

Not true. Our priorities have been elsewhere—China, Iraq, Iran. We have spent no more than before on counterterror, even since the African bombings. Last year Congress voted us more money for counterterror than we asked for, and millions of that we left unspent. Lindsay is not under oath.

He reads for about half an hour more, winding up with a paean to our SIGINT capabilities. "We have a full-point panoply of listening and sensing devices and capabilities . . ." Though this has not much to do with interagency cooperation, his words flummox the assembled senators. They are lawyers, most of them, and are clueless about technology and find discourse on it intimidating. Lindsay knows this.

During the question period, the senators, even our critics, are mostly polite.

When it's Donovan's turn, however, he leans into the mike like a barroom brawler about to deliver an uppercut and launches into a rambling prepared speech on our secrecy policies. This he reads in fits and starts, then asks Lindsay a series of curt questions, also from a written text. "Secrecy is a good way to hide mistakes and incompetence, Mr. Director. Is that not so?"

"Senator," Lindsay answers blandly, "there's a tension between what policymakers need to know and what can harm national security if revealed."

Lindsay wants to expatiate on this, but Donovan springs on him, "I'm not talking about policymakers, I'm talking about the execution of policy, particularly counterterrorism. The work of our once well-regarded Antiterrorism Action Committee has I think deteriorated in recent years. This is a fact, it is simply a fact. This fact is in a general way known, but only in a general way. Secrecy covering bureaucratic fumbling at ATAC, sir. Furthermore, the em-phasis"—Donovan drags out the word and repeats it—"the em-phasis your agency puts on secrecy can conceivably inhibit the cooperation fundamentally needed between agencies for this enterprise to succeed. Is that not so? FBI and CIA still do not cooperate sufficiently, and the reason for that, the essential reason, whatever the cul-tural"—he drags the word out—"cul-tural differences between the two organizations, the essential reason for this is CIA's reflexive stress on secrecy. This, of course, is not the only problem. We see multiple signs of other incompetence in our antiterrorism effort."

As Donovan talks, Lindsay gives him a fish eye and lets him wander.

Coale, who is not happy with Donovan's performance, finally interjects and shuts him down, ending the session.

Lindsay, Len, and I will huddle later for a replay of the action, but I sense they feel the afternoon has gone better than we had hoped.

I wonder about Donovan's speech, though.

Multiple signs of incompetence in our antiterrorism effort. That's a shot at Bill Cleppinger. It is the first public volley in some kind of campaign. I know Donovan.

On the way out, I grab Merritt Grayson in the hall. "What's the deal, Merritt? Why's Donovan got such a stick up his ass about ATAC?"

Merritt gives me that squirrelly, sideways look he's famous for: head turned away, one eye, his left, rolled back directly at you, alert, as if awaiting an attack. What a rodent.

"You've got problems at ATAC," Merritt says, "which you're covering up. Energy problems. You are not proactive. It's causing concern. You guys talk a beautiful antiterrorism game out there, but where's the beef? You haven't taken down anybody significant since Ramzi Youssef." Youssef masterminded the World Trade Center bombing in 1993. We captured him in 1996. "Yeah, him and there was some dope dealer on Cyprus, some guy, had a peripheral role in a hijacking way back." Merritt means Fawaz Yunis, who'd been in on the hijacking of a TWA flight. A young American had been killed on the plane as it sat on the runway at Beirut International. They shot him in the head and dumped his body out onto the tarmac. Yunis, a Lebanese, had been dealing in narcotics when we finally captured him in international waters off Cyprus. He is in federal prison.

"But since then what? I mean what? They even got one of your own people, that woman, in '97." Terri Talbot, murdered in her van in Karachi. "No movement even on her, your own officer. Patterson, you've gotten sclerotic over there. You don't know how to deal with our new enemies. You fought the KGB all your institutional exis-tence, since the 1940s, and so that's who you're comfortable with, the Russkies, not the terrorists. Cold War's over and you don't even know it."

Merritt, looking up and down the hall, gets a confiding tone in his voice and edges closer to me. "This Powers case—you haven't even begun to confront the implications of that. All these allegations floating around, narcotics trafficking and all that."

"We've looked carefully at that," I say.

"Uh-hun. And you're not being forthcoming on it, not with us. Probably not with other agencies. Probably because you don't know shit from Shinola. We think you've got problems on that one," he says, and heads down the hall.

21

JUNE 11
Here I Am

Late this rainy evening Karen drove from D.C., from the *Post* building on Fifteenth Street, to my place, bringing a day pack with cosmetics, underwear, toothbrush, and her next day's outfit on a hanger. No nightie. As always when she appears on my doorstep, her eyes were sparkling, her face fresh, open, eager.

Here I am, her face said. *Here I am for you, lover.*

Lover? That's what she calls me. And she says she loves me. But does she mean it? Really mean it? I don't push her on the subject. I'm afraid I'll push her away.

We've got the TV in my den turned to ESPN, but low. We are snuggled on the sofa, her head in my lap. We are munching popcorn, drinking beer, talking of this and that. Suddenly: "Why'd you go to the Pentagon? You left CIA, went down there to work. How come?"

The reporter, always asking.

"David died," I say. "Crazy reason to get another job, maybe, but I wanted a change. Thought it'd be a good idea. I still think it was."

She asks quietly, "Do you still love Nan?"

Surprised, I say, "No, she walked out on me, remember?"

"Still, you might—still love her, I mean. Something to think about."

"You think about it?"

"Sometimes."

"Well, she's been gone awhile. She said the house made her think of David." Our son is still present in the house—his photograph, taken when he graduated from Yorktown High, hangs in the living room, his toys we never had the heart to get rid of are still in the attic, his bicycle still out in the garage. "Anyway she blamed me for his death—that I do know—and she left."

Nan: "You abandoned him, you prick. Why have kids in the first place if you're not going to give them time? What were you thinking?"

"Well," Karen says, "you've lost a child and a marriage." She pauses on that one. Maybe to think on what lousy boyfriend material I am. I have, as they say, "issues." But she keeps showing up out here in Arlington, fresh-faced and smiling. And I am welcomed with smiles at her place on the Hill.

"Maybe your pain is greater than you admit."

"If you don't think about it, Kare, how bad can it be? I mean, yeah, when Nan left, it hurt. And when David died, it was like having a limb amputated. But you soldier on, you deal with it, you just do."

Her face doesn't agree. She isn't buying it. "But you might still love Nan. Down deep."

"Kare, if I don't feel it, it's not there."

"Mmmm. Hard to tell with you, Big Boy. It's not just your work you won't talk about."

"Way I am."

She goes "Mmmm" again, studying my face, then smiles and says, "You know, I liked your approach when we met. That thing for Finn." She's changing the subject, probably to lighten the mood—okay by me though I know we're going to come back to it. "You said, 'I don't know anybody here so I thought I'd start with you.' They teach you that at the Farm?"

"They taught me to recruit Russians. That's not how you do it."

"You were supposed to go after their women?"

"Nope. It isn't like that. So what'd you think? About me?"

"Ooooh, first of all, I noticed your face. Here's a fierce, serious guy, I thought. And the looks you could get, even that night at the Finn thing. I sensed you could be cranky and grouchy."

"God, I was on my best behavior."

"So I figured—that was the scary part."

She laughs. But keeps studying my face.

First time was at her place, in the big king-size bed that almost fills the back room in her shotgun row house. She'd lit a candle on her dresser, and its small yellow flame, reflected in the mirror, just barely illuminated the room. She took off her bra and panties, leaving on only her slip, and lay beside me. As we loved, she began to murmur softly, "Mum-mum mum-mum mum-mum," a throaty hymn that surprised me at first but which I would come to know well. Then, murmuring that murmur, she brought her leg over mine and we were joined.

The morning after, a Sunday, her head rose above a far-off pillow and our rumpled sheets. She was a smiling mermaid emerging from the sea, her green eyes dreamy, her hair disheveled, like blond seaweed, and I was a sailor bewitched at the sight.

She pulled to my side and buried her face in my neck. As we lay silent, I felt the warmth of her body, felt her soft breath purling down my chest, rhythmic as her heart.

Well, hello.

Friday she's off to speak at an academic conference, University of Minnesota, Gunderson Center for Media Studies. Karen will talk on "Democracy and the Press in the 21st Century." The center does these jamborees once a year, hiring journalistic bigfeet like Karen to fly in and give them the word. I will not see her again until midweek.

22 JUNE 17
TIPOFF

On June 17, 2001, Khalid al-Mihdhar, who had left the United States in the late spring, applied for a new U.S. visa at the American consulate in Jidda, Saudi Arabia. His old visa, under which he had entered the United States in January 2000, had expired. As was routine, the State Department officers who took his application checked his name against a database of known and suspected terrorists supplied by CIA and other agencies under a program called TIPOFF.

Though CIA had information on al-Mihdhar linking him to al-Qaeda—he had attended the al-Qaeda strategy meeting in Kuala Lumpur, in January 2000—the Agency had declined to furnish his name to the TIPOFF program, and al-Mihdhar did not appear on the consulate's terrorist list. The consulate gave al-Mihdhar a new visa.

CIA also neglected to put the name of al-Mihdhar's companion from Kuala Lumpur and California, Nawaf al-Hazmi, in the TIPOFF system, though it had associated al-Hazmi with al-Qaeda as well. Nor did CIA furnish the names of the two men to any other U.S. agency.

23

JUNE 19

"Bill Cleppinger Has an Unbroken Record of Failure"

"Hey, I hear there's a cabal in there going after Bill Cleppinger." It's Meatball on the line. Ten in the morning, early for him.

" 'Going after Bill Cleppinger'? Meaning what?"

"Meaning his head's on the block, some people want him out, re-tired. We gonna have blood on the walls out there?"

"How'd you hear that?"

"Well, Ron Diamond sure did a number on him."

Ronald Diamond was once an assistant secretary of defense and is now in the private sector working as a "security consultant," making hay with his contacts. Over the weekend, in a major speech at a Washington think tank, Diamond tore into Cleppinger by name. *The Washington Times,* which admires Diamond and is a frequent outlet for his ravings, printed the whole text.

"Bill Cleppinger," Diamond said, "has an unbroken r
failure in our struggle against global terrorism. We have los
nel. We have lost agents. We have failed to detect important anti-
American operations. We have failed to put in place the appropriate
warning systems. These are serious failings and the situation has to
be put right. The head of the Antiterrorism Action Committee at
CIA should be removed on the grounds of incompetence and a lack
of the fundamental qualifications to hold that position. The director
of central intelligence should explain why William Cleppinger has
been there all this time, despite a record of one failure after another."

Heavy stuff. Diamond delivered his speech ("New Threats in the
New Century") at the National Security Forum, a well-funded
group who have great disdain for CIA and our fearful, bureaucratic
ways. They have a point—up to a point—but Clep is by no means
the problem, a truth that matters little to them. Their target is the
Agency, and fairness isn't their forte.

Diamond didn't say so in his speech, but he was talking about
Powers and the collapse of NOREFUGE, probably the Talbot shooting as well. Though he is no longer in government and should not
know anything about anything, Diamond has his sources. Some are
here at Langley, some at the Pentagon, some elsewhere. Robert Fowler
is certainly one. Diamond and Fowler are blood brothers. The congressional intelligence committees probably feed Diamond as well.

This speech was coordinated with Donovan's attack last week in
committee. Something's up.

"And, some people are saying Diamond's right," Meatball says,
"too many screwups, not enough performance. Cleppinger gonna
last?"

The poison has started. They're out whispering to the media.

"Far as I know, Bigfoot. Who's been talking besides Ron baby?"

"Oh, people."

"Like who?"

"They're not on the record."

"Oh, right. Courageous people, your 'sources'? They'll talk if nobody can tell who they are, right? And you—can't screw a source, huh?"

"Hey, 'sources and methods,' right? Off-limits, right? Hint: a top officer in Operations."

I wonder who. Sonny maybe. I wouldn't put it past him.

"I'm serious, Paul, I just called Bill about Diamond, and he wouldn't say anything. I thought I'd bounce it off you."

Meatball is earning his nickname today. "Well, I'll have to ditto that."

"No comment?"

"Well put."

Meatball hesitates, then says, "You know, we never settled whether Edward Powers was Agency or not. Was he? Anything ever come out of that, of his death?"

"Shit if I know—ask Public Affairs. Want their number? They're swell guys, might help you out."

"Very funny. Talk to you later, guy."

He hasn't put Powers and heroin together. Nobody's blabbed about that yet. Small victory for our side.

Outside the government, Diamond is our most prominent and persistent critic, but he is not alone. And within the government, Clep has his detractors as well. I've heard the talk. Flack, I know, is coming in from Fowler. The White House wants bodies. Fowler claims all we give them is planning papers. We're not doing enough.

Meatball's "top officer in Operations," whoever he is, may not be alone. Usually when one person starts in, he knows he has allies.

I ease into Cleppinger's office. He's reading a stack of cables and scratching notes on them, his narrow, little reading glasses down on his nose.

"Meatball just called, said he'd talked to you about Diamond and all that."

Clep looks up at me. He says, "Uh-huh," tonelessly.

"They're out there, aren't they? D'he say a 'top officer' said something?"

"He did."

"What do you make of that?"

"Meatball's just stirring the pot a little. Could have been some drunk at a party."

We both know this is bravado. The campaign is on.

---

24 **JUNE 19**
"Smoke in Your Hand"

"Al-Qaeda's moving money," Sonny says.

It's 8 p.m. or so. Sonny's dropped in at my place to talk. I've been home a couple of hours. He's just left work.

We started in my den, a rammer for Sonny, a beer for me, and now, Sonny on his second rammer, we are out in my backyard near the white gazebo in the corner, where the lot falls away. (Nan, ever a roses and white-picket-fence kind of lady, had the gazebo put in.) The evening is cool after a rain, and swallows are flitting over our suburban yards in the failing light.

"Got a thing in on it this evening, cable out of Berlin. I'll show you tomorrow. BOXER pulled out twenty thousand in cash from an account they got there. Account's almost empty now. They may close it."

BOXER is a Moroccan living in Germany. He is a student at a technical school in Hamburg. We consider BOXER an al-Qaeda operative. We've alerted the German police, who have been watching him and our famous al-Kods mosque in Hamburg, where BOXER and friends gather.

Twenty thousand dollars is not a lot of money, though banks do notice withdrawals of this size, which they may or may not report. It doesn't matter much. Governments pay little attention to bank reports. It's only because we've asked the Germans to put a special watch on the account that we've heard about this withdrawal. Our agreement with our German hosts forbids Berlin Station to spy on these individuals, and we therefore have to rely on the Germans for our information. *Semper fi.*

BOXER has probably placed the $20,000 with a hawala somewhere in Germany—there are twenty we know of—and we'll never see it again.

Hawalas are informal cash and credit transfer offices. They are used mostly by Muslim workers from the world's poorer countries working overseas to send what they can save of their wages to their families back home.

To move money from country to country hawalas rely on personal trust, not precise documentation, and they avoid such standard techniques of international banking as wire transfer. A deposit with a hawala in Hamburg can mean instant cash on the street in, say, Detroit. All it takes is a phone call.

In 1998, after our embassies in Africa were bombed and after we fired seventy cruise missiles in retaliation into Afghanistan to kill bin Laden—and missed—al-Qaeda started pulling its cash out of the international banking system. They used their deposits to buy diamonds, other gems, gold—we call it commodifying—and placed the valuables with hawala brokers in Nairobi, Karachi, Abu Dhabi, Detroit, Toronto. Gems and gold can be carried easily past customs officials and can be turned back into cash in any city al-Qaeda has a friend. All they need is a telephone or an e-mail account. The transactions, like hawala transfers, are impossible to track.

Globalization—it has its hidden costs, costs we don't think about. Great for investors, great for terrorists.

Sonny is half-turned from me, silhouetted against the sky. He's staring over the roof of the Evrards' house, which nestles in a hollow under our gazebo.

"Money's gone," he says softly. "Smoke in your hand. We'll never know where it went. But you know they are doing something with that goddamn money."

It is one more indication that al-Qaeda is arranging something, probably something large. We don't know what or where.

Sonny runs his hand along his chin, massaging it. "Big free-form network," he says. "Buncha little independent actors, embedded here, there, everywhere. Like germs. And they mutate." Suddenly he turns back to me, holding his glass in both hands, as if he's having trouble keeping it steady, his eyes troubled, haunted. "We gotta get these people," he says softly, "gotta get 'em."

I ask, "What'd the Germans say on the transfer?"

No response. Sonny just stands there strangely, facing me but not looking at me, lost in some world.

Then, as if he's just noticed it's late, he says, "Hey, I'm gonna take off. See you in the morning, guy. Germans didn't say anything much. Show you that cable."

That's Sonny: fast entrances, fast exits. When I walk him around the side of the house past a couple of runt pine trees, I see he has parked a good fifty yards down and on the other side. Sonny plays his games, too.

---

2 5   JUNE 20
A Stroll Down Connecticut

"Trumpets blew and drums banged when I inquired about Abdel Kareem Yusufzai. Apparently, everyone in Peshawar knows that Powers-Rutherford and Kareem were business partners of some sort," my Pakistani journalist friend Amjad Afridi says.

Afridi and I have had a midmorning coffee in the dark, wood-paneled lounge at the Canterbury Hotel, a small place on N Street that Afridi favors when he's in town. He's here to address two think tanks and the State Department. Afridi wasn't comfortable talking at the hotel, so we are out strolling down Connecticut Avenue toward Farragut Square.

"Now, Powers and Kareem were seen often together in Peshawar and elsewhere. They say that Kareem is a young man in a bad trade. They say heroin. They say he has sited an extracting plant somewhere near Jalalabad. It's highly secret, and I don't know its location. The Taliban leadership doesn't own the plant, but is cognizant of its existence and essentially approves. The plant is a cash cow for them. Kareem pays 'taxes' to them. This seems to be his chief business venture at the moment, and I would guess that Edward Powers was involved.

"These people, the Taliban, are so hypocritical about the drugs. The money looks good to them and so they take it. And of course in America, these ignorant and hypocritical men, with their floggings and stonings of women, their hatred of music and art and all the rest, these men are represented in the press, on television, as typical Muslims and are used to illustrate how backward and how antimodern Islam and we Muslims are.

"But I think we Muslims have a lot to say to others, particularly to others in the so-called modern world. As I read it, an essential point of the Koran, perhaps the most essential, is the need—the religious duty—to build a just and equitable social order on earth, one in which the rulers are responsible for their citizens and where citizens may lead good lives, good in both senses, pious as well as materially successful.

"But of course this stress on social justice in the basic text of our religion is why these people, the Taliban, al-Qaeda, all Muslims perhaps, are so troublesome. We Muslims have a social vision, and it comes from God. It's because of this vision of course that the bin Laden types of the world feel perfectly justified in killing, killing anybody, to get their way, to set up God's prescribed order here on earth."

"A hundred years ago, Amjad, we weren't in each other's faces."

"Oh, yes, we were. At least the British and the French and the Dutch were very much in *our* faces—in North Africa, the Near East, India, Indonesia, black Africa. They were everywhere. We've not managed to get over that—the colonial experience. And now you Americans with your new world order, *you're* everywhere, even talking of empire! And with your military bases you have a very large footprint, especially in the Persian Gulf. I like that expression, *footprint*—it makes one think of a boot, doesn't it?—a boot in our faces. I think this 'American Empire' is unhealthy for everybody."

"Mine is not to reason why, Amjad. I just try to know what's going on."

"Yes, Paul, you are 'tasked' to know the facts. You are directed by your government to focus on oil or 'Islamism' or this or that army's order of battle. And you look at these matters very closely, and that's all well and good, that's your job. But I sometimes think you cannot see the living, breathing reality in front of your faces or the dangers that lurk just off to the side, just out of your view.

"Take poverty and its consequences. Most Muslim countries are poor, some of them desperately so, beggars among nations really. They are wounded societies. Think of Afghanistan, which is the best example. Or Somalia or Chechnya or my country, Pakistan—all these places are so poor, so weak, so ignorant. And so full of strife. They are where the bin Ladens come from, and where they get their troops.

"You know, without the Soviet invasion of Afghanistan there would never have been an al-Qaeda—the organization simply wouldn't have come into existence. Nor would there have been the thousands of young men passing through Pakistan, getting military training. Nor the database of young jihadis willing to kill and die for Islam. Who knew at the time that the Soviet invasion would give us bin Laden and his misdeeds? But it did.

"Obviously we can't just blame the Soviets. There are other more fundamental reasons for the success of bin Laden. In so many parts of my world people feel that their lives are out of their control, that they are manipulated by outsiders—young men especially feel this, feel the humiliation of it.

"Those are the problems: the poverty and the humiliation. This is what I tell them at the State Department, and I suggest that you put it in your next President's Daily Briefing. If you do, you may quote me with direct attribution."

"And Kareem, Amjad? Is Kareem a humiliated young man out to kill the Crusaders? Or just a crook?"

"Those alternatives, Paul, are not inconsistent."

Amjad and I part company at Farragut Square.

26

JUNE 20

"It's Me"

When I arrive at Karen's for a midweek rendezvous, she's out, though Pooch rises to greet me, putting a wet nose to my hand, woofing softly. Formalities over, Pooch gives herself a satisfying shake and heads for the kitchen and her feeding bowl. I see Karen's left me a note on the floor in front of the door: "Errands CVS."

So, as I often do, I go up to her office and plop down in an ancient Barcalounger she inherited from old man Halliday, the most comfortable chair in the house.

On her messy desk, made from a door and two two-drawer black metal filing cabinets, is a postcard she's framed, a Modigliani nude I'd sent her from Rome. "Reminds me of somebody I know," I had written on the back. The nude, a female, is reclining, eyes closed, asleep, perhaps dreaming, arms folded behind her head, groin to the viewer, offered. The woman's hair is a reddish blond, darker than Karen's, but the shape of her face and the contours of her body are the same.

Next to the Modigliani, her answering machine is winking red with at least ten incoming messages. Probably returns. Karen lives by the telephone and seems to work out of her house as much as down-town. On the phone, not with me, she is type-A-plus, particularly when someone's not taking a call. When that happens, I've seen her flare into fury. "Goddamn it, this is Karen Halliday, *The Post. Washington Post.* Look, he wants the call, believe me, toots."

Even though she is tough and a type A, maybe because she's tough and a type A, she cries a lot. She cries when people don't take her calls or return them, she cries when hot leads peter out into the Abyss of the Nonstory. She cries, she tells me, when I am off in some strange place and she wonders if I will ever come back.

Karen's phone rings four times. Her message "You have reached 202 . . ." comes on, then the beep.

Then: "Hi, Kare, it's me."

I recognize the speaker, his Southern voice. It's Jim Jeffries, Karen's ex-lover. "Sorry not to catch you, Kare. I'll give you a call later."

But Jeffries pauses, doesn't hang up. Then: "It was good. I mean like never better. Know what I mean? We could be good together. I mean it, Kare. Please give me a call." He pauses again. Then he hangs up.

"Good"? What was "good"? And "Kare" he called her, a term of endearment I thought I monopolized. "It's me," he said, not "It's Jim Jeffries."

I could erase Jeffries, but I don't. When I think of Jeffries dogging Karen—I doubt this call was a onetime episode—I get angry. I picture Jeffries's boyish face, that pushed-in chin, and want to smash it even farther back down into his throat.

And I get fearful. Don't go, I want to say to Karen. Don't go.

I've never felt that I've ever "needed" anyone. I've seldom said it to a woman, and when I've said it, I've never meant it.

But now? Oh, now I do, I do.

———

From time to time I've noticed a whiff of cigarette in Karen's hair. Jeffries smokes. Jeffries's employer, *The Los Angeles Times,* like every place in town these days, is a smoke-free zone. When I picture Jeffries standing outside the *Times'* bureau on I Street sucking in cancer, I am pleased. I particularly like the wintertime variation: Jeffries down there with two or three other *Times* outcasts huddling in the snow and slush, shuffling their feet to stay warm. That tobacco scent, Karen could have picked it up anywhere, of course. But the fact remains, Jeffries smokes.

A thought strikes me. Hurriedly, desperately, on Karen's PC I Google the Gunderson Center for Media Studies, go to the conference program, and, sure as shooting, find among the luminaries on tap to dispense wisdom James R. Jeffries, *Los Angeles Times.*

Karen didn't tell me. I am pierced to the heart.

Karen and Jeffries were out of town together at the same academic jamboree, were probably put up at the same campus hotel. I stare at, not seeing, the Gunderson Center's slick Web page. It's Karen and Jeffries I see, sitting there at the hotel bar, which is dark, cool, metallic, like J. Gilbert's. They have a drink or two, then move on to dinner. Then, well-fed, maybe a little boozy, they get up from the table. Their eyes meet, the signals get given, and for auld lang syne . . .

Wheels up, rings off, right?

I sit quietly for a time, desolate, then go downstairs and wait for Karen.

When she returns toting her plastic CVS sack, she bounds happily over to me, and we kiss. She notices my lack of enthusiasm, which puzzles her, but she decides to ignore it. She's wearing jeans and a man's shirt outside her belt, the sloppy look I like, and she smells of Amerige, a perfume I gave her, the wearing of which is usually a signal that red-hot sex is in the offing.

She goes up and takes her messages. When she comes back down, the look on her face is matter-of-fact and unperturbed.

Then I drop my bomb. "I was upstairs," I say coolly, "when Jim Jeffries called." I stare at her.

"Oh," she says. She stiffens and looks away, her face clouding. She's silent for a time, then looking back at me, her eyes worried and pleading, she says, "Oh, God. That's just . . . I know what it sounds like, Paul. It's nothing, it's just Jim. You have to know him. He's talking about the way it was."

"Sounded recent. What was 'good,' Kare? That's what he called you, wasn't it, 'Kare'?"

"Don't you do that," she says, staring at me incredulously.

"What was 'never better'?"

"I said don't do that. I don't like being interrogated. And I'm not so happy you were listening. It reeks, come to think of it."

"Hey, I go up there innocent as a lamb to stretch out. He calls. What the hell am I supposed to do, flee the room? Stick my fingers in my ears? He . . . called."

"Paul, people have to trust."

"People have to . . . Kare, I heard the goddamn call!"

"Oh, Paul, how can you?"

"Kare, you're the one he called. 'Never better'! Jesus Christ, what does that mean? What was 'never better'? Tell me."

"Paul, I won't be interrogated."

"Why didn't you tell me Jeffries was on the program out there in Minnesota?"

"How'd you . . . Oh, I can't believe this."

"Why didn't you tell me?"

"I didn't know."

"Aw, bullshit."

We're standing close. I'm breathing hard, hot-faced now, shaking. Karen is quiet, her eyes solemn. Reaching out, she puts her fingers to my lips, a gesture she has, tender solicitude of some kind. Has she done that with Jeffries?

She lets her hand drop. "Paul, I just hate this . . . this mistrust. Can't you see how hurtful it is?"

"Hurtful? Kare, I'll tell you what's hurtful—hurtful's being betrayed then being lied to by someone you love. That's hurtful."

"Oh, for God's sake! You want to give me a polygraph? Paul, I have no interest in Jim, none. I love *you*. *You're* my lover."

"You love me now?"

"Can't you tell?" She tries to put on a sexy-mischievous grin—the Amerige—but the smile doesn't work, fails, falls away. Her eyes go worried and pleading again, brimming now with tears. When she tries to put her arms around my neck, I snap my head back, grab at her wrists, and throw her hands down. "We'll . . . We'll talk," I choke out.

I head for home down Independence, past the Rayburn Building, where Karen and I first met at that party for Tommy Finn, a lifetime back.

27

JUNE 24
Brixton

There. He's there.

On a windy, rainy Sunday morning, MI5 officer Peter Osbourne spotted Abdel Kareem Yusufzai coming down out of the British Rail station in Brixton, in south London. Kareem was back in sight.

Kareem, wearing thick-ankled running shoes, Levi's, and a green mackintosh for the London wet, walked out the wide entrance of Brixton Station, turned left and left again, and headed south on Railton Road.

Osbourne followed Kareem. Osbourne was thirtyish and overweight, his hair long, unwashed, and unhealthy looking, his walrus mustache badly trimmed. Dressed for street duty in Brixton, he wore sneakers, a khaki parka, denim trousers, and had the air of the happily unemployed.

Osbourne followed Kareem down Railton Road past a string of shops in a long, dirty redbrick building: a Barclays Bank, a Supa Clean launderette, a Ladbrokes betting parlor, a sandwich place called the Montego Take Away, a Londis convenience shop. Sunday morning, all the shops closed.

Brixton all the way, Osbourne thought. Brixton is Clapham without the glitz. Hah hah.

Crossing to the opposite side of the street, but keeping Kareem in sight, Osbourne passed a vacant lot, surfaced in cracking asphalt, where a black man was working on a car. The car's hood was up and both its front doors were open wide. Next to the car, the man, or someone, had set trash alight in a metal oil drum.

Brixton.

Osbourne passed a string of small, dark, two-story brick flats. From the open window of one of them came rap music; somewhere peppers were frying in oil.

A couple, a black girl, her hair in cornrows, and a white boy, coming up Railton Road passed Kareem, who was now fifty yards or so down the way, giving him no sign of recognition. When they came opposite Osbourne, the girl shouted at him from across the street, "Can you tell me, is Marcus Garvey Lane along here?"

She was from the islands. That accent. Pretty girl if you don't mind cornrows.

"Marcus Garvey Lane? Oh, yes, up there to your right." The girl smiled, Osbourne smiled back.

Osbourne came to a lone frame building with a board sign over its door that read COLLECTIVE RESISTANCE, and he lingered there to let Kareem move farther ahead. Stapled to the door of Collective Resistance was a note written in ballpoint ink on paper: "Ignited aerosol, any sort will do, glue being best, is just the ticket for council bailiffs. Make them Feel the Heat of the People's Anger. Britain is in the throes of a class struggle and violence is a necessary and legitimate means to an end. Fuck your British imperialism and dirty Blairism-Capitalism. Kill Blair."

Next to Collective Resistance was another single-standing building. Its ground floor was a shop called Islamic Liberation Books. In the shop's dusty window were displayed books with titles like *Usama bin Laden Commander of the Faithful, The Crimes of the Zionist Americans, The Necessity for Jihad, Muslims Enrich Science, Internalizing the Glorious Koran.*

At a cross street Kareem turned left toward a BritRail flyover and vanished.

Osbourne speeded up. *We'll make it. No panic.*

When Osbourne got to the cross street, Shakespeare Road, he caught sight of Kareem again, walking through the flyover.

Kareem turned into the yard of a run-down, grimy brick house and disappeared inside. The house had been painted off-white long, long ago. Its front garden had gone to weeds. A pane in one of the windows on its upper story was cracked.

Osbourne walked past purposefully, having, it seemed, business elsewhere.

Under urging from the American CIA, it was deemed best, once Yusufzai had been found, to subject him to surveillance before taking any action on the domestic complaint.

They watched the house for a week from a van they'd placed behind a high chain-link fence in a British Telecom car park opposite and got shots of everyone who entered or left the house. They noted that the phone and power lines ran along the north side of the street and that the phone distributing unit was close to the BritRail flyover. The power meter, which looked old-fashioned and low amperage, was attached to the east side of the house.

There was one door in front and one at the rear, which exited into a trash-cluttered yard. A wooden gate led from the yard into a walk behind. In one direction, west, the walk dead-ended at the rail line but in the other ran behind all the houses in the street.

It wouldn't require much, they concluded, to take this place down and everyone in it.

Their van was painted in acrylic with fantastic New Age scenes: lush green meadow and forest, peace symbols, an ankh sign. A bumper sticker read LOVE HAPPENS.

---

2 8 JUNE 24
The Van

Nine p.m., empty house, no Karen. Sitting in my kitchen this Sunday evening, I dine according to my prole tastes—hamburger, Safeway coleslaw, a couple of bottles of Budweiser.

Karen and I haven't talked. I don't want to pick up the phone. Neither obviously does she.

It's over.

I turn out the kitchen lights and go stand by the bay window of my dark living room. North Pollard Street is deserted except for one vehicle, a van, parked fifty or so feet down the way in front of the Konners'.

I saw the van once before, a week or so back. It was early in the morning then, too early, I thought, for workmen.

But now here it is again, late at night. The van is unmarked and dull white, like thousands of others in the great Commonwealth of Virginia. But here it is again. Where it does not belong.

I think of the warning from Security, and I get that cat's claw at the back of my neck.

Al-Qaeda knows who I am and they know my address.

Watch your goddamn back.

Time to take a closer look at that van. It's almost certainly some innocent interloper in the neighborhood, but I want its plate number and make anyway.

In Tehran, once, terrorists tailed my chief of station, George Holloway. The tail, actually a succession of neatly bearded young men, staked out his villa in the winding, narrow lanes in the north of the city and watched his comings and goings. When George noticed he was being watched, he went out to get a look at the people who were looking at him. The two, George and tail of the time, smiled at each other as they passed in the night.

This went on for a time, the tail staking out George's villa, George going out, and the two nodding and smiling as if old friends. Finally one night, George went out wearing a raincoat, carrying under it a sawed-off shotgun. Without warning, he let fly with both barrels at his tail, purposefully missing the man, though blowing a large circle of plaster off the high wall of a neighboring villa. They, whoever they were, called off the stakeout, and George never saw a tail again.

I hurriedly climb the stairs to my bedroom to retrieve the one gun I own, a snub-nosed Smith & Wesson .38 Special, which I keep unloaded and broken open, hanging by its trigger guard on a hook in my closet.

Nan liked the shiny, silvery thing, its maleness, its threat of violence.

When I look out my bedroom window, the van is still there.

From an ammo box I keep in my night table I take six slugs and quickly insert them into the cylinder, then go back to the closet and throw on my over-the-shoulder holster. Though it's a warm, muggy evening, I put on a blazer to cover the weapon. Like George and his raincoat.

When I get down to the street, the van is gone.

I'm hallucinating, seeing little men, I tell myself, as I look up and down hilly, leafy North Pollard. Lesson taught at the Farm: it's when you *don't* see them that you have to worry.

Back indoors, I get a call from the ATAC night duty officer, George Brandes. The British have phoned over. They say they have found Abdel Kareem Yusufzai, that they've got him under surveillance. With Lindsay's consent—they reached our DCI at a dinner party—they will not arrest Kareem immediately. They will watch his movements, see whom he visits, who visits him. After a suitable period, maybe a week, they will pick him up for attacking Mary Ogilvie.

A beautiful, beautiful break here. We may get Kareem to talk to us after all.

"Fine," I tell Brandes. "Real fine."

---

2 9   JUNE 26
Eddie Calls

Eddie Dietz dreams of the Valley of the Shadow of Death. The dream keeps coming back, he tells people.

Eddie's dream: You're alone, you're in a gray land filled with gray-trunked, leafless trees that look ashen, as if they have been burned in a big fire.

On the branches of the trees sit gray birds that stare. At you. The birds are silent.

You have to move through the gray land and the gray trees and past the staring birds, and as you do, the birds move their heads in silence to watch you pass. Eddie thinks the birds are vultures, but they are all different kinds, so maybe, Eddie says, they aren't just vultures. The thing is, they fill all the branches of all the trees, and they stare at you.

You always make it through the valley and to the other side. Over there, some of the trees have small green leaves on them, but you aren't sure the leaves really belong to the trees—maybe they do and maybe they don't, Eddie says, maybe they're just on vines or something. They—the vines—are gray, too.

Then you wake up. That's it.

Even after waking, you know that the birds are back there, silent, motionless, staring, and you always have to go back and walk through the valley and the birds are always there.

Eddie Dietz is one weird number. He has just told me about this dream of his, which he says he has frequently. He is edgy and spooky as he paces my living room this June evening, a glass of whiskey in his hand, babbling about himself, his life and loves, and about Ed Powers. Eddie, as he walks, has this herky-jerky body language, as if he's had too much of something, not alcohol, something else, and he looks scared to death.

Eddie speaks in a rush sometimes, sometimes falls silent. Through it all, silent or not, Eddie keeps nodding and agreeing with himself.

I listen to him, trying to figure out if there is any truth to his stories about Ed Powers. I believe Eddie's dream, I'm not sure about the rest.

Eddie called me late last night from a booth somewhere in western Virginia. His voice sounded muffled and faraway even though he was shouting. In the background, I could hear trucks passing. Eddie said he knew I was Lindsay's special assistant on terrorism and said he knew things I "should be aware of."

"Gotta talk," Eddie yelled into the phone, "no choice, life or death. Guy got killed six months back. Went down in the drink. Arabian Sea. His name was Bates, Wayne Bates. I knew him. He was ex-CIA. He was Ed Powers's guy. The flight was arranged by Afghans. It was one of a bunch of flights. I know all about it. I know the people who arranged it. Afghans. It was ammo for the Taliban. Nobody's listening. I tried to talk to BATF about all this, tried to talk to FBI, CIA. Nobody's home, man. Somebody's gotta listen."

Eddie had worked for Ed Powers. After Powers was killed, Eddie's name turned up on our list of Ed's acquaintances, and we went looking for him. By that time, Eddie had left Powers and, jobless and broke, was drifting around northern Virginia, moving from one cheap motel to another, drinking. In March, Stu Kremer's people found him living on a horse farm outside Warrenton, doing chores for the owners.

Stu's people went out to the farm twice to talk to Eddie, but found him boozy and incoherent, maybe psychotic. They didn't trust him. Though they took notes and wrote up a report on the conversations, they dismissed Eddie and what he had to say. "Crazy as a coot," Stu told me, "regular loony tune. Not credible."

On the phone last night Eddie said he had to come into town to see me. "It's guns and dope," he said. "Can you understand? Afghanistan. Guns in, dope out. I can tell you that. Can't go into it . . . um, now."

Eddie wanted to see me at night, because he could "dry-clean the surveillance" better in the dark, and preferably at my place, not Agency headquarters, because he didn't trust the Agency and thought people there were trying to "deep-six" his evidence, maybe were even out gunning for him. "They're coming around, they trying to track me. Gotta keep moving, gotta keep moving. Uh, this is real. I mean, this is real, no shit."

I let Eddie rave over the phone about the danger to his life and about Powers and his crimes, yelling in that booth out in the Virginia night. "Powers's airline wasn't an airline. Never owned any goddamn planes, everything was just leased. It wasn't just Ed Powers, it was a bunch of others, other crooks, buncha Russians, Arabs."

And so, here is Eddie in my living room, drinking the whiskey I have given him, walking up and down, nervously eyeing our big bay window that looks onto North Pollard Street, keeping his distance from it, afraid of what might be out there.

This is Eddie's story:

He was born in Orlando, Florida, March 28, 1963. He grew up in Gainesville in a middle-class family. His father was a civil engineer, his mother a stay-at-home mom.

Eddie was a good boy in high school, a churchgoing Methodist and an Eagle Scout. He went to Virginia Tech and studied electrical engineering, for which he had real talent. At some point in his college time, though, he gave up his Methodism for the pleasures of binge drinking and, when he could afford them, upscale drugs. Despite his new habits, he managed to graduate with reasonable grades and went to work for a succession of high-tech companies in northern Virginia, restlessly moving from one to another, probably drinking too much, probably doing drugs.

He met Ed Powers when he was employed at a business communications firm in Herndon called Global Reach. Powers regularly made the rounds of high-tech companies in the D.C. area, claiming he could round up government clients for them.

Eddie sat in on a session with Powers and got to talking with him afterward. Powers told him about the companies he owned—four at the time—and, ever the bullshitter, spun tales of well-paying derring-do out on the fringes of civilization. Eddie, who had always wanted foreign adventure as well as the kind of money you can make in Ed's world, was captivated by the stories Ed told. He got Ed's business card and proceeded to campaign for a job. He called Ed repeatedly, sent him his résumé, and got his friends to get in touch with Ed and vouch for his brains and good character.

Ed was impressed with Eddie's eagerness and apparent smarts, so he took a chance and hired Eddie as "assistant manager" and sent him out to the Dubai office.

There in fancy quarters in the Dubai Chamber of Commerce Building, Eddie did routine import-export work for a time—air conditioners, perfumes, lingerie. He hadn't been in the Dubai office for long, though, when he saw the paper on some of the other deals

Powers was doing—orders for rifle ammo in million-round lots, an order for fifty thousand AK-47s. Most of these deals had shadowy Eastern European suppliers and implausible end users in Africa and Latin America.

The deals scared Eddie, and like Andrea, he started worrying about Powers's operation and what it might mean for himself. Was what he was doing right? Was he liable for anything? Had he gotten himself into something illegal?

The more Eddie saw, the more Eddie thought about it, and the more he thought about it, the more frightened he got. Finally he quit to go home, minus his end-of-contract bonus.

Before leaving, he copied on the sly a large number of Powers's office documents, sneaking into the Dubai Chamber of Commerce at night to photocopy material, reams of it, that he thought might incriminate Ed Powers and save his own neck.

Back in the States, he typed up memorandums on what he knew about Powers's businesses, then, following his churchgoing, good-boy bent, began hounding journalists around town, trying to get them interested in Ed. With not much success. Ed and his dealings never made the papers.

Broke and bitter, out of touch with family and avoiding friends, Eddie started hitting the bottle and drifting around the wilds of Virginia.

And called me.

"Wayne Bates," Eddie says, uttering the syllables like an incantation. "Wayne . . . Bates . . . pil-ot. I knew Wayne, he was a cool head. Wayne Bates died for Ed Powers. Taliban rep in Dubai was on our case. Major flight of arms in from Ukraine. Major stuff. Major, major, major. Paks bought it—that is, paid for it, but bought it for the Taliban. Paks wanted deniability, right? Ed gave them that, in spades man. Want deniability?—come to Ed Powers. Wow. Um, yeah."

Here is what CIA knows: On the night of Tuesday, October 17, just two months before Powers died, a charter flight piloted by one Wayne Bates, an ex-U.S. navy flier, took off from Dubai International Airport headed for Karachi, Pakistan. The plane was a leased Russian aircraft, registered in Liberia. Bates's co-pilot was Alex "Alyosha" Kozlovskiy, a Russian. The flight, which had arrived in Dubai from Ukraine via Istanbul, had two other crew members, apparently freight handlers from Ukraine. We don't have their names.

The cargo manifest checked through by Dubai authorities stated that the plane was carrying "used clothing" and "specialized construction materials."

When the plane was some two hundred nautical miles due east of Dubai over the Arabian Sea and about halfway to Karachi, it disappeared from the air traffic radar screens of Fujairah and Muscat airports, whose air controllers have responsibility for aircraft flying to and from the Persian Gulf. No distress signal was received in Fujairah, Muscat, or Karachi, nor did ships in the area report sightings of the plane going down or of wreckage in the water.

The plane simply disappeared, its crew presumed dead.

"I got stuff on them. I can show you stuff," Eddie says, his sad eyes ever in motion, the eyes of a man used to not being believed.

Eddie gave Kremer's people the same story he is giving me, that he "had stuff"—letters, contracts, phony export licenses—and he showed them some of the photocopied documents he'd lifted from Ed's offices in Dubai.

Kremer and a couple of lawyers from our General Counsel's Office thought Eddie's "stuff" was junk, mostly innocuous-looking freight-hauling contracts and insurance documentation.

Eddie kept saying, Don't you see? Don't you see?

Kremer and the others from the Agency told him, No, they didn't see.

I'm not so sure. I wonder about that "stuff." And I wonder about that charter flight that went down in the Arabian Sea. Eddie has the paper hidden somewhere out in the Shenandoahs. I tell him I'm interested. Eddie, who hasn't sat down, moves toward the door. "Here's my phone number," he says, and gives me a page torn from a small notebook. The number written on it has an 804 area code. "You won't get me, you'll get a desk, but that's okay, guy there'll give me a holler or leave me a message. Ask for Bobby. I'm in number four."

I let Eddie out my door and he disappears in the night, maybe to go dream his dream somewhere out in Virginia.

You always listen to madmen and drunks if they know what they're talking about.

30
JUNE 27
Arrival of the Muscle V

On June 27, 2001, Saeed al-Ghamdi, a Saudi citizen, and Fayez Banihammad, a citizen of the United Arab Emirates, arrived at Orlando International Airport in Florida.

Like Ahmed and Hamza al-Ghamdi and Ahmed al-Haznawi, Saeed al-Ghamdi was from the al-Bahah region and shared the same tribal affiliation.

In 2000, al-Ghamdi attempted to enter Chechnya to fight the Russians, but at that time Chechen fighters were turning additional foreigners away. Al-Ghamdi then made his way to Afghanistan, where he underwent military training by al-Qaeda, probably outside Kandahar. At some point while in Afghanistan he volunteered to undertake suicide missions for al-Qaeda. He was filmed in the same video that showed Hamza al-Ghamdi and Ahmed al-Nami and that aired on Al-jazeera satellite television. Unlike the other two, Saeed al-Ghamdi has a speaking role, in which he calls the United States "the enemy." He is also seen studying maps and flight manuals.

Fayez Banihammad grew up in the U.A.E. He left home in July 2000, telling his parents that he wanted to participate in a holy war or relief work. He had not seen them since that time.

Both Saeed al-Ghamdi and Fayez Banihammad used the Saudi Visa Express program to gain entry into the United States.

JUNE 27

31 Scenic View

Wednesday morning, about ten thirty. The sun is out, the air still sweet and cool, though the day will be hot. I have driven out to Front Royal through the rolling Virginia countryside and into the Shenandoahs to a place called Simmons Ridge, just off the interstate.

The Scenic View Motel, Eddie Dietz's place, is six identical weather-beaten cabins and a two-story office and manager's residence. The cabins form a semicircle around a potholed, gravel drive and look west over Route 11 toward the long Massanutten Mountain Range.

The cabins are a dirty white. They have black wooden shutters, metal roofs, and small front porches. On some of the porches there are chairs and on one an outdoor grill. Behind the cabins, paralleling the interstate, runs a single rusty rail line.

Eddie Dietz country.

Across the road, the land falls away quickly and you can see the farms far below in the valley. As the wind blows the clouds, patterns of shadow shift over the mountainsides and across the lime green valley floor. Two big hawks are circling the valley, riding the drafts that sweep up from the low fields and over the ridge the cabins are on.

Just as Eddie is letting me into cabin four—"Hey, come on in, man, great, yeah"—to a smell of liquor and stale cigarette smoke, a young guy, long-haired, red-bearded, wearing a red-orange, billed cap, comes around the corner of Eddie's cabin carrying two one-gallon paint cans. He glares at Eddie, then at me, then goes on about his business, looking away, muttering. Eddie being Eddie has spooked these people.

Pointing at the narrow bed, its single faded, light coverlet neatly pulled across, Eddie says, "Okay, man, this is it." On the bed he has laid out his "stuff" in ten or eleven neat piles, some in crisp, clean manila folders. "Secrets of the secret, man, fucking inner sanctum. Um, yes."

As I leaf through the photocopies, Eddie stands looking out the one side window, his right hand up on the dusty venetian blind. A swath of light from where he has displaced one of the slats cuts across his face. He has a worried look. The look seems permanent.

The documents Eddie has copied are expense-account statements from the InterTech Washington office and Ed's other companies, some I've heard of (InterTech, Triple A Airlines), some new to me (Transnational Shipping, Greentree Investment Advisers, United Air Consultants). Also, bank account statements (Riggs in Washington, Barclays in London, GCBI in Dubai, Sharjah, Abu Dhabi). Also, credit-card charge receipts and monthly statements, receipts for airline tickets, car and limousine rentals, hotel and restaurant bills.

When Ed Powers was murdered, our Inspector General's Office got heavily interested in him. The IG had heard rumors of Powers's doings well before he died and was nervous about almost everything Powers was up to.

"The arms-trafficking allegations, the other allegations, are a matter for the FBI," John Mauer, our IG at the time told me, "given that the subject was not an Agency officer. We'll take our cue from the Bureau, and we'll certainly cooperate fully with them, do anything they want us to do, but it's for them to go forward on this. We don't want to muddy the waters with a dual investigation."

Mauer, no longer IG, is a tall, distinguished fellow in his seventies. He's of the East Coast, Ivy League, patrician elite and has the usual manner of his time and class. He's smooth as a lube job.

Mauer's office produced a short report on Powers's relationships with the Agency, which we received at ATAC and which lies undisturbed in Bill Cleppinger's safe. The IG's report contains little save personal interviews, most of them easy on the interviewees. Nobody bothered to assemble documents on Powers or put together any kind of paper trail.

When Big Ed died, Mauer circled the wagons.

Eddie looks down at me from the window. His face says, Don't you see? Don't you see? Don't you understand how important this is?

I do. With this stuff we can follow Ed on his travels for the last two years of his life. We can see some of what he bought and sold—chemicals, ammo, weapons.

The IG, Mauer, didn't want to deal with this, didn't want it part of the record. Neither, therefore, did Stu Kremer.

The copies on the bed are for me, Eddie tells me. When I pile them up, they're a foot high. I will haul them home and personally slog through them before turning them over to DI analysts.

---

32   JUNE 28
ROCKER

"It's crushing. We had everything on him, twenty-four/seven, very close, very tight," my MI6 counterpart, Nigel Henderson, is saying on the phone. "We don't know how it happened."

Barely four days after MI6 tell us they've found Kareem, they tell us they've lost him. They've concluded he's no longer at the address in Brixton, and they don't know where the hell he is. Henderson tells me they've got an all-points alert out on Kareem—crypted ROCKER—at airports, train stations, the Chunnel, everywhere.

The inhabitants of the house where Kareem was staying, three Pakistanis and two Yemeni Arabs, all young men, claim they met him at a mosque in Brixton. He told them he needed a room. They don't know him well, they say. He was just a poor chap and fellow worshiper. None of the young men are on British suspicious persons lists.

Shortly after Henderson's call, a roundup cable from chief of station London reaches my desk: MI6 AND SPECIAL BRANCH REPORT ROCKER HAS MANAGED TO ELUDE SURVEILLANCE AND IS CURRENTLY BEING SOUGHT.

I feel washed-out, almost sick to my stomach at this. How could they have let him slip?

Clep, Sonny, and I hold a session on the news in Sonny's office. Clep is subdued, Sonny agitated. "Screwups like this are just unforgivable. The goddamn British, I'm telling you, incompetence is the bedrock of their existence. It's what they live for, it is what they do."

The Desmonds, most of them, have been in this country for five generations and have been well-off for three, but like a lot of Irish-Americans, they don't forget where they've come from, and they always have it in for the British. Memories don't go away.

We conclude Kareem has slipped away in the night. Henderson cannot even guess at the value of the freight he's lost.

When I give Lindsay the news, his usually animated, inquisitive face goes flat, as if somebody let the air out of it. "Well, damn," he says limply, then, recovering a little, he says, "Okay, it's not the end of the world. Keep on humping, guy. We'll get him." Lindsay's face and voice show he's none too sure of that. Neither am I.

JUNE 28
I Call Meatball

When I get back to my desk, I see that my secretary, Ivy, has left me a pink Please Call slip. Meatball. The news from London has me so down I don't want to talk to anyone, let alone the fourth estate, but I'm nervous about what Meatball wants. I get him at his *Times* number downtown.

"Hey, Marshall. Paul Patterson. What's up?"

"Hi, Paul. Ah"—I hear him fish around through papers on his desk—"there's a guy out of the Agency who's being looked at. Drug stuff."

Drug stuff. They've thrown it to Meatball.

When a reporter calls with a hot story, you don't stonewall him or cut off the conversation. You want to listen to him, find out what's out there. Your best move after that is to try to massage the piece a little, get your licks in, move it your way.

"What do you mean, 'looked at'?"

"Ah . . . committee investigators on the Hill. Participating in the South Asian heroin market. Could go to Justice, be a major thing."

"News to me, Bigfoot."

"You don't know anything about it?"

"Why the hell should I?"

"I said, it's an Agency guy, he's out of Near East Division."

"I don't believe it."

"No, no, no, no, no, I heard it from people who know."

"Who is it?"

"I don't have his name yet. He's not active. He's retired, gone private with some kind of company. I thought maybe you could help. Can you think of anybody?"

I can think of Ed.

"Wouldn't tell you if I could, Bigfoot, but this sounds like Hill bullshit to me."

"Well, it's happening—there's something major going on, Paul. Your shop's got some troubles coming."

"Bullshit again."

"Paul, I know my sources, I know they're right."

Meatball's always so fucking sure of himself, always walking through the world with this knowing smile, as if he's got the line on everything and so cute you want to pinch his fat cheek.

"Sources. Like who?"

"Sources."

"Yeah. Well, what else are they saying?"

"It's got something to do with current officers, people in Near East South Asia. He's got ties to Agency personnel. They're protecting him. Could even be payoffs involved, payoffs to the Agency people."

Maybe that's what Merritt ("We think you've got problems") is pushing these days. Corruption in the directorate. Donovan will make some kind of move with it, you can tell, you can just feel it.

"Aw, don't give me that crap, Marshall."

"Look, I mean it, Paul, there's some stuff going on, major, major stuff. You sure don't seem up on things."

Here's a thumb in your eye, Meatball. "Hah hah. Well, I got work to do, anything else?"

"No, just the dope thing. It's real, guy."

"Uh-hun, fat chance. Well, I'll do some asking, Marshall, put you out of your misery. How's Kathy? Kathy okay?" Katherine Robertson writes for the *Times*'s Home Section.

"Sure is. Sends her love. Take care, guy."

"Roger."

Clep shakes his head in disgust when I tell him about the call.

"It's Ed Powers," I say.

"Yep. And it's Merritt putting this stuff out, probably running Meatball's investigation—shit, probably writing that asshole's leads for him."

---

3 4
JUNE 28
"A Little Bluesy"

I'm late getting in this evening after dinner at Café Oggi in McLean and a movie, *Pearl Harbor,* feeling crummy. How could they lose Kareem? How could they? And Meatball—where is *he* headed?

My answering machine is flashing with a message, and when I hit PLAY/STOP I hear, "Hi. It's me."

Karen. Her voice. Breathy, a little hoarse, that trace of Kentucky. "Sorry I didn't get you. You okay? You in the country? Or shouldn't I ask?" She coughs to clear her throat. "I don't know, Paul . . . I'm just sitting here. It's a nice night." A pause, a sigh. "A little bluesy . . . about things. You know? I don't like the way things went. It's been a week now, and I think we should talk. Umm . . . right. Just wanted to tell you what I was thinking." This last Karen says in her busy reporter's mode, as if ending an interview. "You wanna give me a call?"

My machine pings, then says, "Thursday, June twenty-eighth, ten forty-six p.m."

She's just called. I push PLAY/STOP again. Second time around, her voice, soft, Southern, breathy, kicks off a sequence of memories: first date, first fuck, good times; then righteous anger—at her, at Jeffries; then . . . then desire, a warm flow of it welling up in my groin. I slip into a low, empty mood, a feeling of irretrievable loss, as in those first nights after Nan left.

You cannot know the other. You just have to make assumptions, and these carry you along until you have to change them. Karen will never admit to succumbing to any yah-hah with Jeffries—that's a given. Though she protests loudly—"Jim Jeffries isn't anything to me"—she never quite says she didn't fuck the guy. Ordinarily, I'd take that refusal to deny as bulletproof evidence that she and Jeffries seized the moment out there on the prairie, but I know Karen. When she gets her dander up, she will not cooperate, maybe in this case by refusing to deny doing something she may in fact not have done. "Paul, I will not be interrogated."

Still, my assumption is, something happened out there. It did. And she's lying about it.

But why am I so pissed at her? I'm a big boy. I'm no stranger to flings myself. I've listened to the most outrageous lying all my adult life, and I'm a fair practitioner of the art myself. So why am I so angry? Why, why, why?

I don't return the call.

35

JUNE 29
Arrival of the Muscle VI

On June 29, 2001, Abdul Aziz al-Omari and Salem al-Hazmi entered the United States at John F. Kennedy International Airport in New York. Both were Saudi nationals.

Like Waleed al-Shehri, Mohand al-Shehri, and Ahmed al-Nami, al-Omari was from the southern province of Asir. He had a degree from the Imam Muhammad Ibn Saud Islamic University, was married, and had a daughter.

Salem al-Hazmi, born in Mecca, was Nawaf al-Hazmi's younger brother.

On arrival in New York, the two proceeded to Paterson, New

Jersey, where they moved in with Nawaf al-Hazmi, Hani Hanjour, Majid Moqed, and Ahmed al-Ghamdi. Khalid al-Mihdhar would soon join them.

Both al-Omari and al-Hazmi entered the United States under the Saudi Visa Express program.

JUNE 29

3 6 "You . . . Can . . . Get . . . In"

Clep wanders into my office after lunch. He's in one of his states.

"NOREFUGE is in free fall," he announces.

As Clep settles into my wing chair, the scent of juniper berries wafts over my desk. Clep, I figure, probably has three martinis on board, his usual noontime load these days. He's perspiring. His face is pink, and he's surly with a kind of all-purpose anger.

"You read our latest tome in from Islamabad Station?" Clep means the quarterly Station Operations Report. "We have run out of Afghans."

Not so, but I know what he means.

The latest SOR is Carl Lindquist's work, and as you would expect, considering the author, it is an optimistic and forward-leaning document. Carl, to be fair, has a point or two.

Carl notes we have managed to tune in to al-Qaeda cell phones, capture some of their faxes, track some of their e-mail. To an extent, we know where and how they bank. We've seen some of their wire transfers, cash deposits, and withdrawals. We know where their houses are in Jalalabad and Khowst, towns over the border in Afghanistan. We have breathtaking satellite and spy-plane photos of camps they run in eastern Afghanistan. All good.

But, Carl does not say, beyond the electronic take and the satellite imagery, none of our human informants can talk to the al-Qaeda membership and tell us the news about Osama bin Laden. Some of our better agents seem to have gone into occultation since Powers's death. Not even Carl can disguise this.

Cleppinger jabs his finger at my desk. "Killing Powers was a most effective piece of work. When that asshole got himself popped, down came the NOREFUGE structure, such as it was. Powers's death was enough to scare the manure out of our friends on the Af side of the border, who suddenly have gotten fewer in number, and our al-Qaeda targets become ever more mysterious."

Clep goes silent for a moment. His policeman's eyes stray around the room. Then he says, "Forget CATHEDRAL."

CATHEDRAL, fruit of Cleppinger's baroque mind, is a small part of NOREFUGE. CATHEDRAL is a plan to get certain Afghan clerics—we know their names, their addresses, and their pedigrees—to act as an early-warning system for attacks on us by some of their followers, an idea not as crazy as it sounds.

The scheme is, we'd pay the clerics for information on impending operations against us. We'd run the payoffs through Saudi private citizens, maybe Saudi mullahs on the Saudi payroll, whom the Af clerics trusted. The Af clerics would never know, or at least never need to acknowledge to themselves, that they are working for Uncle. At most, the clerics would think they are liaising with the Saudi service—treacherous enough from al-Qaeda's point of view, but they would not be supplying the infidels of the USA. And to our clerics, the cash would look good.

Tip-offs on actions would come to us through those same Saudi friendlies or through pliable Afghans, all of them on payroll. Nice false-flag op, everybody happy.

Riyadh and Islamabad stations made some efforts, apparently honest ones, to get CATHEDRAL rolling, but because we couldn't find the right Saudis, because we didn't have enough Afs or Paks, the scheme has never moved. CATHEDRAL sits in a red-bordered operation file folder in Lindquist's office in Islamabad, with copies in Peshawar, Riyadh, and HQ Langley. Powers's death has probably pushed it further into oblivion.

Clep closes his eyes. At first I think he is dropping off, slipping into a juniper-and-vermouth dreamland after a satisfying burst of anger. (Clep once fell asleep during an after-lunch session with the DCI of the time, Dick Helms, who wanted to can him for it forthwith, but was talked out of it.)

Clep's eyes pop open. He belches again and wipes at his perspiration.

"I'll tell you, Patterson, when I was in Cairo, I had a grunt from Islamic Jihad on our payroll. Kid, scruffy little bastard. I got him through a pal of mine, Saudi businessman. Well, fixer—he put spot oil contracts together for the dopier sort of Egyptian. Atef Juffali—know him? Anyhow, he knew this Saudi kid studying in Egypt, radical, mean-talking. Juffali thought it would be fun for me to hear what he had to say about Islam, corruption on earth, Jews, Crusaders, and all that.

"So I meet the kid. Kid has a neat little beard, neat little mind. Get to know him a little. Kid liked hanging out in East Cairo, liked hearing radical yap in the mosques. It gave him a rush to pretend to be a commando. It also gave him a rush—and here you gotta be able to sense this, gotta know when it's in play—it gave him a rush to be talking to a superpower, namely me.

"Well, he's in California now, got a filling station or something outside Sacramento. Turns out what the kid really wanted was for somebody to listen to him and ooh and aah over what he had to say. Plus money. He wanted money. I saw he got what he wanted. And as a result, we had a talkative man in Islamic Jihad for a time. Point is, you can get these guys, some of them, anyway. They're not all the same, they're not all total fanatics. You . . . can . . . get . . . in."

Sonny's voice breaks in over the intercom. Twelve hours back, he tells us, my friend Amjad Afridi was torn apart: suicide bomber, Shiite mosque off Korangi Road in the eastern suburbs of Karachi. Afridi had been interviewing the imam.

News reports say the blast cratered the imam's office and took out windows all around the neighborhood. Sixteen people were killed, including Amjad, who never knew what hit him. My friend of twenty years is gone.

Clep and I rush to Sonny's office, where Sonny's just starting to play a short clip of coverage from PAKTel, a Pakistani satellite news service. Warren Cutler, Karachi Base chief, who phoned us about the bombing, recorded the clip and forwarded it to us.

We see shots of angry young Shiites roaming Karachi, trashing whatever property they can find. The voice-over, in Urdu, though the broadcast has English subtitles, says Pak Rangers have fired on some of them. PAKTel doesn't show this.

At one point we hear that the journalist interviewing the imam was decapitated, and I think, yes, decapitation, it's what they are doing to themselves. I told Amjad I thought they'd kill him, and they did, not knowing what they were doing. Now Amjad's in the City of the Silent, as his Urdu poets would put it.

I think of Amjad's intelligent, decent face, of his belief in a benign Islamic social order. Where's Amjad's social order now? Perhaps it's good that he never lived to be disillusioned.

"Blind, stinking bad luck," I say. My voice can't convey the bitterness I feel.

"Typical Pak scene," Sonny says quietly. "Crazy, just crazy. And hopeless."

Amjad thought the truth should be told. Like Karen, he thought the truth would make you free.

Loss of my old friend pushes me down into some bad zone. At home, when I think of Amjad's death, the loss of Kareem, both piled now onto my rocky dealings with Karen—she's lost and gone forever, too—I get good and drunk on bourbon and red vermouth and stumble to bed, colliding once with an armchair.

3 7

JUNE 29

Laptop

"Always had trouble with the African stuff," Andrea says.

We're in the Clyde's at Tysons, an eatery several cuts up from Bennigan's. Andrea's choice again. She's talked with Stan Bress, Ed's old lawyer and now hers. Bress has done some checking and has told her she's safe from prosecution, which means she probably is.

As with me, things seem not to have been going well for Andrea, despite Bress's encouraging words. She's swollen under the eyes, her voice is raspy. On her second chardonnay now she's weepy, no longer a health nut. She's explaining something to me, and I'm trying to figure out what.

"You see those pictures in the paper, on TV," she says heavily. "You know, the wars there in Africa, Sierra Leone or wherever, you see those pictures of the little boys, little girls, with their hands cut off, staring into the camera, wondering why. Well, they happened to be born among the wrong crew, that's why. Chop, there goes your arm, kid, chop, there goes your hand, chop again, both hands. Teach 'em a lesson, right? Or maybe just for the fun of it. All those militias. Crazy. Well, Ed flew weapons for some of those people."

She looks away. "Oh, Jesus, I mean, you feel so shitty. I knew he was doing it. I mean, if I looked hard, I could have known. So I didn't look hard. Ed—fucking Ed, with all that talk. Charm the birds out of the trees, right? Charmed me. What a liar!"

He had the gift of believing his own lies. People who can do that are the best liars in the world.

We know Ed flew for African groups. Some of the time he did it for us, for groups we supported. Those men on the beach in the photo Lurch showed me were some of the people Ed flew for with our blessing.

"Ed knew. He organized a company called United Air Consultants."

UAC. Eddie Dietz's stolen documents mention the company and show a few of the UAC bank balances.

"You think Triple A was crooked, you should have seen UAC. UAC leased all its planes. Guess who from? From Ed, from Triple A.

"UAC and Triple A were two sides of the same coin. God, we cut checks for the crews from the same ledger. I mean, come on. I mean, he was leasing to himself—that's what he was doing. I mean, course there were silent partners with side deals, side contracts, Arab sheikhs, Russians. The deals would be registered in weird places, Sharjah, Panama City, places like that. But even so, Ed was in on all of it, always had his finger in the pie. UAC was Ed. Records are not good on any of this, as you might imagine. And when Ed died, I heard they, the office guys in Dubai, destroyed a lot. Shredded and burned stuff, all the files. Ed held all this close to his chest, anyway. Only person who knew the whole deal was Ed. Makes you sick."

She looks at me seriously. "Paul, Ed had this laptop. He'd carry it around sometimes, Dubai or wherever, but he was very, very careful with it. Lot of the time he kept it in the UAC offices out in the damn jungle somewhere. He would not carry it around in Europe or the States. All that African stuff was on it, and it was too dangerous. So mostly he'd leave it at the field office, in Sierra Leone. That's where he kept it. He wouldn't have erased it. I mean, they killed him. The laptop's probably still around somewhere."

I drink to her with my eyes.

3 8
JULY 4
Al-Mihdhar Returns

On July 4, 2001, Khalid al-Mihdhar arrived at John F. Kennedy Airport from Jidda, Saudi Arabia.

A year before, in June 2000, al-Mihdhar had left his companion Nawaf al-Hazmi in San Diego, where both were undergoing flight training, and proceeded to Yemen to visit his family for about a month. He then traveled to Afghanistan, where he met with Osama bin Laden and other al-Qaeda leaders. In June 2001, al-Mihdhar left Afghanistan for Mecca, Saudi Arabia, staying in that city with a cousin for another month. Then he flew to the United States.

On arriving in New York, al-Mihdhar gave his intended address as the Marriott Hotel in New York City, but instead spent one night at another New York hotel, then traveled to Paterson, New Jersey, and moved in with his old companion from Kuala Lumpur, Nawaf al-Hazmi, and al-Hazmi's roommates, Hani Hanjour, Majed Moqed, Abdul Aziz al-Omari, Salem al-Hazmi, and Ahmed al-Ghamdi.

3 9
JULY 4
After the Fireworks

Sundown, ghost of the day. The house seems particularly lonely and cavernous this evening of the Fourth, so from the fridge I collect a bottle of chardonnay and head out to the backyard and Nan's wooden gazebo. The air is heavy with the threat of rain.

Beyond the Evrards' slate roof, the neighborhood falls away down toward Donaldson Run. Our hilltop lot and some helpfully thick bushes keep us from seeing much of the neighbors, and them from seeing much of us: a spy's backyard.

The Evrards', as they do every year, had a large and exuberant cookout, and the smell of grilling burger, though faint, still hangs over the land, as does the sulfury, gunpowder scent of the fireworks that have been popping off all up and down North Pollard Street since morning.

Ed's laptop is floating somewhere out in the great world, and right now, as I sit in this graceful white gazebo in north Arlington, Africa Division is out trying to grab it. I should be way high over this, but I am not.

Karen. Her absence, like Nan's, like David's, has become a presence. I think I've climbed down from whatever peaks of anger I'd been on. I think I want her back.

So, a little sloshed on the chardonnay, I maneuver to Karen's number on my cell's ice-blue screen and punch the green-colored YES. One ring. Two. I wait till the fourth, then, not wanting to leave a message, I punch the red-colored EXIT. Which I guess is about where we are, Karen and I.

She's out somewhere. Maybe banging Jeffries.

I sit for a time brooding on that possibility, then for distraction, return to the den, carrying my still-chilled but now half-empty bottle of chardonnay, and click on the festivities down on the Mall, always a kind of variety show that I've never much liked. Neither did Nan. We never watched.

I catch a trio of black women winding up some hip-hop number they were doing. Just as Barry Bostick, who's hosting the show, prances on to thank them—they're the Pointer Sisters, I learn—buckets of rain begin cascading from the heavens, soaking the audience on the west face of the Capitol, a lot of whom head for shelter, though some stick it out. The rain's starting out here in Arlington, too. Heavy drops are beginning to thud on the windows and I hear wind cutting through our trees.

After a time, though, the rain lets up, and right on schedule shortly after nine the fireworks start: five fast, silvery rockets shooting up into the sky and exploding into starry balls of gold, red, and green, the orchestra playing Sousa marches all the while.

I watch for a time, edgy and morose, then start feeling bad enough to call Karen again and leave her a message after all. So again I punch YES on her number and wait for her machine, trying to think of a message to leave when, surprised, I hear, "Hello?"

I catch my breath. "Oh. Hey. Hi, Kare, it's Paul. How are you? How're you doing?"

A pause. She says, "You sure don't return calls in a hurry."

I don't respond to that. She cries, she told me once, when sources don't return her calls. I wonder, feeling a small nudge of guilt, if she's cried because I haven't called.

I say, "Wanted to check in, Kare. How're you doing? You okay?"

"Umm. I guess. So where are you?"

"Timbuktu."

"Oh. Well, how's life in Timbuktu?"

"Pretty arid."

Another long stretch of dead air, this one threatening to last till the dawn's early light. Finally Karen breaks in, "You're not very talkative."

"No."

"Wanna know something, Big Boy?"

"Shoot."

"We had good times."

I want to say "Well, who fucked it up?" but don't.

She goes on, "Paul, you're a tough guy. I mean tough on yourself. In all kinds of ways. A-a-a-and you're tough on other people. You always look for the worst in them. That can be a sock in the puss sometimes. You just don't understand how hurtful that can be."

"Well, maybe I do," I say glumly, knowing she won't buy it and not really believing it myself.

More dead air. Then Karen asks, "Well, is that it?"

"Look," I say, "I been thinking . . . Uh . . . Want to get together? To talk?"

"Like on neutral territory?" she asks coolly. "With bodyguards?"

"Kare, I'm serious. I'd like to meet. Maybe talk about things. Want to?"

I hear her breath, a couple of soft, hushing sounds in the receiver, which she must be holding to her lips. Those lips. Then she says, "It's Independence Day."

"Uh, Kare, I don't get it, what do you . . . ?"

"It's the Fourth—Independence Day. Might be good for us to be independent. Of each other, I mean. That's what I think." She pauses. "Why don't we let it go? So long, Paul."

She hangs up. After a time my cell's little screen goes back to being icy blue, inviting me to make another call, but I don't.

40

JULY 7
The Tourist

On Saturday, July 7, 2001, Muhammad Atta flew from Miami, Florida, to Zurich, Switzerland, continuing on to Madrid, Spain. He passed through Spanish customs quickly, but stayed in Madrid airport a full five hours. Just before leaving the airport, he reserved a room at a hotel in Madrid, the Diana Cazadora, through an airport travel agency. He paid cash for his room, using an alias and giving a false address in Cairo as his residence. He made three calls from his room, probably to coordinate with a young man named Ramzi bin al-Shibh, whom he was to meet in Spain.

The following day, July 9, Atta rented a car and left Madrid for

Reus, on the Mediterranean coast, where he picked up bin al-Shibh and drove to Cambrils, another town on the Mediterranean coast. The two registered at a hotel in Cambrils.

Bin al-Shibh, a twenty-year-old Yemeni national, had flown to Reus from Hamburg, Germany. A friendly, outgoing young man with a cheerful face, bin al-Shibh was a close friend of Atta's and a leading figure in the group of Islamist radicals who frequented the al-Kods mosque in Hamburg.

Bin al-Shibh had repeatedly requested visas to enter the United States, but each time had been refused, because American officials suspected that he, as a young, male national of an impoverished country, was simply looking for work in the United States.

Bin al-Shibh was in fact a trusted al-Qaeda operative, who acted as an emissary between the al-Qaeda leadership in Afghanistan and the group's sympathizers overseas. He had spent much of the spring in Afghanistan and Pakistan helping move young al-Qaeda volunteers such as Satam al-Suqami, Waleed al-Shehri, and Majed Moqed into the United States.

Atta and bin al-Shibh spent a number of days together on the Spanish coast.

On July 16, bin al-Shibh flew back to Hamburg, using a ticket Atta had bought for him earlier the same day. Atta left Spain on July 19, flying Delta Airlines to Fort Lauderdale, Florida.

During Atta's stay in Spain, his U.S. visa had expired. When he arrived at Fort Lauderdale airport, he requested and was given a tourist visa.

41

JULY 10
Legitimate Targets of Islam

On July 10, 2001, an agent in the FBI's Phoenix Field Office e-mailed a memo to the chiefs of the Osama bin Laden Unit and the Radical Fundamentalist Unit at FBI headquarters in Washington, D.C., and to two agents on international-terrorism squads in the New York Field Office. In the e-mail, the agent suggested the "possibility of a coordinated effort by Osama bin Laden" to send students to the United States to attend civil aviation schools. The agent had noticed what he called the "inordinate number of individuals of investigative interest" attending flight schools in Arizona.

The agent had long suspected that al-Qaeda might have an active presence in the state. Several bin Laden operatives had lived in or traveled to the Phoenix area, and one of them—Wadih El-Hage, a bin Laden lieutenant—had been convicted for his role in the bombing of U.S. embassies in East Africa in 1998.

In April 2000, the agent had interviewed a young Arab national who was attending flight school in the Phoenix area. On the walls of the student's apartment the agent noticed a poster of Osama bin Laden and another of wounded Chechen mujahideen fighters. The student told the agent that he considered the U.S. government and military to be legitimate targets of Islam. The student, who was taking expensive aviation training, was from a poor country and had not studied aviation before his arrival in the United States.

In his e-mail to FBI headquarters the agent made four recommendations: that a list of civil aviation schools be compiled, that FBI establish liaison with those schools, that his theories about bin Laden be discussed within the intelligence community, and that the FBI seek authority to obtain visa information on persons applying to flight schools. The memo went unread in Washington, and the agent's recommendations were not acted on.

42

Samuel Is Dying

Southeastern Sierra Leone, hill country. I am in the custody of two boy soldiers. One is about sixteen, the other's voice hasn't broken. They are armed. The older is carrying an AK-47, the younger has a long knife. We are in a shed, part of a compound of four or five flimsy structures, built at the edge of a potholed, single-runway airstrip. I am in protective custody here because Samuel is off somewhere in the scrubby bush and has not alerted his airport people to expect me. His arrival, I am told, is imminent.

The shed we are in is utterly empty, and for the last hour the three of us have sat on the dirt floor swatting flies and watching the sun go down. July in Sierra Leone is hot as blazes.

I am here to meet Samuel Kontay Edgerton, once an Agency protégé, who now commands a small, defeated army. In his better days, Samuel had shown what an Agency cable called "leadership potential," and we cultivated him for that. Samuel also had friends on Capitol Hill, and in the past, in those palmy days, Samuel would be extracted from this wretched country and brought to the United States to testify before House and Senate committees—Human Rights, African Affairs—and have his words taken seriously by congressmen, church groups, and reporters.

He was my man in Africa. In Washington I hauled him around for secret sessions with intelligence committee members and was his minder at Langley.

If Samuel trusts any American, he trusts me. I don't know why.

Samuel has not done well. He has run afoul of most of his com-
rades in the Revolutionary United Front, who had little regard for his
leadership potential and who, at one point, kept him prisoner in a
freight container at an army barracks just outside Freetown. After
three months of life in a container, Samuel escaped. He has brought
the remnants of his group, the New Africa Rally, here to a small piece
of territory around this landing strip. Samuel and the NAR survive
by finding and selling diamonds. They have no future.

To launder money and to avoid the international banking system,
al-Qaeda operatives buy Samuel's diamonds in Africa and sell them in
Europe when they need cash. They sometimes even turn a profit,
though that is not the point.

Ed Powers came through here often. He rented a small room in
Samuel's compound for United Air Consultants and staffed it with a
string of dubious Lebanese, Liberian, and Yemeni clerks, who have
vanished. Here, too, is where he kept his laptop.

I have been preceded to this place by an Agency officer named
Bailess from Monrovia Station in Liberia, the closest one we have.
CIA has almost no presence in black Africa. As far as what goes on
here is concerned, we rely on the British, French, and Israeli services
for information. Otherwise, we read the papers.

When Bailess tried to talk Samuel out of Powers's laptop, Samuel
got testy and sent Bailess empty-handed back to Monrovia Station.

Samuel has been radioed, however, and has been told to expect
me for a serious discussion. He knows we want the laptop and he can
probably guess why. His position is weak.

The charter company that flew me here from Monrovia, Air
TransAfricain, is Belgian-owned. It is not one of ours, but we use it
frequently. The pilot is an overweight South African named Timperman. He flew me here in an ancient Fokker two-engine prop jet. He
sports cowboy boots and wraparound sunglasses. When he flies these
bush missions, he straps a Ruger .45 automatic to his left thigh, butt
to the front so he can grab it quickly, "just in case," he says.

Timperman, who is laconic on principle, spoke little to me on the flight up from Monrovia, except to tell me how he hates Africans. "They're shit," he said with no sign of emotion, "human shit."

When we landed, Timperman disappeared into Samuel's airport customs shed, where they have vodka. It's rather lordly of Samuel at this point in his career to have a customs service, but there it is.

Samuel's airstrip was built long back by a Swiss mining company, whose field geologists had found titanium dioxide and diamonds in the rolling, dusty hills around here. Because of Sierra Leone's perpetual civil war, however, extracting and transporting the mineral and diamonds proved far more expensive than the Swiss had projected. Five years ago, the company withdrew its white engineers, sacked its African miners, and departed. Samuel and the NAR moved in.

The last time I came through, I saw a group of young men, eight or nine of them, barefoot and wearing only shorts. There had been fighting of a desultory sort somewhere, and Samuel's people had actually taken prisoners.

These were sitting at the edge of the compound's drainage trench, quietly perspiring in the sun. They were strung together at the neck with rope, and their hands were bound. They had the sad faces of men who knew they were going to die and who didn't want to think about it.

Now that it's become dark, I hear an electrical generator *hap-hap-happing* somewhere. It supplies power for the lighting—one lamp outside in the compound courtyard, one in the customs shed, the rest for Samuel.

One of my guards, the boy whose voice hasn't broken, has fallen asleep, still grasping his long knife. The other stares at me neutrally. I do not detect any malice in his young eyes, but he would most certainly do me grievous harm if I got up and headed for the door. I'm close to sleep myself when, outside, someone barks a command I do not understand. The two soldiers get up and motion for me to follow them, and we walk out into the African night.

The moon is opalescent through the overcast. At the end of the landing strip, orange flames flicker upward from three oil drums like hands grasping for help. Low, scrubby brush, tangled and indistinct in the moonlight, stretches away over the flat land. Beyond lie hills that in daylight are rust-colored, but in the night are simply dark, angular shapes rising into the sky.

My guards take me into a low building next door, also without furniture except for an orange plastic Eames chair in the corner facing the wall.

Peter comes in. Peter is Samuel's "aide-de-camp" and worshiper, and his arrival means that Samuel is somewhere about.

"Hello, Peter," I say.

Peter's face is a curtain. Peter is in his twenties now. I knew him when he was sixteen. We've never hit it off. Peter is wearing an olive-green military T-shirt, camouflage pants, and rubber sandals. His canvas belt is cinched tightly around his skinny waist so that it draws his trousers into thick pleats. Peter has light skin, light almost reddish hair, and—there's always a demented note in this strange place—he smells of aftershave.

Peter has decided to point a semiautomatic pistol in my face. The weapon is 9mm. I can't identify the make.

"Hey, hey, easy," I say, hands up.

With his left hand, his eyes never leaving mine, Peter motions for me to turn and face the far wall.

"Yeah, yeah," I say seriously, moving, I hope, as told, and because I think my passport may mollify him, I say, "Papers are in the right pocket."

I'm not sure how much English Peter speaks so I grin and grin, and keeping my hands halfway up and immobile, I motion with my eyes downward at a Velcro-topped pocket on the right thigh of my trousers that contains my passport. I turn slowly, hoping this will reassure Peter.

Peter goes "Ha-ha-ha"—he's not laughing, it's some kind of rebuke—and repeats his hand motion, this time more vigorously, waggling the pistol, though keeping it pointed at my head. Bad guess—I moved too slowly, so quickly around I go.

When I have turned, I feel Peter's hand in the middle of my back, then feel a light push, meaning—I'm guessing—that I should move forward, which I do, deliberately, and I stop, my face inches from the wall, which is made of plaster. It smells of damp and mildew. Some of the plaster has fallen away.

Peter's left hand probes my shoulders, moves up to my neck, rests there, withdraws. Now at my neck, where Peter's light fingertips have just been, I feel metal. The feel is neither hot nor cold, just a hard presence.

Then nothing. The piece is away.

I feel Peter's hand again on my neck. The hand pats my left shoulder, then my right, moves back across my shoulders, intrudes into my left armpit, pats down to my waist, glides across the small of my back, pats up my right side to my right armpit.

The hand pats my buttocks, moves into my crotch.

I want to kill Peter, just kill him.

The hand pats down my left leg, rises back to the crotch, then pats down my right.

When Samuel comes in, he dismisses Peter, who leaves sulking.

"Hullo, Bob," Samuel says. "Good trip I hope."

"Hi, Sam. Pretty good." Samuel lets me call him Sam.

Samuel's shiny black face looks like polished ebony, but his eyes are yellowed and bloodshot, and his cheeks are thin and hollow. A scraggly, graying beard circles Samuel's mouth. Apart from his political problems, Samuel himself is pretty much done for. We and our British informants think it's AIDS. I wonder if Peter has the virus.

Samuel takes me back into his stark war room. There's not much furniture: a wooden table, four folding chairs, an easy chair upholstered in dark blue nylon and foam rubber, a small black metal desk with chrome-plated legs.

Like an old man with arthritis, Samuel lets himself down slowly at the desk. I take the easy chair. Samuel, I notice, is wearing the old Rolex we gave him years back.

"You want whiskey?" Samuel looks at me mock-expectantly and, before I can answer, says, "We don't have any." Samuel smiles at his joke and issues a short, creaky African laugh. "Good old vodka—workingman's choice." Reaching under his desk on the floor, Samuel brings up a bottle of Stolichnaya. " 'Beer, beer, beer, it makes you want to cheer.' Isn't that right? That's right, yes? But leave it to vodka, which is of serious medicinal value."

Samuel is being light. After vomiting this evening, Samuel will go to bed and drift. Samuel is dying.

Samuel's British adviser, Rick Luzac, an aging SAS warrior who washed up at Samuel's camp years back like slop on a beach, isn't around. I'm pretty sure Luzac has deserted Samuel. Samuel is alone except for us.

I tell Samuel I want the laptop. Ed's dead, I tell him. Whether this is news to Samuel or not, I can't tell, but Samuel doesn't show much reaction. We will extract you one more time, I tell him. That and $25,000 is the deal.

Samuel's eyes half close. He's not thinking about the laptop or Ed or much of anything.

With Sam in tow I go into the adjoining room, whose door is lettered UNITED AIR CONSULTANTS FIELD OFFICE. Another door is open onto Sam's dirt runway. I hear a plane outside, and I think it's Timperman, who wants to get the hell out and, juiced on vodka, isn't afraid of taking off at night.

With Sam's help, I find the laptop in a deep drawer of one of two desks in there, each like Sam's. As I plug the thing into Sam's jittery

electrical supply to power it up, Sam wanders from the room, probably heading for his Stolichnaya.

The laptop is Ed's. I hack around in it and find spreadsheets,
notes, photos. It's King Solomon's mines and probably the key to Ed.
I think Kareem may be in here as well. I close out, pack it up, and
head for the door to the runway.

"You stop!"

Peter.

I turn and see Peter and one of the boy soldiers, the one with the
long knife. Peter has a Kalashnikov at his hip, which he is pointing at
my chest.

"You stop," Peter says again. "You give me that."

"No."

"Yes. You give me that."

Peter thinks the machine is valuable. It is, but he can't know why,
he can't know what's on it. He probably wants to sell it.

Peter, his eyes serious, edges around the room studying me, getting between me and the open door to the runway. The boy soldier
hovers behind him.

Peter once led a squad of boy soldiers in one of Samuel's attempts
to take Freetown. They captured other children who belonged to the
enemy and, as Andrea said, randomly cut off their hands and arms, occasionally a lower limb. Some of the children they killed. Those who
survived the massacre had scars on their heads and necks that lay open
like grimacing mouths.

"That is mine," Peter says.

"It was Samuel's. He gave it to me."

I hear the Fokker's engines. Timperman is leaving. He may disappear into the black African sky and not come back.

Peter wipes perspiration from his eyebrow, dabbing with his middle finger. "He could not give it to you. It is mine."

"Peter, this was mine once, and I gave it to Sam. Now I'm taking
it back, that's all. Let's ask Sam."

Maybe he thinks there are games on this thing. Maybe it's the games he wants.

"He cannot say. Give it me."

The boy soldier flashes his knife, swooping it in the air over his head. The blade is broad down toward the tip to make the tip heavy, to give it more heft for slashing. The boy's face has clouded into an imitation of adult menace, a kind of put-on anger that is supposed to be intimidating. It is.

"Do you want a better computer, Peter? I can get you a better one."

Peter says nothing to this, but points at the laptop with his slender left hand and gestures for me to give him the machine. The boy soldier is nodding in support, smiling now, the angry look gone from his face. His smile is just as scary.

You got a will? Someday or other, dice'll roll wrong.

Peter is tensed, watching me. The boy soldier touches the blade of his knife to his left fingertips, as if testing its sharpness. His face is without emotion.

I look over at Peter's face. As I am wondering how the hell to play this, Peter's face crumples, and I am hit with a gusher of blood. Peter's arms and knees go limp and his Kalashnikov rattles to the floor, though he remains standing.

Timperman's second shot smashes into the back of Peter's head, which brings him down. The boy soldier dives for the floor, hugging his knife and kicking his dusty black feet in terror, hiding his face with his arms, sobbing, "No, no, no!"

The flight back to Monrovia gets shaky once or twice when we hit turbulence, but Timperman handles it well enough.

"Hello, Bob."

"Hello, Omar," I say. Omar Lateef is sitting across from me in our safe house, a large villa of many rooms and almost no furniture, one of four or five we have around Dubai. Omar is regional manager, Gulf Commercial Bank International in Dubai, where Gulf Commercial—GCBI, we call it—is headquartered. Omar is our highest, best single source in Gulf banking.

I am in Dubai on a quick jink to the East after leaving Samuel at his airstrip. Bill Squires, our second-in-command in Monrovia, got me a change of clothing, escorted me around customs, and somehow disposed of my gory shirt, pants, and boots. When I talked with Clep over the secure phone at Monrovia Station, he told me we were interrogating Omar in Dubai, and I decided to attend. Ed Powers made great use of GCBI, and Omar is talking. I know Omar. I have some questions for him and want to watch his performance. Clep wanted me to come back to Langley immediately ("Jesus Christ, you're getting shot at too much, I mean it"), but I pulled rank, and here I am.

July clouds lower over this sweaty coastal city, where the temperature is 105 and the humidity 95. Our safe house is permanently battened down, the windows closed, the curtains always drawn. As ever, window air conditioners rumble and drip moisture down into the deserted street.

Carl Peterson, a CIA officer from Dubai Base, and Roger Vanderslice, an Agency polygraph specialist, who has flown here from New Delhi, are conducting the proceedings. Tom Curtiss, legal attaché, Islamabad, is in for the session. Curtiss has pale blond hair, a narrow, intent face, staring eyes. His handshake is bony and not quite there.

The five of us are in a kind of living room on the second floor. Four chairs and a two-person sofa, each made from plywood and canvas stripping, circle a plywood coffee table. Peterson and I have just arrived.

"Bank okay, Omar?" I ask. "How's business? I hear things aren't so good."

"The bank? Oh, yes, Bob, the bank. The bank is, as I'm sure you know, experiencing some negative results. In fact, financially things have been quite traumatic."

Omar's uncle, the great Ali Heydari, is the founder of Gulf Commercial. Heydari is a self-conceived visionary, Islamic mystic, poet, and philosopher. To us, he's an international financial fraud, pimp, and murderer. To facilitate his banking business and build up "goodwill" for the firm, Heydari procures Asian and Russian young women for the Emirates' various emirs, sheikhs, and plutocrats. A few of these young women have been flown here only to disappear forever.

GCBI has recently suffered major liquidity problems, having lent much of its money to its owners. It has also lent to its local auditors and to a wide variety of Persian Gulf sheikhs, few of whom have been forthcoming in repayment.

Its depositors, mostly laborers and the owners of small businesses in the U.K. and the British Commonwealth, caught wind of the bad loans and two months back made a run on the institution. Many depositors have just lost their life savings. Heydari, founder-director, has been blamed for the debacle and is currently in a U.A.E. jail, from which he may never emerge alive.

Because of his position in the bank and his relationship to the founder-director, our man Omar is in a world of hurt and may be headed for a U.A.E. jail himself. He badly wants our protection.

Curtiss and Vanderslice have polygraphed Omar several times in a string of sessions lasting over a number of days. Curtiss wants a coherent tape made of Omar's various stories. The current session is on Powers.

Omar is hooked up once again to an Agency polygraph, a small box no larger than Ed Powers's laptop computer. He is sprouting wires from his arms and fingers; three elastic tubes bind his chest.

Resting on the coffee table next to an unopened bottle of Johnnie Walker Black, a reward for Omar after his performance, is a tape recorder, its little red light glowing.

"Okay, let's go," Curtiss says. As Roger fiddles with the dials of the polygraph, Curtiss runs through a few preparatory questions— How old are you? Where were you born? and the like—to gauge Omar's nervousness and calibrate the machine. He glances at Roger, who gives him a thumbs-up.

Curtiss then reads, slowly and carefully, from a yellow legal pad on which he has written a string of questions, some of which I've supplied. Omar, slowly and carefully, answers.

"Did there come a time when you met a man named Rutherford?"

"Yes."

"Did you know who Mr. Rutherford was?"

"I knew he was associated with some companies in Panama, in the U.S., with an airline."

"Did you know the name of his airline?"

"Yes, it was called Triple A."

"How did you meet Mr. Rutherford?"

"He came to call on me. He wanted to open an account, and he wanted a line of credit."

"How much did he want as a 'line of credit'?"

"I don't remember, but something ridiculous, because he didn't want to offer any security for it."

"What did you tell him about that? What happened when he asked for that money?"

"I asked him to leave."

"Did he offer any security at all?"

"No."

"Did there come a time when he came in later with a cash deposit?"

"He did. He did come to see me."

"What happened with that account?"

"Well, he opened an account. He put in a cash deposit, against which he took a loan, a line of credit, with a substantial margin, of course. Subsequently, he never came back. When it more or less reached, when the interest amount reached the outstandings, the loan was adjusted."

"Did you ever see him again?"

"I never saw him after that one meeting I had with him."

"Why would somebody do that? Why would somebody walk into a bank with a large bundle of cash and then immediately borrow against it and disappear, giving up the interest to the bank?"

"In the first place, I don't know whether he came in with cash. It could have been a bank transfer. But this was a normal type of business in Dubai—a cash-collateralized advance, as we call it."

"Why would somebody do that? What would the purpose be? If you want to use your money, what you would do is to make a deposit and then withdraw the money as you need it, rather than borrow it out and pay the interest and then let the loan be extinguished by the deposit."

"I can only conjecture as to what his motives were. But it can be a business-related transaction which is normal in Dubai."

"What sort of business transaction?"

"Inasmuch as there could be a partnership, there could be various corporations set up. The man does not want to show his partner that this is his own money that he is putting up, and does not want to show that he is taking a loan from a bank. It could be a third-party transaction."

"Isn't it possible that he is trying to conceal the source of the funds, because they originated in some sort of shady deal of one kind or another?"

"It could be possible."

"When did Rutherford make this deposit?"

"I don't quite remember, Tom, but it was certainly before we had heard about his company or his aircraft being lost."

"Did you know at the time he came in to deal with you that he was involved in gunrunning?"

"No."

"Did you have any information that he was involved in the narcotics business?"

"No."

"Mr. Rutherford was killed, was murdered."

"Yes."

"What were the circumstances of that? Do you know anything about it?"

"Do you mean his death?"

"Yes."

"I was not there at the time. I just read about it in the newspapers."

After Omar is led out, clutching his Johnnie Walker, Curtiss and Roger hang around briefly, then leave Peterson and me alone in the Agency property.

"Remember Bill Bonner? 'Wild Bill'?" Peterson asks.

"Sure do." William Bonner, like William Cleppinger, is an Agency legend. He worked South Asia for a couple of decades, spoke good Hindi, and was close to falling in love with the region.

"Bonner had this tape recorder," Peterson says, "big goddamn machine, big as a Lincoln Continental—this was way back when of course. Well, he'd haul it into an interrogation and make a deal about plugging it in, running the wires around, setting the tapes, getting the mike placed, taking levels and all that, and fuss and fuss, all the while making the subject more and more nervous, making the subject wonder what the hell's going on here.

"So after all his fussing Bonner would look up into the poor bastard's eyes, Kumar or Kuldip or whoever, and he'd say, 'Hey, Kumar, this make you nervous? Tell you what, why don't we just keep this guy off, no sweat.' Kumar relaxes, just like Bonner wanted, and now he's off mike, he spills his guts, talks and talks, says all kinds of stuff he's so relieved, stuff he'd never have said otherwise. All the while Bonner's running a little jobby in his vest pocket with a mike in his lapel. Pretty funny. Well, I just hope Omar's telling the truth. Ask me, boxing him's a pile of shit. These people cannot be caught by polygraph. They are immune."

There is a theory around the Agency—I don't subscribe to it, but Peterson does—that Easterners, Iranians in particular, cannot, when lying, be found out by polygraph. All the stigmata of the guilty liar that these machines are supposed to detect, the increased perspiration, the heavier, faster breathing, the racing heartbeats, the clenched muscles—the Iranians supposedly show none of these when glibly weaving their moonbeams. Omar is no Iranian, but, Peterson tells me, he is close enough.

Peterson says, "It's not even . . . I mean, it's so naked. Powers walks into GCBI last fall and pulls this shit. It's so outrageous maybe it's actually smart—doesn't look smart, but what do I know?"

Peterson means Powers's money laundering. Omar, however, a discreet banker, can't or won't tell us where Ed's cash deposit came from. He says he doesn't know. Our polygraph indicates he's telling the truth. He probably is.

I think the source is Kareem. I think we are coming close.

As ROBERT LANGER, I head back to the States in the morning on commercial carriers, Gulf Air to Cairo, Delta to Dulles. With the lousy connections, the trip will take twenty-four hours.

44 JULY 24
TIPOFF II

On July 24, 2001, an FBI analyst assigned to work at CIA headquarters noticed an Agency cable indicating that Khalid al-Mihdhar, a young man known to have al-Qaeda connections, had a visa to enter the United States. The analyst, curious now, found a report from the Immigration and Naturalization Service that al-Mihdhar and his companion Nawaf al-Hazmi had entered the United States in January 2000.

The analyst requested that the two be put on the TIPOFF watch list of suspected terrorists—their names were added to the list on August 24—and shortly thereafter the FBI began a search for the two. Though both were living in San Diego under their real names, the FBI did not give high priority to the search and failed to find them.

45 JULY 26
"Nonperforming"

Stu Kremer brings the word: SciTech has dumped Ed Powers's hard drive. "The drive's a mess. Two gig of data and programs—hundreds of folders, nine-thousand-plus files, including the porno downloads. We are to conclude among other important details that Ed had this thing for lesbians."

Though Ed had encoded some material with a commercial cryptographic program, it was one NSA had broken into long back. NSA has a slew of these programs and has their keys on file. Reading Ed's mail was not difficult.

The drive contains Ed's doodlings, letters, appointments, travel plans, spreadsheets, e-mails, financial records, some for companies we know (AAA Airlines, UAC, InterTech), and some for companies we've never heard of (TK Corporation, Vandalia Associates, Lorain/ CAL Industries, Crescent Technologies) and seem never to have existed, save in Ed's enthusiastic imagination.

Stu plops onto my desk two fat folders of printouts of Ed's hard drive as analyzed by DI arms control and banking specialists. "Have fun," he says, and leaves with a smirk on his face.

From the right side of the stacks of paper protrude numerous little pink, purple, and yellow stickers, notes scribbled by DI analysts categorizing the contents: "Chemicals," "Sierra Leone," "Diamonds," "NAR?" "UAC leasing contracts," and so on.

It's chaotic and hard to understand. When I can, I will try to collate this material with Eddie Dietz's "stuff" on Big Ed's movements through space and time. I have little doubt that what Eddie copied will match this material one for one and will probably explain a lot of it.

As I glance through the DI's short cover report on the dump, I find this on Sam and UAC:

"The main arms intermediary for the New Africa Rally, better known as Samuel Kontay Edgerton (see tagged items), is an Antwerp-based Belgian firm, Steen Ingénieurs. They are relatively new, having been established five years ago, and are ambitious and highly capable. The following from a Steen e-mail describes a typical transaction with Edgerton:

" 'The consignment from Steen Ingénieurs, SA for NAR, Sierra Leone, is 300 AK–47 assault rifles, 15 9mm M65 pistols, 2 sniper rifles with night-vision sights, 2 night-vision binoculars, 25,000 rounds of rifle ammunition, 6,000 rounds of pistol ammunition, 10 RPG–7 rocket launchers, 100 antitank grenades, 100 ordinary grenades, and 25 PM 79 antipersonnel mines. The commercial invoice will describe goods as per contract no. 046-hps 10.11.01 to keep within the required framework of our Swiss bank.' "

UAC's Swiss bank, the one with a "required framework," is a small boutique financial house in Zurich, Bank Hügen. We are familiar with Bank Hügen—we use it ourselves from time to time—but that does us no good in learning what Big Ed and Sam were up to. The Swiss won't talk, not even to preferred customers like us. It's Ed's hard drive that gives us the skinny.

A man named Ibrahim Niasse in Senegal is the recipient of Sam's diamonds. Senegal is on the West African coast, two countries up from Sierra Leone. Niasse, a curious customer, is a man our French counterparts know well. He weighs three hundred pounds, lives in a large compound of six or eight buildings in Dakar, Senegal's capital city, with—he is Muslim—a changing cast of wives and a large, ever-increasing troupe of children. He is guarded by a private army.

The French tell us Niasse is an al-Qaeda operative. His agents in Liberia and Sierra Leone are Arabs, apparently North Africans. According to the French, Niasse's Arabs get the diamonds to Europe, to Antwerp and Amsterdam, and sell them there at European prices.

Commodification.

Niasse's agents pay Sam, partly in cash in Sierra Leone, partly by deposit into a bank account in Antwerp. Through the Antwerp account, Sam buys weapons from Steen Ingénieurs, which are flown in to Sam by UAC. A record of the sale is e-mailed to an Internet account maintained by Ed and finally passed on to Sam in the form of hard copy signed by Ed and stamped with the UAC corporate seal. I'm not sure Sam in his fog understands all this.

UAC also flies for the Taliban.

By our reckoning, UAC has delivered at least fifty tons of weapons—antipersonnel mines, RPGs, assault rifle ammo—over the past couple of years to Taliban forces in northern Afghanistan. UAC pilots were paid $10,000 for each trip plus an extra $1,000 "per landing"—sometimes a flight would take them to more than one high-risk airfield in Afghanistan. The flights operated out of Dubai and Sharjah under deals made with Afghan traders in the Emirates.

The flight that went down in the Arabian Sea last October, the one Eddie Dietz told me about—"Wayne . . . Bates . . . Pil-ot. I knew Wayne, he was a cool head. Wayne Bates died for Ed Powers"—shows up in a note on Ed's hard drive. The flight was a UAC charter, and, as Eddie claimed, was carrying arms to the Taliban in Afghanistan.

Another note on the hard drive mentions an earlier UAC flight, again Dubai to Karachi, this one in September and also piloted by Wayne Bates. This flight carried four tons of acetic anhydride, one and a half tons of sodium carbonate, and seven drums of chloroform. These are chemicals needed for refining opium into heroin. The registered end-user was a Pakistani textile firm in Karachi. The firm seems not to exist.

The flight, we think, never went to Karachi. We think it went to Jalalabad in eastern Afghanistan, where the chemicals were offloaded and taken to a heroin processing plant—sounds like Kareem here—protected by al-Qaeda.

NAR, the Taliban, al-Qaeda. Diamonds, heroin, arms.

Our Ed.

Long back, I worried about dealing with men like Powers, about including them at the table. At some point I must have stopped worrying. It doesn't matter who they are or what they do, I decided. Get the product. It's a higher law.

One yellow sticker catches my eye and gives me a jolt. It reads, "Who K?"

I quickly, hopefully check to see what the sticker marks. It is attached to a short series of day notes Powers wrote on his dealings with someone he names K.

"February 18, 2000: K talked, interested."

Then another:

"June 10 talked K phone, K Karachi, okays. Wants to see, knows he'll be pitched. S at hqs informed."

A third note:

"August 16 pitch K. S at hqs informed."

Cat's claw at my neck. The operational dates and actions—the initial meeting, the call, the pitch in Karachi—tally with our lone, lorn WILDCARD cable.

There is a fourth and final note:

"December per S at hqs K relationship U.S. Government terminated, payments ceased. Per S I turn vouchers over to ISI Afghan liaison committee. S at hqs: K nonperforming. S as usual ballsy with other people's balls. Be a great pleasure, watch K little fucker squirm."

"K" is Kareem, most certainly. And "S" at hqs? "S" sounds a lot like Declan St. John Desmond, who answers to the name Sonny.

This is operation WILDCARD the way Powers saw it.

Kareem has been back on the payroll, has been one of ours recently. Just last fall. Those "vouchers" have to be pay vouchers. Kareem would have signed them or put his thumbprint on them. Ed would have collected them and, since this operation was consummate loosey-goosey, would probably have kept them and not turned them over to CIA personnel for safekeeping.

The first thing we learn in elementary spy school is that we are to get absolute control over our agents: we want their peckers in our pockets. One of our methods of control is to demand that our informants sign pay vouchers and return them to us. Then, if they don't bring us what we want or refuse to take the chances we want them to take or simply want out of the relationship, we can, if we choose, threaten to let the wrong parties know of said informants' said relationship with us. The signed pay vouchers are our proof. The threat often does the trick.

In December, we, in the person of Ed Powers, passed along copies of those vouchers to Pakistani InterServices Intelligence and its Afghan Liaison Committee, that is, to the Paks who handle the Taliban and al-Qaeda. To what end? Why? What did we mean by "non-performing"?

And if we cut Kareem loose and sold him out, did Kareem get wind of it?

I think now of my last talk with Meatball and feel a cold spike driven through my gut. *There's a guy out of the Agency who's being looked at. Drug stuff.* Meatball was talking about Ed Powers, though he didn't know it. *It's got something to do with current officers,* Meatball said, *people in Near East South Asia. They're protecting him. Could even be payoffs involved, payoffs to the Agency people.*

Drug stuff.

I don't think Sonny was on the take, that's just not believable. But protecting a heroin operation, Ed's and Kareem's maybe, to get into al-Qaeda—that I wouldn't put past Sonny. Escudero, the DEA guy in Islamabad, is complaining to congressmen that we're protecting sources from the law. Merritt Grayson on the Hill is telling us we got trouble over drugs and won't tell us what.

It's Powers and Kareem.

I remove the sheets containing Powers's day notes from Kremer's folder, slipping them and the one yellow Post-it reading "Who K?" into an unmarked manila folder of my own, and put them in my office safe. I cannot see yet what these notes mean or what this operation was about, but one thing I do know: Sonny won't tell me.

"Final Decree of Divorce *a vinculo matrimonii*.

"THIS CAUSE which has been regularly matured, set for a hearing and docketed, came on this day to be heard upon the Bill of Complaint for Divorce filed by the Complainant, Nancy R. Patterson."

And so on. It is 7 p.m., still light out. When I sifted through the mail this evening, there it was, a letter from the Circuit Court of Arlington County, not stuck to my door by a county functionary this time, but delivered like any ordinary piece of mail—a telephone bill, a mail-order catalog—by our postman, a Vietnamese immigrant named Le.

It is over. After twenty-four years of marriage, I have no wife. I get a strange, floating sensation, a sense of disconnection from the earth, from anything solid and material.

But still I think of Nan as my wife. When will I stop doing that?

I look at our picture of David there over the mantel, which Nan put up and which I have not taken down. Graduation, Yorktown High. He is seventeen. His face, under the high school mortarboard, is her face, the long Radford elegance.

David, born when Nan was thirty, died when she was forty-seven. When she bore David, the delivery was horrific. She endured thirty hours of back labor and was for months thereafter afflicted with much physical hurt. A year later, after seeing a therapist and talking it over with me, she had a tubal ligature. No more kids.

A summer evening comes to mind. Nan and I are out in the backyard of this house in north Arlington. David has been dead one month.

Nan, tipsy with wine, is in an airy, cornflower-blue cotton dress and is walking barefoot on the lawn. The moonlight illuminates the white streak in her black hair, that starburst that begins at her left temple, runs back, and loses itself in the tangle. She is carrying an empty wine goblet made of heavy, opaque, ice-blue glass, one of a set of six we'd bought in Tehran, so long ago, in the first year of our marriage, when the world was wide and open.

Walking with concentration toward our white gazebo, moving too carefully because of the alcohol she has consumed, Nan says, "Oh, Paul, we were a family once, long back," then, giving me a sudden desperate look, she breaks away from me and glides silently, aimlessly over the dark grass, waving the empty goblet.

"But what's become of us?" she asks. "What are we now?" She drops the goblet onto the grass and stands looking over the neighbors' roof. When I put my arm around her, she leans her light body against mine, sobbing, sobbing.

And now, sitting here holding my decree of divorce from the bonds of matrimony, I think of David, of Nan, of that life I had. And I wonder, What became of us?

---

47 **JULY 29**
Walk-in Wonders

Cleppinger, I, and some other people from the Agency are spending Sunday morning with a man named Suleiman Badri in an Agency safe house in the Virginia burbs.

Badri, perspiring as he talks, is rubbing his skinny upper arms with his hands, chafing them nervously and excitedly as if he's cold, chilled by our air-conditioning, but I think it's nerves. He is wearing new clothes, light trousers and a Polo shirt we've furnished him from Hecht's and sneakers from a Foot Locker in Ballston Commons.

Our hideaway is a modest town house, one in a row of lookalikes on a cul-de-sac named Shawn Leigh Drive. Shawn Leigh is in a complex of short, nondescript streets north of I-66, on the western fringes of Vienna, Virginia. The development is populated by young people on the rise and older people on the move, transients who do not stay for long. Shawn Leigh's a friendly enough street if that's what you want. Or a place where you can be anonymous, if that's what you want.

Badri is what we call a walk-in wonder. Walk-in wonders are the way we learn many of our secrets. Somebody we've never heard of simply shows up and pounds on our front door.

Badri is thirty or so, slender and fine-boned. He has large, intelligent eyes. Maybe a little too intelligent—you always wonder about walk-ins.

Badri handled al-Qaeda money moving through Yemen. Because of the informality of the al-Qaeda cash transfer system, he had hands-on access to large sums of cash, sometimes tens of thousands of dollars. A year back he began skimming off al-Qaeda funds for himself.

The al-Qaeda leadership, he is pretty sure, have found out about his embezzling. He thinks they were biding their time before settling their score with him. Eight days ago in the dusty port city of Aden, southern Yemen, he left al-Qaeda and came over to us. Four days ago he arrived here in humid, green Virginia.

Our Agency debriefer is Rick Landry, an ATAC professional. He has a loose-leaf notebook containing the day's interrogations, put together by our Research and Analysis personnel.

Because Badri is who he is, our R&A people are running computers and spitting out questions for the man, page after page of them. We are asking Badri about hundreds of names and addresses, dates, and operations. We have questions on the al-Qaeda hierarchy, their cash-transfer methodology, their financial backers, their network of camps, everything we can think of that he might know.

In an adjoining room we have an Arabic-language translator—Arabic is Badri's second language after Somali, but we have no Somali linguists—whom we can haul in if necessary. There is no need. Badri's English, his third language, is good enough.

Like all our walk-ins, Badri wants to prove himself, show us he's real. This is our first session with Badri in the States, so we start this morning with the easy ones. "You were born . . . ," Landry says.

"I was born," Badri responds, "in a village, small village. Close to Mogadishu."

Badri is a coastal Somali. He has no tribal name.

"My father was a fisherman. He died. He was sick. I don't know what. He died. I was six, maybe seven."

Badri's mother then brought the children, five of them, to her father's house, a compound without running water or electricity, in Mogadishu. The compound was large, and a large number of people lived there, mostly family, but also servants. Badri's grandfather, a man named Osman, was a merchant, who imported and sold the cheaper kinds of electronic gear, new and used.

Badri's grandfather recognized early on that Suleiman was bright and had a special affection for the boy. The old man sent Suleiman to a school in Mogadishu, where he spent some years, though he didn't graduate. He did manage to learn passable English, at school and also by listening to the radio and watching television in coffee houses.

When Suleiman dropped out of school, he worked for a time for his grandfather, but left to take a number of menial jobs in Mogadishu city, then got a position as clerk with the Mabruk Trading Agency, an Islamic financial services firm. At Mabruk he helped with hawala transactions, transferring cash to and from Somalia, and taught himself some bookkeeping. He began to earn a modest salary.

Feeling his life was in order, he took a wife, a second cousin named Na'eema, from among his relatives living in the compound and in short order fathered a child, a boy. The boy was born shortly after the Nairobi and Dar es Salaam embassy bombings, so Badri named him Osama.

Badri began attending Arabic-language and Koranic classes at night in a mosque, the Al-Azhar, near his grandfather's compound, where he met an Arab teacher, a Saudi from Asir Province named Abu Qutaiba, an eloquent and persuasive preacher, who was also an al-Qaeda operative.

The meeting changed Badri's life.

Abu Qutaiba was a short, chunky man, with a round face and a ferocious beard. He was partly lame. His voice was "musical," Badri says, "beautiful." Wednesday nights Abu Qutaiba held forth to a special group of young Muslims, some Somali, some from elsewhere in Africa, in a starkly lit side room in the mosque, a room used ordinarily for study, where Somali boys would sit on the floor bending over Koranic texts, chanting them, memorizing them.

To his special Wednesday group, young men beyond school age, Abu Qutaiba spoke of jihad. He spoke of the "armies of the Crusaders," meaning the Americans in Saudi Arabia, who are occupying Arab land, "spreading like locusts, eating its riches." The Americans, Abu Qutaiba said, are occupying the lands of Islam in the holiest of places, dictating to its rulers, humiliating and impoverishing its peoples.

Abu Qutaiba spoke of the great devastation inflicted on the Iraqi people by the Crusader-Zionist alliance and the vast number of those killed in Iraq by war and blockade, exceeding now 1 million persons. Despite this murder, said Abu Qutaiba, the Americans are repeating the massacres from the air, not content with the protracted blockade imposed after the ferocious war and devastation that had already been inflicted on the people.

The Americans' aims behind these wars are economic. Their other aim, he said, is to serve the Jews' petty state, Israel, and divert attention from the Jews' occupation of Jerusalem and murder of Muslims there. The best proof of this is the Americans' eagerness to destroy Iraq, the strongest neighboring Arab state, and their endeavor to fragment all the states of the region—Iraq, Saudi Arabia, Egypt, and Sudan—into paper statelets. The disunion and weakness of these states would guarantee Israel's survival and the continuation of the brutal Crusader occupation of the Arabian Peninsula.

To kill the Americans and their allies, said Abu Qutaiba, civilians and military, is a duty for every Muslim who can do it in any country in which it is possible to do it. This killing is permissible in order to liberate the al-Aqsa Mosque in Jerusalem and the holy mosque in Mecca from their grip and to move their armies out of all the lands of Islam, defeated and unable to threaten any Muslim. This is in accordance with the words of Almighty God: "And fight the pagans all together as they fight you all together" and "fight them until there is no more tumult or oppression and there prevail justice and faith in God."

"We foretell a black day for America," Abu Qutaiba said.

We know the language. It is bin Laden's, issued by him in a pseudoreligious decree in 1998. Badri, our man, has it close to memorized.

In the same side study room in the mosque, Abu Qutaiba had a Sony TV and VCR, which he used to show videos on various Islamic subjects—on the hajj, how to pray, and an old Anthony Quinn film, *Mohammad, Messenger of God,* in which Quinn played a Companion of Muhammad.

Abu Qutaiba showed other kinds of tapes, too, al-Qaeda tapes. One we know well. I've seen it several times. It has circulated everywhere—North Africa, the Arabian Peninsula, Pakistan, India, Central Asia—and is famous. It is entitled *The Need for Jihad Against the Crusaders and the Jews.* We call it "The Osama Hour" (it actually lasts fifty-three minutes).

In the tape, repeatedly, Israeli soldiers shoot dead an Arab boy while his father tries to shield him with his body, both cowering behind a cement block in Gaza. It's the famous Muhammad al-Durra incident.

We then see Israeli soldiers beating Arab children. In one sequence, an Israeli soldier stuffs the body of a dead Arab child into a black garbage bag—this is somewhere in southern Lebanon, who knows when.

We hear children screaming and see dead Arab boys lying in a ditch, their eyes open, seeming to stare at the sky. A woman whose face is soaked in blood looks vacantly away from the camera.

The voice-over tells us Jews are "dogs," Jews are "pigs." The Jews kill Muslim men, women, and children.

And the Jews are backed in their work by the United States (a shot now of Bill Clinton), by pliant, complicit Arab governments (shots of fat Saudis, of Hosni Mubarak).

The voice-over is deep-toned and masculine, conveying a controlled, deeply felt rage.

There is an answer the voice-over says. Come to Afghanistan. Make a hijra, like Muhammad moving from Mecca to Medina. Leave where you are. Come here.

We see shots of training camps. We see adolescent boys with purposeful faces, crawling under barbed wire and dragging Kalashnikovs as live ammo snaps through the air above them. Older men roll in the dun-colored earth, rise, and hurl grenades downrange. Men manning a Soviet antiaircraft gun maneuver the thing around, peer through its sights, raise and lower the twin barrels.

We see an active shooting range. Board targets, some of them images of Bill Clinton, rise randomly, and a man holding a pistol in both hands, American style, shoots once at these targets, twice, three times.

We hear religious singing: "Overcome the Jews, overcome the Crusaders, overcome the oppressors. Overcome them, overcome them."

Cut to bin Laden, who speaks to the camera. He has a soft, gentle voice, soft, liquid eyes. He seems almost shy. "You should not love this world," he intones. "Loving this world too much is wrong. It is the other world you should love. You should not be afraid to die. To die as a martyr is to go to the other world. It is the right act for a true Muslim. It is praiseworthy."

Toward the end of the tape we see dead American soldiers lying in a street in Mogadishu; the bombed-out U.S. army installation at al-Khobar in Saudi Arabia; a state funeral for U.S. soldiers and embassy personnel at Arlington Cemetery.

Finally, Palestinian children throw stones at Israeli soldiers, who duck and run for cover. Then we see smiling children, no Israelis, while on the voice-over there is singing: *Ma' dam, ma' dam, ma' dam,* "with blood, with blood, with blood."

There is nothing the Americans can do, is the message. If we are not afraid to die, we can strike at them, defeat them. With blood.

Ours. Theirs.

We often attribute some kind of abstract, context-free, almost metaphysical evil to these people, and we think we are in a religious war. That's a mistake. Islam has a way of mixing politics and religion, raising the stakes for both, and making the war look religious when it is in fact intensely political.

Badri wanted jihad. He thought he had to participate personally in the struggle. He left his wife and child for five months in 1999, traveling first to Pakistan, where he contacted al-Qaeda agents in Karachi. He then entered Afghanistan, going first to an al-Qaeda training camp near Kandahar, where his talents, particularly his facility for bookkeeping, and his Islamic commitment impressed an al-Qaeda recruiter named Abu Musa.

We don't tell Badri, but Abu Musa is dead, killed in that roadside ambush Ed Powers and his tribals had intended for bin Laden.

On Abu Musa's recommendation, Badri was sent in late 1999 to

Yemen, where he took up residence in the port of Aden, joining a small cell of al-Qaeda operatives in that city, and began work at the Yemeni branch of Mabruk Trading. In the spring of 2000 he arranged for his wife and child in Mogadishu to join him.

Our first question for the few al-Qaeda people we have been able to talk to is always, Is al-Qaeda planning an attack? We asked Badri first in Yemen, later here in Virginia.

In Yemen, Badri said, "I think yes. It is their plan, but I do not know it. I do not know of the plan. It is large, something large." He gives more or less the same answer here.

In Yemen, Badri also said he knew of a man named Abdel Kareem. "The Afghan," Badri called him.

"So the Afghan, Yusufzai," Landry says, "Abdel Kareem Yusufzai—that's his name, isn't it?"

"Yes."

"Tell me about him. What did he do?"

"He stayed a day. Maybe two."

"Where?"

"In the New City. A good apartment."

"An al-Qaeda apartment in New City?"

"They have some apartments. This is one."

"Do you know it?"

"Yes."

"Describe it."

Badri tells us what he knows of the house and its approximate address. We've already found it. It's in a hilly quarter on the north loop of Aden harbor. What he says checks.

Three men came through at the same time, two months back, all from Peshawar. Two of them were Egyptian Arabs. The other was the Afghan, Abdel Kareem.

From Yemeni security we know Kareem was using his real name

and traveling under his real Pakistani passport. The Arabs used coun-
terfeit passports.

Kareem was carrying money, some $23,000, Badri says. Kareem
placed the money with Mabruk Trading, which functions as a bank as
well as hawala service. As was his wont, Badri turned most of it over
to the hawala dealer, but held some back.

"He also carried passports."

"What kind?"

Badri seems puzzled.

"What kind, what nationality?"

"Oh. Saudi, Moroccan, Tunisian. Many countries."

"Who'd he see besides you?"

"I don't know. He came and left very fast."

"How long did he stay?"

"One, two days. I saw him once only."

"He had been through before?"

"Yes."

"When?"

"Some times. Six months before I think. Some times."

Landry lets this pass. He'll come back to the other times Kareem
came through.

"But, this time," Landry says, "two months ago, it was money he
was carrying and documents."

"Yes. He was carried the money. And passports."

"For al-Qaeda?"

"Yes."

After more questioning on the Arabs, the session ends. Badri is
tired. We let him rest.

In time Badri will get another identity and a new life and will be
sent somewhere out West. His wife and child in Aden will be brought
in as well; what they will do once they get here I have no idea. We
will give him some money, but only some. After a while he'll be on
his own, though we'll check in on him from time to time.

On the way back to Arlington, where he's dropping me off at home, Clep says, "Kareem was documents handler. It's time to work up a snatch. Gotta find him, of course, and the lawyers have to sign off, but it's time. When we get him, we will politely inquire as to what brother Kareem knows about the sad end of Ed Powers. And where the hell Liamine Dreissi is."

Late night. I'm nursing a bourbon on the rocks in my dark living room. My TV is on to the tail end of a Cardinals-Giants game, though I've got the sound muted and I'm not watching.

Where is Kareem? And who is he? He's a courier for al-Qaeda and an informant for us. I think. And yet Sonny decided to burn him. Why? Doesn't make sense.

The doorbell rings. It's close to eleven. I'm not expecting anyone and I'm alone.

Cat's claw at the back of my neck.

I think, *Watch your goddamn back.* I think, *Individuals of potential significance.* And since I have no way to see who's on the front porch except to open the door, I give serious thought to my silvery Smith & Wesson hanging in the closet upstairs.

Paranoia, I decide, and with what feels like a touch of bravado, I open the door and find—Karen.

She's wearing Bermuda shorts and a sloppy man's shirt. Her hair is pulled back in a ponytail. And she is on my front porch as of old. *Here I am,* she seems to say. A wave of desire courses through me.

"Hi," she says flatly. "Like they say, just happened to be in the neighborhood and thought I'd drop in. Joke. I mean, is it okay? You're not busy?"

"No. No, no. Sure, come on in, Kare."

She enters the living room, familiarly, goes over to the couch, and sits, tensed and serious, in her old place.

She says calmly that she's had time to think. She says maybe we've fallen into something that's a mistake. "Like, it all went wrong very fast. And we could both be sorry. It would be a pity to end what we had, which was good"—she gives me an appealing look—"truly good."

" 'Never better'?"

"Don't. Please don't, Paul."

She swears Jim Jeffries means nothing to her, and I tell her, "I know."

But I don't know. I do know that I want her and that in the end I will lie to myself and to her to get her. When I raise the "age thing," my no-go area, she smiles, shaking her head dismissively. "You seem pretty young to me, Big Boy." I will allow myself to believe that she means it.

And so we arrange our truce. As I sit beside her on my old couch, she rocks in my arms, eyes closed, like a person absolved of guilt. Maybe that's what we all want, to be absolved of guilt.

48
JULY 30
Get Kareem

Monday morning, our first Get Kareem session, William Cleppinger presiding. We are in the Director's Briefing Room, seventh floor, new building, sitting around Lindsay's enormous conference table. A long bank of ever so slightly tinted windows overlooks the forests of Langley and beyond. Blue sky, no clouds: American idyll.

Officially this session is just a regular meeting of the interagency Counterterrorism Security Committee, but today the subject, Abdel Kareem Yusufzai, is special, and we have, in addition to the usual crew, called in the heads of our CounterIntelligence Center and of our Operational Security Office, Lurch from the FBI, and Perry Rollins, our in-house DEA liaison. General of the Army Frederick Mayrhofer, Central Command, Security Division, is also here.

Lindsay, who is touring stations in the Far East, will not make the scene. No matter. When I briefed him, he approved going forward with a major push to seize Kareem. The White House is ecstatic. The White House wants Kareem labeled an operative of Osama bin Laden and wants his head in a basket.

Fowler, invited by Lindsay, is out from NSC. Though it is on our turf, Fowler had requested to chair the meeting. He was refused, of course. He is unhappy about this. A deep wad of resentment has sunk like lead into his gut, keeping him lowered in his chair, deeply sober, facing Cleppinger, as Cleppinger, his usual self, red-eyed and dyspeptic, conducts the proceedings. Fowler, who lunches at his desk on salads and caffeine-free diet cola, is as much an ascetic as Cleppinger is a boozer and an eater.

Sonny, as plans officer ATAC, is here, too, sitting next to Fowler. Sonny's mostly for show—he has better things to do than attend sessions like these—but Lindsay wants to impress the Oval Office with our high seriousness. As Lindsay's terrorism guy and stand-in, I'm to do the talking.

We've distributed a one-page agenda that looks thin: time, date, place, participants by title, not by name, and then: (A) Presentation by Mr. W. Cleppinger, (B) Presentation by Mr. P. Patterson, (C) Discussion." This is bureaucratic minimalism, but it is our style for these things.

Cleppinger, winding down his introductory remarks, says, "Paul Patterson here, uh, most of you knew Paul before this morning's meeting, so I won't go into his long résumé, I'll just say he knows whereof he speaks and we all know it, and he will give the presentation on the principal. Paul."

I'm on.

At the end of the table we have a wide-screen TV, which I operate from a laptop using PowerPoint and on which I have a dazzling series of photos to show.

"This is our man," I say. I click onto the demo screen Kareem's latest photo, the one taken by our German friends in Hamburg, showing Kareem, with his hands on the table in that café, his head back in that laugh. "Until recently this individual was under British surveillance in London. He has eluded them, however, and is now on the run."

I mention the other man in the shot, Dreissi, and tell what we know of him: a professional killer, a known al-Qaeda operative, who arrived in Pakistan just before Powers's death.

Now shots of the mosque in Hamburg, the street café, the friends of Kareem's, including the lizard-faced man in the Egyptian galabia, his arm up around Dreissi's neck. "If we can get Kareem," I say, "get him talking, we can move against all these worthies."

Unblinking, Fowler leans forward. He's staring hard at the demo screen. He looks as if he can barely contain himself.

"Our subject," I say, "was born Abdel Kareem Yusufzai in 1960 in Kabul, Afghanistan." I project an early photo of Kareem, from when he was nineteen or so and working for us. "He is an Afghan national. He has five living brothers and two sisters, some in Pakistan, some in the U.K. We've talked to a number of them. He seems to have broken off all contact with family in the West. British police believe this to be the case as well. The extended family is huge. In fact, though Kareem's a city boy, his family is a tribe, and he has relatives on both sides of the Pak-Afghan border.

"In 1978 he entered Kabul University, the Engineering Faculty, but after the Soviet invasion of Afghanistan—this was in late 1979— he fled with his family to Pakistan, then to the U.K.

"In 1980 he enrolled in an applied electronics course at Hammer-smith and West London College, London." Shot here of an austere, dark redbrick complex, a kind of urban junior college, much frequented by foreign students. "As far as we can tell, he wasn't much of a student. Two years later he left London for Peshawar in Pakistan to work for the Afghan resistance, and there we think his life was formed.

"Even at that early age Kareem became a fixer—he arranged arms shipments, made sure deliveries got to the field. He raised funds, brought in money for the resistance, and helped place volunteers from Islamic countries, mostly Arabs—Algerians, Egyptians, Yemenis. We think he was dealing heroin even then."

Guns in, dope out.

"In time he came to know the major financial players—rich Saudis, donors from other places in the Persian Gulf, all those little sheikhdoms that are rolling in money—Dubai, Abu Dhabi, Sharjah. And he got to know the Gulf banking system and a regionwide network of financiers. He's highly competent, highly energetic."

I keep an eye on Sonny. His face is bland and expressionless—just plain Sonny. I'm thinking of WILDCARD, of "nonperforming," of Sonny and Powers trying to burn Kareem.

"We think Kareem is a courier for Osama bin Laden and al-Qaeda," I say. "We believe he was involved in the bombing of the USS *Cole* in Aden harbor." Shots of bin Laden, the *Cole.*

"We also believe Kareem arranged for the death of Edward Powers, an American businessman on contract to CIA."

I show a forensic shot of Powers's face taken against the flat, antiseptic white of a hospital gurney. Frizzing up from what is left of his exploded scalp are tufts of his red-blond hair in crazy disorder, matted with blackened blood and gray-green brain. Powers's lower jaw twists away to the right. What should be his chin is a dark, iridescent smear. To the right of his head, placed there evidently by some Pakistani pathologist, rests a small collection of recovered skull fragments.

"Pakistan is a dangerous place," I say, "a hotbed of political Islam and on the popular level, highly anti-American. We have lost other people there."

Shots now of the consular employees killed in Karachi, of the four oil company workers, and finally, of our murdered CIA officer Terri Talbot. Her brown hair, frosted at the tips, is caked with blood and plastered against her young face. Clep, who mentored her in Cairo, stares hard at the screen; Sonny, who was station chief, Islamabad, when she was working in Karachi, looks away.

"We don't know the perpetrators of these killings, though we suspect the professional killer Liamine Dreissi"—I show again the shot of Kareem with Dreissi—"was involved in the shootings of the oil company executives. In Ms. Talbot's case there has been some movement. A little over a year ago Pakistani police caught two minor players of the team who carried out the murder. They have given some information on the crime. We do not know who killed her." We have little information on the Talbot murder. The investigation has stalled.

The shots of Powers, Terri Talbot, and the others have subdued my audience. We all want to get the killers.

Back to Kareem: "This picture"—I flash on an old photo of Kareem taken in Peshawar—"was taken twelve years ago when the Afghan war was winding down and Gorbachev had announced the Soviets were pulling out of Afghanistan. These next"—I flash through a quick series of shots of Kareem walking in the street, Kareem emerging from a run-down house, Kareem in front of the Brixton Mosque—"were taken in south London by British security people quite recently. As I say, he has eluded the British, but might still be in the U.K." When I say this, I notice Cleppinger giving me a look: fat chance.

Fowler's tensed again, pinching his lower lip between thumb and forefinger, staring his unblinking stare at the photo of Kareem in front of the mosque, which is actually a shabby Victorian row house, the door columns and lintel painted green. There is just one small sign: BRIXTON MOSQUE AND ISLAMIC CULTURAL CENTRE."

I mention Mary Ogilvie, but not by name ("a highly reliable source in London"), the Jordanian take on Dreissi ("security officials in a Middle Eastern capital"), and Badri ("a defector now in the United States") and describe in a general way the information these sources have given us.

"Kareem," I say, "is a violent man, a Muslim radical, what we call a bearded engineer—he's got a little education, but not a lot, a little familiarity with the outside world, but not a lot. He is sure of himself and intolerant. He is also vain. And he hates America with a depth some of us find surprising when we first come upon it. He is proud of the Islamic moral sense. He is also a drug smuggler, a counterfeiter, and a murderer. Bundle of contradictions."

As I talk, I realize that the portrait I am sketching for these people is the Agency received wisdom about Kareem. I'm no longer so sure of that wisdom. I do not know who Kareem is, what he's done, or why he's done it. Those "vouchers" trouble me deeply—I have stewed over them all weekend, wondering what they mean.

Watch K little fucker squirm.

"Bearded engineer"? Maybe. "Islamist"? Could be. But opportunist seems more like it. The portrait I've just given, I realize, is Clep's and Stu Kremer's. Not mine.

Early on in my black career I asked an older officer, Dick Marin, DDO at the time, if there was one inviolable rule in CIA, one law at the Agency you just never broke. I caught him off guard with the question, and he had to think for a moment. Then he told me, "Never lie to a superior. Most young officers aren't any good at lying. You've got to be trained at it so that you can do your job right. But when it comes to lying in the organization and especially to superiors, you must not do it. We don't want you to be so good at lying that we can't detect it ourselves."

"Ed Powers helped us," I tell these people, "supplied us with information on al-Qaeda, the Taliban, and Kareem himself. Helped initiate operations against al-Qaeda."

Including our troubled op NOREFUGE, I think, though I don't mention this to the committee. "Now Powers is dead. CIA considers it highly likely that al-Qaeda killed Powers and that Kareem brought about the killing."

Each sentence I say is true. Ed did help us. The Agency does believe al-Qaeda killed him for it. And the Agency thinks it is probably Ed's work on NOREFUGE that got him killed. But as I utter these truths, I think they amount to a falsehood. I know better. I doubt al-Qaeda killed Powers, in retaliation for that ambush south of Kandahar or for anything else. I think Ed died because he tried to betray Kareem, our agent of long ago and of not so long ago, on instructions from Langley, and Kareem got him for it. As I said to Clep that dark Christmas Eve, when we'd just gotten word of Powers's killing: it was some kind of payback. Not the kind I suspect now, though.

To learn the truth I have to run a clandestine op against Sonny Desmond. I'll inform Lindsay of this—it's my job, after all—but not just now. There's no telling how Lindsay will react if I do. And if by hook or crook Sonny finds out someone's looking at WILDCARD, he'll make evidence disappear.

One way to learn the truth, to learn why we betrayed Kareem, is to go find him and ask him.

"So we have to bring Kareem in," I say, "and we are going to try mightily to do just that. We have decided to offer a $500,000 reward for information leading to his capture, and we are publicizing it in the region. We are also working up an operational plan for tracking, finding, and decommissioning the principal, either by arrest or some other means."

General Mayrhofer likes this. Fowler, despite himself, seems pleased.

I'm done with my misleading speech, feeling tired and a little unclean. I have lied a lot in my life, perhaps even constructed my life as a large collection of untruths, Nan's considered view, but never before have I lied in-house. I took Dick Marin's injunction seriously.

I tell myself I am lying now to protect an important and delicate op, an op I'm running against Sonny Desmond, which will fall apart if too much truth sees the light of day.

Get the product. It's a higher law.

I can't think too much about this.

I turn to Lurch. "Rudi, the consensus is, I believe, that if we can find Kareem, we can nail him—that right?"

Lurch says, "Correct. Testimony of the individual here in the U.S., material from the U.K., this other material, we've got enough on the little bastard. We can indict, try, and convict him right here in a U.S. court. Slam dunk."

As we segue into a question-and-answer period, Fowler is ruminative and remains quiet. General Mayrhofer asks about the problems of arresting people overseas, which Lurch fields in his booming voice, going into the pros and cons of extraction versus extradition, how such things have to work under U.S. law, problems that can come up with the host country.

Rollins talks about the drugs coming out of Afghanistan, which, though they're heading mostly for Europe, are worrisome. People like Kareem facilitate the trade. I keep silent, of course, on Big Ed and those UAC flights.

Inevitably, Fowler comes on. He has waited for the end to sum things up, his way of asserting control.

"Well, I think this is all very good," he says. This is Fowler's typical patronizing talk; Cleppinger's face shows no movement—I'm sure he's in deep pain. "In fact very impressive work. I'm wondering, though—you say 'working up an operational plan.' We don't have one now. That's so, isn't it? We don't?"

"What's so?" Cleppinger asks blandly.

"That we don't have a plan. At this point, after all this intelligence, good though it is, we have yet to work up even a tentative track-and-seizure operation. Am I correct?"

Cleppinger is very cool. "'At this point'?" he asks slowly and seriously, an attitude put on to irritate Fowler, which it clearly does. "'This point,' Bob, is premature."

Cleppinger, who has called Fowler "Bobbo" at other sessions, restrains himself today. "At the proper time, we will get up a full-court press. That time is not yet. We do not know where the individual is. We have a program, a detailed plan, for finding him. When we do learn his whereabouts, there will be numerous ways of getting ahold of him, as Rudi has set out. Until we find him, though, operational planning per se—I mean in any elaborate fashion—just isn't in the cards."

"Fair enough," Fowler says, a tight little smile on his face. He doesn't ask about Cleppinger's "detailed plan." Just as well, because it doesn't exist. The $500,000 reward for information leading to Kareem's capture is the extent of our detailed plan. We've put the offer up on the State Department Web site.

Then Fowler says, glancing from face to face around the table and smiling, "Well, I commend CIA and everyone else who's contributed to the work on this individual." More patronizing talk; Clep just stares. Fowler continues, "We are facing a shadowy enemy. They are everywhere and they are nowhere. They are in cells, these hard-to-penetrate cells, and we do understand the difficulties of getting in at them. They are disciplined. They are a force to reckon with, and they are the cutting edge of the Islamic world in its clash with our world. But we do have to track them and somehow be able to deal with them. It is, I know, a very hard task."

Then he says—Clep and I are waiting for this, we know it's coming—"They think—now, I'm talking here about the non-Western world, not just about the Muslims—the non-Western world thinks differently from us. They and we have had different histories, at least since the Renaissance. The cultures that now we call 'less developed' have escaped the impact of Newton, of all our scientific thinking. That thinking is the basis of our worldview. We in the West deeply believe that the real world is external to the observer, that knowledge consists of recording and classifying data, the more data the better. And the more accurately the better."

General Mayrhofer, who's probably never heard this kind of talk before, looks puzzled and furrows his thick eyebrows as if he can't get a fix on what Fowler is saying. Lurch and Rollins look bored. Sonny and Clep sit quietly, Clep with his hands folded on the table, Sonny staring studiously at the wall.

"But the peoples of the East," Fowler says, "of non-Western cultures generally, don't think that. They think the real world is almost entirely internal to the observer. That's why they lack technology, haven't undergone technological development, why they don't have consumer goods and so on. So their worldview has been a profound negative for them. On the other hand, in some ways it also gives them great power. After all, they can imagine the world they operate in. Doing that gives them enormous flexibility. They can alter reality simply by shifting their perspective. And they do this. They do it in ways we can't understand and don't even perceive when it's going on." Fowler nods sagely, agreeing with himself.

"But we in the West have to know reality. Our culture forces us to try to come to terms with the external world, to know objective truth. And knowing it isn't easy. It's hard work, very hard work."

Fowler's speech is unbelievably dim-witted. You wouldn't think a high-ranking American official could be so loony, but Fowler is walking, talking proof. I have heard him descant to this effect often before, as have Sonny and Clep. It is standard-issue Fowlerism. When he finishes, he purses his little rosebud lips in satisfaction.

Cleppinger's face is a blank. Sonny keeps staring at the wall.

Semper fi.

Cleppinger scoops up his notes and ends the meeting.

As we leave, Sonny says to me, "Fowler—checked his brains at the door, didn't he?"

"Long time ago, Sonny. Way back."

Shortly after the meeting, Clep pulls me into his office and shuts the door. He's quitting, he tells me. I'm the first to know at Langley after Lindsay.

"Not fun anymore. Stopped being fun when I took over ATAC. Really did. All we do here is tread water. Our ops are going to hell, and I can't move the troops to do better. And the intel we produce is no damn good. Our analytical people—shit, they're all inbred, like a village of morons with bad genes piling up. Makes them shiftless. They sit around a table and weasel-word their drafts into horse pucky. It's all 'if on the one hand, this, if on the other hand, that.' It's junk. Nobody downtown can use that stuff."

"Diamond?" Ron Diamond, the "security consultant" and one-time assistant secretary of defense, who made that take-no-prisoners speech a while back tearing into Clep.

Clep blows a puff of breath. "Yeah, Diamond. And Donovan. And the little turd Merritt. Goddamnit, at this age and stage, I just don't need to be kicked in the nuts every damn day."

"What are you going to do?"

"Oh, I'll stick around. Lotta friends here. Putter around the garden. We thought of Florida, but it ain't for me. Bunch of old fucks down there, and I don't golf. Bea hates the place, too. Maybe do some consulting, security or something. Hell, I don't know."

Clep's replacement is to be Dennis Dennlinger, a colorless bureaucrat from the Intelligence Directorate. He won't last.

I sit alone in my office, thinking of Clep, of Fowler. In his day Clep was a tough guy. He once had a fight over something insignificant with the deputy chief of mission of our embassy in Tunis. Clep gave his final opinion by pulling a Glock 9mm out of his desk drawer, aiming it between the DCM's eyes, and clicking off the safety. The DCM stayed cool in the encounter—"You goddamn cowboy," he claims to have said—but then complained up the chain. Clep survived that scrape and numerous others through his long years with the Agency. But he hasn't managed to survive Ron Diamond and friends.

Clep departs, Fowler stays, and I can't think we're better off. Clep knew the world. Fowler does not.

Honest to God, that clown wouldn't know how to walk down the street in some of our better countries.

We, who are rich and powerful, define the world in the terms we like and seldom deign to notice when our definitions are challenged by the poor and weak, a class of beings whose views we ignore. So the world for us becomes what we say it is. But it is our "world," not the world, not the real world.

There is a real world out there.

And it is not what we think it is.

49

JULY 30
IDs

By the end of July 2001, a group of fifteen young Arab men, fourteen from Saudi Arabia and one from the United Arab Emirates, had arrived in the United States and had gathered in two locations.

Those who entered the country through Orlando and Miami airports settled in the Fort Lauderdale area, near Muhammad Atta, Marwan al-Shehhi, and Ziad al-Jarrah. Those arriving in New York and Virginia joined Hani Hanjour in Paterson, New Jersey, as did Nawaf al-Hazmi, who arrived in January of 2000 in Los Angeles. Almost all had spent a year or so in al-Qaeda training camps in Afghanistan.

Four of these young men—Fayez Banihammad, Saeed al-Ghamdi, Abdul Aziz al-Omari, and Salem al-Hazmi—entered the United States under the Visa Express program; some others had used stolen passports.

After arriving in the United States, several obtained photo IDs, in New Jersey and Virginia. A number of them established bank accounts, acquired mailboxes, rented cars, and started visiting gyms. Some used aliases, some their own names.

Evening, Fourteenth Street Bridge. I'm leaning on the rail, looking upriver toward Rosslyn and the heights of Georgetown. The river here is wide and shallow, its flow imperceptible.

I've biked in from my place after work, which I do sometimes, weather permitting. It's good exercise, a seven- or eight-mile junket, and the return, a steep climb up away from the river, is even better.

A fat, gunmetal-gray tube comes screaming low over my head, a US Airways flight heading down to Reagan National. I hear its tires scranch on the runway when the plane touches down and a moment later catch the bitter smell of burning rubber carried upriver by the wind.

A squad of trim young men in shorts jogs past in step, chanting numbers—"Hut . . . two . . . three . . . four . . . Hut . . . two . . . three . . . four"—heading over the bridge toward the Jefferson Memorial in the District. Their haircuts are high and wide, their faces strangely innocent. Marines, I think. I must have looked like them once.

Semper fi.

The afternoon has been hot, muggy, and electrical, our typical Washington July, but the threatened storm never came, and what's left of it now is a mere haze that hovers over this green city like a layer of gauze.

As I stare at the water, I think of Powers's day notes on Kareem—I cannot figure them, cannot parse their significance. The Meeting. The Call. The Pitch. And those vouchers, especially them. What do they mean?

Watch K little fucker squirm.

You can follow Powers's movements with Eddie Dietz's "stuff." Powers is in Athens in February, the right time for The Meeting, and there, too, in June for The Call to Karachi. In August he travels to Pakistan and is in Karachi on the sixteenth for The Pitch. Everything jibes, slam dunk as Lurch would say.

And S at Langley—I'm pretty sure I know who S is. But what was the op?

Kareem, my old gofer, was an agent of ours, implanted deeply in al-Qaeda. He held a position of trust—all that al-Qaeda money he carried, the passports. He may even have been close to bin Laden. Then we—Sonny and Ed—tried to burn him, tried to get him killed. Why?

Kareem, I'm pretty sure, will tell me before Sonny will.

Hanging just south of the silvery gray towers of Rosslyn is a waning moon and below it, the Evening Star, a single bright planet.

PART III: SPY

(AUGUST 6–SEPTEMBER 10)

AUGUST 6

1
"Rush Job"

HE IS IN GREECE. HE IS COMING TO PAKISTAN. I DON'T KNOW HIS DATE,
HIS DATE OF LEAVING GREECE YET.

WHERE IN GREECE?

ATHENS.

WHERE IN ATHENS?

I DON'T KNOW THE ADDRESS. BUT HE IS IN ATHENS. HE IS COMING
TO ISLAMABAD. IN TWO, THREE DAYS. HE WILL SPEND SOME DAYS IN
HERE, THEN HE WILL GO TO PESHAWAR. AFTER THAT I DON'T KNOW WHAT
HE WILL DO. I WILL SEE HIM AT AIRPORT. HE WILL STAY AT THE LALA GUEST
HOUSE, WHICH IS IN THE RAMNA 6 MARKET AREA.

The cable from Islamabad Station arrived at Langley around three in
the morning. The night duty officer at ATAC called me at home—
alone, no Karen—and I'm at my desk by four or so, adrenaline
pumping.

Our break: a bounty hunter, a young man from South Africa
named Suleiman Razavi, maybe thirty years old, of indeterminate
origins though South Asian of some sort. He's in Pakistan supposedly
to study religious law at the Islamic University in Islamabad. He is, he
says, a militant.

He tells us he has been hired by Abdel Kareem Yusufzai to help
carry out attacks on American air carriers.

Razavi has heard of the $500,000 reward we are offering for Ka-
reem's neck and has decided that he prefers earthly cash to jihad

credit. At 11 a.m. Pakistan time Razavi approached our regional security officer Mike Beaudry in Islamabad, who passed him on to Carl Lindquist. Carl immediately cabled us a transcript of his talk with Razavi and a request for fast action.

When I phone Lindquist, he says he finds Razavi's story plausible.

Pancho Reiner, on the line in Peshawar, is not so sure. "It's what he says, but of course he's going to have some goddamn story like this—what else? End of the day, he wants the money. I detect a level of caginess here. Razavi has shown us no evidence, none whatsoever for this air carrier caper. And we know what a crook Yusufzai is. Till we get evidence one way or the other, I make the aircraft attack a 'maybe.'"

"Why would Razavi tell us some story?" Lindquist asks. "For the five hundred thousand dollars all he needed to do was deliver Kareem."

"They all embroider, makes him look better," Pancho says.

Razavi and Kareem have been in touch, IMing each other through cybercafé e-mail services, Kareem from Athens, Razavi in the New World Internet Club, Ali Plaza, Nazimuddin Road, Islamabad. Razavi has presented us with hard copy of the exchanges. The messages out of Athens seem genuine enough, but they're not in the least incriminating.

That doesn't matter. Lindquist, Reiner, and I conclude that Kareem, for whatever purpose—anti-U.S. mayhem, some business deal—is coming to town, and we can pull off a snatch.

Lindsay, at his desk at seven prepping for an 8 a.m. meeting with the president, is all smiles when I bring him the news. "Yeah, yeah, yeah," he says. "Real rush job, huh?" As I talk, he gets up and paces in front of his big window, feeling good, again and again punching the palm of his left hand with his right fist, saying, "Right . . . right . . . right," as I talk. This will play well this morning in the Oval Office.

"I should go," I tell him. "The operation will involve heavies from the Pakistani Ministry of Interior, and we need somebody there with clout representing the U.S. government and CIA. A mere chief of station doesn't hack it. Also, FBI will be wanting to run the show, and we need representation because of that." Our ambassador will remain in the dark.

We have enough assets in the area for the bust, and I am therefore the sole officer from Langley heading out for this. When I leave Lindsay, he's putting in calls to the president and the attorney general. We draft a cable to Islamabad Station telling of my arrival tomorrow afternoon.

Other than Lindsay, Bill Cleppinger is the only officer at Langley who's clued in on the operation. He chortles at the prospects of grabbing Kareem. "Good hunting," he says simply. He agrees, naturally, to keep Sonny out of the loop.

I call Karen and postpone a Wednesday-evening date until I don't know when.

"Rush job," I tell her.

"Fun, I hope."

"Yeah. Oh, yeah. Should be."

A pause, then she says, "Paul, you take care—you hear me?" She has real worry in her voice. She knows something's on.

"Always do. I'll be away—maybe a week," I tell her, "though it could stretch out, can't really tell just yet. I'll be in touch." Then I say, meaning it, "I love you."

I fly out of Andrews Air Force Base at 7 p.m. on an Agency Gulfstream. I'm wired, nervous as hell. On the way over I try to sleep—the plane has small chambers with beds in them that you can stretch out on—but can do no more than a little ragged dozing.

The plan: We, with help from the Pakistani Interior Ministry, will take Kareem down in his hotel, the Lala Guest House, which is tucked away in a back street in the north of Islamabad. The Paks will supply most of the troops. I will hear the final arrangements when I arrive.

Now and then our commo officer shakes me gently, though I'm not sleeping, to give me messages on the operation from Langley and Islamabad. Nothing significant in the plan changes.

At 4:30 p.m. local time we set down in Islamabad International, where Mike Beaudry, our security chief, meets me and briefs me on the action as we are driven into town. The snatch is a go. We have surveilled the Lala. Kareem is there, alone. Razavi, our militant, has made contact with him.

We will not take him right away. Kareem may have people other than Razavi to see, and we want to watch the hotel at least this evening and take Kareem in the morning.

Kareem, if we get him, will be transferred to our custody immediately on arrest and zipped away to the States in a military Boeing 707 we have waiting at Islamabad Airport. He will be sedated the entire trip and will be strapped to a hospital gurney.

The Lala this night is under watch by Pakistani plainclothes officers.

I put up in the embassy guesthouse, where I immediately meet with Carl Lindquist. I'm nerved out but eager to be in on the bust. Lindquist is also high on the operation.

"Razavi met Kareem this morning at the airport," Lindquist says. "He escorted Kareem into town with his one piece of luggage. They got to the Lala at eleven thirty a.m."

Lindquist shows me surveillance tapes of Kareem arriving at the airport, getting out of a cab at the Lala. Though he has come in on a stolen Moroccan passport in another man's name, it's Kareem all right, my old gofer. He is unshaven. He looks puffy-faced, afflicted with a long weariness that comes from more than lack of sleep. The cash reward for his head has flushed him out, sent him moving our way. He's scared.

When Lindquist leaves me, promising to alert me if anything changes, I finally drift into sleep and a fitful, headachy soup of bad dreams arising from my own tense weariness.

Lala Guest House, Ramna Market, a little before 7 a.m. Mike Beaudry and I are in an embassy car with dark, opaque windows parked across the square from the Lala. With us are two embassy security officers and two FBI gumshoes. We are all armed. Like Lindquist and Beaudry, I am carrying a Beretta 9mm. Nobody talks much.

Ramna Market is a pleasant little commercial square. The storefronts here open to passersby under broad-boughed, leafy trees. As we sit, vegetable and fruit vendors are pushing their carts into place and setting out their wares. It's hot already.

Beaudry tells me the Lala occupies all the upper floors of its building, starting with the second. The ground floor is the Sparkle Video Shop. To get to the Lala, you enter through a thick glass door next to the Sparkle and walk up one flight of stairs to the hotel's first floor, where there's a clerk and a desk. Across the square from the Lala, a little up from where our car is parked, is the Spring Guest House, where Razavi lives with his wife.

About 8 p.m. yesterday Razavi and Kareem went out for dinner. Kareem told Razavi that he'd be in town for three days. Operationally, it might make sense to follow Kareem's movements in town, listen to whatever phone conversations he might make, let him hit a cybercafé or two if he wants, but we opt to take him this morning. We want Kareem, the Pakistanis have acquiesced. We'll brook no screwups.

If Kareem has a guardian angel or two in the Pak security services, they seem not to be onto this operation. Kareem is still in the Lala.

The drill: Sixteen Pak Interior Ministry troopers are waiting in three unmarked Range Rovers parked separately, each about a hundred meters from the main Ramna Market Square. They will pull into the square, and when they do, we will all rush the Lala and grab Kareem.

The Lala has only one exit, those front stairs. In case Kareem tries a jump from his bathroom window, a car full of Pak troopers has been stationed behind the hotel.

About 6 a.m. I got out of bed and forced a breakfast down— canned grapefruit juice, Cheerios, canned milk—but hardly tasted any of it. Mike Beaudry tells me he's been up half the night as well.

No one at the embassy knows the show except Mike, our security officers, the FBI liaison office, and me. We've maintained communication with Razavi. We've told him we're going to surveil Kareem for a day or two.

Pak liaison has done a routine check on the guest book at the Lala. They look at the guest books of all these small hotels about once a week, mostly to trip up Afghan smugglers and shake them down. Kareem has signed in as Muhammad Ali Tariq using his stolen passport.

Suddenly a Pak officer speaking in English radios from one of the Range Rovers. "We are proceeding with the action," he says. "It's the action."

The three Range Rovers move at normal driving speed into the square and halt just in front of the Lala. We pull around the square and join them.

Then things go very fast. The Pak officer, a colonel, leads his troopers out of their Range Rovers and they storm through the Lala's one door and surge up the stairs. Mike and I and the other Americans jump from our embassy car and start running for the Lala, too. I have my Beretta out, safety on. My stomach is churning, but I feel good.

Four of the Pak troopers stay outside on the pavement and secure the door—no one will enter or leave the building until the action is over.

We reach the second floor quickly, just behind the Paks. The colonel, who has drawn his gun, is asking the desk clerk something in

Urdu. The clerk, a skinny guy, wide-eyed and terrified, points to the stairway and says something, and we all rush to the next floor, sounding like an army going up the dusty, yellow-carpeted stairs. The Pak troops are waving guns now, mostly short machine pistols with long, straight magazines—MAC10s, I think. The Paks are excited, their dark eyes flashing.

All the rooms here are one step higher than the floor of the hall. Each has a little stoop in front of its door. The colonel mounts one at room number eighteen and pounds on the door. When it opens a crack, the Paks shove it in and rush the room yelling bloody hell in Urdu, followed by the Americans.

Inside, we find one man, very young, in his underwear.

It's not Kareem, not anyone we know.

The Paks grab him all the same, beat him around, and throw him to the floor on his stomach, as he's screaming in high-pitched English, "Why this? Why this? Who are you? Why this?"

One Pak trooper, short and beefy like Mike, puts his knee in the small of the man's back as two others bind his hands with plastic strip cuffs, bind his legs, and blindfold him. He is terrified, still struggling, yelling in English, "I am innocent, I am innocent."

The guy is panting now and begins to vomit on the floor and gives out choking coughs. They turn him over and pull him head-first, faceup, out the door and down the stoop—his heels bump twice—and drag him down the hall toward the stairs.

In the room: twin beds, two suitcases, one of them open, a TV set, and over the bed an air cooler.

No Kareem. We can't find him. Beaudry, beside himself, wild-eyed, is yelling, "What the fuck? Goddamn it to hell, what the fuck?" and, shoving Pak troopers out of his way, dashes into the bathroom.

I leave the milling troopers and American security people and go alone out into the hall. Across from room eighteen the door is open, and there, not five feet from me, standing immobile, is Kareem.

Kareem brings a pistol up smartly, holding it American-style, two-handed, right index finger on the trigger, left guiding the aim, steadying the pistol, a heavy-looking automatic.

I see the end of the barrel and Kareem's intertwined fingers. The piece is aimed at my face, like that time in Tehran, long, long ago, and the smiling crazies on the motorcycle.

Kareem is not smiling. His eyes are grim, his face stony and concentrated. Then puzzlement and something like wonder come over his features. He recognizes me, knows my face from long back, and astonished, he hesitates for an instant—miracle—then: flash and sound together, deafening in the closed space. My first shot catches Kareem in the stomach, my second hits higher, and Kareem slumps from the door, tumbling into the hall, and sprawls on the dusty yellow runner in the corridor, panting, slowly panting, his eyes focusing on nothing.

He's gone. Dying away from us.

I've killed him.

3

AUGUST 15
Two Knives, Padded Gloves, and Shin Guards

On August 15, 2001, an employee at Pan Am International Flight Academy in Eagan, Minnesota, telephoned the FBI's Minneapolis field office because he and other employees at Pan Am were suspicious of a student named Zacarias Moussaoui. Moussaoui had none of the usual qualifications for study at Pan Am, which specialized in commercial-pilot training on large jets. Moussaoui, who had left the Airman Flight School in Norman, Oklahoma, some weeks before and had moved to Minnesota, was unable to fly even single-engine aircraft.

When they interviewed Moussaoui, FBI agents quickly learned that he had deposited $32,000 in a local bank account, but could not plausibly explain how he had gotten the money. His passport showed travel to Pakistan, and he became "agitated" when asked if he had ever traveled to neighboring countries such as Afghanistan. He had in his possession two knives, padded gloves, and shin guards. When asked about his religious beliefs, he became "extremely agitated."

The Minneapolis agents suspected Moussaoui might be involved in an aircraft-hijacking plot. Because his visa had run out on May 22, he was in violation of U.S. immigration law. The FBI arrested him on August 16.

Agents in the Minneapolis office wanted to search Moussaoui's personal belongings, but feared they would be unable to get a criminal search warrant. They tried instead to seek a search warrant under the Foreign Intelligence Surveillance Act.

To get a warrant under FISA, the FBI would have to demonstrate to a judge in Washington that there was "probable cause" to believe that Moussaoui was the agent of a "foreign power," though not necessarily of a foreign state.

The FBI official in Washington who was supervising the investigation was not a lawyer and did not understand the definitions of "probable cause" or "foreign power." There was indeed probable cause to seek a search warrant under FISA, but FBI headquarters refused to go before a FISA judge for a warrant.

As a result, agents in Minneapolis were unable to search Moussaoui's personal effects, among which they would have found a letter from Yazid Sufaat, the high-level al-Qaeda operative who had hosted the meeting of terrorists in Kuala Lumpur in January 2000 attended by Nawaf al-Hazmi and Khalid al-Mihdhar.

---

4 **AUGUST 16**
Fourth Rammer

"Too bad we didn't get him alive," Sonny says. "What *could* we have gotten out of him?" The look on Sonny's face is supposed to show regret, but I sense an underglaze of satisfaction there. Kareem dead is just fine with Sonny.

We're in my basement den, Sonny on the sofa, me in the captain's chair across the coffee table from him. Late evening, my invite.

Sonny's had two end-of-the-day rammers, and now, slouched back in the sofa, he's looking at his third, poking at the ice with his fingers and slushing it around. The vodka's from an old bottle of Absolut that Nan bought long back and that's still here. I'm drinking chardonnay from one of those heavy, ice-blue glass goblets Nan and I bought so long ago in Tehran.

Looking over at Sonny, I say, "You know, I don't buy the bomb-plot business, that they were going after the airlines and all that. We got no evidence, just a story from an informant—one guy—who's not very reliable. And that's it, no other indicators. Story's bullshit."

Sonny shrugs. He's agnostic on the point.

Not so the ATAC Working Group. The WG has ginned up a postmortem action report that takes the bomb plot as a given. The gist of it is, Abdel Kareem Yusufzai, Afghan, was an al-Qaeda agent. He delivered cash and passports to the terrorists who bombed the USS *Cole*. He was "implicated" in a plot to destroy U.S. air carriers in South Asia. With his death resisting arrest, a "potential terrorist attack on American interests" has been "preempted."

A sanitized version of the report, duly signed by Dennis Dennlinger, acting head, ATAC, has been sent over to Bob Fowler, and via Fowler, to the Oval Office. We hear the president is pleased.

Sonny sits there sipping at his rammer and munching from a bowl of salted peanuts, not saying much. He looks bone weary after one of his long days, but his shirt's a little out over his belt, his tie loosened—the rammers, I think they've relaxed him.

Time.

I get up and from our big, dark oak buffet where they're lying I take the printouts of Powers's day notes on Kareem, bring them back to the coffee table, and without comment drop them in front of Sonny.

I get a look. Sonny bends his skinny torso forward, and as he reads through the printouts, he nods, bobbing his head a couple of times, then looks back up at me expectantly. He knows we're going to get into something this evening, something he hasn't figured on. His blue eyes play over my face, then lock onto mine. Where's this evening going? his eyes ask. What's this all about? Staring at me, saying nothing, he gives me that canted smile. Classic Sonny.

"Powers," I say. "He kept this stuff on a laptop. I got the laptop. Ain't much, but it's WILDCARD, right? The meeting, the call, the pitch? And you're S."

Sonny hesitates, then throws his head back in a silent guffaw, nods again a couple of times. The appreciation animating his face looks genuine to me. He gives me a sly, bad boy's grin and says, laughing now, "That's good, that's very good. I like it," and, seeing the look on my face, says, "No, no, I like it, I really do."

I say, "Kareem was on our payroll."

"Sure was."

"We got no records of that, Sonny. Where'd Ed get the money?"

"Discretionary funding, NOREFUGE account. 'Agents' expenses.' On the books, reported through Powers."

I recall the list of "contacts" Powers had. Kareem's name, of course, was not among them.

"Phony names, those agents?"

Sonny eyes me. "You recording this?"

I shake my head.

After a pause Sonny says simply, "Ed's deal."

Oh, Sonny's one of our best. If you've got a dangerous or tricky job you want done, Sonny's your man. Just keep a lawyer around.

"How come, Sonny? Why'd you keep it so secret? Kareem was a former agent—he'd been on the books before, you knew that, you could have put him on again. What the hell was the problem?"

Sonny's look is defiant. "Could've, didn't."

We'll come back to this.

I say, "And nobody here at Langley knows shit about Kareem being on payroll."

Sonny remains silent.

"Well, I hope he was useful—was he?"

Sonny nods obliquely. "The deal made sense. Ed knew Kareem—met him in Athens—knew Kareem was tight with the Taliban, had some contacts with al-Qaeda personnel. So we hired him, paid him on a retainer basis."

"Yeah. And when Ed paid Kareem he collected vouchers from him."

"So he did."

I pick up Powers's last day note and read it to Sonny: " 'Relationship U.S. Government terminated, payments ceased. Per S I turn vouchers over to ISI Afghan liaison committee. S at hqs: K nonperforming. Be a great pleasure, watch K little fucker squirm.' "

I look over at Sonny. "You burned him. Why?"

Sonny smiles tightly. "No, we didn't. Read it again."

" 'Read it again'?—what does that mean?"

"It means, 'Read it again'—'Read it again and this time read it carefully.' "

"Sonny, stop this fucking around."

"What does Ed say?" Sonny asks, being patient with me, smiling again that tight, little "gotcha" smile, enjoying the moment. "Ed says, 'I turn vouchers over.' Doesn't say 'I turned vouchers over.' World of difference. Ed never gave those vouchers to anybody, never got the chance. Died first. Sure, turning them over was in the works, we really were going to burn Kareem. Hell, why not? He wasn't giving us shit. We pushed at him for more info. We needed it—bin Laden, goddamn it! Al-Qaeda! So we pushed at him and pushed at him and kept on pushing at him. But the little shit balked, put us off, complained about the dangers—can't say I blame him—finally told Ed to shove it.

"So Ed made his threat. Early December, Peshawar. Told Kareem if he didn't produce, those pay vouchers'd be shown to the wrong people. Then Ed went back to London. Gave me a call, said he had Kareem wired, had him scared to death, too scared to do anything except work for us. Had him by the clock weights. You know Ed—always superconfident, always thinking he's way ahead of everybody else. Well, late December Ed goes back to Peshawar to work Kareem one last time. Dies.

"Kareem killed him. I don't know how—maybe he did use Liamine Dreissi. Makes sense. Dreissi was a known murderer. Dreissi and Kareem were great friends. Dreissi was in country at the time. Your friend in Jordan, Abu Nejmeh, the Palestinian—he named Dreissi as the perp. All fits. Maybe wouldn't hold up in a court of law, but in our world—you know as well as I do—in our world this level of proof is about the best we ever get.

"So, after the deed's done, Kareem hightails it to London, hides out there for a time. He gets wind we're after him—that five hundred thousand dollars—goes under, gets a phony passport as Abdul the Bulbul Amir from Morocco. Tries to travel to more hospitable climes using his buddy network. But he chooses the wrong buddy. Buddy tips us off. We bust Kareem, Kareem gets killed in the melee."

Sonny nods a couple of times as if he's satisfied with the story, with the "level of proof." I check Sonny's face and see no doubt in it. Belief is there.

"Kareem's dead, Sonny. We're never going to know."

"We know."

"Intuition, huh?"

Sonny shrugs again. "End of Kareem, end of story."

"End of Ed Powers, too," I say.

Sonny barks a laugh. "You miss Ed? Think he's some kind of loss to the human race?"

"Loss to us."

"Different concept." Laughing again, Sonny waves his empty glass. "Got any more of this?"

As I go to the bar, Sonny calls after me, "Ed Powers was scum of the earth. You use 'em, of course, *comme il faut*. But if you lose 'em, it's no big deal in the ethical arena, right? Right?"

I say nothing as I pour vodka over fresh ice, looking at Sonny reflected in the big mirror behind the bar. He's smiling still. I don't know why. When I take this to Lindsay, Sonny will be shitcanned, career over, maybe even lose the pension. But that's Sonny—ever cool, ever in control—when you're tensed, be relaxed, when you're down, be up, don't ever let the fuckers know.

I go back, give Sonny his rammer, and sit opposite him, silent for a time. Then I say quietly, "Sonny—hey."

Sonny blinks. "Hey?"

"Yeah—'hey.' Kareem, Sonny—all the secrecy about Kareem. Doesn't make sense. What gives? What was the problem? Why'd you keep it all so secret?"

Sonny takes a swallow of vodka and runs his fingertip around the rim of the glass, as if trying to make it sing. Then, no guile in his face, softly, almost whispering, Sonny says, "I knew Kareem. Knew him pretty well. Met him in Pakistan when I was station chief, '97."

Surprise. Sonny always has something in reserve, you never know what.

"You knew Kareem! Sonny, you prick! You never told anybody, I mean anybody! In this whole business, start to finish, you never said a goddamn word!"

Sonny blows a puff of air bleakly. "Got to know Kareem about the time of the Talbot murder. Terri Talbot? Killed in Karachi? Terri's murder's kinda how Kareem and I met. We had Terri at the consulate down there—Karachi—doing visa interviews. Ever meet her? Sweetheart, all-American-girl type—real friendly, real outgoing. Terrific interviewer. All that innocence—that was what really charmed people, got 'em talking. And she learned all kinds of stuff. And recruited some good agents while she was at it, put a lot of people on the informant rosters. People'll do whatever for a U.S. visa, right? Not that charm was the whole story with her—she was one tough cookie, too. Had a first-class medal for marksmanship, green belt in tae kwon do. I mean, the kid was an ace, just the kind of officer we want." He shakes his head. "Her death—what a waste."

This is what we know:

Just after 7 a.m. Tuesday, February 11, 1997, CIA officer Teresa Weber Talbot walked out of her apartment in Clifton, a suburb of the wealthy in south Karachi, and got into a gray, U.S. government van to be driven to work at the American consulate in that city. Her driver was a local hire.

He stopped for a traffic light above the Clifton roundabout on Abdullah Haroon Street. When he did, a yellow taxi pulled diagonally ahead of the vehicle, blocking it, and from the taxi windows, front and rear, two men fired back into the van with AK-47s. One of them then jumped from the taxi, ran up to the van, and from close range, perhaps a yard away, fired a second burst into the vehicle, then ran back and got into the taxi, which then sped north. Terri and her driver had no chance. Altogether, thirty-one rounds entered the van. Eight rounds struck Terri; the driver took five.

How the terrorists knew the vehicle was one of ours we never learned. The van was unmarked, and its license plates did not identify it as embassy. Six months before, to foil terrorists, all diplomatic vehicles in the country were issued ordinary-looking plates.

Two officers in a Karachi police car had been cruising south in the opposite flow of traffic and had seen the shooting from across a median strip. Though their car had a radio, the officers didn't use it. Instead, they drove to a nearby police station to report the incident, wasting a good five to ten minutes on the way. No disciplinary action was taken against them.

On the afternoon of the shooting, someone identifying himself as a spokesman for a group called Army of God telephoned the Urdu-language newspaper *Jang,* the largest-circulation paper in Pakistan, and claimed responsibility for the deaths.

One day later, Karachi police released sketches of three men said to be suspects in the killings and had them printed in *Jang* as well as three other major Urdu-language papers and in *Dawn,* an English-language paper with countrywide circulation.

The sketches were based on descriptions given by the owner of the taxi, which the three killers had stolen in the north of town around 6 a.m. and which they drove off followed by a fourth man on a motorcycle. The killers were thought to be in their mid to late twenties. Karachi police found the taxi in Fatimah Jinnah Road, a ten-minute walk from the site of the murder.

Sonny, his eyes not meeting mine and speaking so softly I barely hear him—what is with him?—says, "Two weeks after Terri and her driver were murdered—this is '97, early—lo and behold, a fella named Kareem, Abdel Kareem Yusufzai, walked into the U.S. embassy in Islamabad. To get in, he pretended he wanted a visa, but then he told the consular officer handing out applications—Warren Krieger—Kareem tells this Warren, real quiet 'cause he's standing in a line with a whole buncha Paks, Kareem says he knows something important, that he's gotta talk to CIA. Well, Warren sends him to embassy security, and embassy security listens to him and figures, yeah, maybe he really ought to talk to CIA.

"CIA's me. So I talk with him. Tells me he's worked with us before, talks about a 'Mr. Bob,' who was this great guy. Later, by the way, when I check the docs on Kareem, I find out 'Mr. Bob' is ROBERT LANGER, who is none other than Paul Patterson, veteran of the Afghan wars"—Sonny lifts his rammer to toast me—"and certified great guy. I also see Kareem hasn't been around for a while, record's pretty scanty since the Soviets left Afghanistan. I figure he drifted away from us after the war.

"So anyhow, in the embassy, Kareem's talking, I'm listening. Tells me he's fallen in with this group, this Islamic group he's met at some hole-in-the-wall mosque on the north side, up by Mauripur Station. Tells me he's in over his head with this bunch. Says this group's the Army of God, Jund al-Haqq in the lingo, the bunch that killed Terri. Told me he had a minor hand in it, in the murder, that in order to show he was okay to these guys—who were beginning to scare him—he let some foot soldiers stay in his apartment. Said he regretted the killing, said he was really worried, 'cause maybe he could get in trouble and was losing sleep over it. Wondered what he could do. So he came in, said he wanted to help us find the killers. In return, he wanted our promise we'd keep it between us and him—not tell the Pak police, and if the Pak police came after him on this, we'd put in a good word for him.

"Course, at the time we had this 'exceptional approval' bullshit. You know the deal—wanna hire questionable characters, gotta run it up the line, get the DCI and the counsel general to sign off on the hiring.

"Well, on Kareem . . . Well, I never ran it up the line. Told myself, 'Hey, guy's worth a try, but maybe back at Langley they won't necessarily think so.' I mean, every goddamn time you get a good idea, ten lawyers jump outta the closet and tell you why you can't do it. Not like the old days. So I just said, 'Fuck it, I'll slip this guy some cash, see what he says.'

"Nothing on paper, of course. Just me talking with this Kareem character and paying him a little. Paid him outta station slush, no real records." Sonny smiles weakly. "I think on the financials I referred to him as 'technical media.'

"Anyhow, Kareem tells me some stuff about Army of God, gives me a description of the ringleader, gave me his name—nom de guerre of course, not his real name, which Kareem said he didn't know—gives me a little background on the guy, on the group. So I pay him, happy to employ him, pass on what I get to the Pak security people without telling them where I got it. They pick up a couple of Army of God people on the basis of it, minor people, but people. Kareem and I part company friends, everything hunky-dory.

"Then, maybe . . . what? Eighteen months back? Something like that?—Paks make some more arrests, get those two, two of the gang who killed Terri Talbot. Paks get confessions from them. One of them drove the taxi, other followed on his motorbike. They said they had a large team—bunch scoping out her apartment, one handling weapons. Weapons were sterile—we're in Pakistan, right? Can't trace anything to anybody. One bunch doing logistics, bringing in the real hit team, organizing the strike, training for it, drilling—I mean, the bastards were organized. Then after the murder, hiding, getting out of the city.

"Our two friends couldn't name the killers, too well run an operation. Everything's compartmentalized, everything's need-to-know. This is the report we get from Pak police. Doesn't amount to that much, so here at HQ nobody pays much attention. Neither does the asshole Carl Lindquist, who at this point is now acting chief, Islamabad Station. And that's it.

"But that's *not* it. I ask myself, 'Is the report the Paks supplied to us the whole deal?' Course not, never is. So I want to see the raw Pak police reports, everything they've got on the case, start to finish. I call Lindquist, tell him to get the reports. Lindquist says he's tried and tried, Paks won't cooperate, no can do. So I fly to Karachi. I get a police colonel I know to get me those files, takes me about five minutes to talk him into it. Lindquist! I don't get 'em all, I don't think, but I get a lot. I requisition the consulate translator and typist, put 'em to work. I get the reports translated into English, every one of them. Like I say, there's a lot, maybe two hundred pages. So there I am sitting in my hotel room in Karachi and reading through the stuff as it gets done, gets translated, page by page. Boring as shit mostly.

"But, hey, wait a minute . . . wait a minute. I come across this interview, last doc I see, interview with one of the perps, guy who drove the car. Perp described the man who ran the operation, said he was Afghan, from over the border. Didn't know his name, perp said, didn't know where he lived, though he seemed to have a place in Karachi. But, he said, the guy's face was marked, scarred. One of those Aleppo boils on the right cheek and a scar on his left. Triangular, like an arrowhead."

My heart shrinks.

"The Paks—they don't know his identity. But, shit, I do. Guy who ran the op, killed Terri, it was Kareem. Who covered his tracks by coming to me for protection—protection! And I gave it to him, never told the Pak . . ."

I'm on my feet, not thinking of Kareem or Sonny, not thinking of anything, as my wine goblet—a heavy, blue projectile—crashes into the mirror behind the bar, and long cracks, jagged as lightning bolts, streak from the center of the mirror to the edges, and shards of glass in delayed reaction fall tinkling onto the bottles arrayed below.

I am burning, quaking with rage—at Kareem and his audacity, for killing one of ours, then asking us for protection from the consequences. At Sonny for playing the fool, giving Kareem that protection. I could kill Sonny, who, barely noticing what I've done, sitting inertly, his face expressionless, gives out a false laugh, a single, breathy *huh* sound. "These people," he says, "people like Kareem, you play the game with them, you take chances. And if you take chances in this life, sometimes you lose. Got to. And Kareem—Kareem screwed us, really, really screwed us."

"Sonny, you dumb fuck . . ."

"So contemptible," Sonny says, not listening. "The little shit—working for us, working for them. Agent, traitor, agent again, traitor again—Kareem could spin into one, then into the other, go back and forth. Well, what's in a name? Huh"—that single, breathy false laugh again. "It's what you do that defines you. Who you are in this world, who you are is how you function. How you function is what defines you. Truth of life."

Suddenly exhausted, drained, I drop into my chair. I think of the Kareem I knew, the beardless boy stepping up to me in that back courtyard at Dean's Hotel, pulling close, looking me in the eye, and reciting his résumé in good English: "I am Abdel Kareem Yusufzai, I am engineer," and all the rest. I think of Kareem going from gofer to commander to heroin dealer to killer, always with infusions of our cash. An Afghan-American story.

"Well," Sonny says, "in our business, you don't look for honor, do you? Not in the targets." He takes off his glasses, those glittery trifocals, and rubs the bridge of his nose. His face looks naked and exposed, his washed-out, blue eyes unprotected and vulnerable, that haunted look more obvious, more there.

"You know," he says, "we had this piano. I ever tell you? Pancho Reiner once had this goddamn big piano, baby grand, had it air-freighted over the Himalayas to Katmandu when he was stationed out there. Think of it—baby grand! Katmandu!"

"Sonny, what's this got to do . . . ?"

"When Pancho got assigned to Pakistan"—Sonny's voice has gone low again, crazy-soft, spooky—"he brought the damn thing along to Islamabad and left it at the First Road staff house, didn't want to take it to Peshawar—don't ask me, the guy's so mercurial—he just left it there. So, hell, we think, great, we got the use of it. Ancient black thing, all scuffed up. Funny, believe it or not, there are three or four really good piano tuners in Islamabad. You wouldn't expect that, but there are."

Sonny's rambling now, talking as if in a daze, and it's my turn as I stare at him to wonder where this evening's going, what it's about.

"So at embassy get-togethers—embassy's a small society there, you know how it is—nothing formal, just in-house things, at these get-togethers, she'd bang away at it."

"She? Terri Talbot?"

"Wasn't bad at all," Sonny says, talking to himself, I think, paying me no attention. "Better'n Pancho. She'd play party songs and what-not, old traditionals, 'As Time Goes By,' 'Bewitched, Bothered,' 'Falling in Love Again,' and everybody'd relax, have a good time, stand around the piano. Even sing—lotta times she had sheet music with the words, she'd come over bringing the sheet music. She was young. Fresh. Perky. Smile like a sunrise. Kind of person who'd get excited over a checker game, wave at people in the canteen she'd only met once—that kinda gal."

She.

"Clarisse loved her, loved having her over. She'd bang away . . . at that piano . . . Play stuff . . . Smile . . ."

Suddenly Sonny starts rocking forward and back, gulping air. He jams his left elbow into his skinny side, seems almost to fold over.

I know where this is going. I'm watching a train wreck.

"I sent her to Karachi . . . good pickings down there . . . city's so . . . so full of intrigue, so . . ."

Sonny thrusts both his hands up to cover his eyes, to cover the tears streaming down his cheeks as he tries to hold back, to still him-self, but his shoulders quake and he is wracked with deep sobs, in pro-found, inconsolable grief.

And now I see.

SEPTEMBER 5

5 Armed

On September 5, 2001, Marwan al-Shehhi, Mohand al-Shehri, and Ahmed al-Ghamdi registered at the Milner Hotel on South Charles Street in Boston, Massachusetts. On the same day, Waleed al-Shehri, his brother Wail al-Shehri, Satam al-Suqami, and Abdul Aziz al-Omari checked in at the Park Inn in Newton, a few miles south.

Two days later, on September 7, Saeed al-Ghamdi, Ahmed al-

Haznawi, and Ahmed al-Nami arrived in Newark, New Jersey, on a Spirit Airlines flight from Fort Lauderdale, Florida, and checked into a hotel.

On the same day, Hani Hanjour and Majed Moqed checked into the Budget Host Valencia Hotel in Laurel, Maryland.

In the early hours of September 9, Ziad al-Jarrah joined Saeed al-Ghamdi, Ahmed al-Haznawi, and Ahmed al-Nami at their hotel in Newark.

Also on September 9, Muhammad Atta registered at the Milner in Boston, staying the night and meeting there with al-Shehhi. Atta also talked by cell phone with al-Jarrah in New Jersey.

On September 10, shortly after noon, Atta left the Milner, picked up al-Omari at the Park Inn in Newton, and drove north to Portland, Maine, where the two registered at the Comfort Inn in South Portland, not far from the Portland International Jetport.

Next morning, Muhammad Atta and Abdul Aziz al-Omari will fly from Portland International Jetport to Logan International Airport in Boston and there transfer to American Airlines flight 11 for Los Angeles. Atta's lizardlike face will be caught by airport surveillance cameras in Portland.

Satam al-Sugami and Waleed and Wail al-Shehri will join them on the flight. Also present in Logan International will be Marwan al-Shehhi, Fayez Banihammad, Ahmed al-Ghamdi, Hamza al-Ghamdi, and Mohand al-Shehri, who will take United Airlines flight 175 for Los Angeles.

The two teams of young men in Boston will board their flights at about 7:30 a.m. After boarding but before takeoff, Atta will call al-Shehhi on UA 175 by cell phone and speak with him briefly.

About the same time, at Newark International Airport in New Jersey, Ziad al-Jarrah, Saeed al-Ghamdi, Ahmed al-Haznawi, and Ahmed al-Nami will board United Airlines flight 93 for San Francisco; and in Dulles International Airport in the Virginia suburbs of Washington, Hani Hanjour, Khalid al-Mihdhar, Nawaf al-Hazmi, Salem al-Hazmi, and Majed Moqed will board American Airlines flight 77 for Los Angeles.

All nineteen young men have tickets for first-class seats close to the cockpits. At the check-in gates, nine of the nineteen will be flagged for screening as suspicious persons, but all will be allowed to board their flights. Most of the nineteen will be armed with knives and pepper spray.

EPILOGUE

SEPTEMBER 10
A Man Named LANGER

Clep's farewell dinner is not at the Tysons Marriott or Holiday Inn, frequent venues of ours for these things. Instead, Clep's wife, Bea, has arranged an intimate affair downtown in the Mayflower, in a small, elegant dining room on the ground floor of the hotel. There are only ten of us. She decided to hold it there, I know, as a way of dissing all the people in town, the Donovans, the Diamonds, the others who ganged up on Bill. What it cost her is beyond my powers to estimate, like the price of Hamawi's yacht, but it must have been a bundle.

Bea absented herself from the felicity—it's to be dinner for "the boys" she told me when she invited me by phone before sending the engraved invitation. Stu Kremer and Jim McClennan are here, a few others from Bill's old days in Cairo and Tunis. Sonny was invited for old times' sake but begged off.

It is a quiet affair with no formal orations, unlike some of our end-of-career celebrations—boozy, roaring sodalities of Langley's noted gunslingers, with much laughter and backslapping, congratulatory speeches, good-natured yells at the podium, and other alarums and interruptions.

Tonight is just conversation, mostly about old days, first postings, strange and marvelous occurrences at the Agency. No bitterness, no recriminations. They seem out of place.

We don't talk business. McClennan avoids the subject of Powers and the Hill's suspicions of the man. As the conversation flows, though, I can't help thinking of Ed and UAC, of those chemicals—

the acetic anhydride, the chloroform, the sodium carbonate—shipped to that nonexistent textile plant in Karachi.

Powers, guys like him, have their own agendas. They're always a little off the flight path. You never know how far.

But Ed's dead, Kareem's dead, even the poor fuck loser of a pilot Wayne Bates ($1,000 for extra landings) is dead.

The waters, I'm pretty sure, are going to close over Ed's narco-trafficking. There is almost no paper on it, and what there is, Ed's day notes, will never come to light. Donovan, McClennan, Meatball—they're spinning their wheels.

Since Bea had to reserve the room for a Monday night, the dinner doesn't last late. We talk through dessert and coffee—decaf for most of us—then walk out into a hazy, starless night.

As I am crossing Rhode Island Avenue, I hear a raspy voice behind me: "Patterson, hey, Patterson, hang on. Where ya headed?"

Clep. He wants to talk.

He catches up with me in midcrossing, huffing from the run, and we halt at the corner on the other side to let him get his breath.

"Hey, now nobody's around, what's the score on Powers?" Clep knows something's happened—he's gotten word from somebody—but he doesn't know what. "Anything new? Who did it, Patterson? We know who killed Powers?" Clep's face is conspiratorial. You can tell me, his face says, me, your old buddy. Sure you can.

When something as banal and as human as love intrudes itself into our professional world, we find it shocking, but it happens. Terri Talbot and Sonny overlapped four months in Pakistan, time enough as I well know for an affair. When I called Clarisse Desmond in Great Falls—she has chosen to stick around the area—and told her Sonny'd been over and had broken down and wept, Terri's name was a trip wire.

"Sonny's little piece," she snapped. "I mean, I'm sorry, truly sorry about what happened, but she was just the last straw. With Sonny's ways, I mean with the work, the endless hours, the weekends—it wasn't a life. I mean the countries he chose for us to live in, children forever sent away to some school or other, beaucoup other things, we just didn't have a life. There were so many disappointments in all that."

As Clarisse talked, I thought of her meaty little legs, her button nose. She has a pathological fear of dogs, I recalled, though I don't know why I recalled it.

My mind then drifted back to that rainy afternoon in J. Gilbert's, Sonny drinking his rammers and bullshitting me about Powers—"So maybe he simply screwed somebody in Peshawar—in some 'business' deal—and got whacked for it"—trying to throw me off the Powers trail and at the same time probing me about Andrea.

Why did he bring her up? Was he testing me, seeing if I'd betray something? Signaling that he knew? Who knows, maybe he was just looking for a fellow guilty husband, hoping to find some kind of comfort in the shared secret of a common transgression.

"Then that baggage came along," Clarisse said. "Well, she was the last straw. After she died, Sonny was just impossible. Down in the dumps? Why, he'd go off and sit by himself in the dark, and cry, yes, cry, didn't try to hide it. Paul, I don't blame her, I really don't. She was a naïve, an innocent, into something way over her head. But— there it was, Sonny's betrayal. I was fed up, last straw. I told Sonny it was over."

WILDCARD was Sonny's deal from the beginning, a bogus operation, never on the books in any real sense. The elaborate cover Sonny cooked up at Langley, the phony pocket litter and credit cards, the backstopped number, the cables to station—one of which Stu Kremer belatedly turned up—all the rest of it, fooled Powers nicely. Powers thought he was working for Uncle. He wasn't, he was working for Sonny.

Powers had bumped into Kareem somehow, probably at an arms bazaar (WILDCARD/1 WAS FIRST APPROACHED IN FEBRUARY BY RUTHERFORD IN ATHENS). When Ed worked the sharp-eyed Afghan a little and found out he had Taliban connections, Ed touted him to CIA as agent, of course not mentioning the crooked deals he and Kareem were dreaming up.

Sonny naturally was interested in Ed's promising new recruit, but when he learned the new recruit was Abdel Kareem Yusufzai, the man who had murdered the woman he loved, Sonny went berserk—quietly and on the sly, Sonny-style. Sonny, whose mind does not move in straight lines, decided Kareem's reappearance was a godsend, that he'd string Kareem along, keep him in view, and one way or another exact revenge. Those vouchers were the way.

Of course, going after Kareem the way he did *(ballsy with other peoples' balls)*, Sonny managed to kill Ed Powers in the process.

Collateral damage.

And Sonny snookered me, too. In that cheap, walk-up hotel in Islamabad, I managed to act—unknowingly—on Sonny's behalf as executioner of my old gofer Kareem, the man who'd worked for us, the man who'd worked against us.

We'll never know what Kareem could have told us—of al-Qaeda, of that gang in Hamburg, of the lizard-faced Egyptian in his galabia. Or of Liamine Dreissi, who is gone we know not where. Dreissi's on our watch lists, of course, for what that's worth, and maybe someday we'll get him. But for now, like so many al-Qaeda operatives whose names we have, he's a phantom, moving in shadow.

I could get Sonny fired for what he did. I could even get him put behind bars. But I won't, and Sonny knows it.

When I got back from Islamabad, after preliminary debriefings at Andrews Air Force Base and Langley and a quick trip to my own house to clean up, I called Karen, then drove to her place bone-tired on a sweet-smelling, end-of-summer night. We embraced in her kitchen door, groin to groin.

"Heya, Big Boy."

"Heya."

"You look like a ghost."

"Maybe I am one, Kare. Sometimes what you see is what you get."

She sensed something had happened in the Great Out There, something she wasn't allowed to know. I told her what I could, which in this case was little. She will never even know where I went.

I also passed on to her the latest communiqué from the Nan front, which my now ex-wife proudly left on my home answering machine. She and Charley Bennett are tying the knot. It will be a small family affair down in Farmville, Charley's point of origin. Nan's sister, May, and brother, Teddy, will represent the Radford family. They may even spring old lady Radford from her house in Greenwich and cart her down for it.

As for Karen and me, we'll continue together. Jeffries, I think, is no longer in the picture, whatever happened or didn't happen out there on the tundra. I do worry, though, about the age difference, which may ultimately do us in. But Karen seems not unhappy on that score. She still styles me her "new old man," after all, and jokes about it with her friends—reassuring in a way, though I don't really like to hear it. So she and I have a kind of tacit agreement going: I flatter myself that I'm young enough for her; she lets me get away with it, a kind of gift on her part.

And let's face it, most couples stay together by suppressing the truth now and then. About some things honesty just isn't worth it.

Let it go.

Clep asks again, "Who did it?"

If I didn't tell someone that something had happened, it was as if it had never happened.

I shrug. "Beats my ass."

Cleppinger shoots me a look at this, intent and searching, but he is silent. Since he doesn't know what else to do, he hunches up his jacket, his eyes still searching my face. The jacket looks heavy, winter-weight—Cleppinger's sartorial disorganization at play here.

I tell Clep, to be telling him something, that I'm heading for New York early in the morning. Working the al-Qaeda money trail. I'll be seeing Treasury and private-sector banking people along with some FBI analysts and people from the New York State Attorney's Office. I'm traveling under my old name, ROBERT LANGER. We're set to meet on CIA premises—Clep knows the venue, he's been there—a phony investment firm called Turnwood Financial Services we've placed in the Trade Center, high up, North Tower, and, a bit of irony here, on the same floor as the Arab-American Chamber of Commerce, one of our controlled groups. Anyhow, I tell Clep, that's the news.

I say, "We'll talk," and I turn and walk up Connecticut Avenue, as long, long stretches of timed traffic lights flash out of the haze. The fancy stores up the street north of Dupont Circle are closed now, but I will come back, maybe on the weekend, and buy something unaffordable for Karen.

I think Cleppinger is still standing there on the corner watching me, but I do not look back. When I get to N Street, I turn right.

I vanish.